BATMAN ADVENTURES

SHADOWS & MASKS

Written by:
Vito Delsante
Dan Slott
Gabe Soria
Ty Templeton

Colored by:
Lee Loughridge

Illustrated by:
Terry Beatty
Rick Burchett
Dean Haspiel
Ty Templeton

Lettered by:
Phil Felix
Jared Fletcher
Rob Leigh
Nick J. Napolitano

BATMAN ADVENTURES VOL. 2: SHADOWS & MASKS
Published by DC Comics. Cover and compilation copyright © 2004
DC Comics. All Rights Reserved. Originally published in single magazine
form as BATMAN ADVENTURES 5-9. Copyright © 2003, 2004 DC Comics.
All Rights Reserved. All characters, their distinctive likenesses and
related elements featured in this publication are trademarks of
DC Comics. The stories, characters and incidents featured in this
publication are entirely fictional. DC Comics does not read or
accept unsolicited submissions of ideas, stories or artwork.

CARTOON NETWORK and its logo are trademarks of Cartoon Network.

DC Comics, 1700 Broadway, New York, NY 10019
A Warner Bros. Entertainment Company.
Printed in Canada. First Printing.
ISBN: 1-4012-0330-2
Cover illustration by Kelsey Shannon
Publication design by John J. Hill

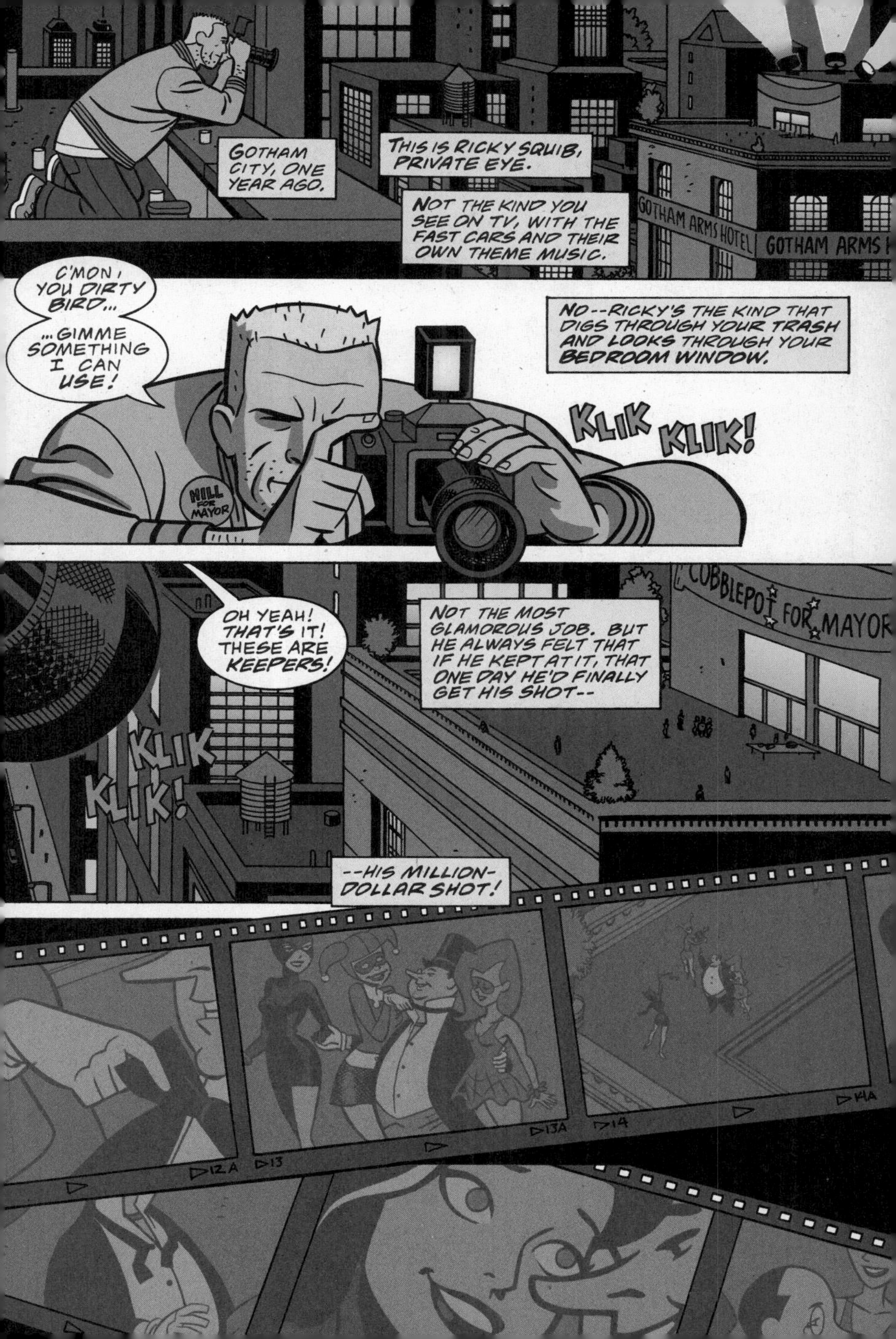
GOTHAM CITY, ONE YEAR AGO.
THIS IS RICKY SQUIB, PRIVATE EYE.
NOT THE KIND YOU SEE ON TV, WITH THE FAST CARS AND THEIR OWN THEME MUSIC.
GOTHAM ARMS HOTEL
GOTHAM ARMS
C'MON, YOU DIRTY BIRD...
...GIMME SOMETHING I CAN USE!
NO--RICKY'S THE KIND THAT DIGS THROUGH YOUR TRASH AND LOOKS THROUGH YOUR BEDROOM WINDOW.
KLIK KLIK!
HILL FOR MAYOR
OH YEAH! THAT'S IT! THESE ARE KEEPERS!
NOT THE MOST GLAMOROUS JOB. BUT HE ALWAYS FELT THAT IF HE KEPT AT IT, THAT ONE DAY HE'D FINALLY GET HIS SHOT--
COBBLEPOT FOR MAYOR
KLIK KLIK!
--HIS MILLION-DOLLAR SHOT!

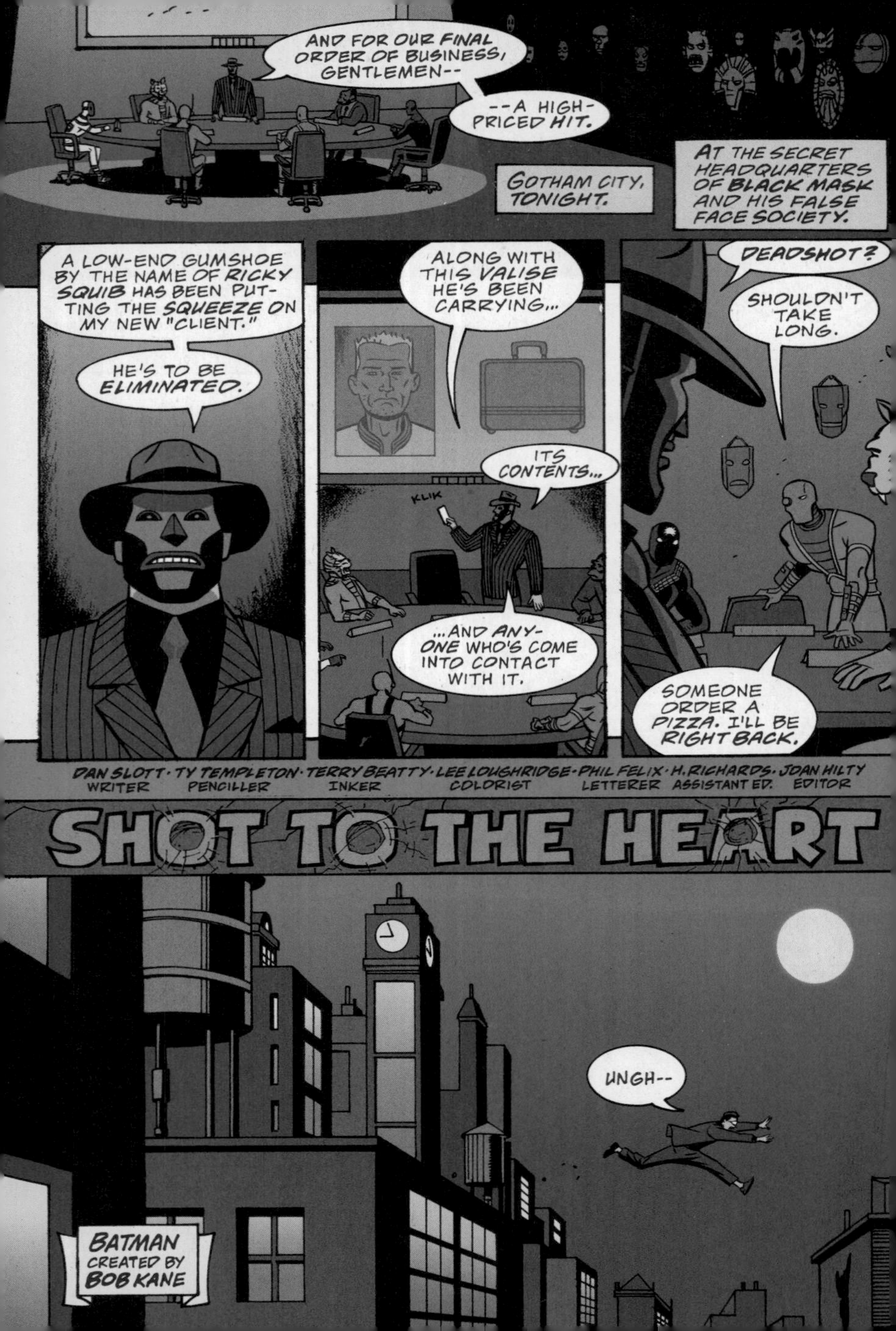
AND FOR OUR FINAL ORDER OF BUSINESS, GENTLEMEN--
--A HIGH-PRICED HIT.
GOTHAM CITY, TONIGHT.
AT THE SECRET HEADQUARTERS OF BLACK MASK AND HIS FALSE FACE SOCIETY.
A LOW-END GUMSHOE BY THE NAME OF RICKY SQUIB HAS BEEN PUTTING THE SQUEEZE ON MY NEW "CLIENT."
HE'S TO BE ELIMINATED.
ALONG WITH THIS VALISE HE'S BEEN CARRYING...
ITS CONTENTS...
KLIK
...AND ANYONE WHO'S COME INTO CONTACT WITH IT.
DEADSHOT?
SHOULDN'T TAKE LONG.
SOMEONE ORDER A PIZZA. I'LL BE RIGHT BACK.
DAN SLOTT · TY TEMPLETON · TERRY BEATTY · LEE LOUGHRIDGE · PHIL FELIX · H. RICHARDS · JOAN HILTY
WRITER PENCILLER INKER COLORIST LETTERER ASSISTANT ED. EDITOR
SHOT TO THE HEART
UNGH--
BATMAN CREATED BY BOB KANE

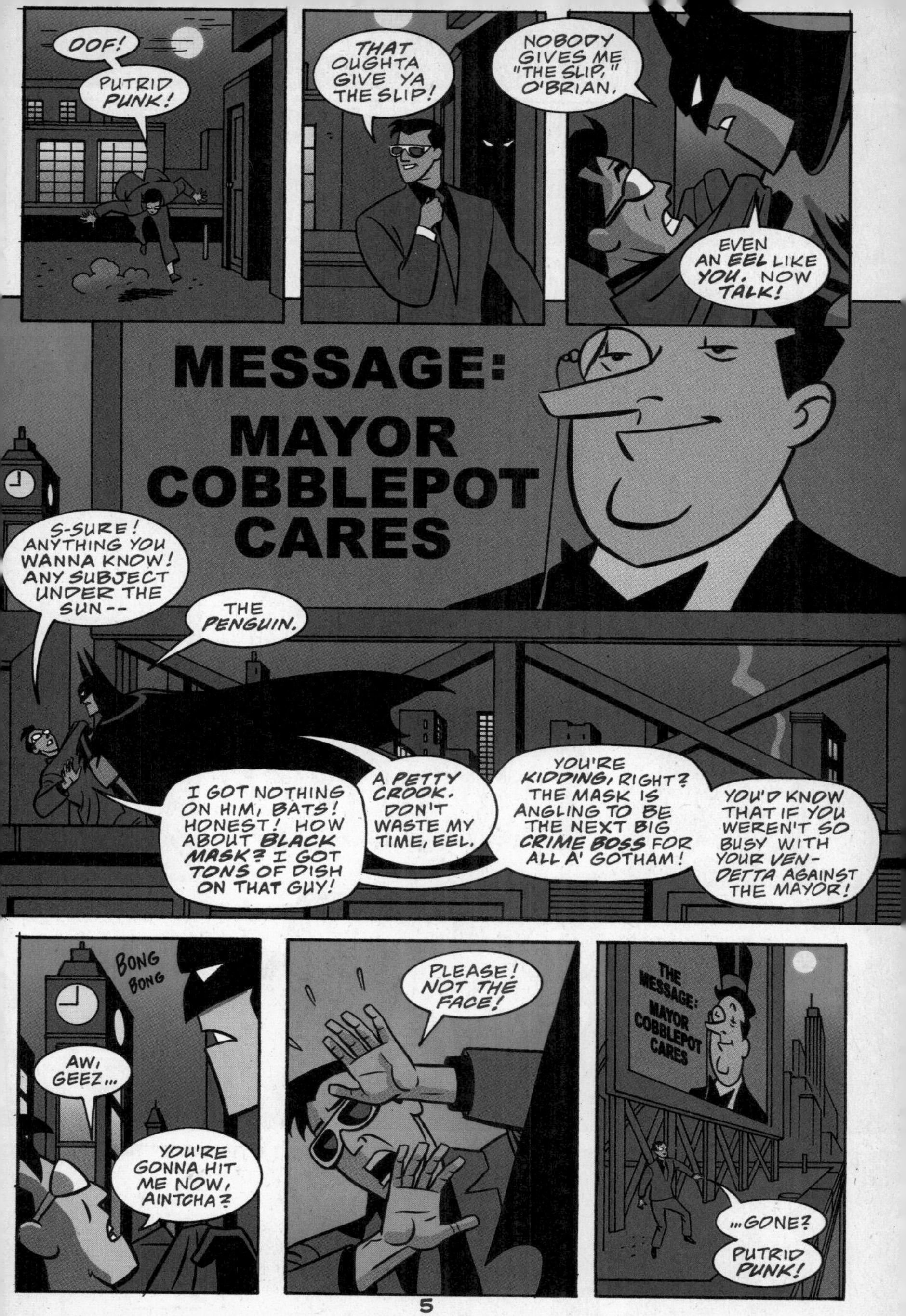
OOF!
PUTRID PUNK!
THAT OUGHTA GIVE YA THE SLIP!
NOBODY GIVES ME "THE SLIP," O'BRIAN.
EVEN AN EEL LIKE YOU. NOW TALK!
MESSAGE: MAYOR COBBLEPOT CARES
S-SURE! ANYTHING YOU WANNA KNOW! ANY SUBJECT UNDER THE SUN--
THE PENGUIN.
I GOT NOTHING ON HIM, BATS! HONEST! HOW ABOUT BLACK MASK? I GOT TONS OF DISH ON THAT GUY!
A PETTY CROOK. DON'T WASTE MY TIME, EEL.
YOU'RE KIDDING, RIGHT? THE MASK IS ANGLING TO BE THE NEXT BIG CRIME BOSS FOR ALL A' GOTHAM!
YOU'D KNOW THAT IF YOU WEREN'T SO BUSY WITH YOUR VEN-DETTA AGAINST THE MAYOR!
BONG BONG
AW, GEEZ...
YOU'RE GONNA HIT ME NOW, AINTCHA?
PLEASE! NOT THE FACE!
THE MESSAGE: MAYOR COBBLEPOT CARES
...GONE?
PUTRID PUNK!

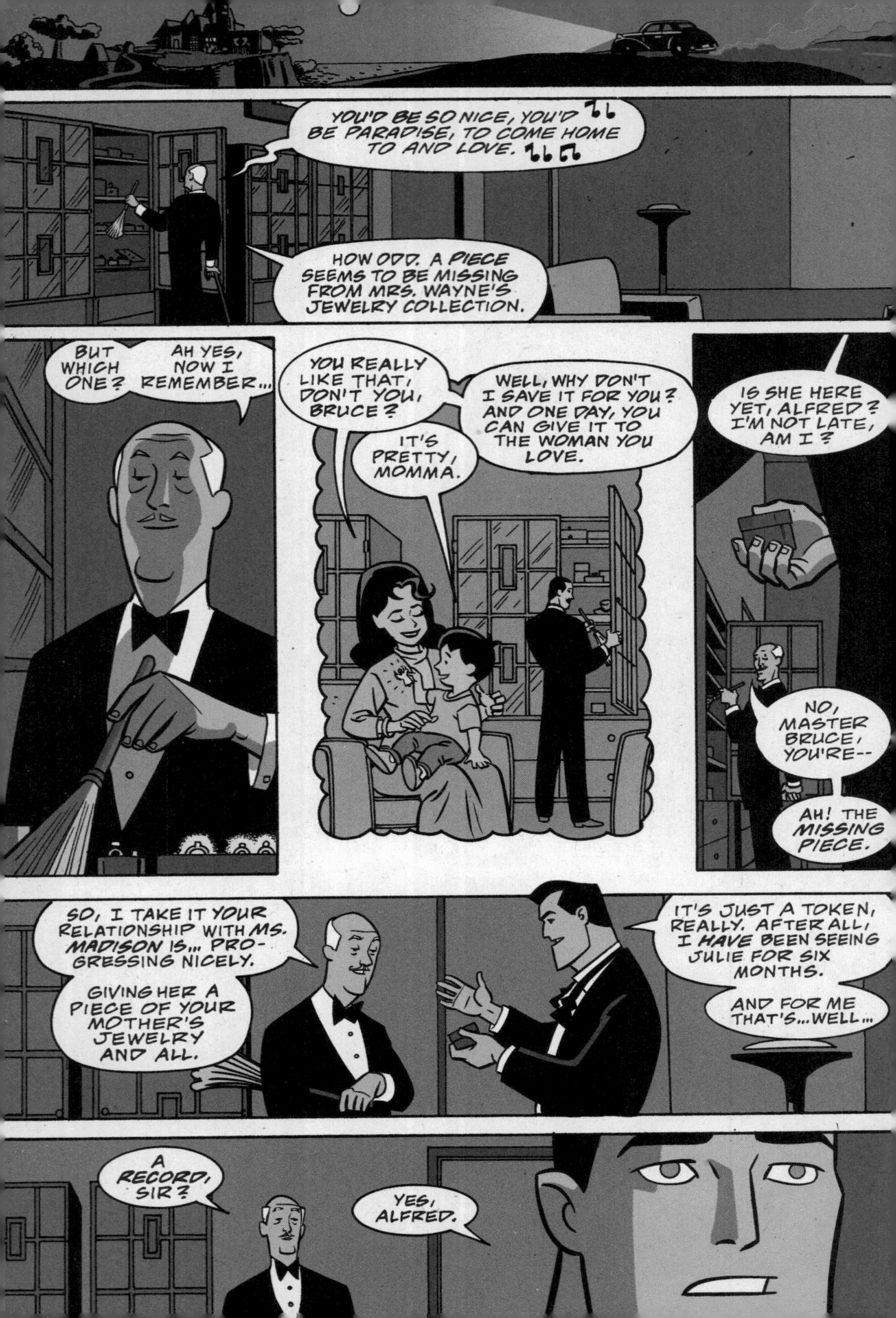

YOU'D BE SO NICE, YOU'D BE PARADISE, TO COME HOME TO AND LOVE.
HOW ODD. A PIECE SEEMS TO BE MISSING FROM MRS. WAYNE'S JEWELRY COLLECTION.
BUT WHICH ONE?
AH YES, NOW I REMEMBER...
YOU REALLY LIKE THAT, DON'T YOU, BRUCE?
IT'S PRETTY, MOMMA.
WELL, WHY DON'T I SAVE IT FOR YOU? AND ONE DAY, YOU CAN GIVE IT TO THE WOMAN YOU LOVE.
IS SHE HERE YET, ALFRED? I'M NOT LATE, AM I?
NO, MASTER BRUCE, YOU'RE--
AH! THE MISSING PIECE.
SO, I TAKE IT YOUR RELATIONSHIP WITH MS. MADISON IS... PROGRESSING NICELY.
GIVING HER A PIECE OF YOUR MOTHER'S JEWELRY AND ALL.
IT'S JUST A TOKEN, REALLY. AFTER ALL, I HAVE BEEN SEEING JULIE FOR SIX MONTHS.
AND FOR ME THAT'S...WELL...
A RECORD, SIR?
YES, ALFRED.

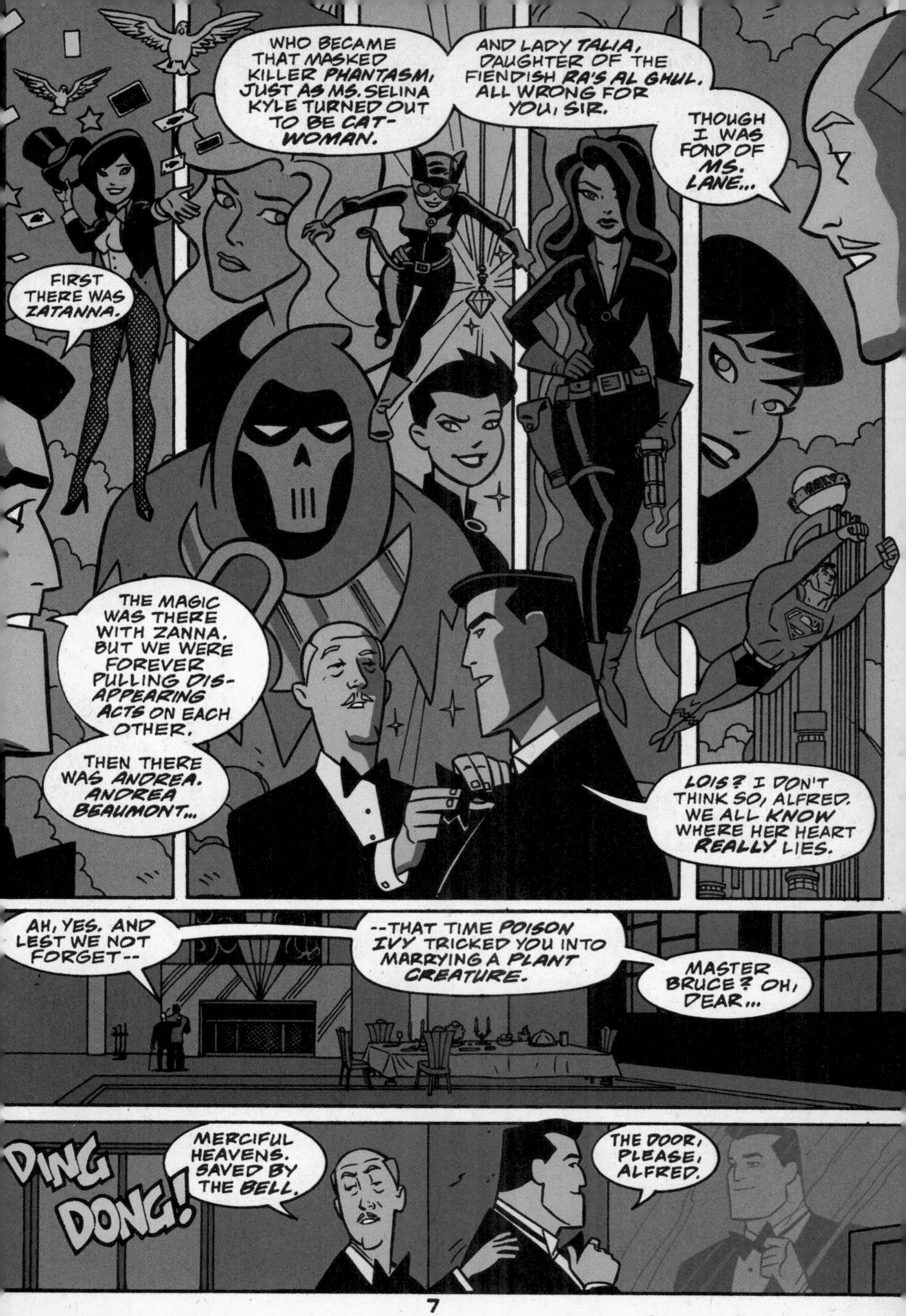
FIRST THERE WAS ZATANNA.
THE MAGIC WAS THERE WITH ZANNA. BUT WE WERE FOREVER PULLING DIS-APPEARING ACTS ON EACH OTHER.
THEN THERE WAS ANDREA. ANDREA BEAUMONT...
WHO BECAME THAT MASKED KILLER PHANTASM, JUST AS MS. SELINA KYLE TURNED OUT TO BE CAT-WOMAN.
AND LADY TALIA, DAUGHTER OF THE FIENDISH RA'S AL GHUL. ALL WRONG FOR YOU, SIR.
THOUGH I WAS FOND OF MS. LANE...
LOIS? I DON'T THINK SO, ALFRED. WE ALL KNOW WHERE HER HEART REALLY LIES.
AH, YES. AND LEST WE NOT FORGET--
--THAT TIME POISON IVY TRICKED YOU INTO MARRYING A PLANT CREATURE.
MASTER BRUCE? OH, DEAR...
DING DONG!
MERCIFUL HEAVENS. SAVED BY THE BELL.
THE DOOR, PLEASE, ALFRED.

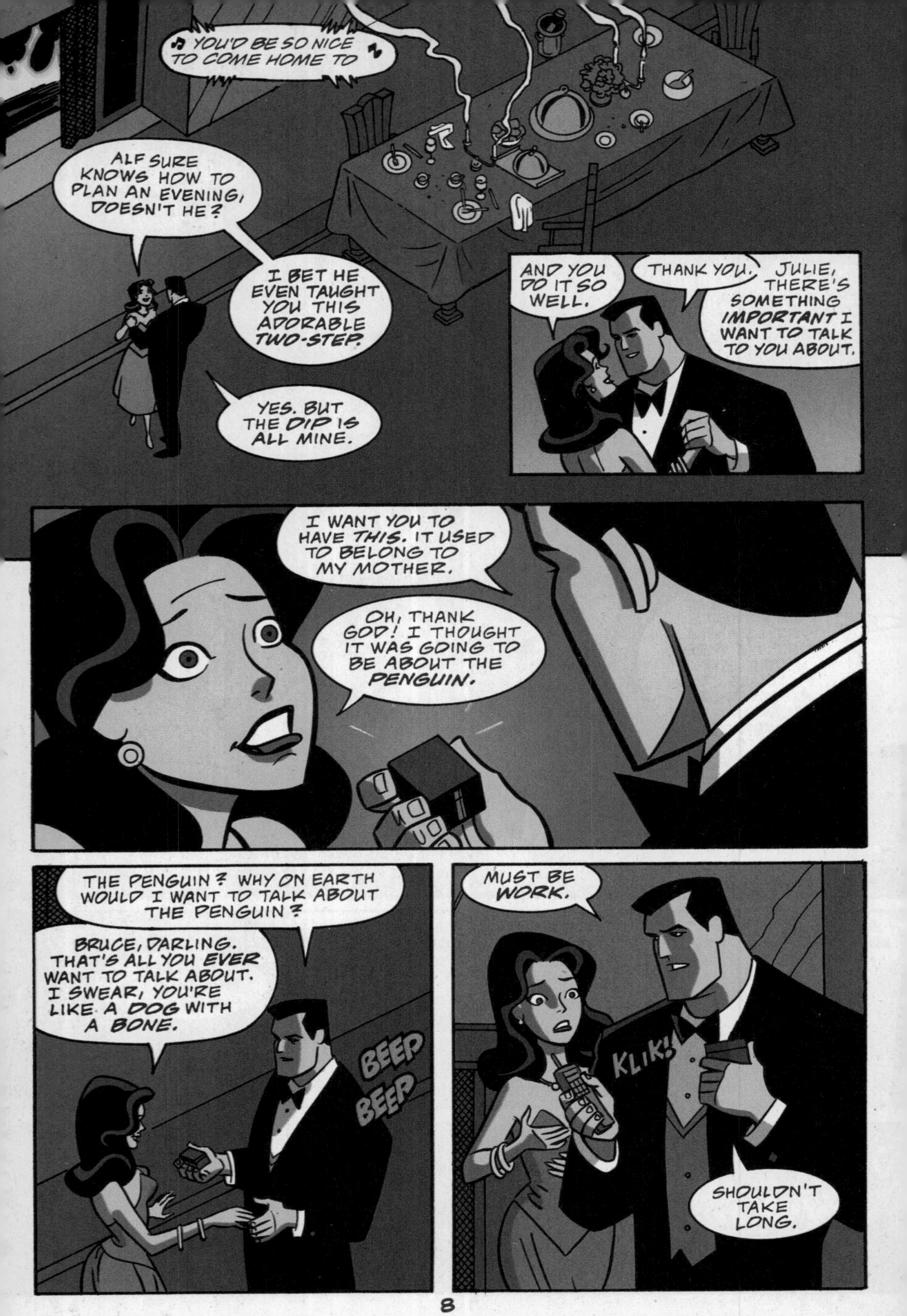
YOU'D BE SO NICE TO COME HOME TO
ALF SURE KNOWS HOW TO PLAN AN EVENING, DOESN'T HE?
I BET HE EVEN TAUGHT YOU THIS ADORABLE TWO-STEP.
YES. BUT THE DIP IS ALL MINE.
AND YOU DO IT SO WELL.
THANK YOU.
JULIE, THERE'S SOMETHING IMPORTANT I WANT TO TALK TO YOU ABOUT.
I WANT YOU TO HAVE THIS. IT USED TO BELONG TO MY MOTHER.
OH, THANK GOD! I THOUGHT IT WAS GOING TO BE ABOUT THE PENGUIN.
THE PENGUIN? WHY ON EARTH WOULD I WANT TO TALK ABOUT THE PENGUIN?
BRUCE, DARLING. THAT'S ALL YOU EVER WANT TO TALK ABOUT. I SWEAR, YOU'RE LIKE A DOG WITH A BONE.
BEEP BEEP
MUST BE WORK.
KLIK!
SHOULDN'T TAKE LONG.

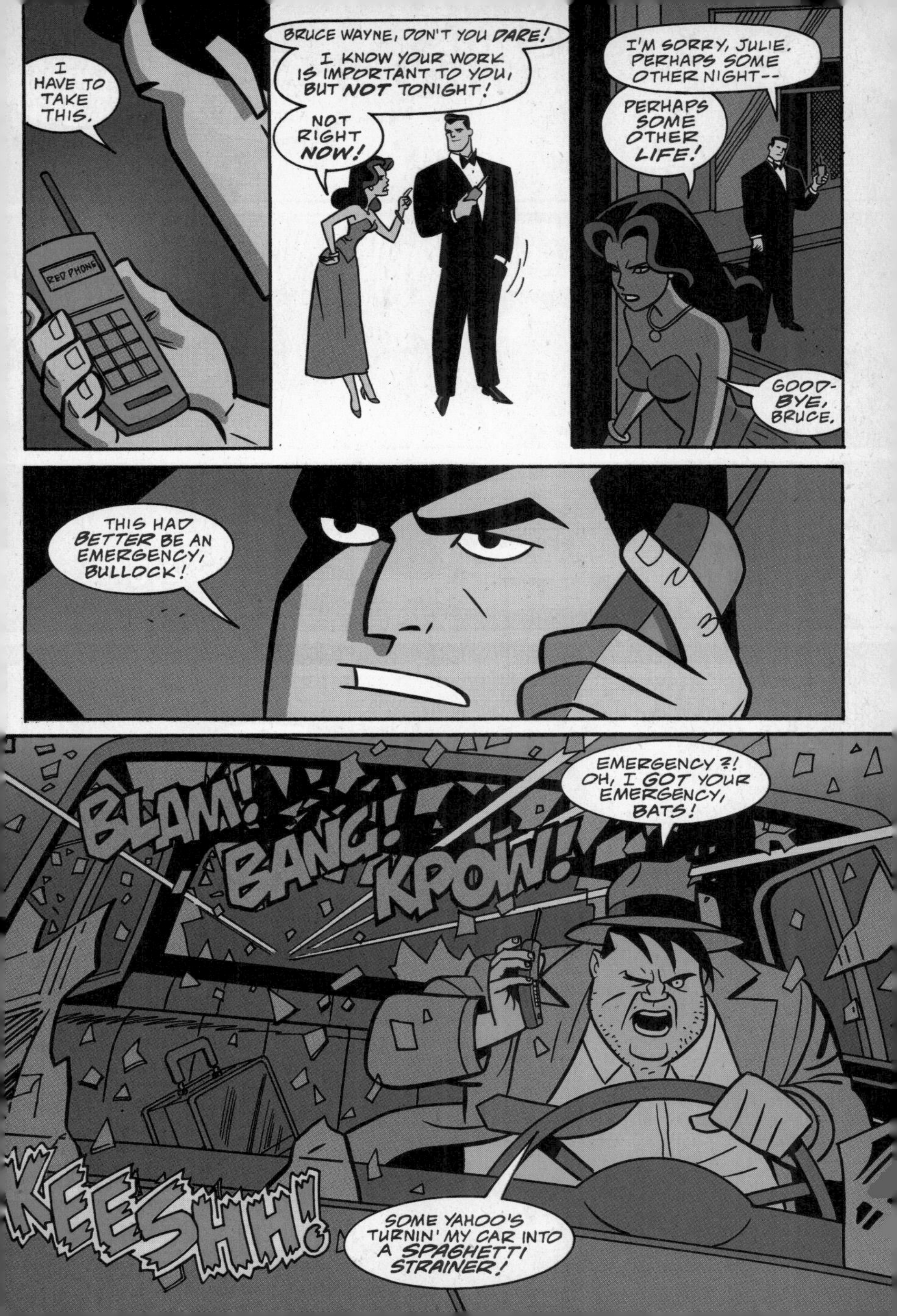
I HAVE TO TAKE THIS.
RED PHONE
BRUCE WAYNE, DON'T YOU DARE!
I KNOW YOUR WORK IS IMPORTANT TO YOU, BUT NOT TONIGHT!
NOT RIGHT NOW!
I'M SORRY, JULIE. PERHAPS SOME OTHER NIGHT--
PERHAPS SOME OTHER LIFE!
GOOD-BYE, BRUCE.
THIS HAD BETTER BE AN EMERGENCY, BULLOCK!
BLAM! BANG! KPOW!
EMERGENCY ?! OH, I GOT YOUR EMERGENCY, BATS!
KEESHH!
SOME YAHOO'S TURNIN' MY CAR INTO A SPAGHETTI STRAINER!

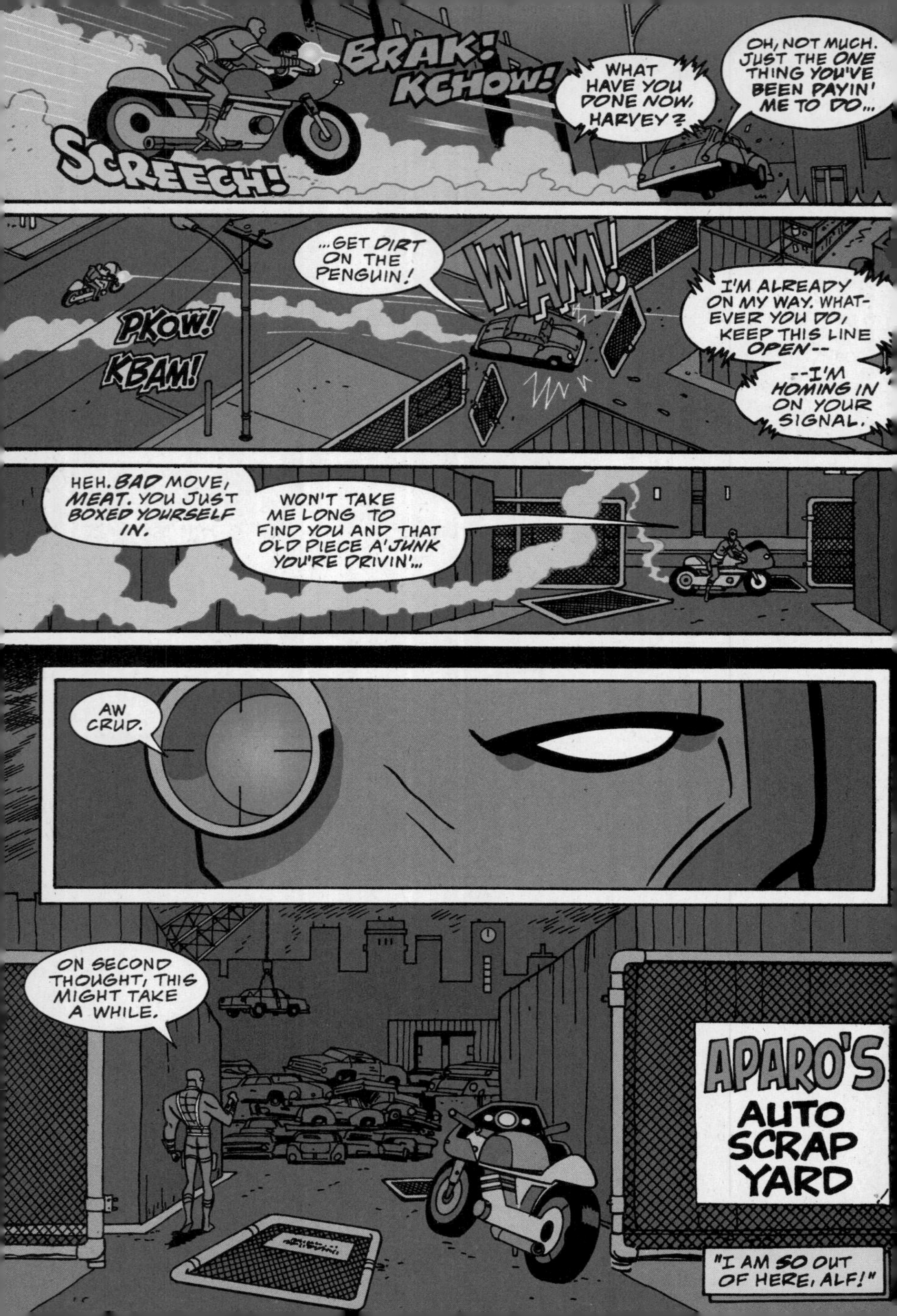
BRAK!
KCHOW!
SCREEECH!
WHAT HAVE YOU DONE NOW, HARVEY?
OH, NOT MUCH. JUST THE ONE THING YOU'VE BEEN PAYIN' ME TO DO...
...GET DIRT ON THE PENGUIN!
WAM!
PKOW!
KBAM!
I'M ALREADY ON MY WAY. WHATEVER YOU DO, KEEP THIS LINE OPEN--
--I'M HOMING IN ON YOUR SIGNAL.
HEH. BAD MOVE, MEAT. YOU JUST BOXED YOURSELF IN.
WON'T TAKE ME LONG TO FIND YOU AND THAT OLD PIECE A'JUNK YOU'RE DRIVIN'...
AW CRUD.
ON SECOND THOUGHT, THIS MIGHT TAKE A WHILE.
APARO'S
AUTO SCRAP YARD
"I AM SO OUT OF HERE, ALF!"

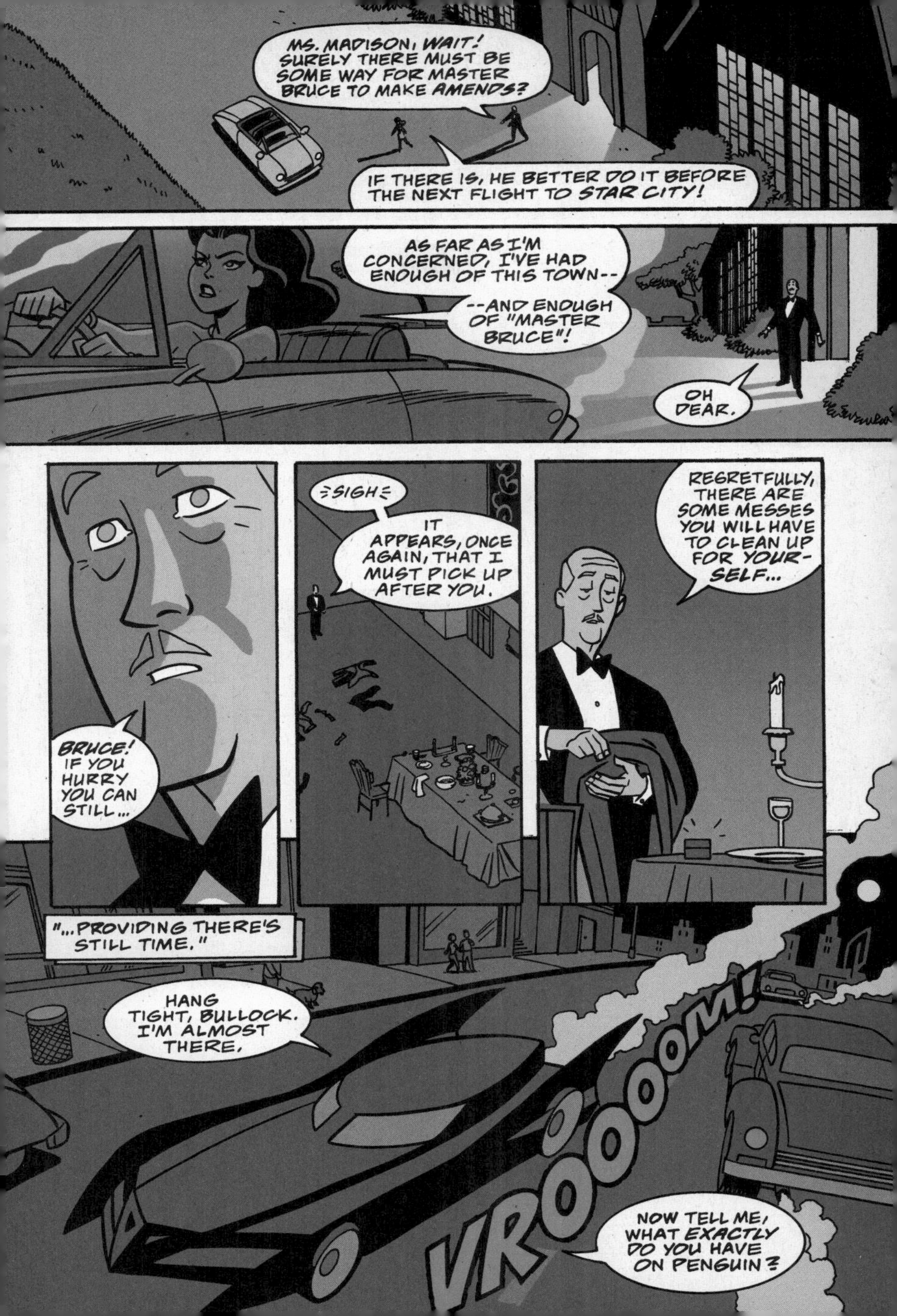
MS. MADISON, WAIT! SURELY THERE MUST BE SOME WAY FOR MASTER BRUCE TO MAKE AMENDS?
IF THERE IS, HE BETTER DO IT BEFORE THE NEXT FLIGHT TO STAR CITY!
AS FAR AS I'M CONCERNED, I'VE HAD ENOUGH OF THIS TOWN--
--AND ENOUGH OF "MASTER BRUCE"!
OH DEAR.
BRUCE! IF YOU HURRY YOU CAN STILL...
SIGH
IT APPEARS, ONCE AGAIN, THAT I MUST PICK UP AFTER YOU.
REGRETFULLY, THERE ARE SOME MESSES YOU WILL HAVE TO CLEAN UP FOR YOURSELF...
"...PROVIDING THERE'S STILL TIME."
HANG TIGHT, BULLOCK. I'M ALMOST THERE.
VROOOOOOM!
NOW TELL ME, WHAT EXACTLY DO YOU HAVE ON PENGUIN?

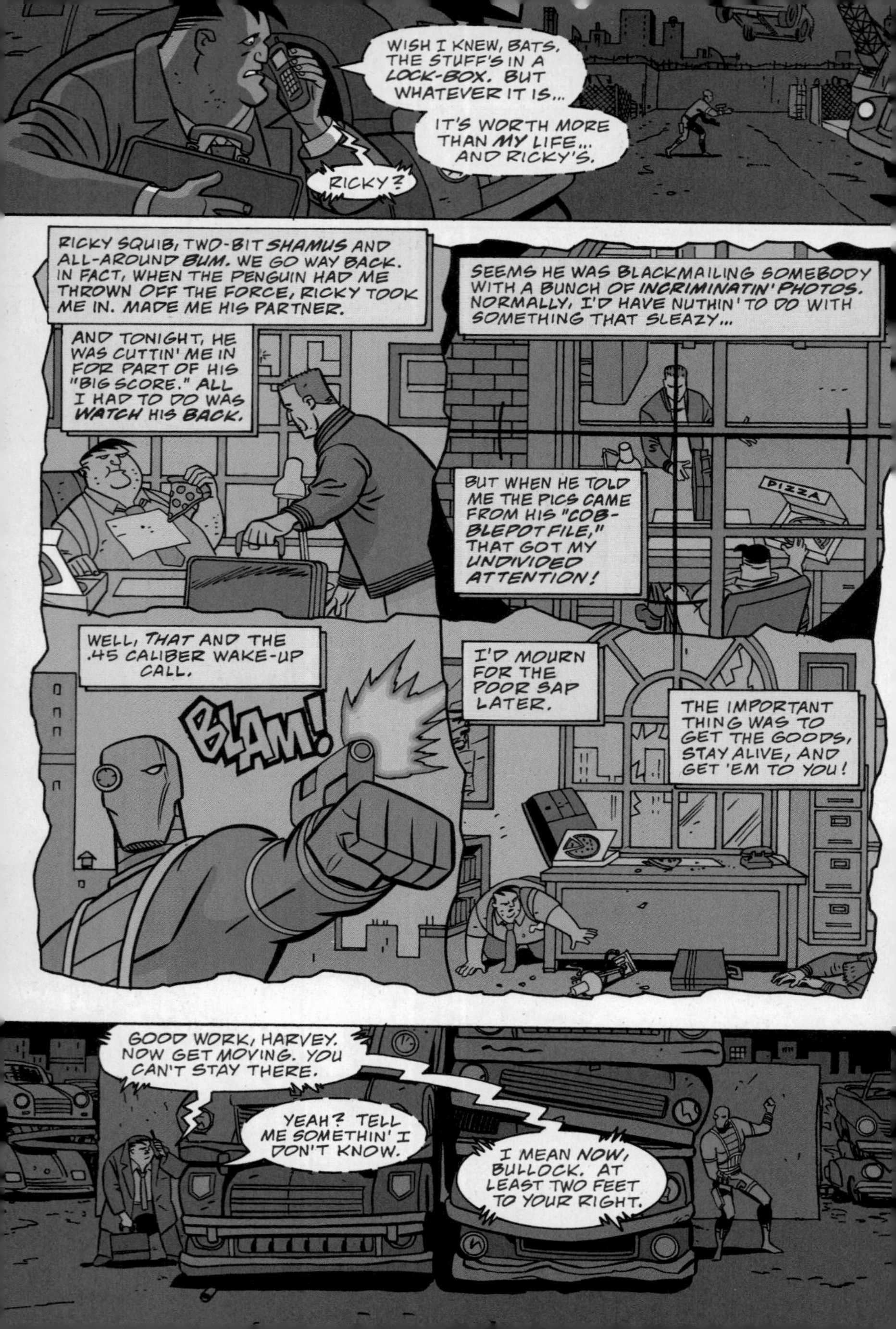
WISH I KNEW, BATS. THE STUFF'S IN A LOCK-BOX. BUT WHATEVER IT IS...
IT'S WORTH MORE THAN MY LIFE... AND RICKY'S.
RICKY?
RICKY SQUIB, TWO-BIT SHAMUS AND ALL-AROUND BUM. WE GO WAY BACK. IN FACT, WHEN THE PENGUIN HAD ME THROWN OFF THE FORCE, RICKY TOOK ME IN. MADE ME HIS PARTNER.
AND TONIGHT, HE WAS CUTTIN' ME IN FOR PART OF HIS "BIG SCORE." ALL I HAD TO DO WAS WATCH HIS BACK.
SEEMS HE WAS BLACKMAILING SOMEBODY WITH A BUNCH OF INCRIMINATIN' PHOTOS. NORMALLY, I'D HAVE NUTHIN' TO DO WITH SOMETHING THAT SLEAZY...
PIZZA
BUT WHEN HE TOLD ME THE PICS CAME FROM HIS "COB-BLEPOT FILE," THAT GOT MY UNDIVIDED ATTENTION!
WELL, THAT AND THE .45 CALIBER WAKE-UP CALL.
BLAM!
I'D MOURN FOR THE POOR SAP LATER.
THE IMPORTANT THING WAS TO GET THE GOODS, STAY ALIVE, AND GET 'EM TO YOU!
GOOD WORK, HARVEY. NOW GET MOVING. YOU CAN'T STAY THERE.
YEAH? TELL ME SOMETHIN' I DON'T KNOW.
I MEAN NOW, BULLOCK. AT LEAST TWO FEET TO YOUR RIGHT.

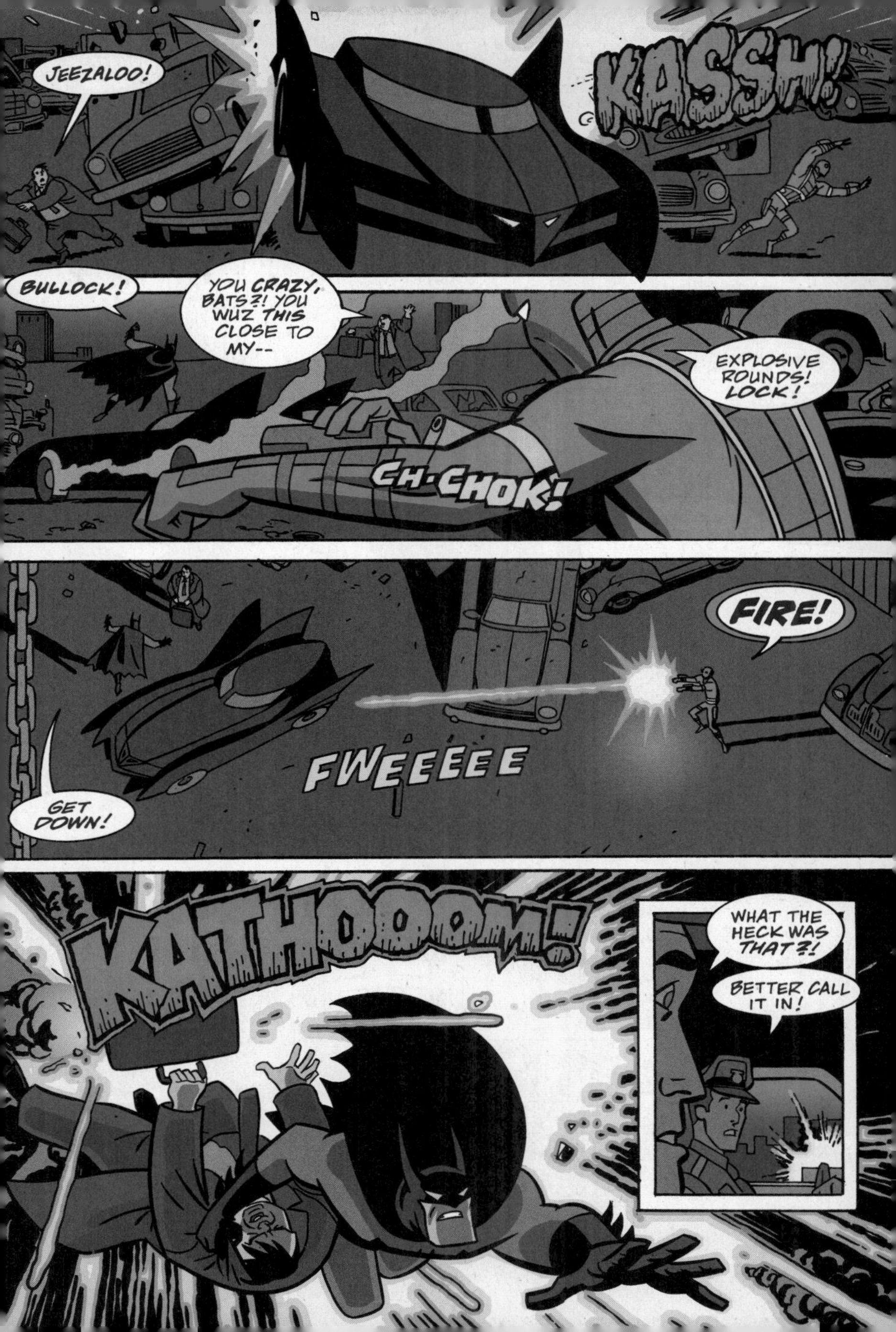

JEEZALOO!
KASSH!
BULLOCK!
YOU CRAZY, BATS?! YOU WUZ THIS CLOSE TO MY--
EXPLOSIVE ROUNDS! LOCK!
CH-CHOK!
FIRE!
FWEEEEE
GET DOWN!
KATHOOOM!
WHAT THE HECK WAS THAT?!
BETTER CALL IT IN!

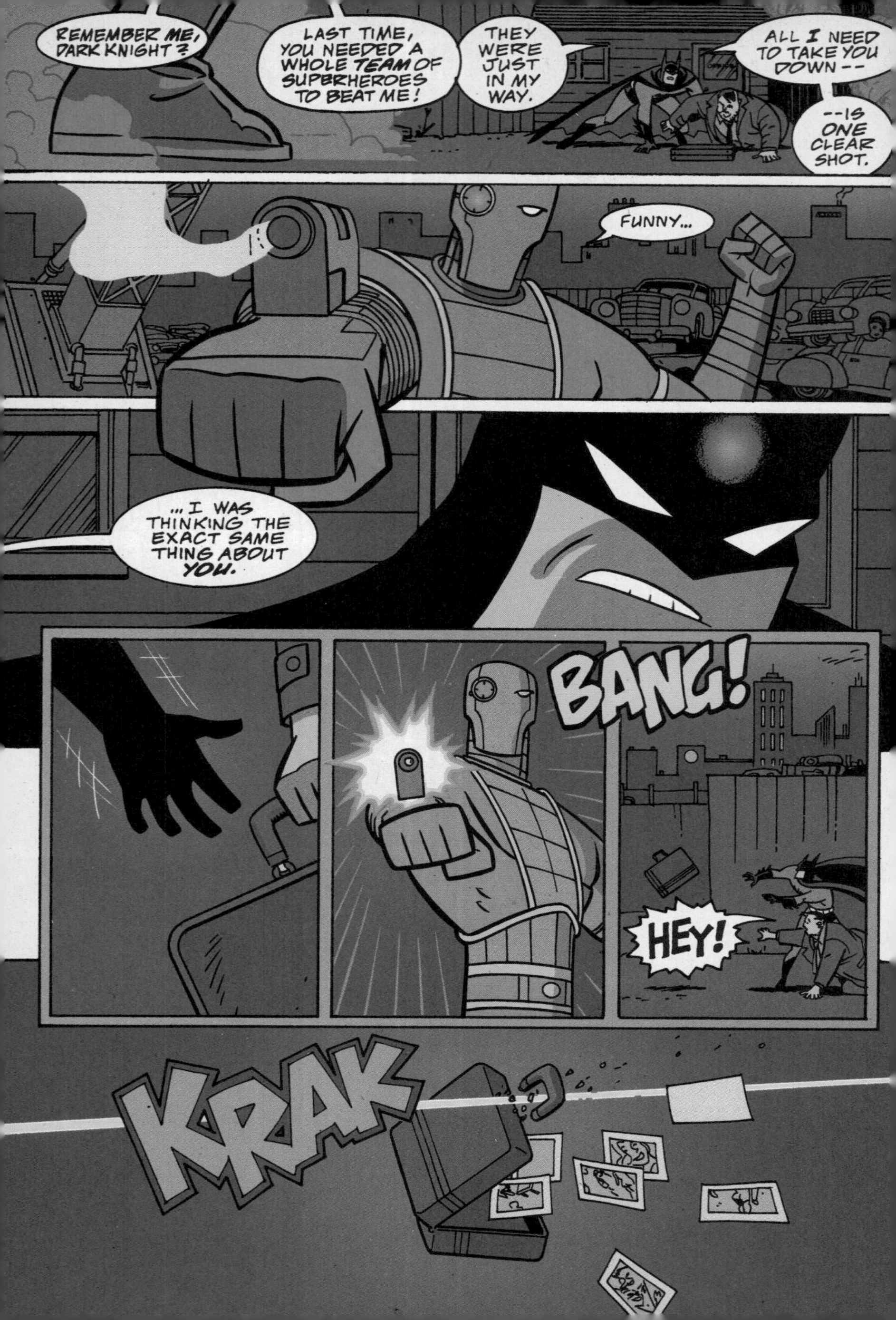
REMEMBER ME, DARK KNIGHT?
LAST TIME, YOU NEEDED A WHOLE TEAM OF SUPERHEROES TO BEAT ME!
THEY WERE JUST IN MY WAY.
ALL I NEED TO TAKE YOU DOWN --
--IS ONE CLEAR SHOT.
FUNNY...
...I WAS THINKING THE EXACT SAME THING ABOUT YOU.
BANG!
HEY!
KRAK

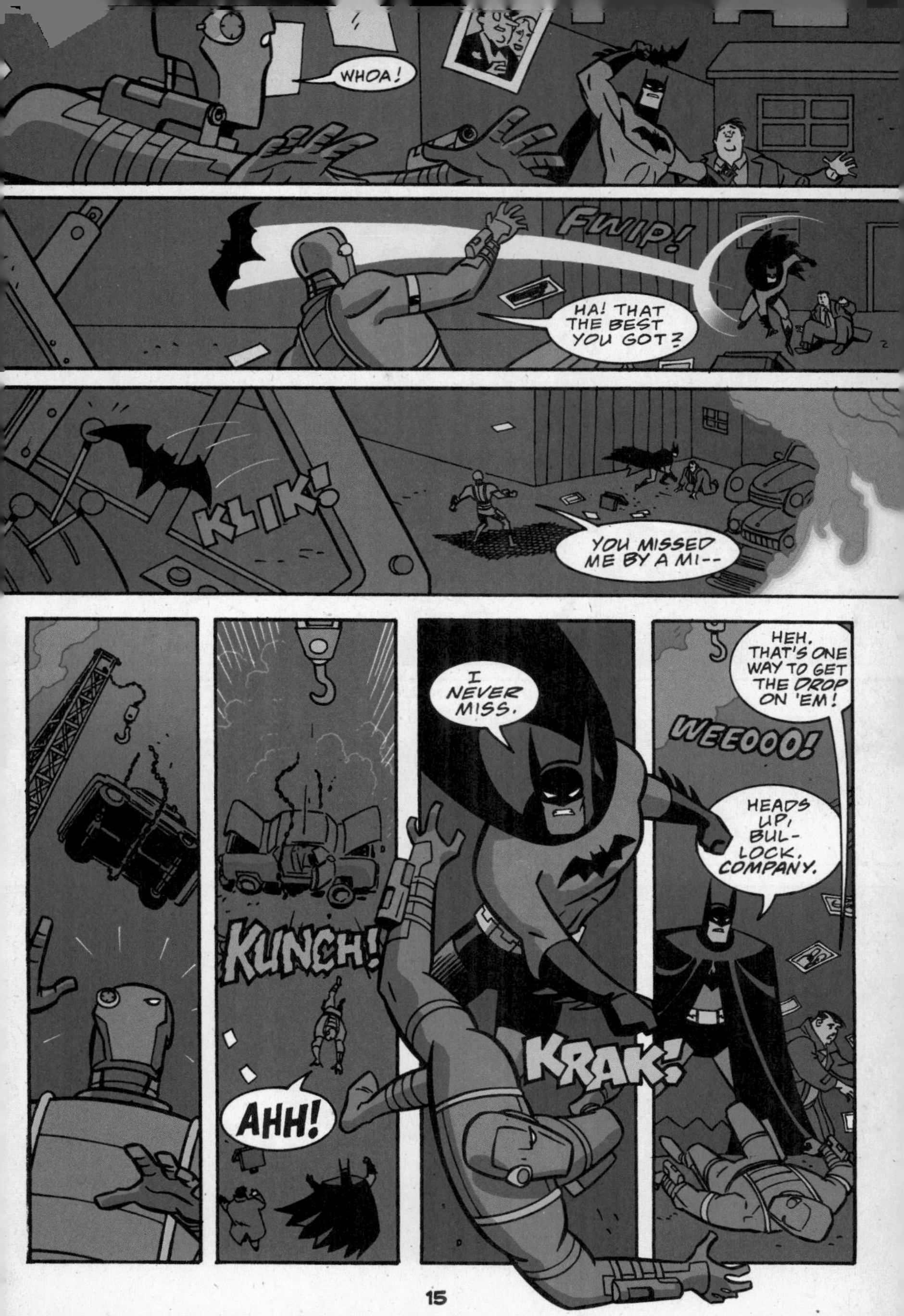
WHOA!
FWIP!
HA! THAT THE BEST YOU GOT?
KLIK!
YOU MISSED ME BY A MI--
KUNCH!
AHH!
I NEVER MISS.
KRAK!
HEH. THAT'S ONE WAY TO GET THE DROP ON 'EM!
WEEOOO!
HEADS UP, BUL-LOCK. COMPANY.

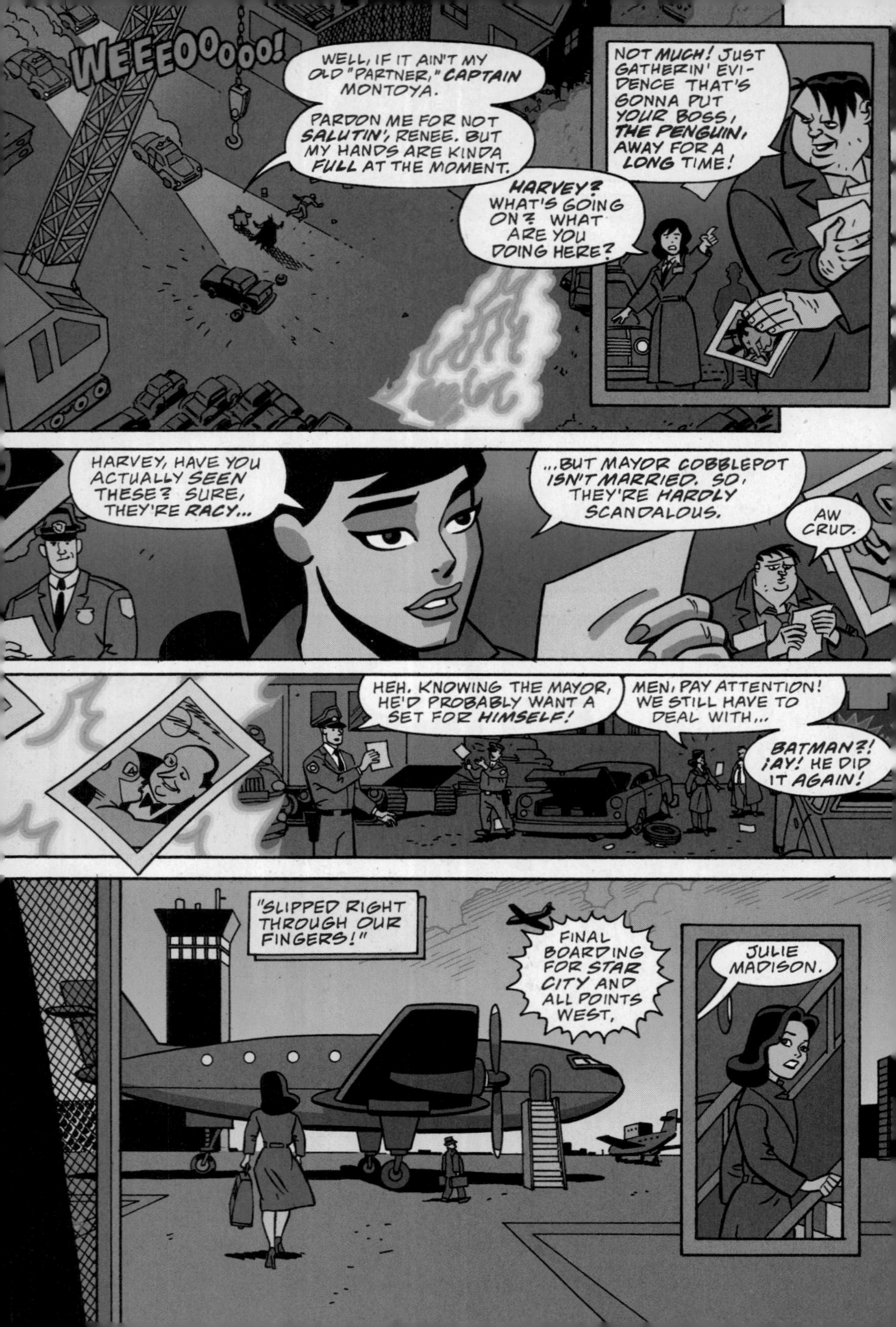
WEEEOOoooo!
WELL, IF IT AIN'T MY OLD "PARTNER," CAPTAIN MONTOYA.
PARDON ME FOR NOT SALUTIN', RENEE. BUT MY HANDS ARE KINDA FULL AT THE MOMENT.
HARVEY? WHAT'S GOING ON? WHAT ARE YOU DOING HERE?
NOT MUCH! JUST GATHERIN' EVI-DENCE THAT'S GONNA PUT YOUR BOSS, THE PENGUIN, AWAY FOR A LONG TIME!
HARVEY, HAVE YOU ACTUALLY SEEN THESE? SURE, THEY'RE RACY...
...BUT MAYOR COBBLEPOT ISN'T MARRIED. SO, THEY'RE HARDLY SCANDALOUS.
AW CRUD.
HEH. KNOWING THE MAYOR, HE'D PROBABLY WANT A SET FOR HIMSELF!
MEN, PAY ATTENTION! WE STILL HAVE TO DEAL WITH...
BATMAN?! ¡AY! HE DID IT AGAIN!
"SLIPPED RIGHT THROUGH OUR FINGERS!"
FINAL BOARDING FOR STAR CITY AND ALL POINTS WEST.
JULIE MADISON.

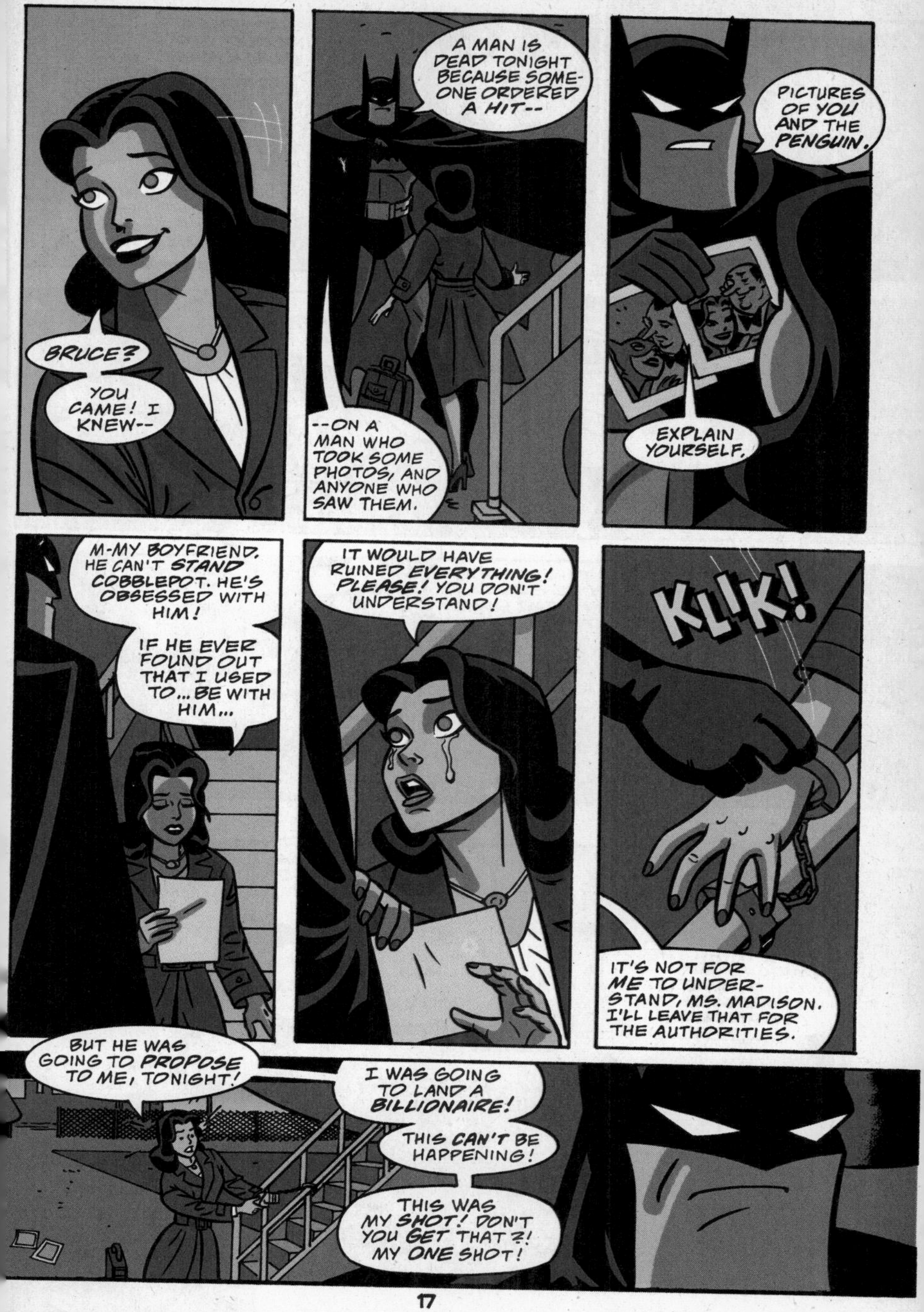

BRUCE?
YOU CAME! I KNEW--
A MAN IS DEAD TONIGHT BECAUSE SOME-ONE ORDERED A HIT--
--ON A MAN WHO TOOK SOME PHOTOS, AND ANYONE WHO SAW THEM.
PICTURES OF YOU AND THE PENGUIN.
EXPLAIN YOURSELF.
M-MY BOYFRIEND. HE CAN'T STAND COBBLEPOT. HE'S OBSESSED WITH HIM!
IF HE EVER FOUND OUT THAT I USED TO... BE WITH HIM...
IT WOULD HAVE RUINED EVERYTHING! PLEASE! YOU DON'T UNDERSTAND!
KLIK!
IT'S NOT FOR ME TO UNDER-STAND, MS. MADISON. I'LL LEAVE THAT FOR THE AUTHORITIES.
BUT HE WAS GOING TO PROPOSE TO ME, TONIGHT!
I WAS GOING TO LAND A BILLIONAIRE!
THIS CAN'T BE HAPPENING!
THIS WAS MY SHOT! DON'T YOU GET THAT?! MY ONE SHOT!

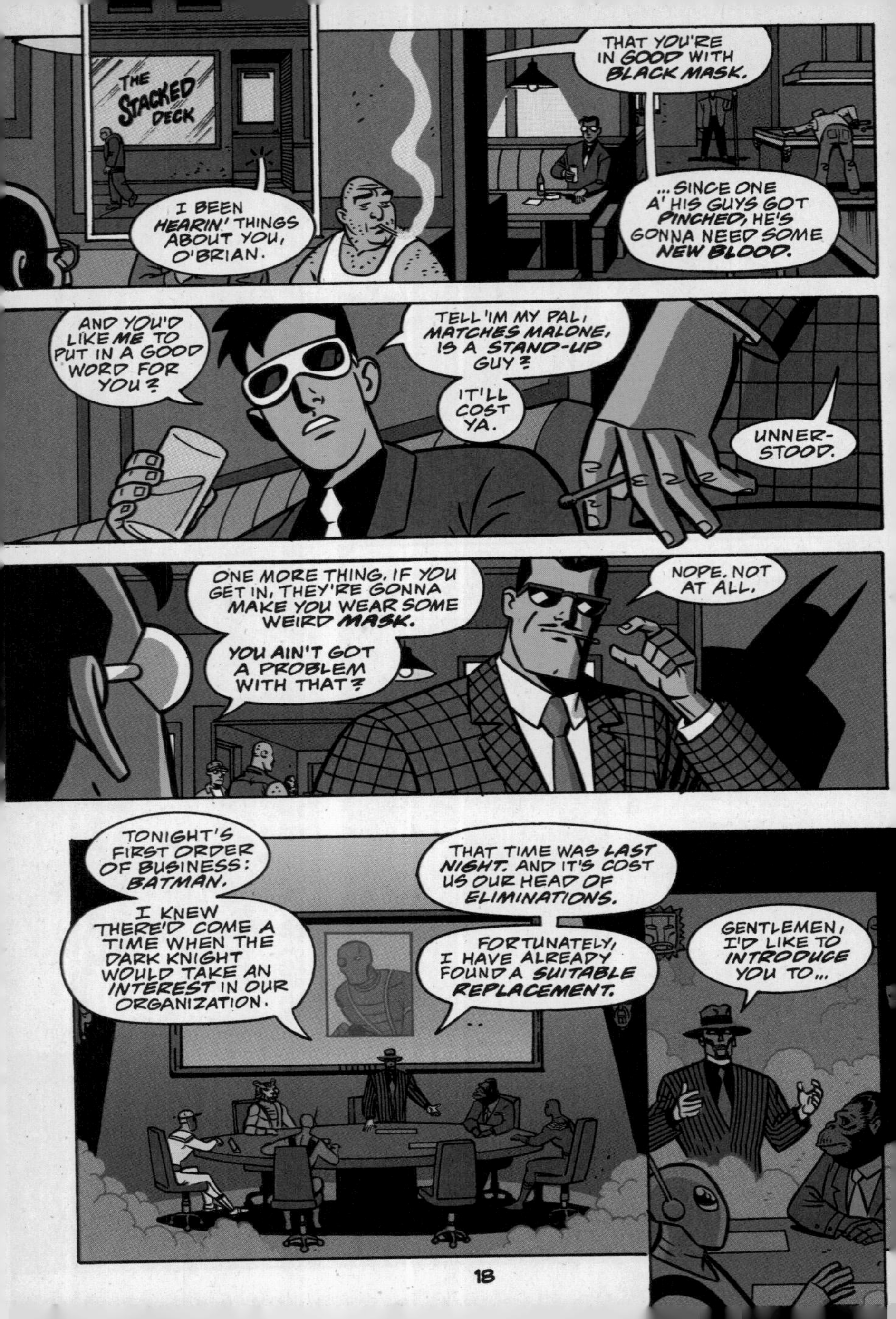

THE STACKED DECK
I BEEN HEARIN' THINGS ABOUT YOU, O'BRIAN.
THAT YOU'RE IN GOOD WITH BLACK MASK.
...SINCE ONE A' HIS GUYS GOT PINCHED, HE'S GONNA NEED SOME NEW BLOOD.
AND YOU'D LIKE ME TO PUT IN A GOOD WORD FOR YOU?
TELL 'IM MY PAL, MATCHES MALONE, IS A STAND-UP GUY?
IT'LL COST YA.
UNNER-STOOD.
ONE MORE THING. IF YOU GET IN, THEY'RE GONNA MAKE YOU WEAR SOME WEIRD MASK.
YOU AIN'T GOT A PROBLEM WITH THAT?
NOPE. NOT AT ALL.
TONIGHT'S FIRST ORDER OF BUSINESS: BATMAN.
I KNEW THERE'D COME A TIME WHEN THE DARK KNIGHT WOULD TAKE AN INTEREST IN OUR ORGANIZATION.
THAT TIME WAS LAST NIGHT. AND IT'S COST US OUR HEAD OF ELIMINATIONS.
FORTUNATELY, I HAVE ALREADY FOUND A SUITABLE REPLACEMENT.
GENTLEMEN, I'D LIKE TO INTRODUCE YOU TO...

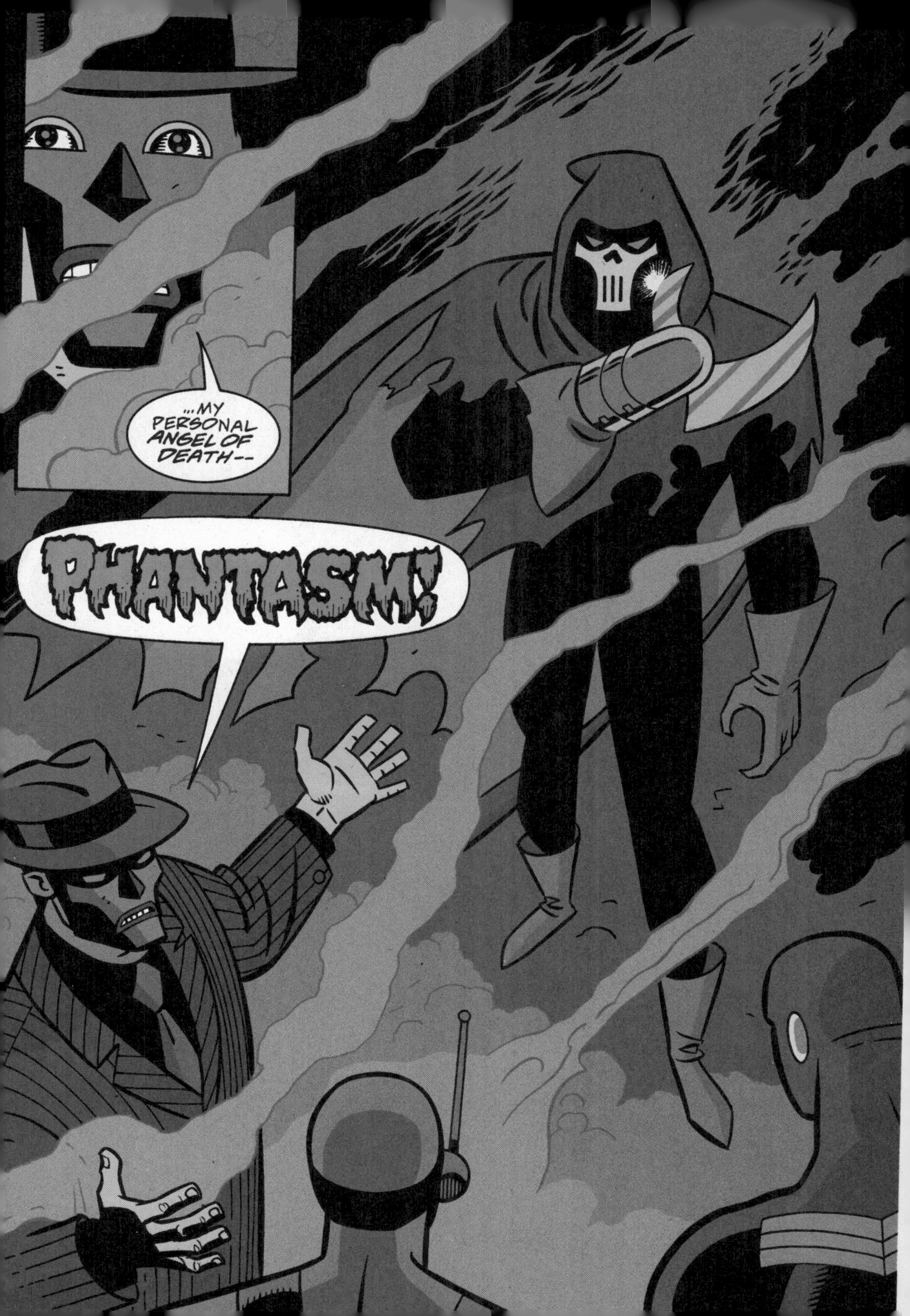
...MY PERSONAL ANGEL OF DEATH--
PHANTASM!

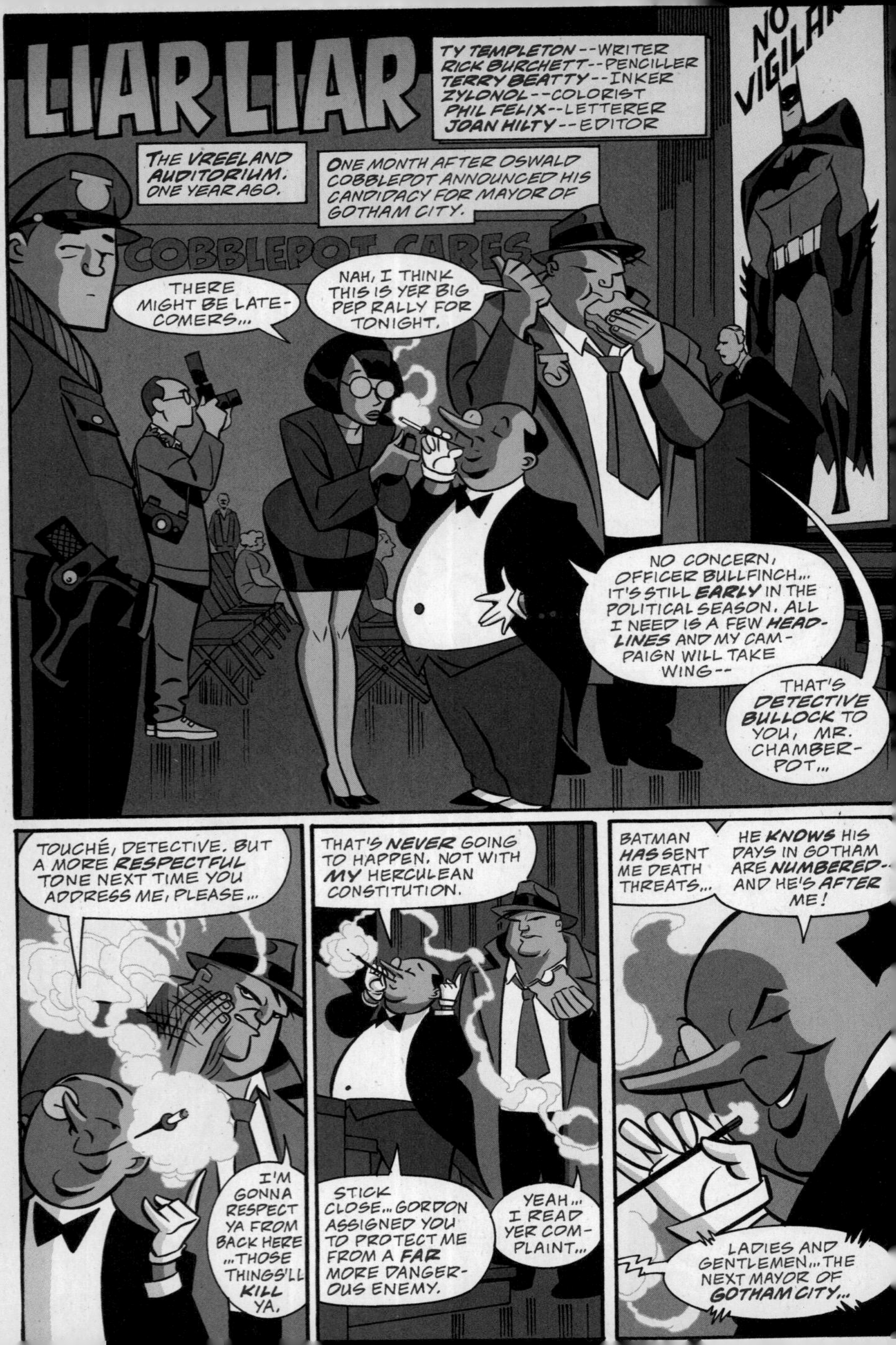
LIAR LIAR
TY TEMPLETON--WRITER
RICK BURCHETT--PENCILLER
TERRY BEATTY--INKER
ZYLONOL--COLORIST
PHIL FELIX--LETTERER
JOAN HILTY--EDITOR
NO VIGILAN
THE VREELAND AUDITORIUM. ONE YEAR AGO.
ONE MONTH AFTER OSWALD COBBLEPOT ANNOUNCED HIS CANDIDACY FOR MAYOR OF GOTHAM CITY.
COBBLEPOT CARES
THERE MIGHT BE LATE-COMERS...
NAH, I THINK THIS IS YER BIG PEP RALLY FOR TONIGHT.
NO CONCERN, OFFICER BULLFINCH... IT'S STILL EARLY IN THE POLITICAL SEASON. ALL I NEED IS A FEW HEAD-LINES AND MY CAM-PAIGN WILL TAKE WING--
THAT'S DETECTIVE BULLOCK TO YOU, MR. CHAMBER-POT...
TOUCHÉ, DETECTIVE. BUT A MORE RESPECTFUL TONE NEXT TIME YOU ADDRESS ME, PLEASE...
I'M GONNA RESPECT YA FROM BACK HERE ...THOSE THINGS'LL KILL YA.
THAT'S NEVER GOING TO HAPPEN. NOT WITH MY HERCULEAN CONSTITUTION.
STICK CLOSE...GORDON ASSIGNED YOU TO PROTECT ME FROM A FAR MORE DANGER-OUS ENEMY.
YEAH... I READ YER COM-PLAINT...
BATMAN HAS SENT ME DEATH THREATS...
HE KNOWS HIS DAYS IN GOTHAM ARE NUMBERED-- AND HE'S AFTER ME!
LADIES AND GENTLEMEN... THE NEXT MAYOR OF GOTHAM CITY...

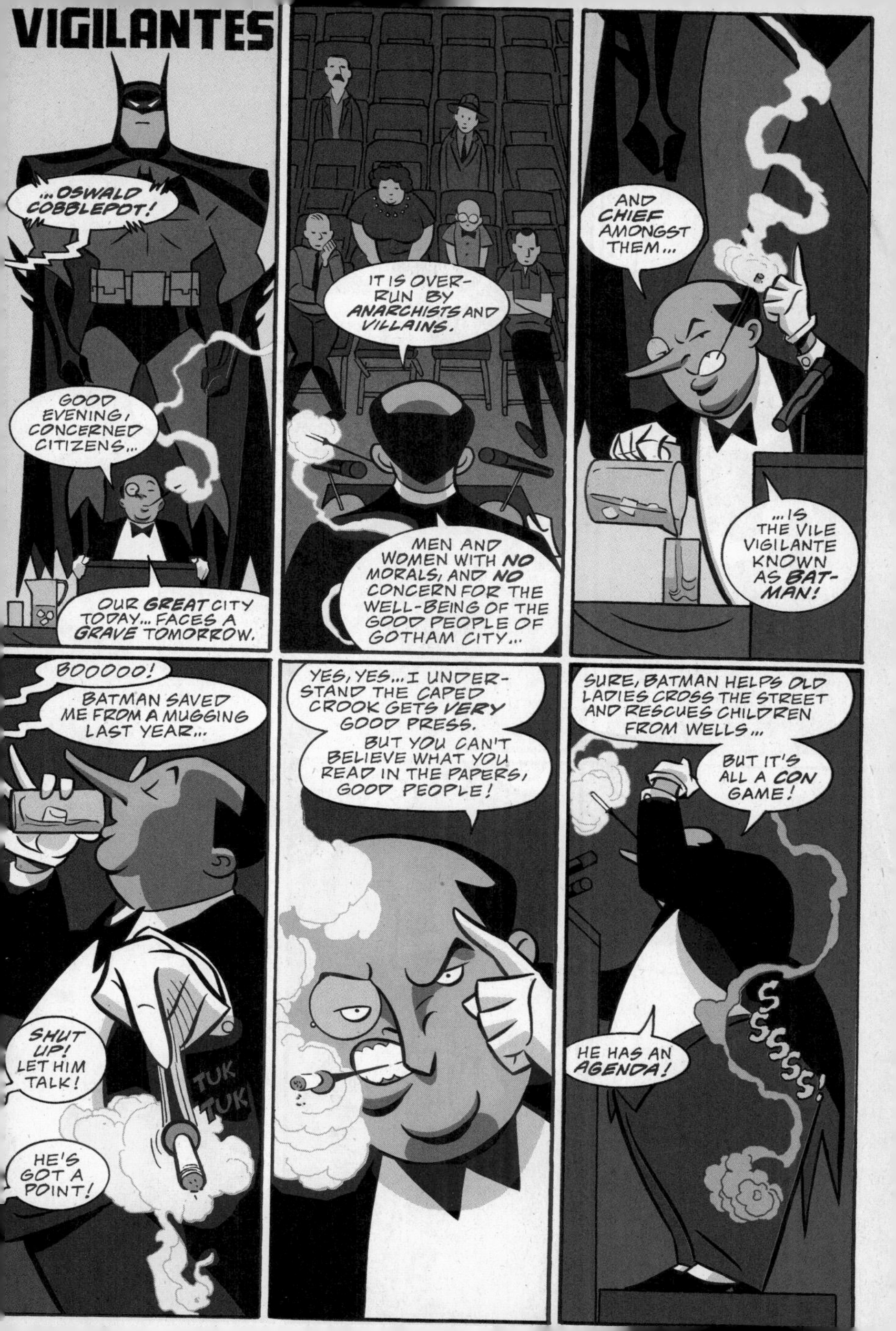
VIGILANTES
...OSWALD COBBLEPOT!
GOOD EVENING, CONCERNED CITIZENS...
OUR GREAT CITY TODAY... FACES A GRAVE TOMORROW.
IT IS OVER-RUN BY ANARCHISTS AND VILLAINS.
MEN AND WOMEN WITH NO MORALS, AND NO CONCERN FOR THE WELL-BEING OF THE GOOD PEOPLE OF GOTHAM CITY...
AND CHIEF AMONGST THEM...
...IS THE VILE VIGILANTE KNOWN AS BAT-MAN!
BOOOOOO!
BATMAN SAVED ME FROM A MUGGING LAST YEAR...
SHUT UP! LET HIM TALK!
TUK TUK
HE'S GOT A POINT!
YES, YES... I UNDER-STAND THE CAPED CROOK GETS VERY GOOD PRESS.
BUT YOU CAN'T BELIEVE WHAT YOU READ IN THE PAPERS, GOOD PEOPLE!
SURE, BATMAN HELPS OLD LADIES CROSS THE STREET AND RESCUES CHILDREN FROM WELLS...
BUT IT'S ALL A CON GAME!
HE HAS AN AGENDA!
SSSSS!

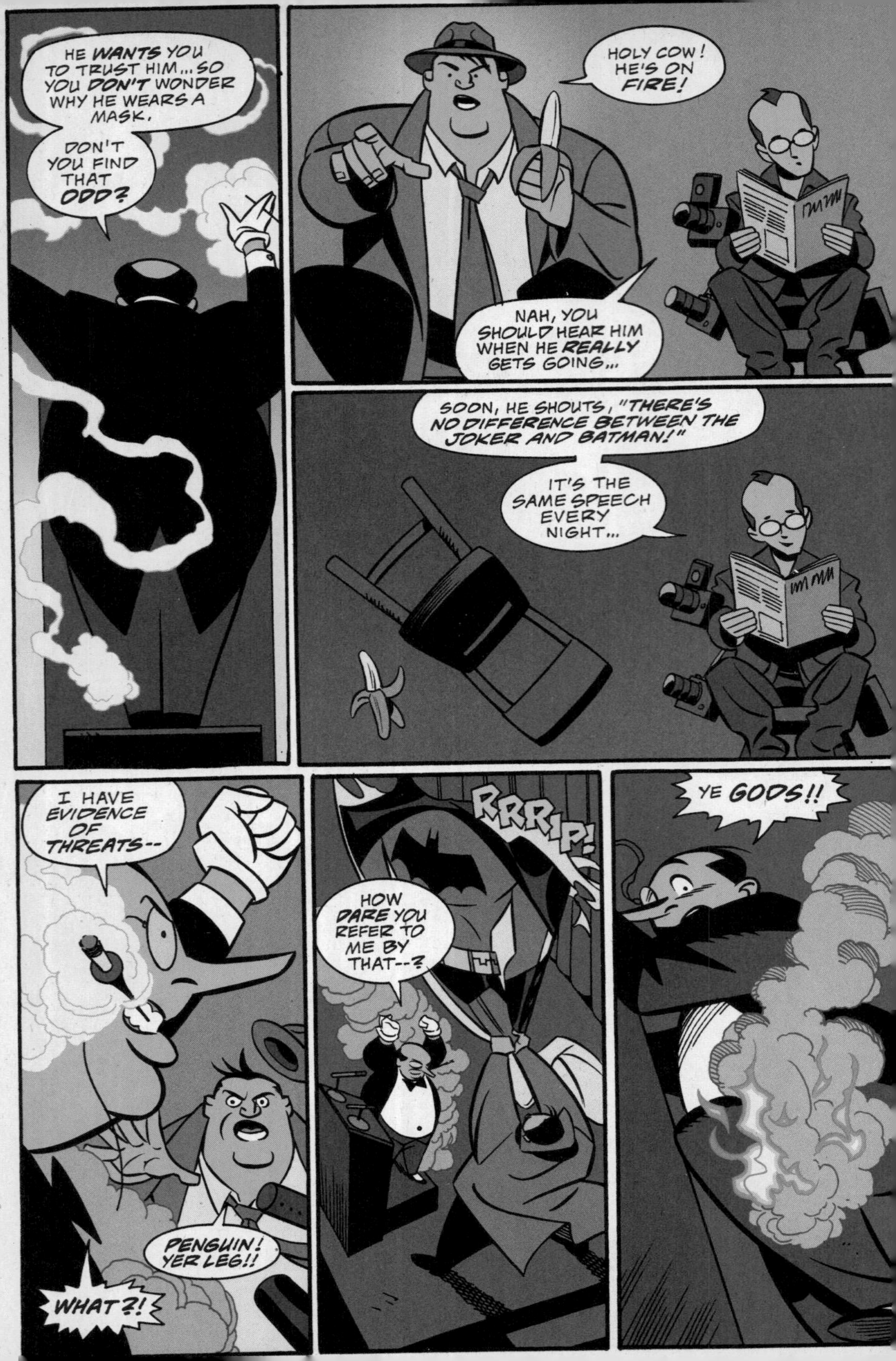
HE WANTS YOU TO TRUST HIM... SO YOU DON'T WONDER WHY HE WEARS A MASK.
DON'T YOU FIND THAT ODD?
HOLY COW! HE'S ON FIRE!
NAH, YOU SHOULD HEAR HIM WHEN HE REALLY GETS GOING...
SOON, HE SHOUTS, "THERE'S NO DIFFERENCE BETWEEN THE JOKER AND BATMAN!"
IT'S THE SAME SPEECH EVERY NIGHT...
I HAVE EVIDENCE OF THREATS--
PENGUIN! YER LEG!!
WHAT?!
RRRIP!
HOW DARE YOU REFER TO ME BY THAT--?
YE GODS!!

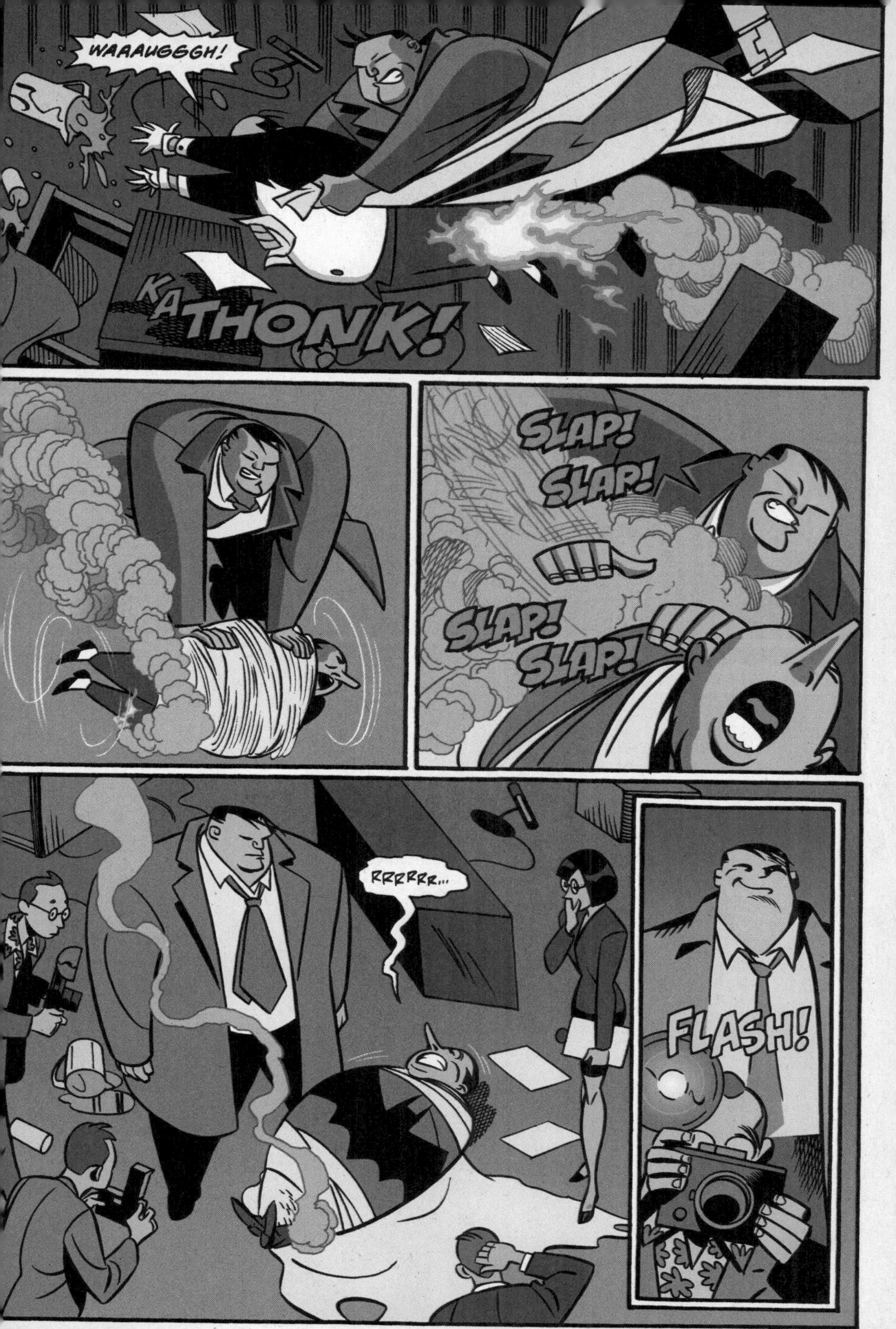
WAAAUGGGH!
KATHONK!
SLAP!
SLAP!
SLAP!
SLAP!
RRRRRR...
FLASH!

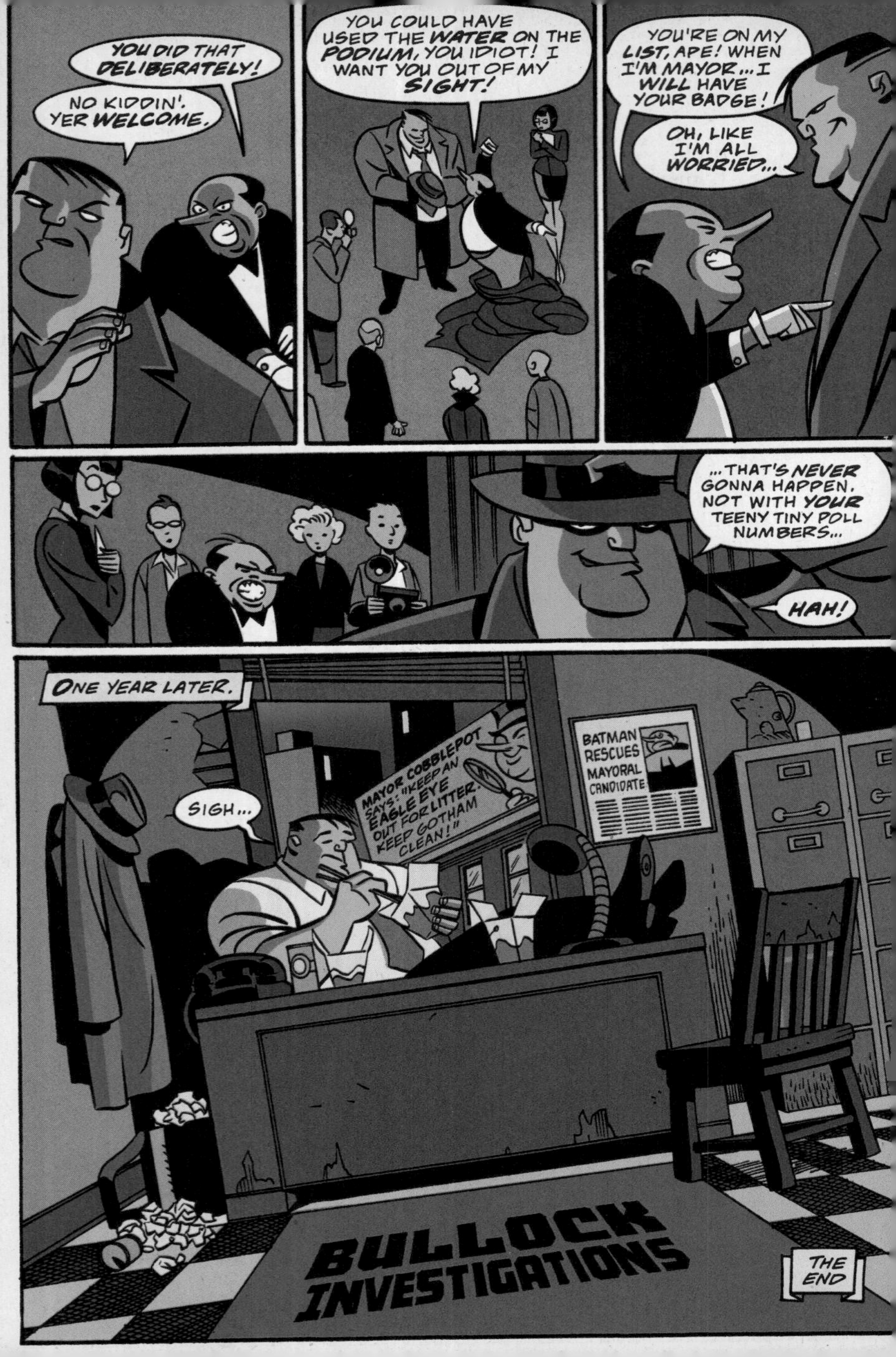

YOU DID THAT DELIBERATELY!
NO KIDDIN'. YER WELCOME.
YOU COULD HAVE USED THE WATER ON THE PODIUM, YOU IDIOT! I WANT YOU OUT OF MY SIGHT!
YOU'RE ON MY LIST, APE! WHEN I'M MAYOR... I WILL HAVE YOUR BADGE!
OH, LIKE I'M ALL WORRIED...
...THAT'S NEVER GONNA HAPPEN. NOT WITH YOUR TEENY TINY POLL NUMBERS...
HAH!
ONE YEAR LATER.
MAYOR COBBLEPOT SAYS: "KEEP AN EAGLE EYE OUT FOR LITTER. KEEP GOTHAM CLEAN!"
BATMAN RESCUES MAYORAL CANDIDATE
SIGH...
BULLOCK INVESTIGATIONS
THE END

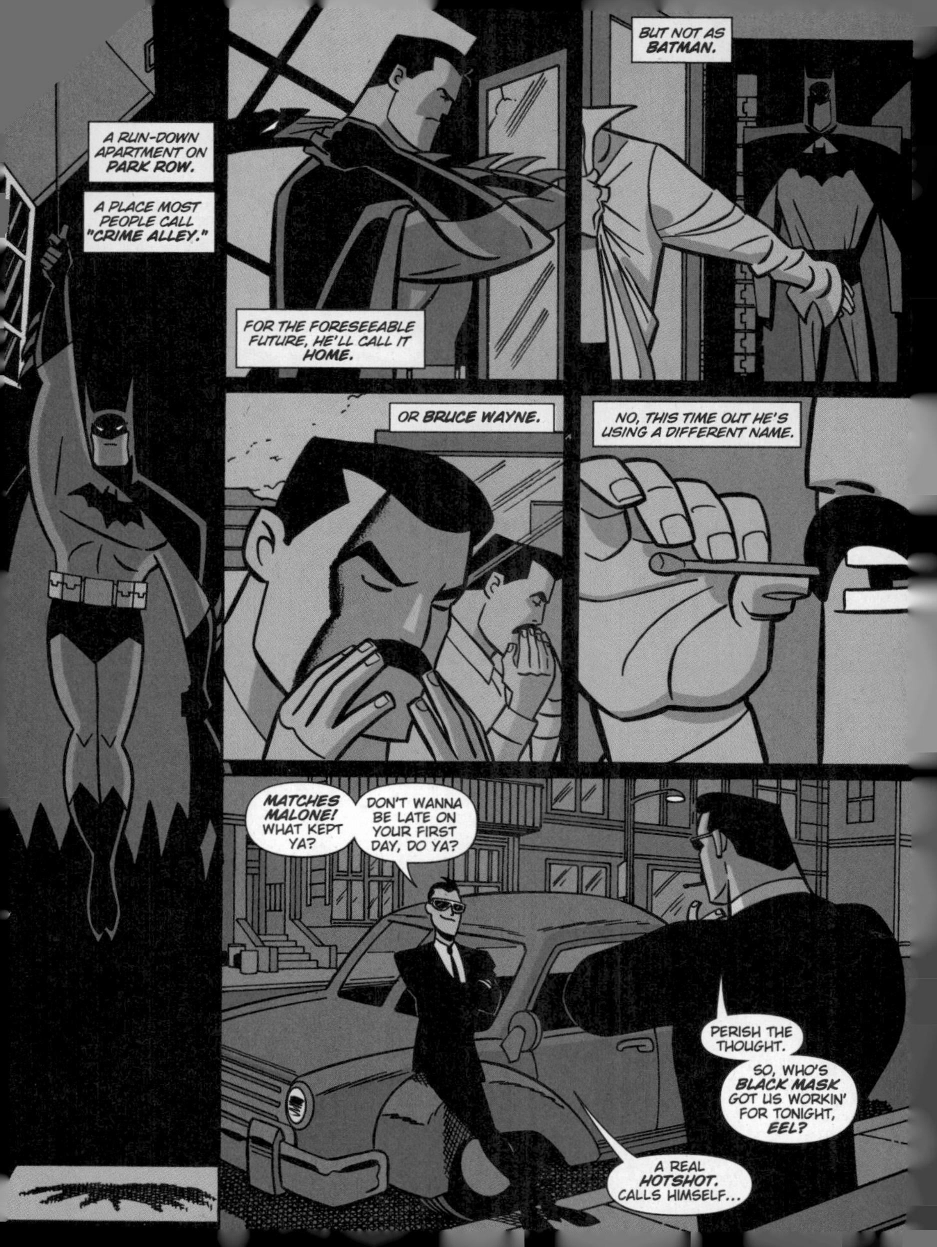
A RUN-DOWN APARTMENT ON PARK ROW.
A PLACE MOST PEOPLE CALL "CRIME ALLEY."
FOR THE FORESEEABLE FUTURE, HE'LL CALL IT HOME.
BUT NOT AS BATMAN.
OR BRUCE WAYNE.
NO, THIS TIME OUT HE'S USING A DIFFERENT NAME.
MATCHES MALONE! WHAT KEPT YA?
DON'T WANNA BE LATE ON YOUR FIRST DAY, DO YA?
PERISH THE THOUGHT.
SO, WHO'S BLACK MASK GOT US WORKIN' FOR TONIGHT, EEL?
A REAL HOTSHOT. CALLS HIMSELF...

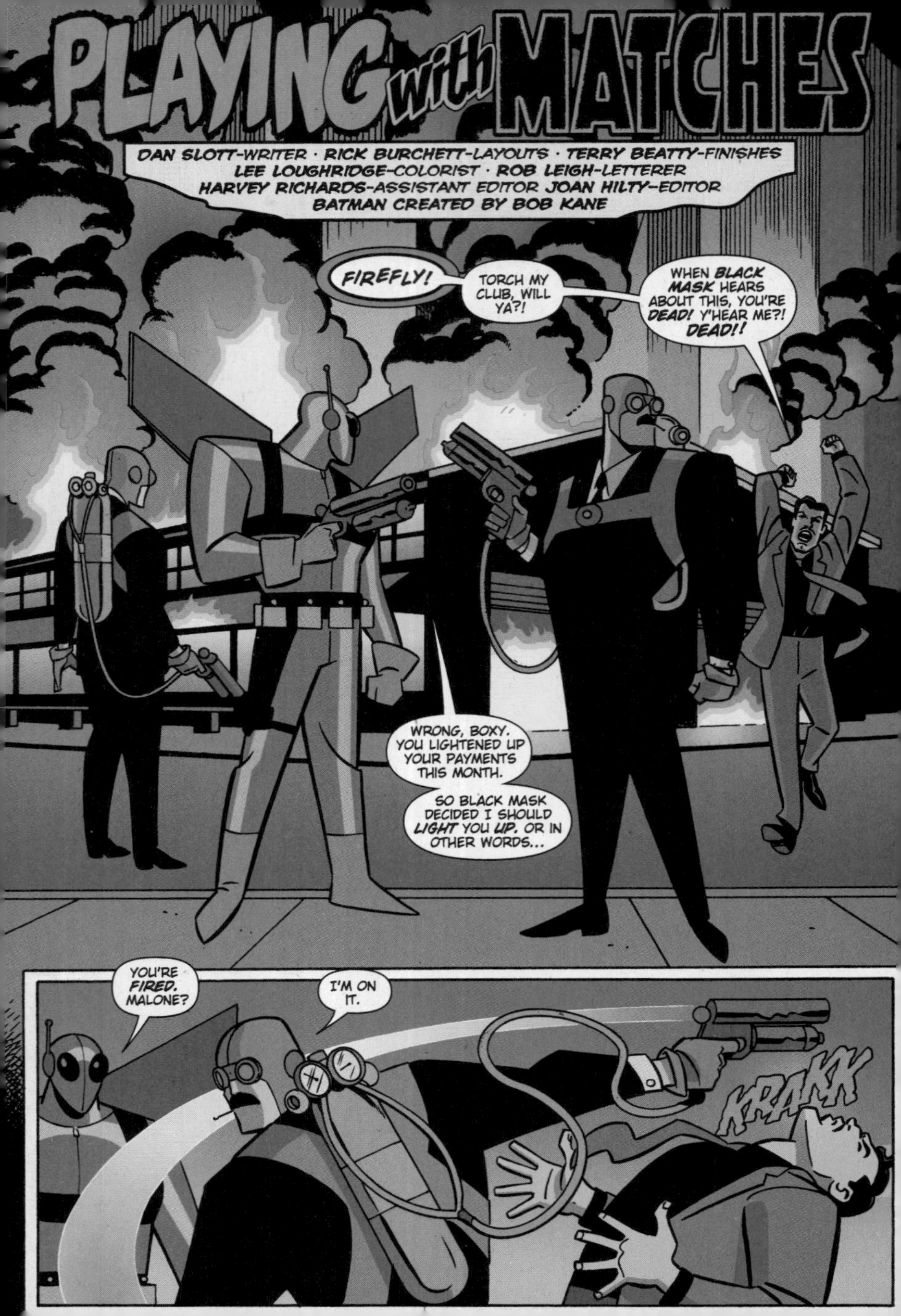
PLAYING with MATCHES
DAN SLOTT-WRITER · RICK BURCHETT-LAYOUTS · TERRY BEATTY-FINISHES
LEE LOUGHRIDGE-COLORIST · ROB LEIGH-LETTERER
HARVEY RICHARDS-ASSISTANT EDITOR JOAN HILTY-EDITOR
BATMAN CREATED BY BOB KANE
FIREFLY!
TORCH MY CLUB, WILL YA?!
WHEN BLACK MASK HEARS ABOUT THIS, YOU'RE DEAD! Y'HEAR ME?! DEAD!!
WRONG, BOXY. YOU LIGHTENED UP YOUR PAYMENTS THIS MONTH.
SO BLACK MASK DECIDED I SHOULD LIGHT YOU UP. OR IN OTHER WORDS...
YOU'RE FIRED. MALONE?
I'M ON IT.
KRAKK

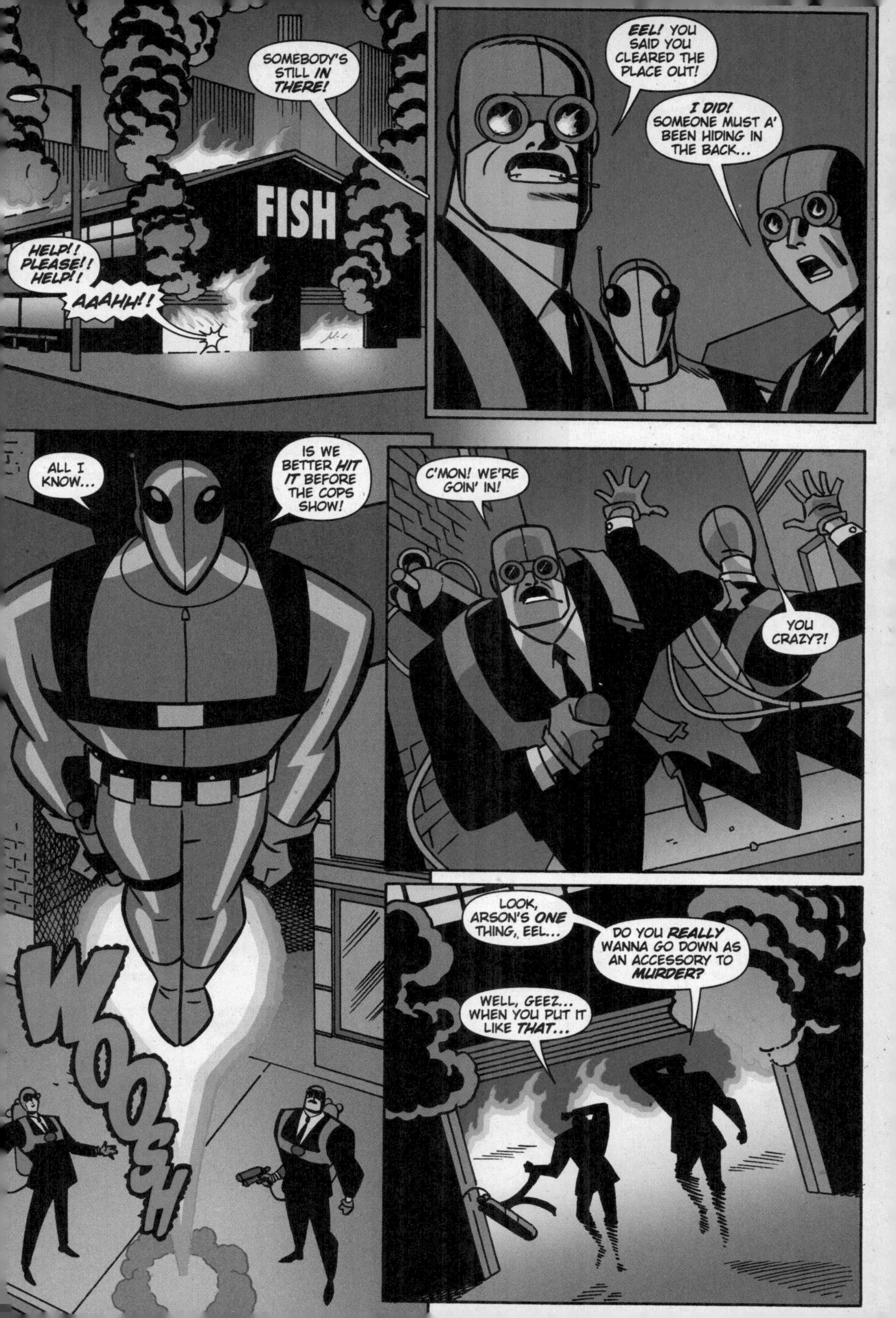

SOMEBODY'S STILL *IN THERE!*
HELP!! PLEASE!! HELP!!
AAAHH!!
EEL! YOU SAID YOU CLEARED THE PLACE OUT!
I DID! SOMEONE MUST A' BEEN HIDING IN THE BACK...
ALL I KNOW...
IS WE BETTER *HIT IT* BEFORE THE COPS SHOW!
WOOOSH
C'MON! WE'RE GOIN' IN!
YOU CRAZY?!
LOOK, ARSON'S *ONE* THING, EEL...
DO YOU *REALLY* WANNA GO DOWN AS AN ACCESSORY TO *MURDER?*
WELL, GEEZ... WHEN YOU PUT IT LIKE *THAT*...

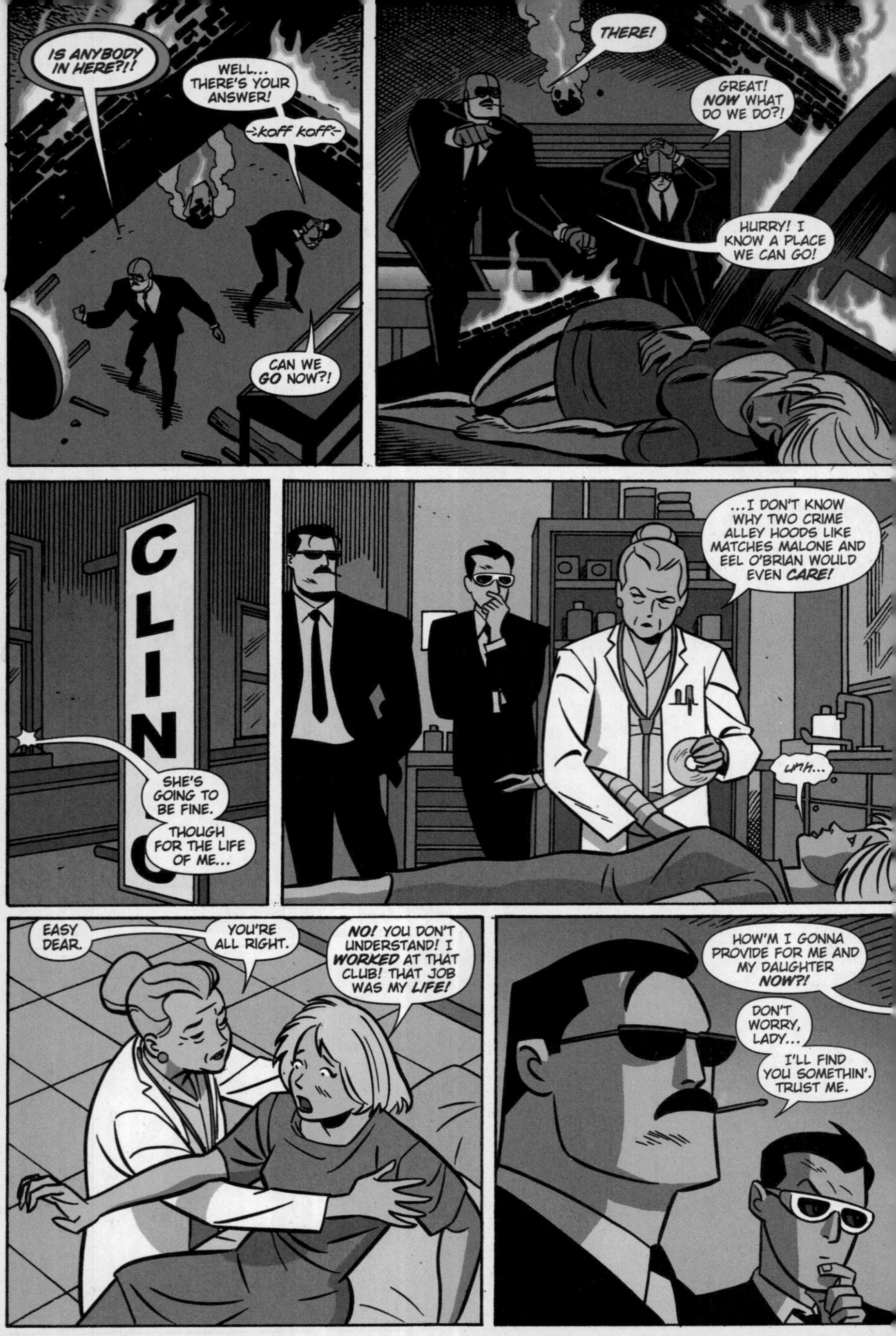

IS ANYBODY IN HERE?!!
WELL... THERE'S YOUR ANSWER!
-koff koff-
CAN WE GO NOW?!
THERE!
GREAT! NOW WHAT DO WE DO?!
HURRY! I KNOW A PLACE WE CAN GO!
CLIN
SHE'S GOING TO BE FINE.
THOUGH FOR THE LIFE OF ME...
...I DON'T KNOW WHY TWO CRIME ALLEY HOODS LIKE MATCHES MALONE AND EEL O'BRIAN WOULD EVEN CARE!
unh...
EASY DEAR.
YOU'RE ALL RIGHT.
NO! YOU DON'T UNDERSTAND! I WORKED AT THAT CLUB! THAT JOB WAS MY LIFE!
HOW'M I GONNA PROVIDE FOR ME AND MY DAUGHTER NOW?!
DON'T WORRY, LADY...
I'LL FIND YOU SOMETHIN'. TRUST ME.

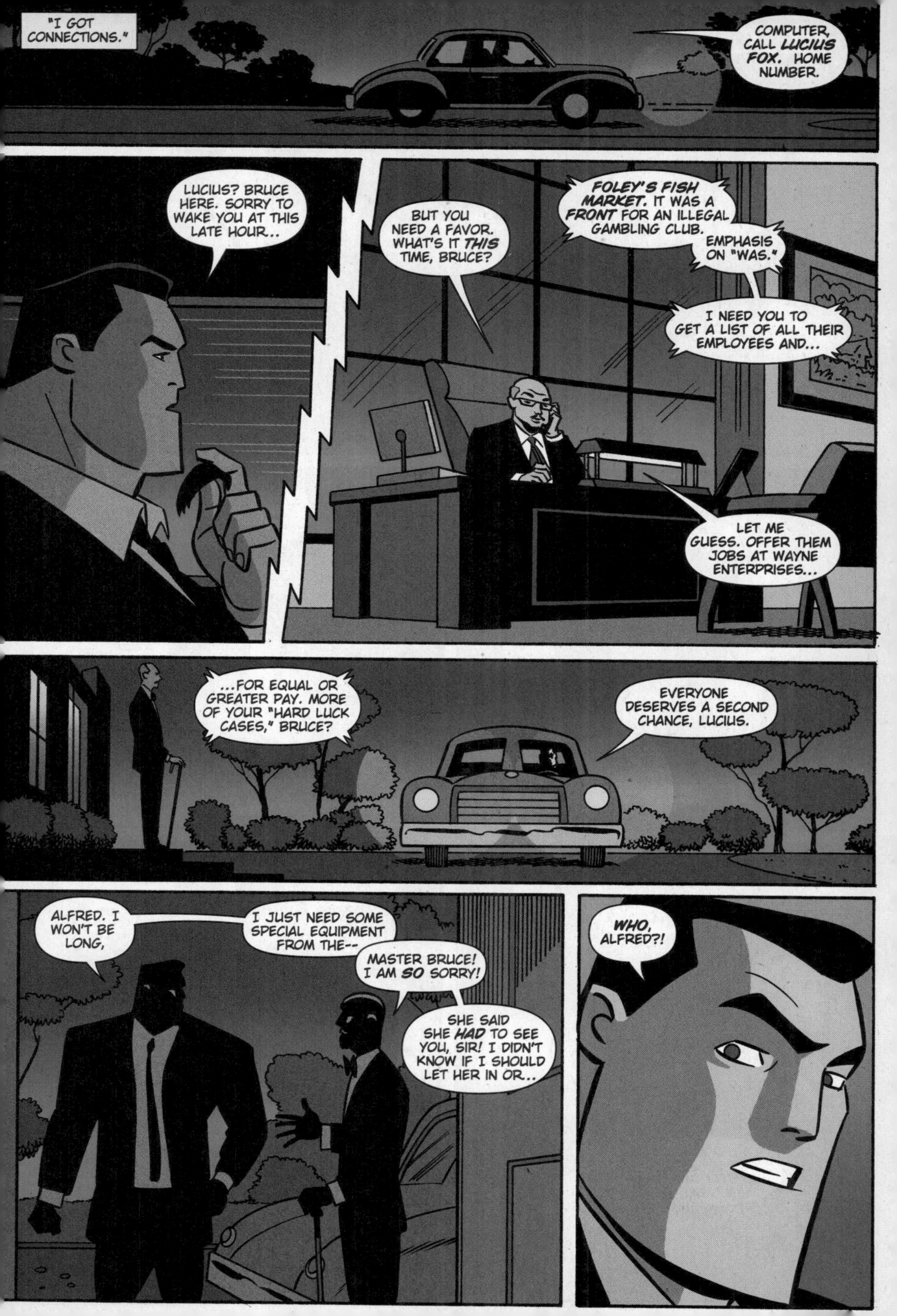
"I GOT CONNECTIONS."
COMPUTER, CALL LUCIUS FOX. HOME NUMBER.
LUCIUS? BRUCE HERE. SORRY TO WAKE YOU AT THIS LATE HOUR...
BUT YOU NEED A FAVOR. WHAT'S IT THIS TIME, BRUCE?
FOLEY'S FISH MARKET. IT WAS A FRONT FOR AN ILLEGAL GAMBLING CLUB.
EMPHASIS ON "WAS."
I NEED YOU TO GET A LIST OF ALL THEIR EMPLOYEES AND...
LET ME GUESS. OFFER THEM JOBS AT WAYNE ENTERPRISES...
...FOR EQUAL OR GREATER PAY. MORE OF YOUR "HARD LUCK CASES," BRUCE?
EVERYONE DESERVES A SECOND CHANCE, LUCIUS.
ALFRED. I WON'T BE LONG,
I JUST NEED SOME SPECIAL EQUIPMENT FROM THE--
MASTER BRUCE! I AM SO SORRY!
SHE SAID SHE HAD TO SEE YOU, SIR! I DIDN'T KNOW IF I SHOULD LET HER IN OR..
WHO, ALFRED?!

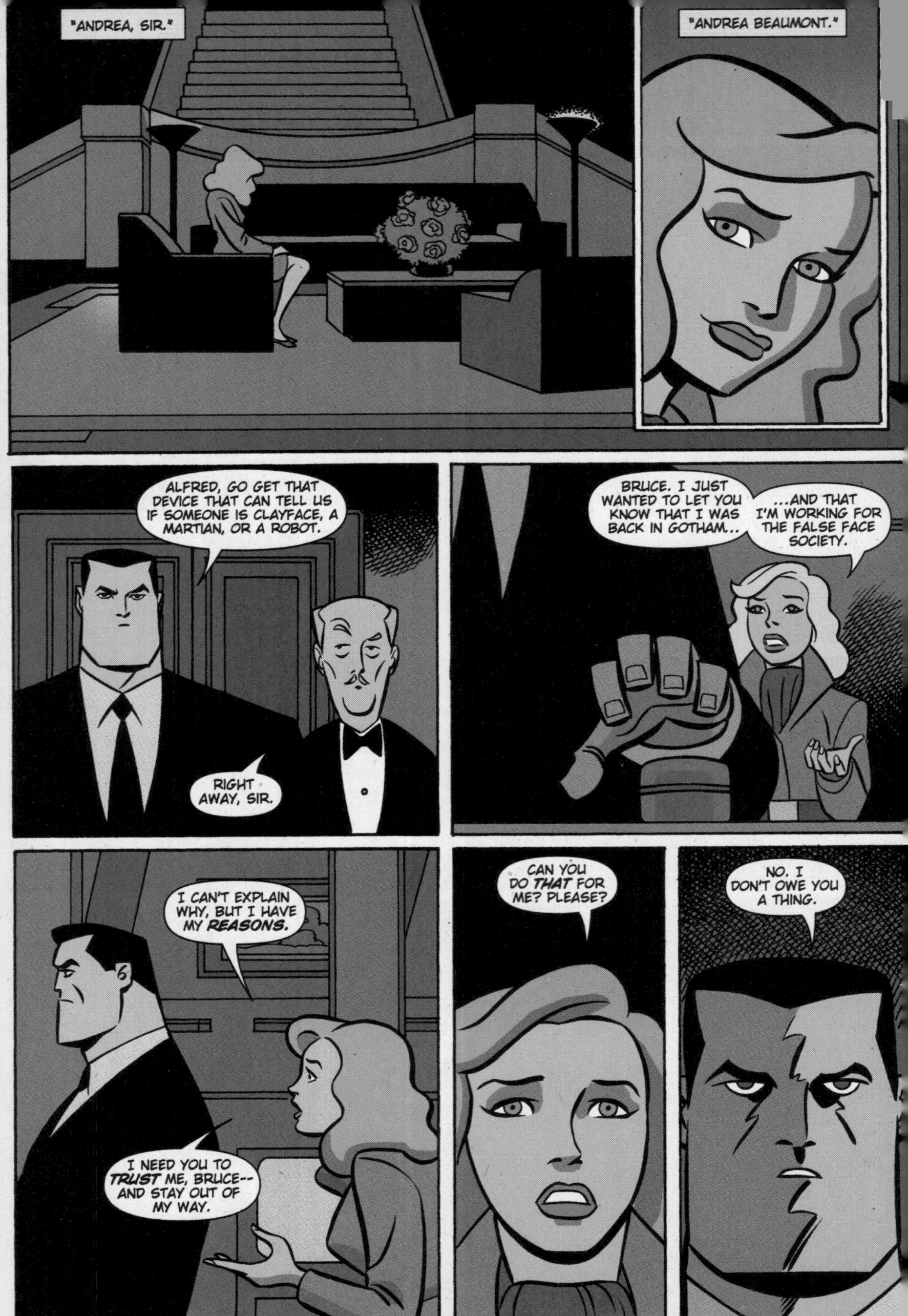
"ANDREA, SIR."
"ANDREA BEAUMONT."
ALFRED, GO GET THAT DEVICE THAT CAN TELL US IF SOMEONE IS CLAYFACE, A MARTIAN, OR A ROBOT.
RIGHT AWAY, SIR.
BRUCE. I JUST WANTED TO LET YOU KNOW THAT I WAS BACK IN GOTHAM...
...AND THAT I'M WORKING FOR THE FALSE FACE SOCIETY.
I CAN'T EXPLAIN WHY, BUT I HAVE MY *REASONS.*
I NEED YOU TO *TRUST* ME, BRUCE-- AND STAY OUT OF MY WAY.
CAN YOU DO *THAT* FOR ME? PLEASE?
NO. I DON'T OWE YOU A THING.

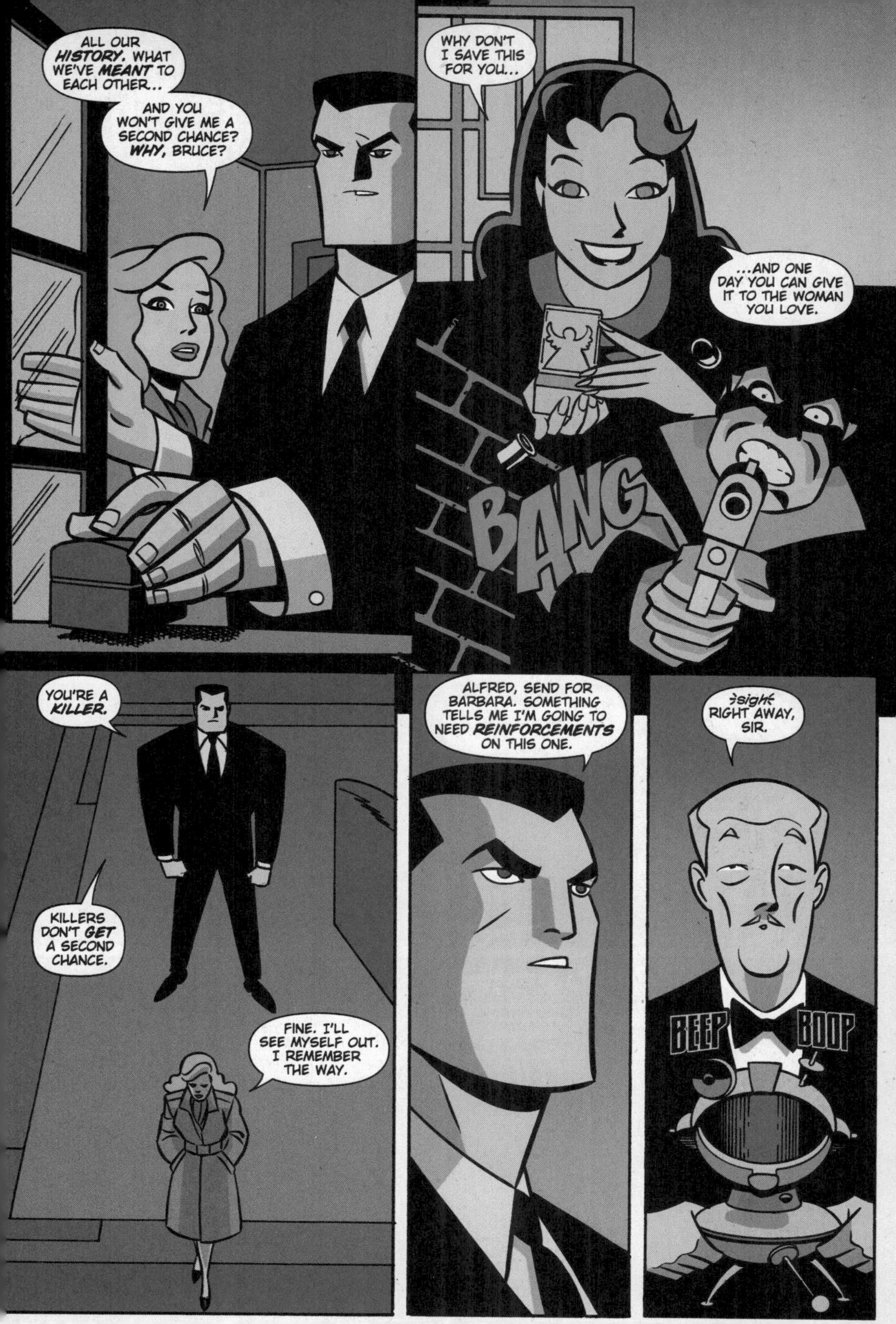

ALL OUR HISTORY. WHAT WE'VE MEANT TO EACH OTHER...
AND YOU WON'T GIVE ME A SECOND CHANCE? WHY, BRUCE?
WHY DON'T I SAVE THIS FOR YOU...
...AND ONE DAY YOU CAN GIVE IT TO THE WOMAN YOU LOVE.
BANG
YOU'RE A KILLER.
KILLERS DON'T GET A SECOND CHANCE.
FINE. I'LL SEE MYSELF OUT. I REMEMBER THE WAY.
ALFRED, SEND FOR BARBARA. SOMETHING TELLS ME I'M GOING TO NEED REINFORCEMENTS ON THIS ONE.
sigh RIGHT AWAY, SIR.
BEEP
BOOP

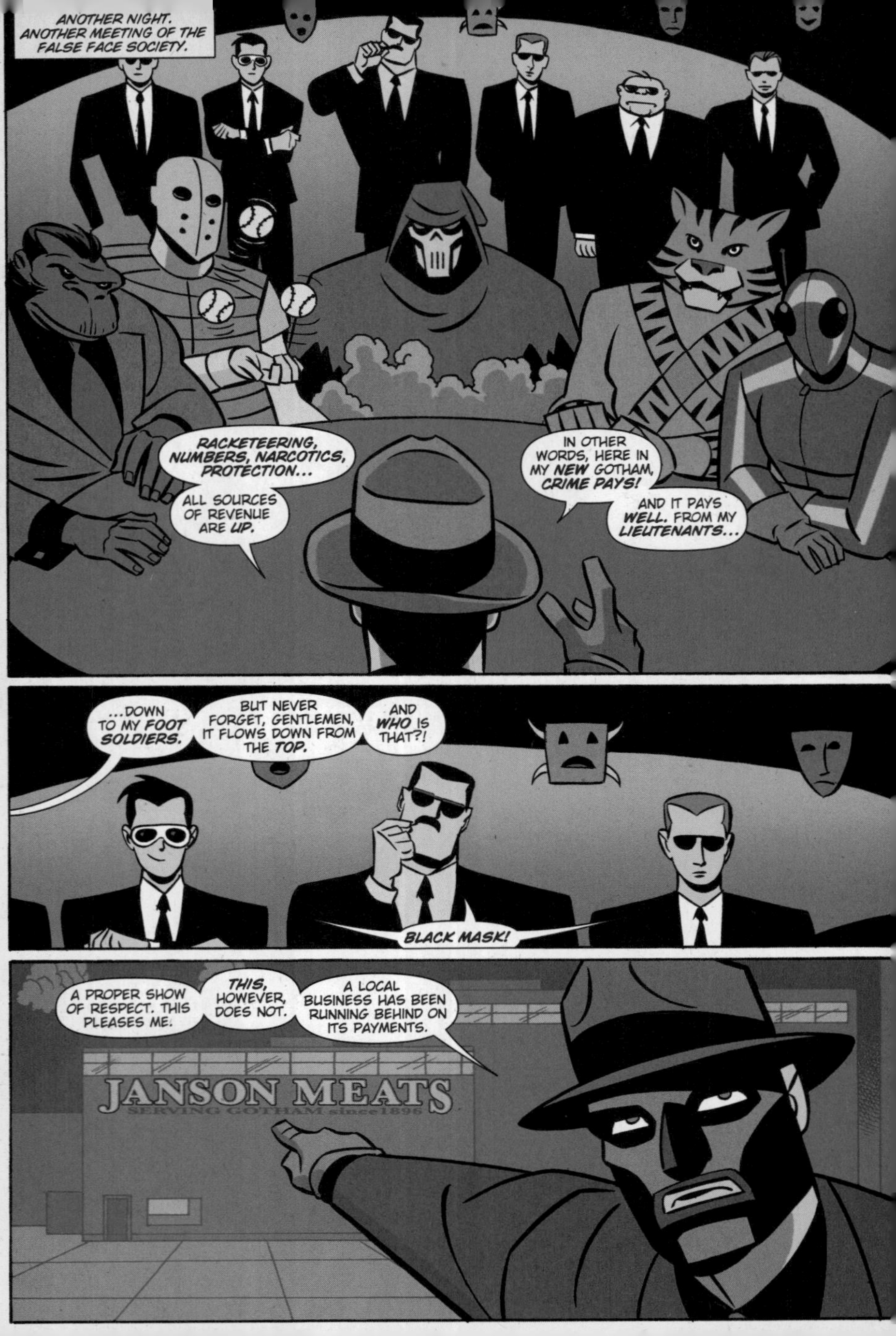
ANOTHER NIGHT. ANOTHER MEETING OF THE FALSE FACE SOCIETY.
RACKETEERING, NUMBERS, NARCOTICS, PROTECTION...
ALL SOURCES OF REVENUE ARE UP.
IN OTHER WORDS, HERE IN MY NEW GOTHAM, CRIME PAYS!
AND IT PAYS WELL. FROM MY LIEUTENANTS...
...DOWN TO MY FOOT SOLDIERS.
BUT NEVER FORGET, GENTLEMEN, IT FLOWS DOWN FROM THE TOP.
AND WHO IS THAT?!
BLACK MASK!
A PROPER SHOW OF RESPECT. THIS PLEASES ME.
THIS, HOWEVER, DOES NOT.
A LOCAL BUSINESS HAS BEEN RUNNING BEHIND ON ITS PAYMENTS.
JANSON MEATS
SERVING GOTHAM since1896

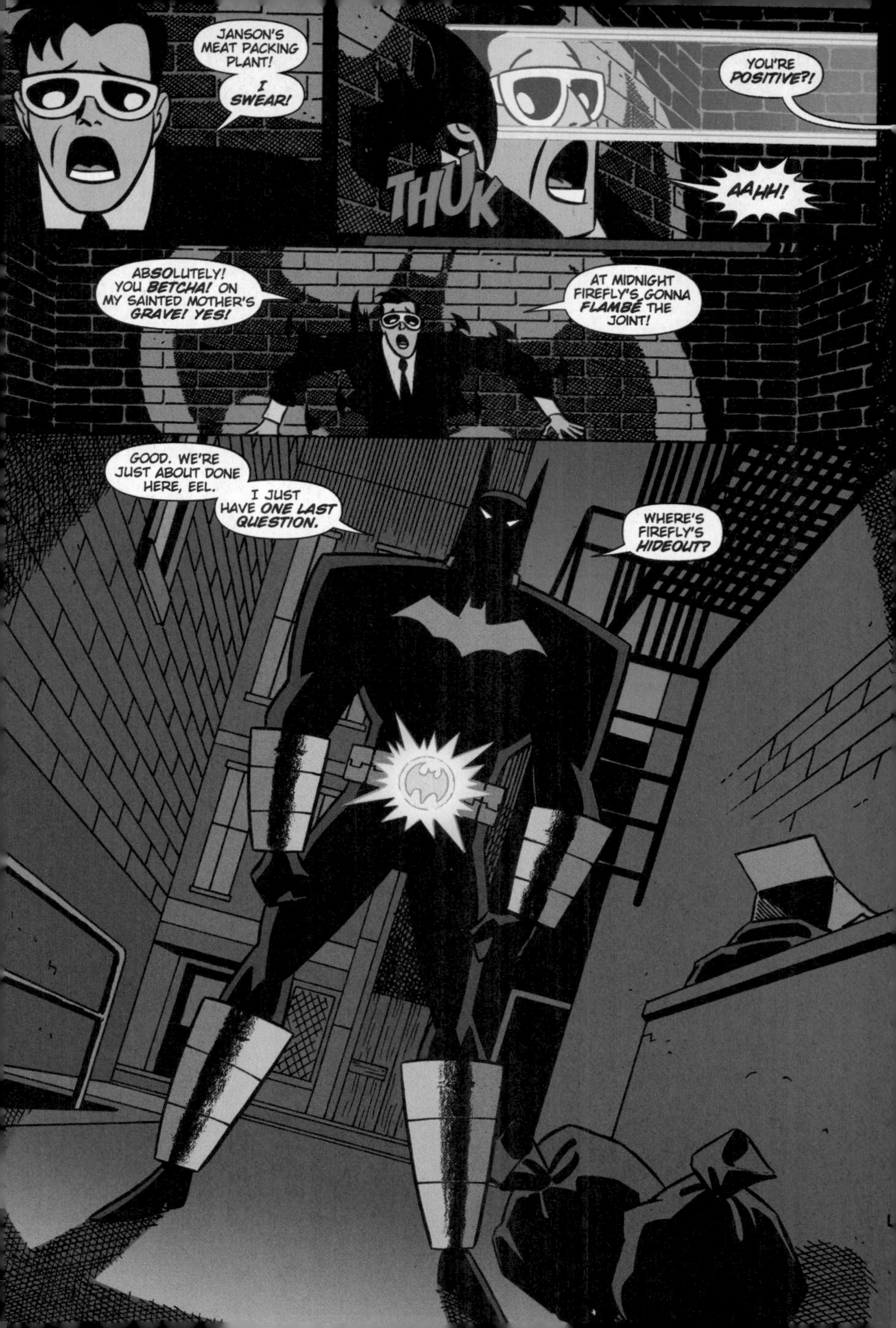

JANSON'S MEAT PACKING PLANT!
I SWEAR!
YOU'RE POSITIVE?!
THUK
AAHH!
ABSOLUTELY! YOU BETCHA! ON MY SAINTED MOTHER'S GRAVE! YES!
AT MIDNIGHT FIREFLY'S GONNA FLAMBÉ THE JOINT!
GOOD. WE'RE JUST ABOUT DONE HERE, EEL.
I JUST HAVE ONE LAST QUESTION.
WHERE'S FIREFLY'S HIDEOUT?

NO WAY, BATS!

I TELL YOU *THAT*, AND FIREFLY'LL MAKE SURE I'M TOAST! *BURNT* TOAST!

CH**UNK**

THE OLD *CLUB INFERNO!* 666 DIXON STREET!

THAT'S *IT!* THAT'S *ALL* I GOT! *HONEST!*

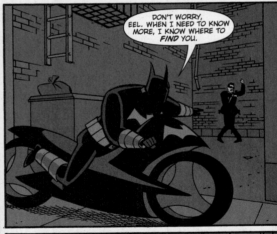

DON'T WORRY, EEL. WHEN I NEED TO KNOW MORE, I KNOW WHERE TO *FIND* YOU.

TELL ME SOMETHIN' I *DON'T* KNOW, YA *PUTRID PUNK!*

VR**MMM**

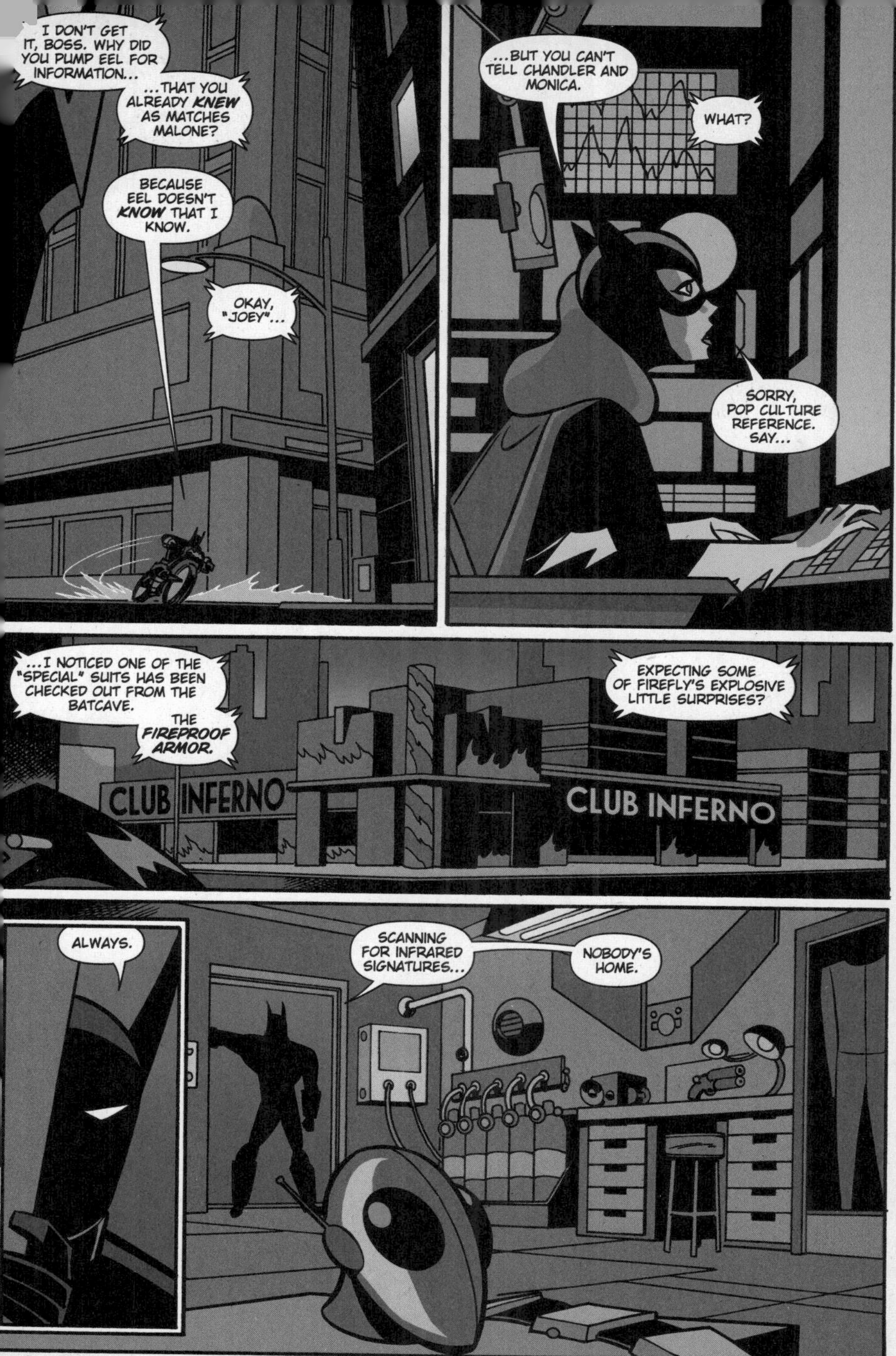
I DON'T GET IT, BOSS. WHY DID YOU PUMP EEL FOR INFORMATION...
...THAT YOU ALREADY KNEW AS MATCHES MALONE?
BECAUSE EEL DOESN'T KNOW THAT I KNOW.
OKAY, "JOEY"...
...BUT YOU CAN'T TELL CHANDLER AND MONICA.
WHAT?
SORRY, POP CULTURE REFERENCE. SAY...
...I NOTICED ONE OF THE "SPECIAL" SUITS HAS BEEN CHECKED OUT FROM THE BATCAVE.
THE FIREPROOF ARMOR.
EXPECTING SOME OF FIREFLY'S EXPLOSIVE LITTLE SURPRISES?
CLUB INFERNO
CLUB INFERNO
ALWAYS.
SCANNING FOR INFRARED SIGNATURES...
NOBODY'S HOME.

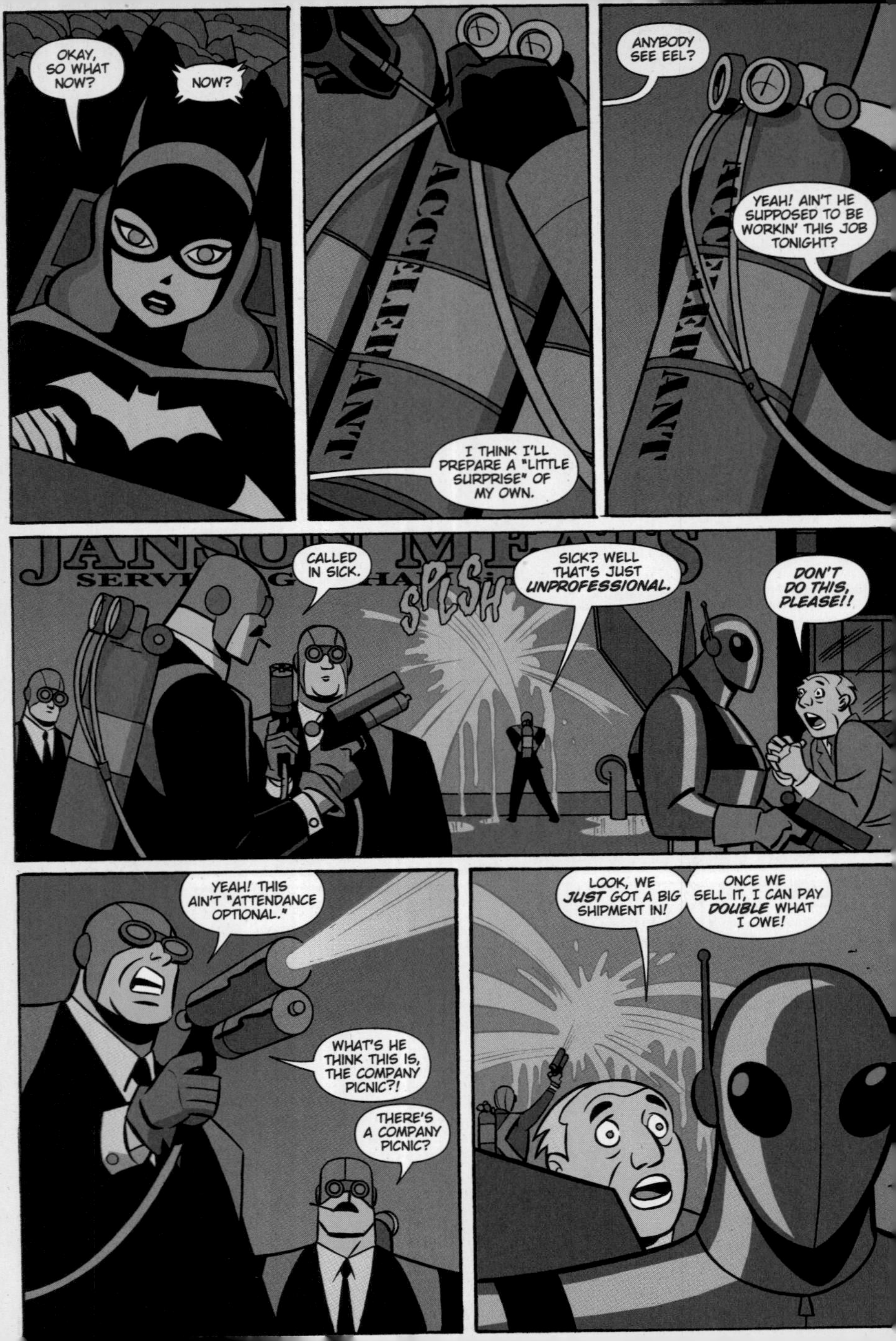

OKAY, SO WHAT NOW?
NOW?
I THINK I'LL PREPARE A "LITTLE SURPRISE" OF MY OWN.
ACCELERANT
ANYBODY SEE EEL?
YEAH! AIN'T HE SUPPOSED TO BE WORKIN' THIS JOB TONIGHT?
CALLED IN SICK.
SPLSH
SICK? WELL THAT'S JUST UNPROFESSIONAL.
DON'T DO THIS, PLEASE!!
YEAH! THIS AIN'T "ATTENDANCE OPTIONAL."
WHAT'S HE THINK THIS IS, THE COMPANY PICNIC?!
THERE'S A COMPANY PICNIC?
LOOK, WE JUST GOT A BIG SHIPMENT IN!
ONCE WE SELL IT, I CAN PAY DOUBLE WHAT I OWE!

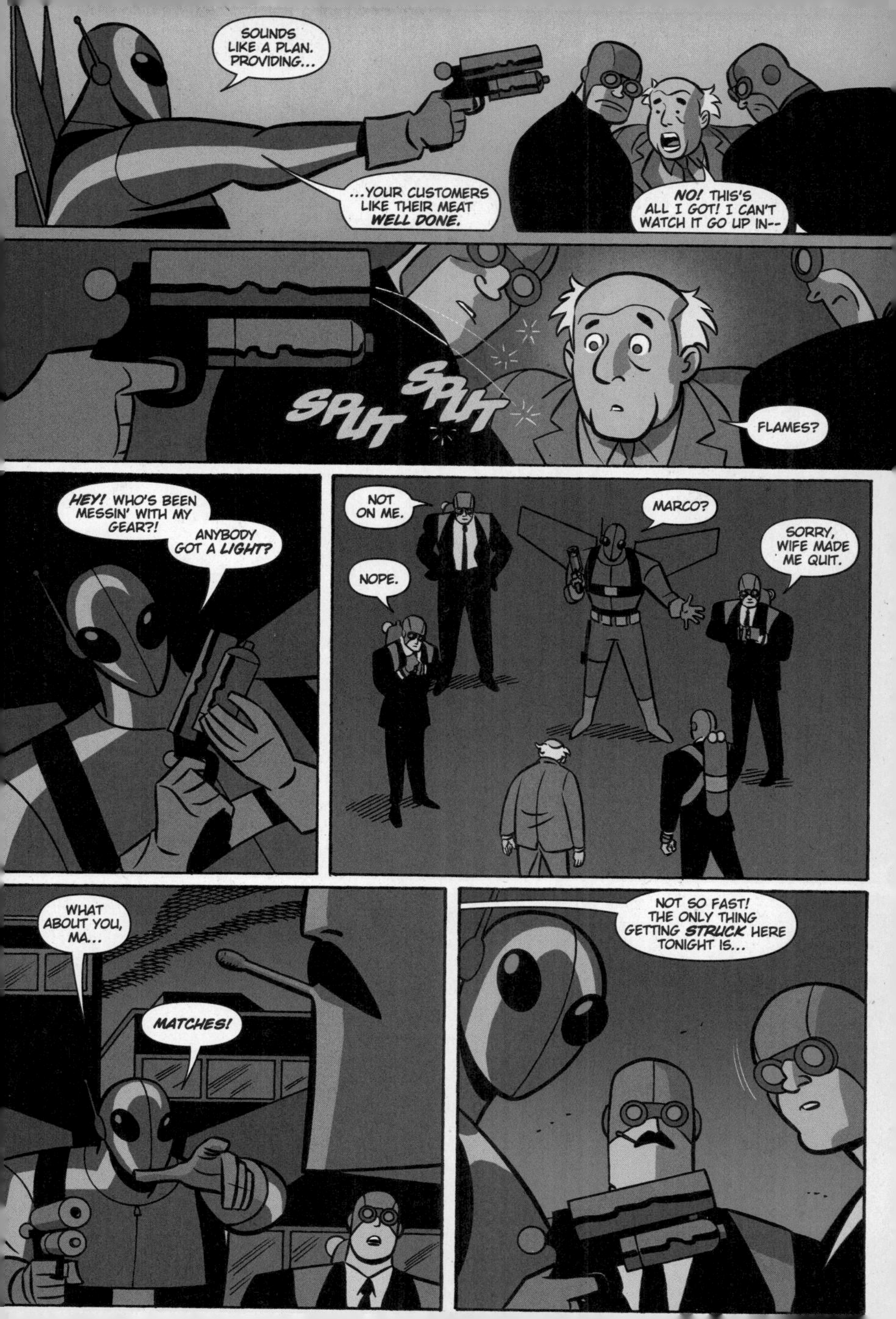
SOUNDS LIKE A PLAN. PROVIDING...
...YOUR CUSTOMERS LIKE THEIR MEAT WELL DONE.
NO! THIS'S ALL I GOT! I CAN'T WATCH IT GO UP IN--
SPUT SPUT
FLAMES?
HEY! WHO'S BEEN MESSIN' WITH MY GEAR?!
ANYBODY GOT A LIGHT?
NOT ON ME.
MARCO?
SORRY, WIFE MADE ME QUIT.
NOPE.
WHAT ABOUT YOU, MA...
MATCHES!
NOT SO FAST! THE ONLY THING GETTING STRUCK HERE TONIGHT IS...

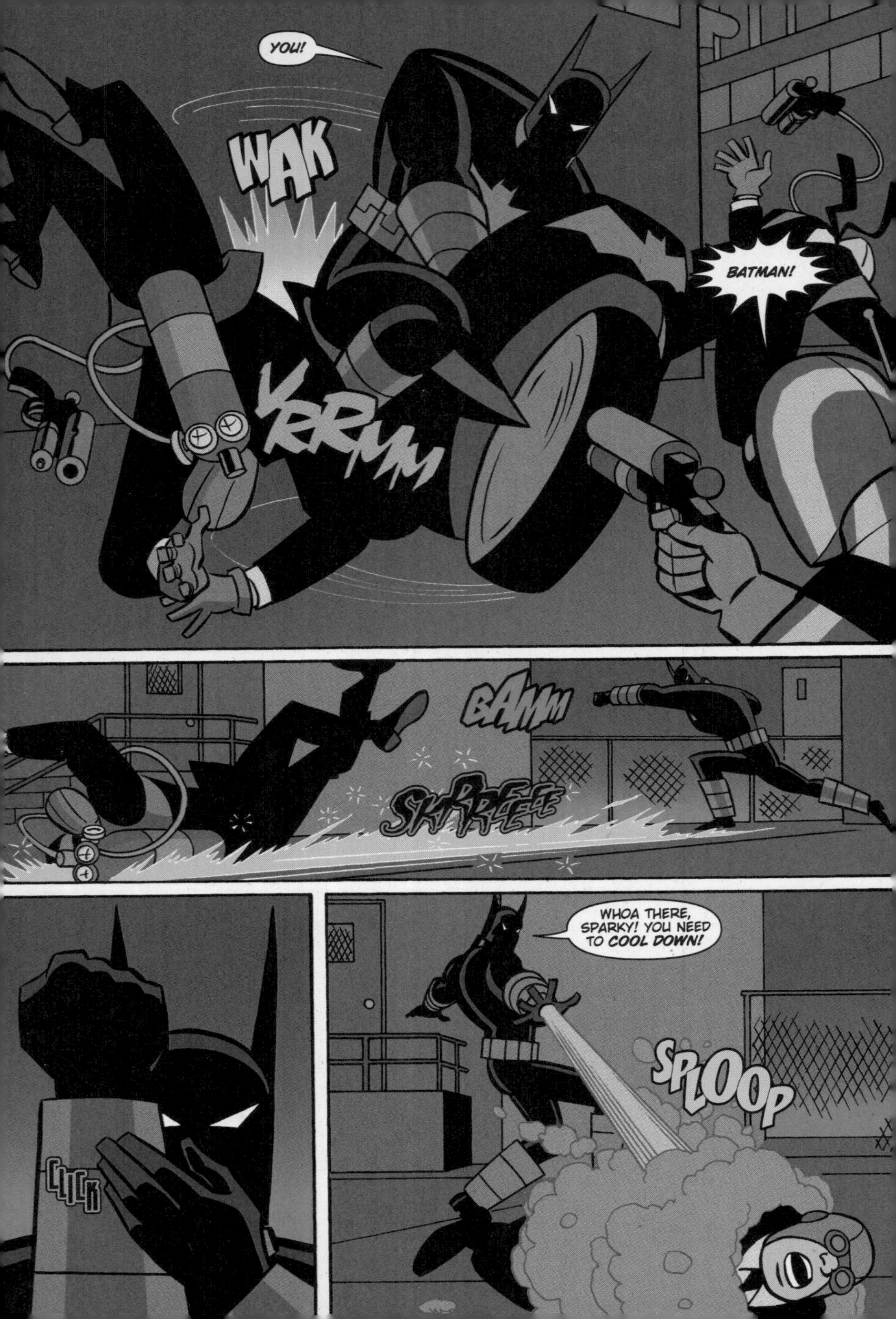
YOU!
WAK
BATMAN!
VRRMM
BAMM
SKRREEE
WHOA THERE, SPARKY! YOU NEED TO COOL DOWN!
CLICK
SPLOOP

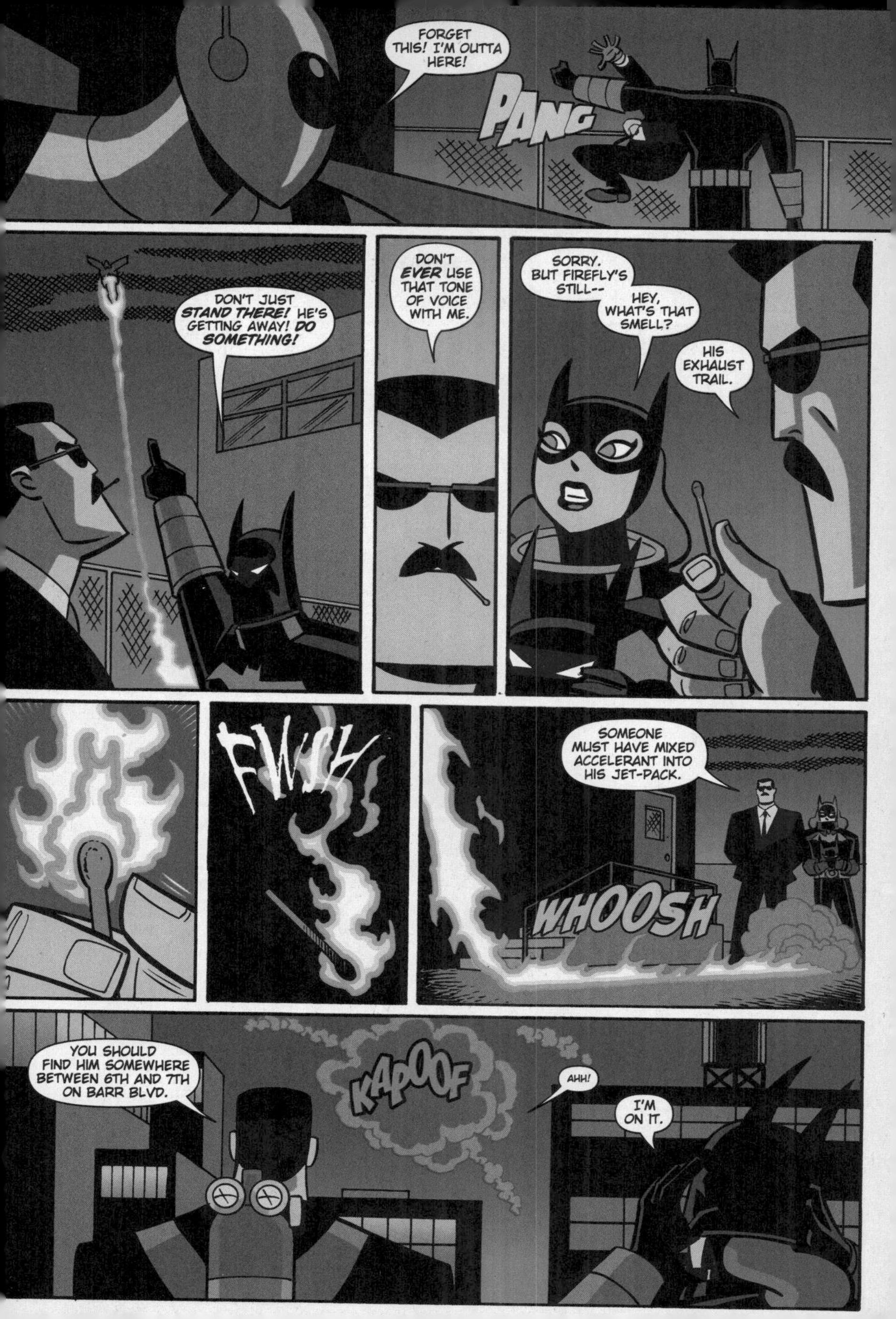
FORGET THIS! I'M OUTTA HERE!
PANG
DON'T JUST STAND THERE! HE'S GETTING AWAY! DO SOMETHING!
DON'T EVER USE THAT TONE OF VOICE WITH ME.
SORRY. BUT FIREFLY'S STILL--
HEY, WHAT'S THAT SMELL?
HIS EXHAUST TRAIL.
FWSH
SOMEONE MUST HAVE MIXED ACCELERANT INTO HIS JET-PACK.
WHOOSH
YOU SHOULD FIND HIM SOMEWHERE BETWEEN 6TH AND 7TH ON BARR BLVD.
KAPOOF
AHH!
I'M ON IT.

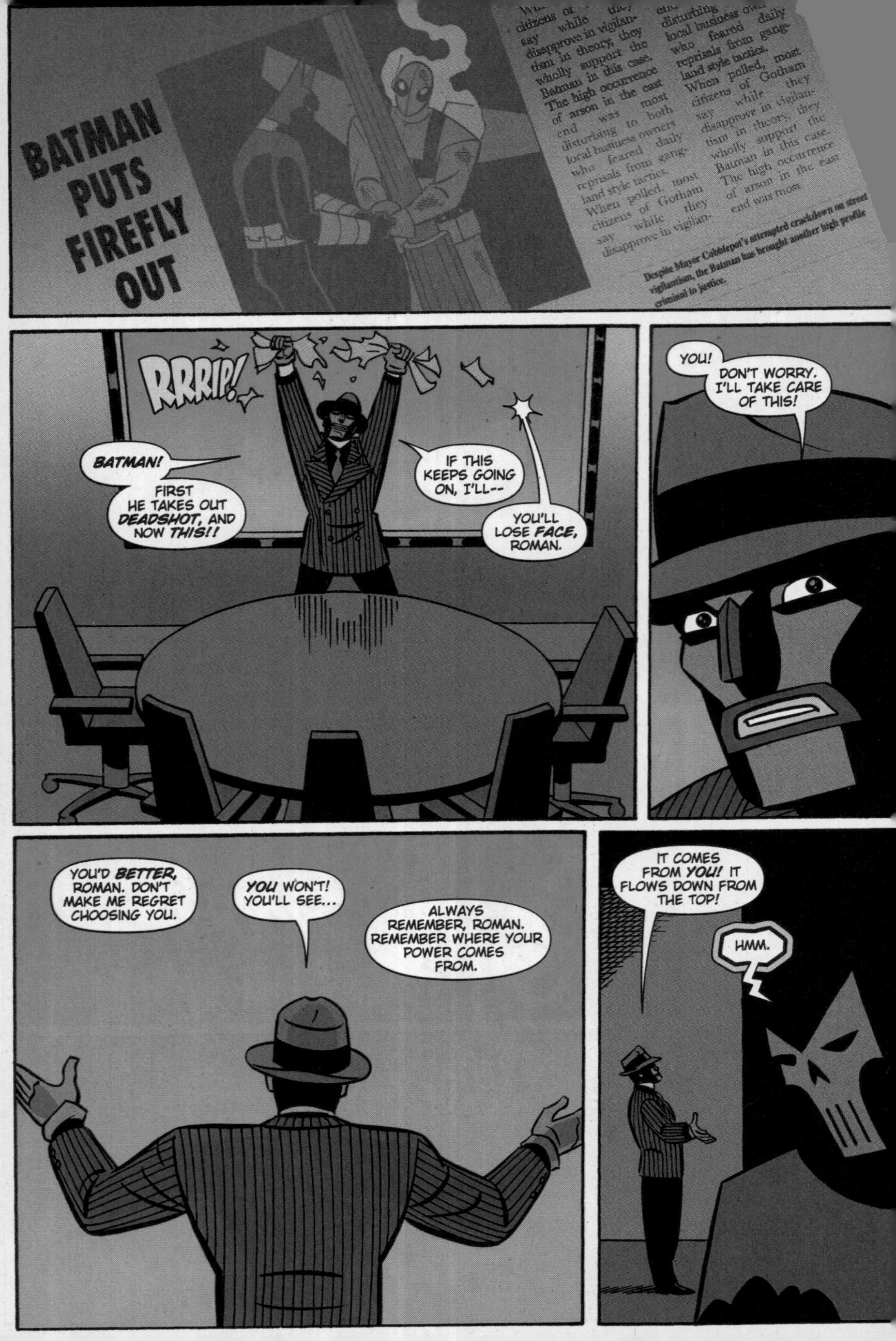

BATMAN PUTS FIREFLY OUT
Despite Mayor Cobblepot's attempted crackdown on street vigilantism, the Batman has brought another high profile criminal to justice.
RRRIP!
BATMAN!
FIRST HE TAKES OUT DEADSHOT, AND NOW THIS!!
IF THIS KEEPS GOING ON, I'LL--
YOU'LL LOSE FACE, ROMAN.
YOU!
DON'T WORRY. I'LL TAKE CARE OF THIS!
YOU'D BETTER, ROMAN. DON'T MAKE ME REGRET CHOOSING YOU.
YOU WON'T! YOU'LL SEE...
ALWAYS REMEMBER, ROMAN. REMEMBER WHERE YOUR POWER COMES FROM.
IT COMES FROM YOU! IT FLOWS DOWN FROM THE TOP!
HMM.

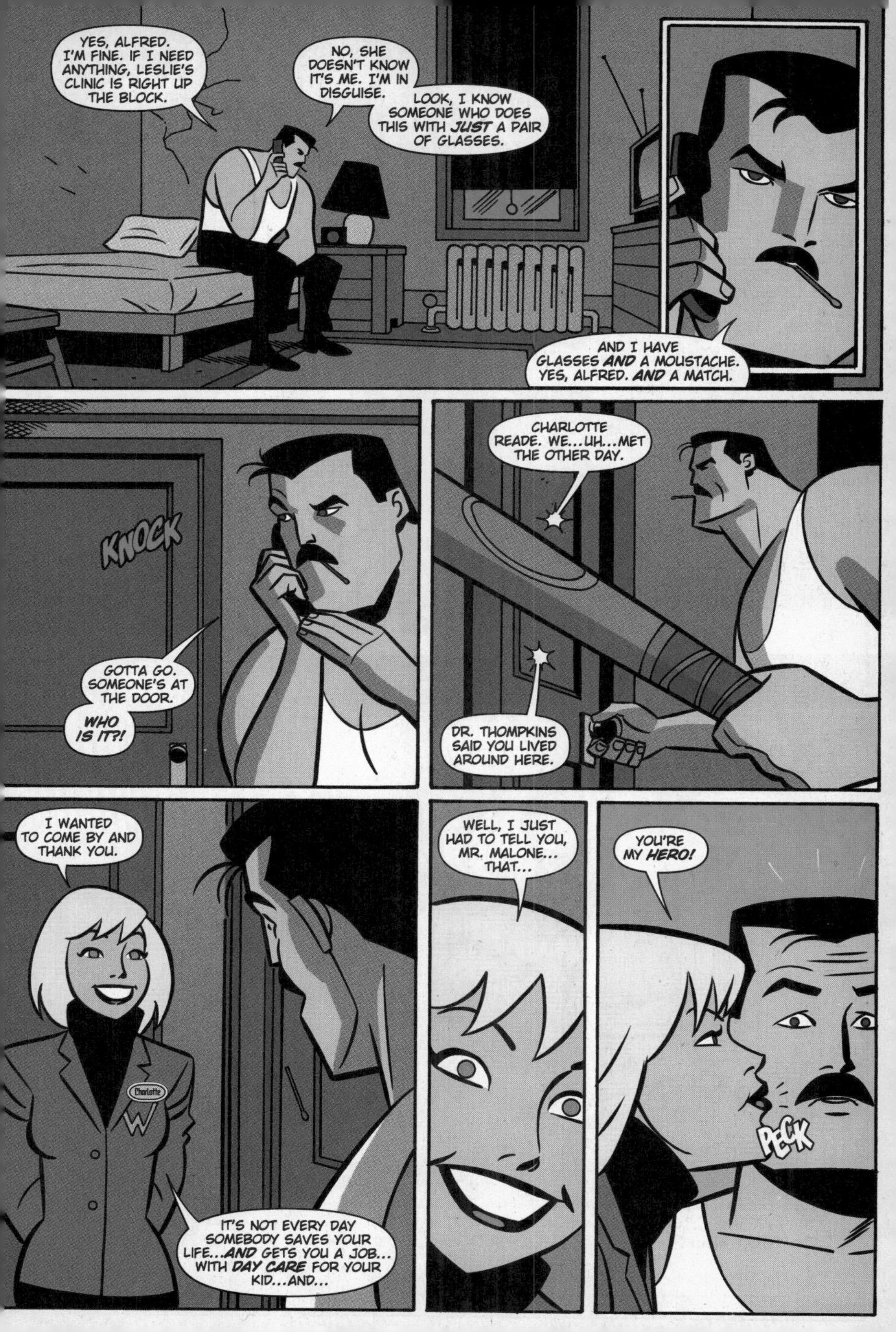
YES, ALFRED. I'M FINE. IF I NEED ANYTHING, LESLIE'S CLINIC IS RIGHT UP THE BLOCK.
NO, SHE DOESN'T KNOW IT'S ME. I'M IN DISGUISE.
LOOK, I KNOW SOMEONE WHO DOES THIS WITH JUST A PAIR OF GLASSES.
AND I HAVE GLASSES AND A MOUSTACHE. YES, ALFRED. AND A MATCH.
KNOCK
GOTTA GO. SOMEONE'S AT THE DOOR.
WHO IS IT?!
CHARLOTTE READE. WE...UH...MET THE OTHER DAY.
DR. THOMPKINS SAID YOU LIVED AROUND HERE.
I WANTED TO COME BY AND THANK YOU.
Charlotte
IT'S NOT EVERY DAY SOMEBODY SAVES YOUR LIFE...AND GETS YOU A JOB... WITH DAY CARE FOR YOUR KID...AND...
WELL, I JUST HAD TO TELL YOU, MR. MALONE... THAT...
YOU'RE MY HERO!
PECK

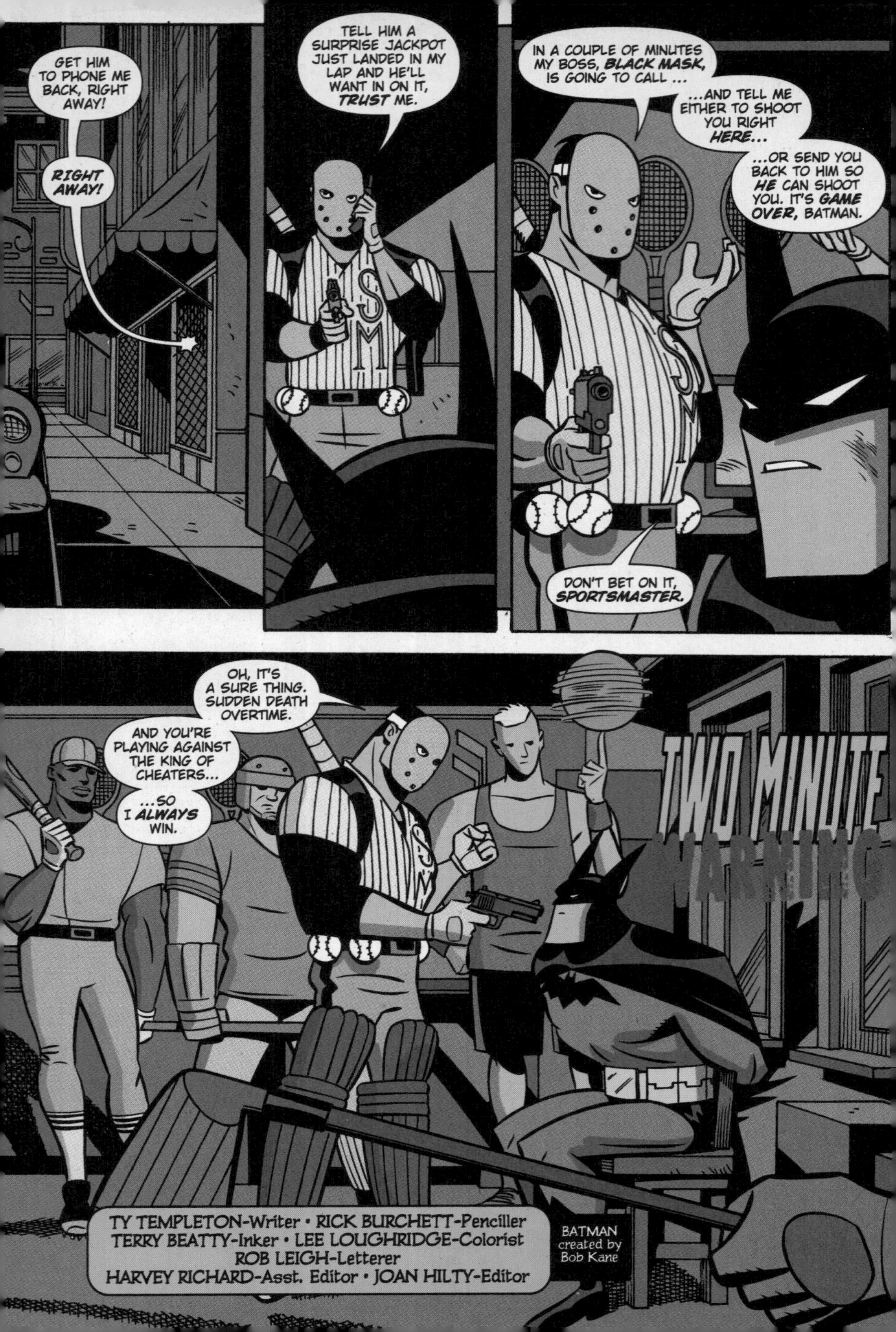
GET HIM TO PHONE ME BACK, RIGHT AWAY!
RIGHT AWAY!
TELL HIM A SURPRISE JACKPOT JUST LANDED IN MY LAP AND HE'LL WANT IN ON IT, TRUST ME.
IN A COUPLE OF MINUTES MY BOSS, BLACK MASK, IS GOING TO CALL ...
...AND TELL ME EITHER TO SHOOT YOU RIGHT HERE...
...OR SEND YOU BACK TO HIM SO HE CAN SHOOT YOU. IT'S GAME OVER, BATMAN.
DON'T BET ON IT, SPORTSMASTER.
OH, IT'S A SURE THING. SUDDEN DEATH OVERTIME.
AND YOU'RE PLAYING AGAINST THE KING OF CHEATERS...
...SO I ALWAYS WIN.
TWO MINUTE WARNING
TY TEMPLETON-Writer • RICK BURCHETT-Penciller
TERRY BEATTY-Inker • LEE LOUGHRIDGE-Colorist
ROB LEIGH-Letterer
HARVEY RICHARD-Asst. Editor • JOAN HILTY-Editor
BATMAN created by Bob Kane

"I DON'T KNOW, BOSS... FOR A GUY ABOUT TO GET POPPED, WHY IS HE SO *CALM*?"

"BECAUSE I'VE BEEN HERE BEFORE AND I KNOW HOW THIS ENDS..."

"WITH MOST OF YOU UNCONSCIOUS, AND *ALL* OF YOU IN JAIL."

"MY ONLY CONCERN IS THAT SOMEONE WILL TAKE A BULLET. YOUR BOSS IS WAVING AROUND A *GUN*."

SHUT UP.

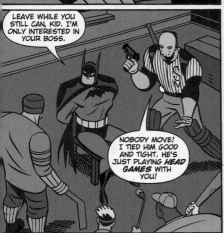

"LEAVE WHILE YOU STILL CAN, KID. I'M ONLY INTERESTED IN YOUR BOSS."

"NOBODY MOVE! I TIED HIM GOOD AND TIGHT. HE'S JUST PLAYING *HEAD GAMES* WITH YOU!"

"THAT'S NOT THE KIND OF GAME YOU LIKE, IS IT, SPORTSMASTER? YOU PREFER CROOKED GAMES AND FIXED FIGHTS, WHERE YOU ALWAYS HAVE THE WINNING BET."

"YOU KNOW MY CAREER? HOW FLATTERING. I *FIGURED* THERE WAS A REASON YOU'VE BEEN SHADOWING MY BOYS LATELY."

"I NEEDED A WAY INTO YOUR HIDEOUT."

"LETTING YOUR BIG APE THINK HE SUCKER-PUNCHED ME AT THE RACE TRACK TONIGHT MADE HIM COCKY ENOUGH TO BRING ME STRAIGHT HERE."

"YOU'RE *BLUFFING*. WHAT CAN YOU DO, TIED TO A CHAIR?"

"I CAN'T PROMISE TO KEEP EVERYONE SAFE ONCE THE SHOOTING STARTS. YOUR MEN HAVE THIRTY SECONDS TO GET OUT..."

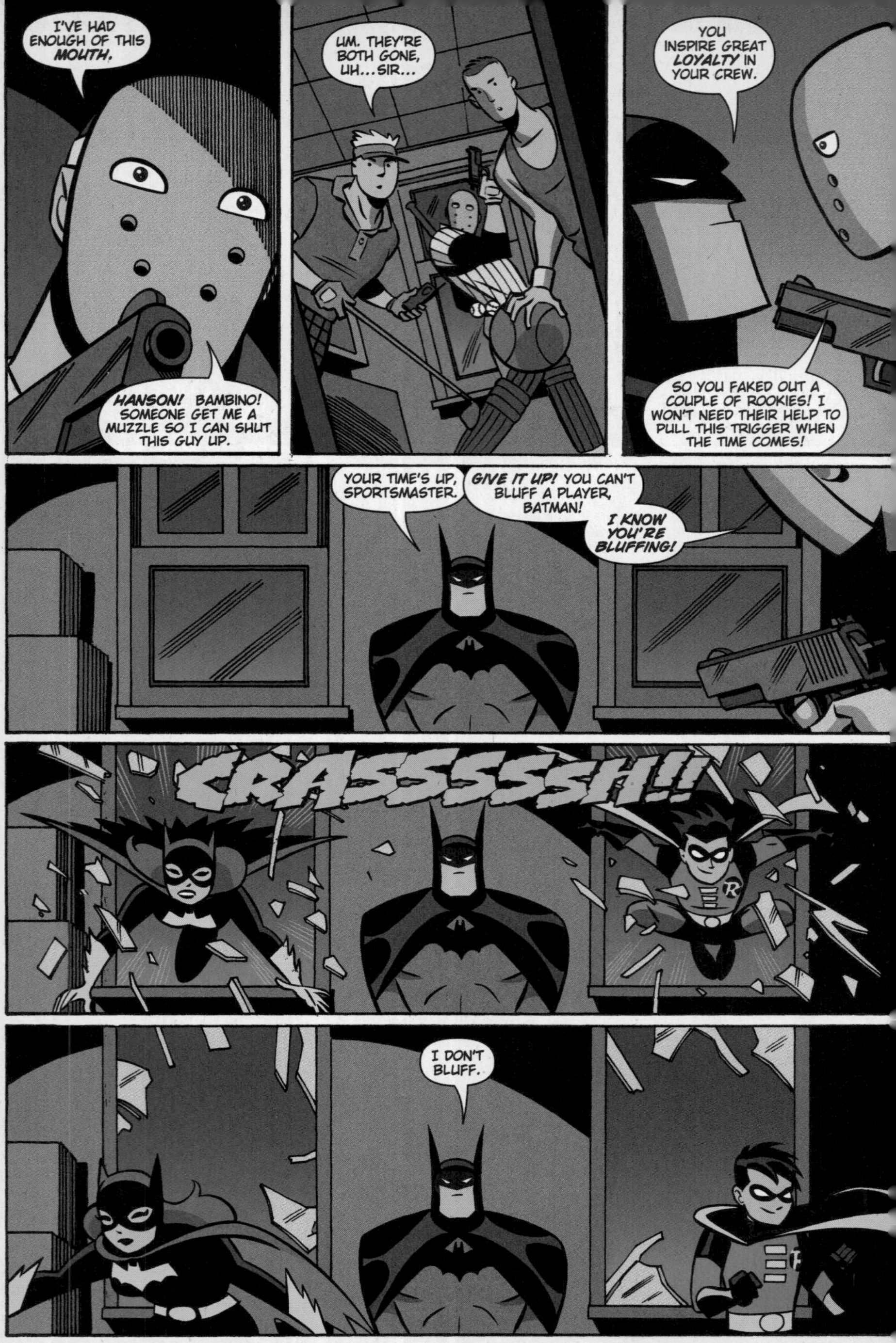

I'VE HAD ENOUGH OF THIS MOUTH.
HANSON! BAMBINO! SOMEONE GET ME A MUZZLE SO I CAN SHUT THIS GUY UP.
UM. THEY'RE BOTH GONE, UH... SIR...
YOU INSPIRE GREAT LOYALTY IN YOUR CREW.
SO YOU FAKED OUT A COUPLE OF ROOKIES! I WON'T NEED THEIR HELP TO PULL THIS TRIGGER WHEN THE TIME COMES!
YOUR TIME'S UP, SPORTSMASTER.
GIVE IT UP! YOU CAN'T BLUFF A PLAYER, BATMAN!
I KNOW YOU'RE BLUFFING!
CRASSSSSH!!!
I DON'T BLUFF.

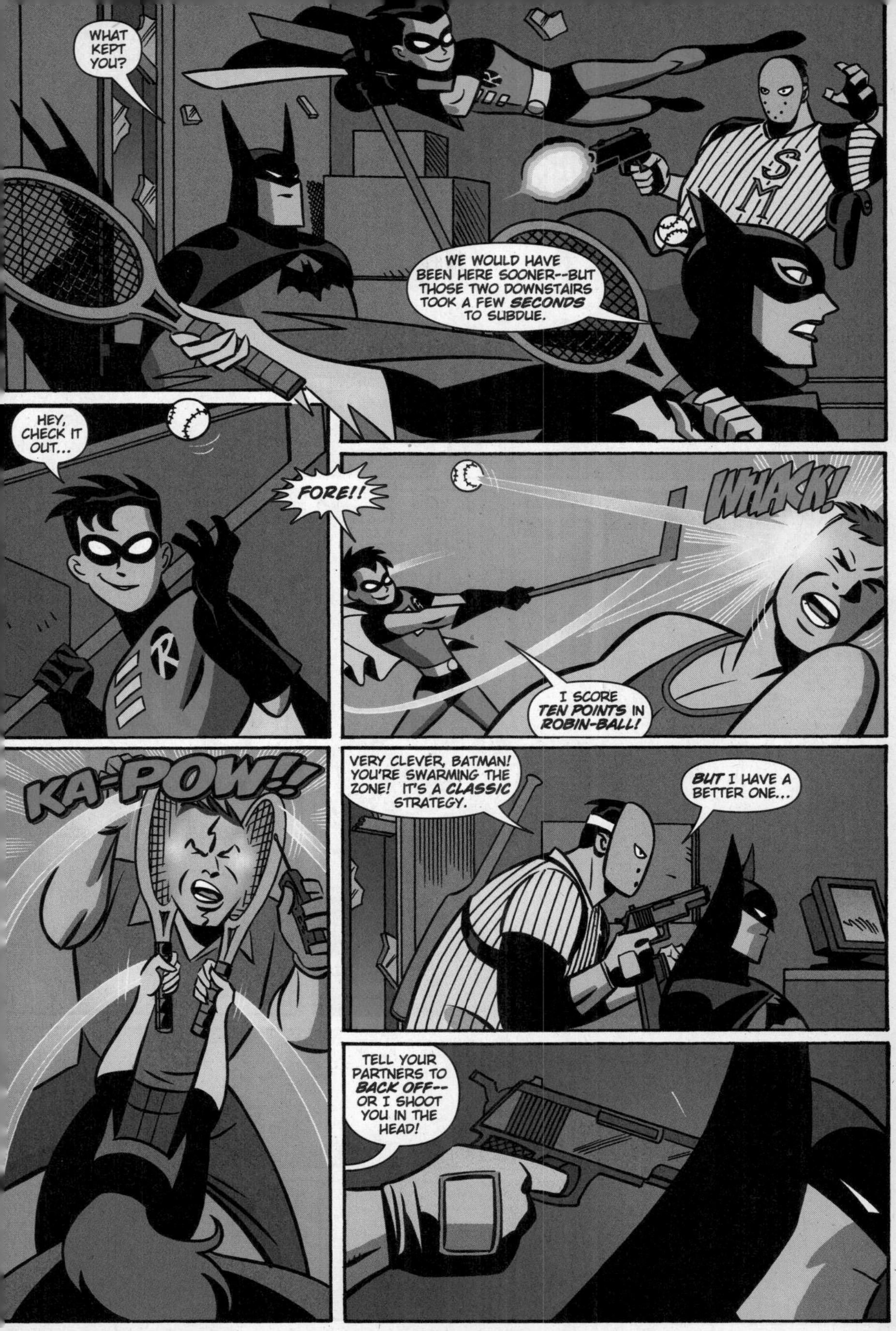
WHAT KEPT YOU?
WE WOULD HAVE BEEN HERE SOONER--BUT THOSE TWO DOWNSTAIRS TOOK A FEW SECONDS TO SUBDUE.
HEY, CHECK IT OUT...
FORE!!
WHACK!
I SCORE TEN POINTS IN ROBIN-BALL!
KA-POW!!
VERY CLEVER, BATMAN! YOU'RE SWARMING THE ZONE! IT'S A CLASSIC STRATEGY.
BUT I HAVE A BETTER ONE...
TELL YOUR PARTNERS TO BACK OFF--OR I SHOOT YOU IN THE HEAD!

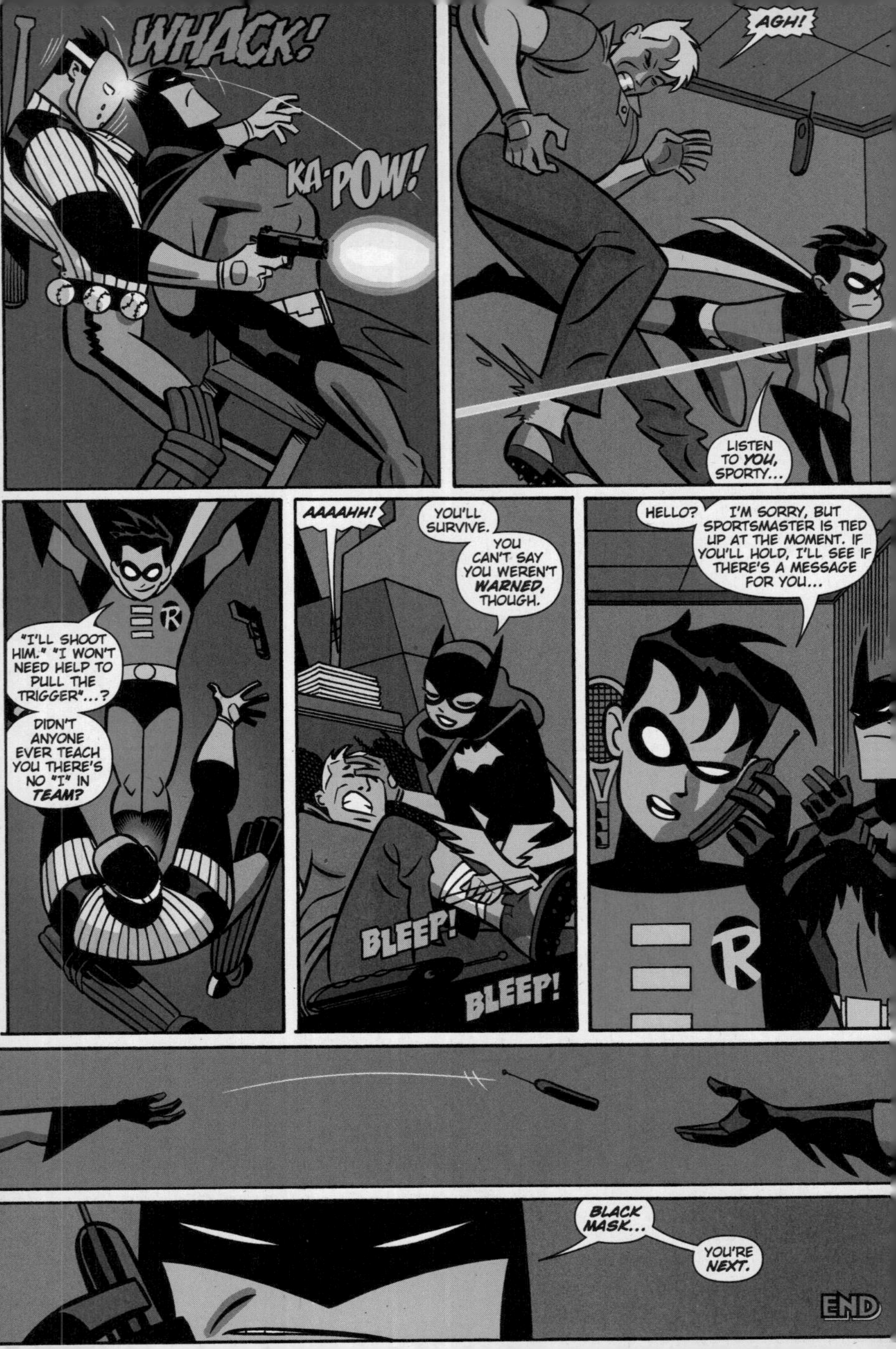
WHACK!
KA-POW!
AGH!
LISTEN TO *YOU,* SPORTY...
"I'LL SHOOT HIM." "I WON'T NEED HELP TO PULL THE TRIGGER"...?
DIDN'T ANYONE EVER TEACH YOU THERE'S NO "I" IN *TEAM?*
AAAAHH!
YOU'LL SURVIVE.
YOU CAN'T SAY YOU WEREN'T *WARNED,* THOUGH.
BLEEP!
BLEEP!
HELLO?
I'M SORRY, BUT SPORTSMASTER IS TIED UP AT THE MOMENT. IF YOU'LL HOLD, I'LL SEE IF THERE'S A MESSAGE FOR YOU...
BLACK MASK...
YOU'RE *NEXT.*
END

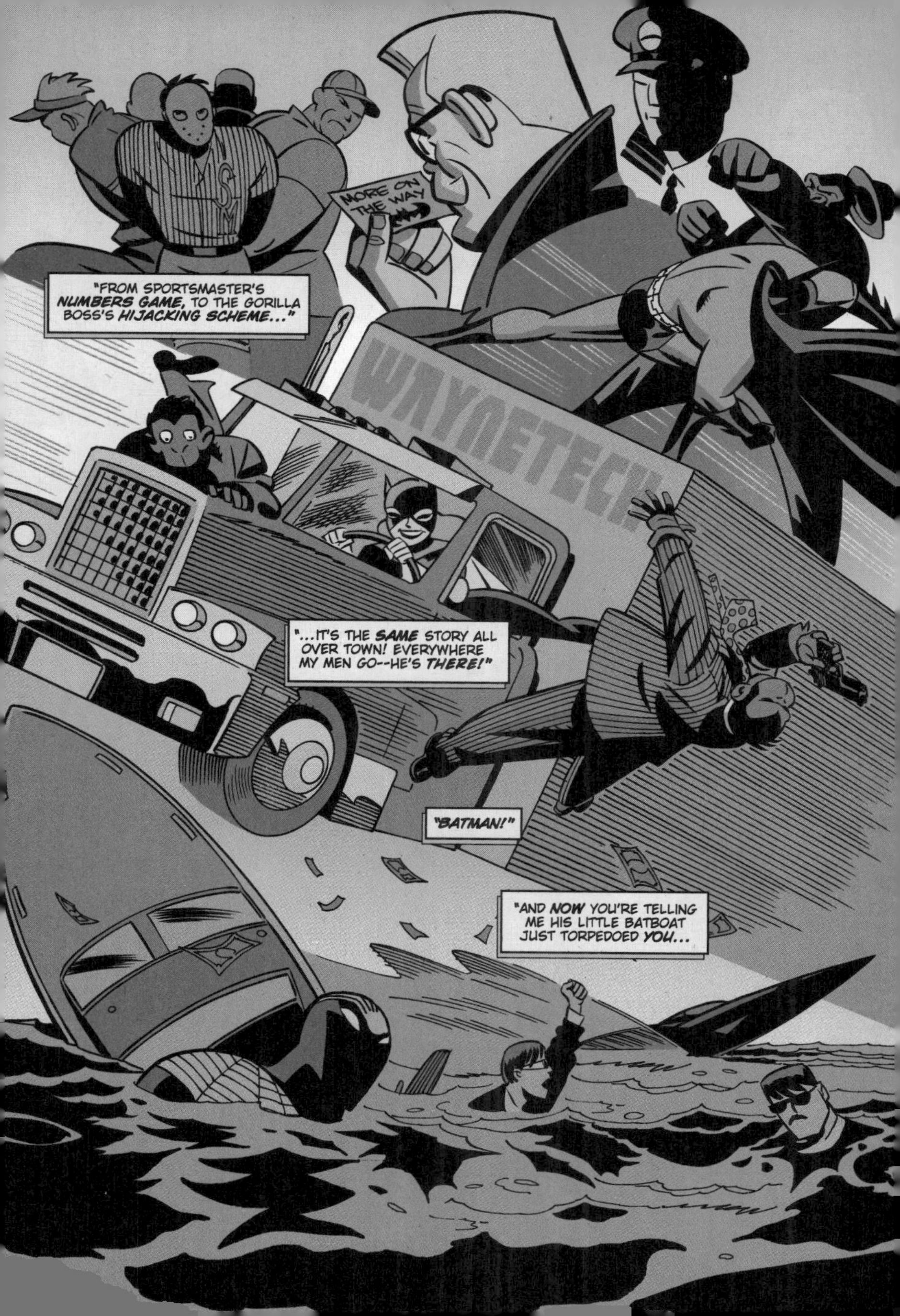
MORE ON THE WAY
"FROM SPORTSMASTER'S NUMBERS GAME, TO THE GORILLA BOSS'S HIJACKING SCHEME..."
WAYNETECH
"...IT'S THE SAME STORY ALL OVER TOWN! EVERYWHERE MY MEN GO--HE'S THERE!"
"BATMAN!"
"AND NOW YOU'RE TELLING ME HIS LITTLE BATBOAT JUST TORPEDOED YOU...

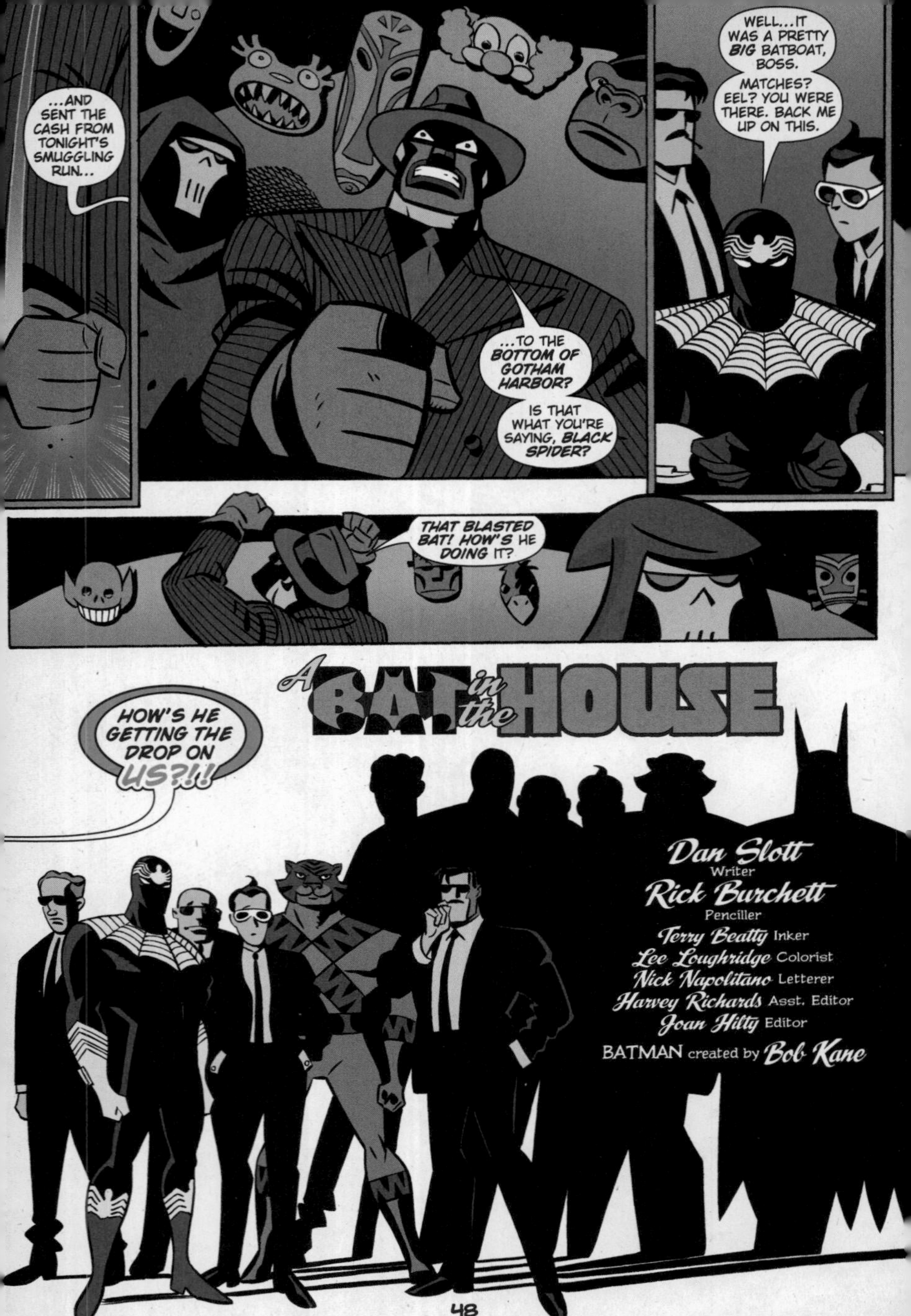
...AND SENT THE CASH FROM TONIGHT'S SMUGGLING RUN...
...TO THE BOTTOM OF GOTHAM HARBOR?
IS THAT WHAT YOU'RE SAYING, BLACK SPIDER?
WELL...IT WAS A PRETTY BIG BATBOAT, BOSS.
MATCHES? EEL? YOU WERE THERE. BACK ME UP ON THIS.
THAT BLASTED BAT! HOW'S HE DOING IT?
HOW'S HE GETTING THE DROP ON US?!!
A BAT in the HOUSE
Dan Slott Writer
Rick Burchett Penciller
Terry Beatty Inker
Lee Loughridge Colorist
Nick Napolitano Letterer
Harvey Richards Asst. Editor
Joan Hilty Editor
BATMAN created by Bob Kane

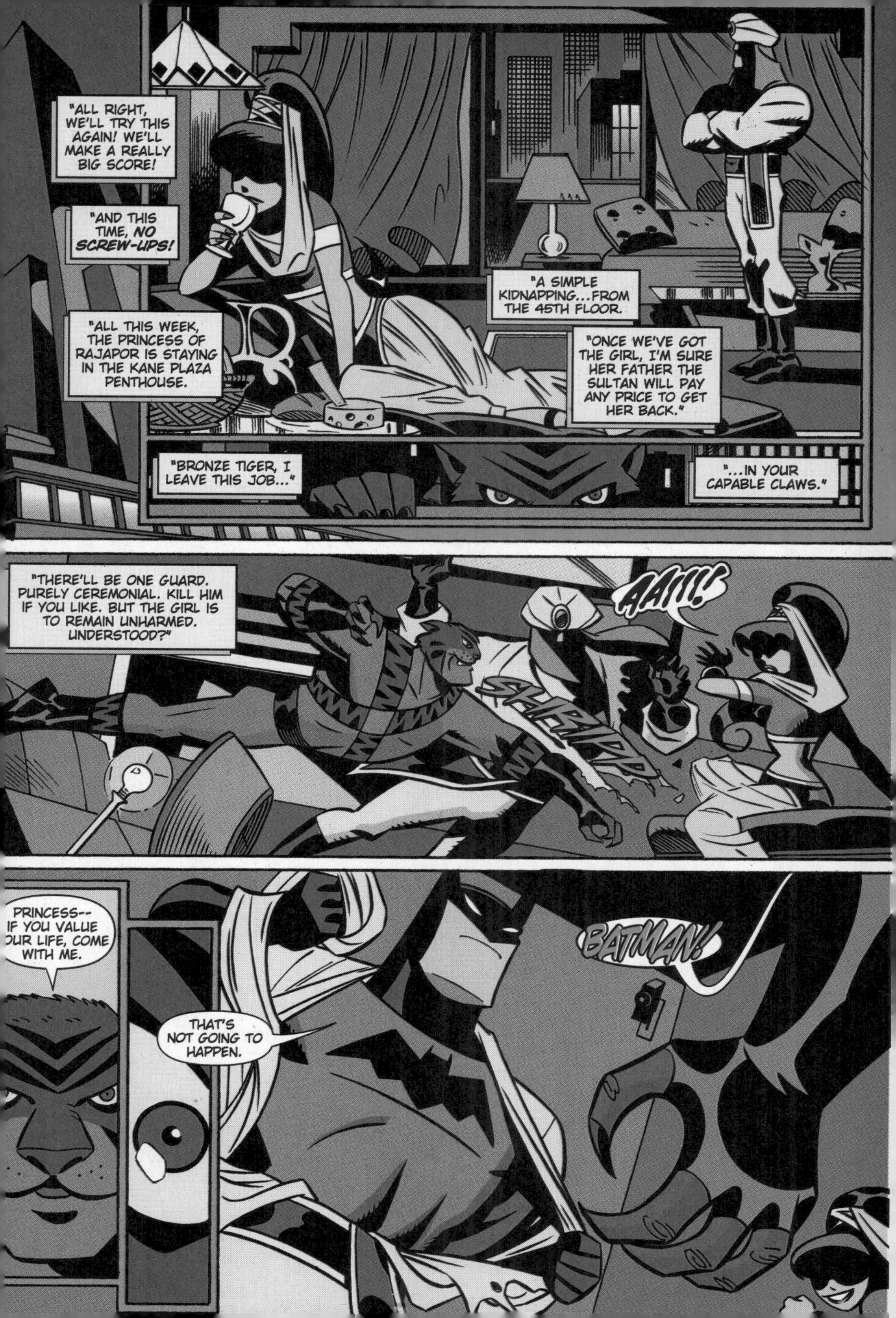
"ALL RIGHT, WE'LL TRY THIS AGAIN! WE'LL MAKE A REALLY BIG SCORE!
"AND THIS TIME, NO SCREW-UPS!
"ALL THIS WEEK, THE PRINCESS OF RAJAPOR IS STAYING IN THE KANE PLAZA PENTHOUSE.
"A SIMPLE KIDNAPPING...FROM THE 45TH FLOOR.
"ONCE WE'VE GOT THE GIRL, I'M SURE HER FATHER THE SULTAN WILL PAY ANY PRICE TO GET HER BACK."
"BRONZE TIGER, I LEAVE THIS JOB..."
"...IN YOUR CAPABLE CLAWS."
"THERE'LL BE ONE GUARD. PURELY CEREMONIAL. KILL HIM IF YOU LIKE. BUT THE GIRL IS TO REMAIN UNHARMED. UNDERSTOOD?"
AAII!!
SHRRIPP
PRINCESS-- IF YOU VALUE OUR LIFE, COME WITH ME.
BATMAN!
THAT'S NOT GOING TO HAPPEN.

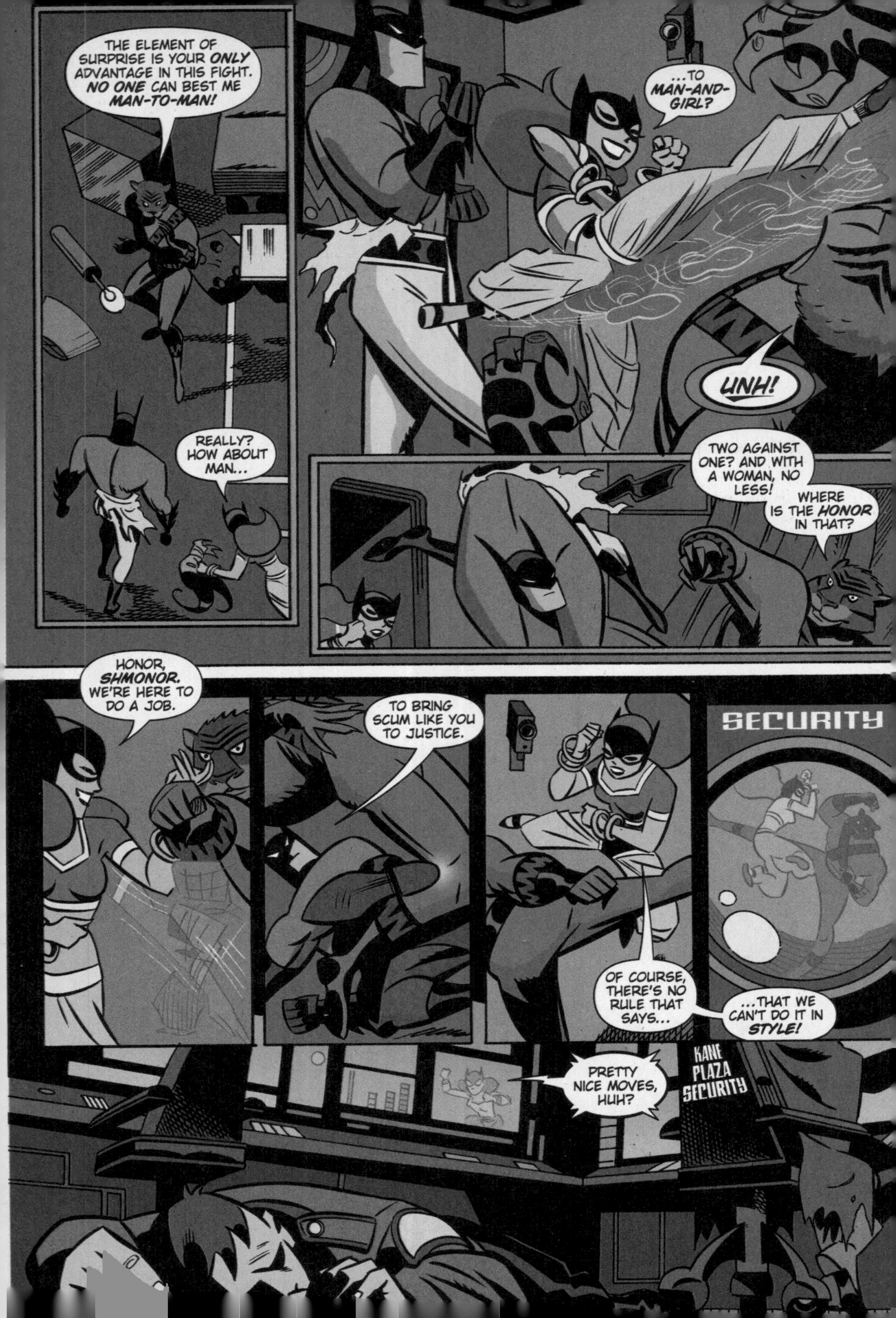

THE ELEMENT OF SURPRISE IS YOUR ONLY ADVANTAGE IN THIS FIGHT. NO ONE CAN BEST ME MAN-TO-MAN!
REALLY? HOW ABOUT MAN...
...TO MAN-AND-GIRL?
UNH!
TWO AGAINST ONE? AND WITH A WOMAN, NO LESS!
WHERE IS THE HONOR IN THAT?
HONOR, SHMONOR. WE'RE HERE TO DO A JOB.
TO BRING SCUM LIKE YOU TO JUSTICE.
OF COURSE, THERE'S NO RULE THAT SAYS...
...THAT WE CAN'T DO IT IN STYLE!
SECURITY
KANE PLAZA SECURITY
PRETTY NICE MOVES, HUH?

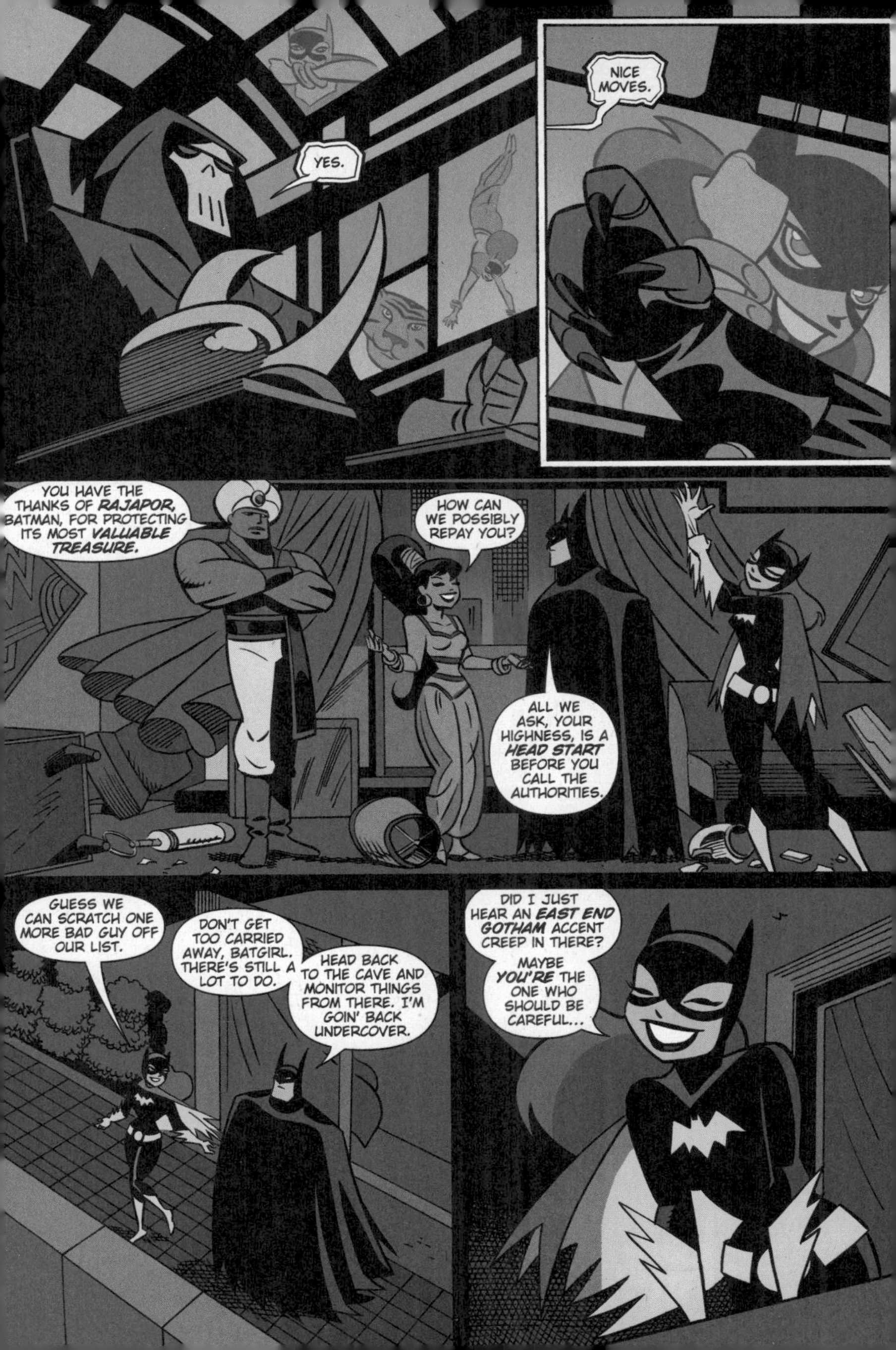
YES.
NICE MOVES.
YOU HAVE THE THANKS OF RAJAPOR, BATMAN, FOR PROTECTING ITS MOST VALUABLE TREASURE.
HOW CAN WE POSSIBLY REPAY YOU?
ALL WE ASK, YOUR HIGHNESS, IS A HEAD START BEFORE YOU CALL THE AUTHORITIES.
GUESS WE CAN SCRATCH ONE MORE BAD GUY OFF OUR LIST.
DON'T GET TOO CARRIED AWAY, BATGIRL. THERE'S STILL A LOT TO DO.
HEAD BACK TO THE CAVE AND MONITOR THINGS FROM THERE. I'M GOIN' BACK UNDERCOVER.
DID I JUST HEAR AN EAST END GOTHAM ACCENT CREEP IN THERE?
MAYBE YOU'RE THE ONE WHO SHOULD BE CAREFUL...

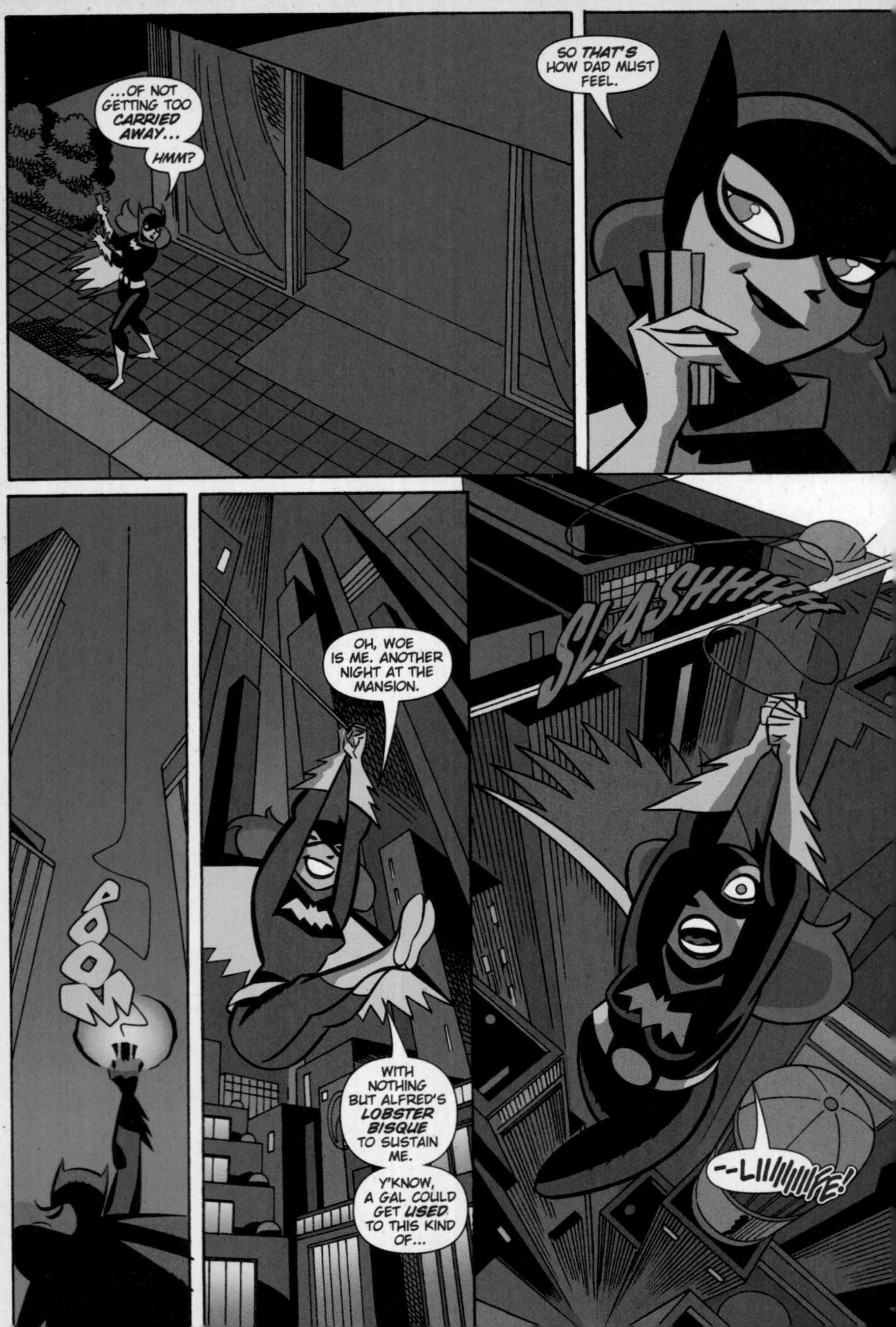
...OF NOT GETTING TOO CARRIED AWAY...
HMM?
SO THAT'S HOW DAD MUST FEEL.
POOOM
OH, WOE IS ME. ANOTHER NIGHT AT THE MANSION.
WITH NOTHING BUT ALFRED'S LOBSTER BISQUE TO SUSTAIN ME.
Y'KNOW, A GAL COULD GET USED TO THIS KIND OF...
SLASHHHH
--LIIIIIIIIIFE!

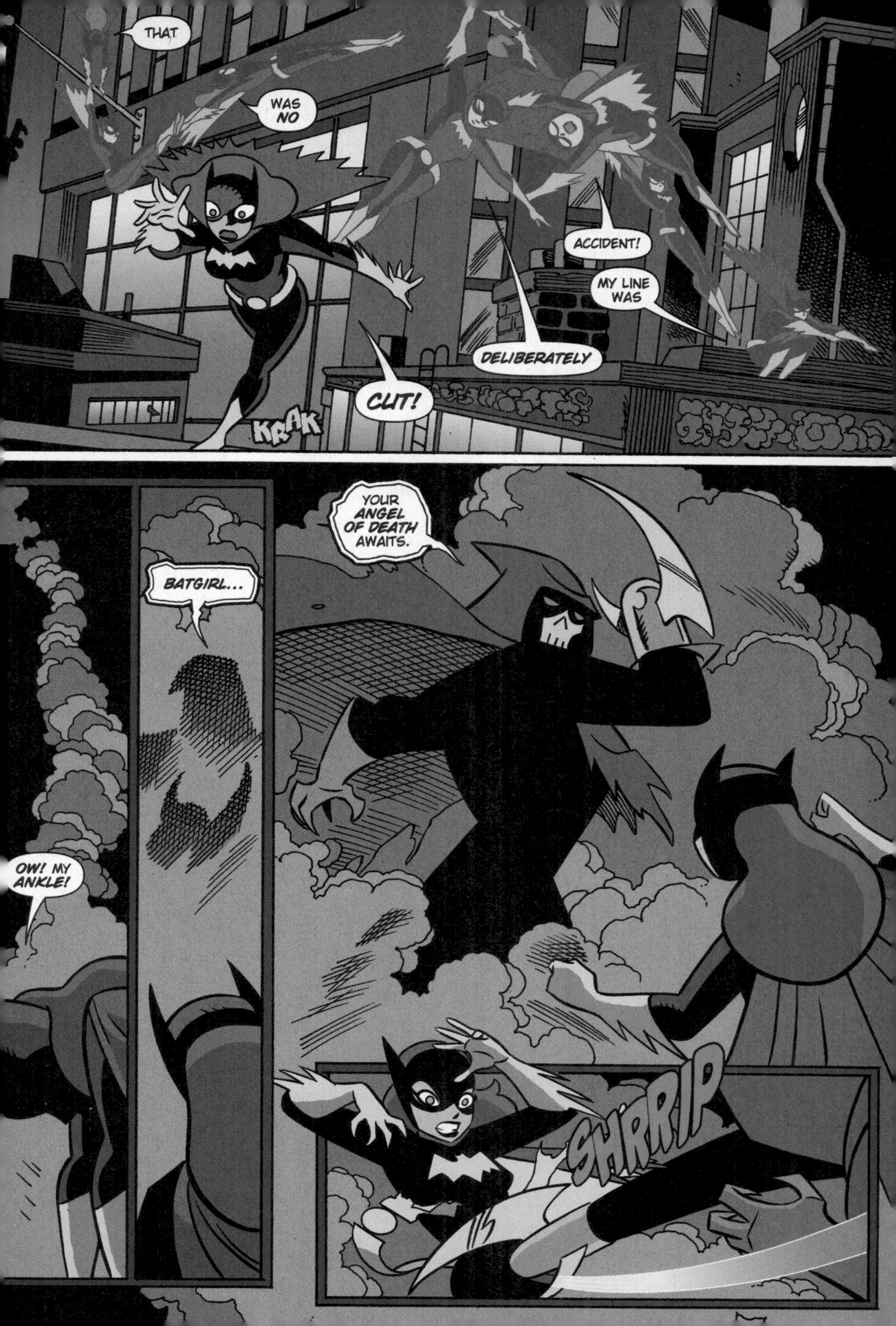
THAT
WAS NO
ACCIDENT!
MY LINE WAS
DELIBERATELY
CUT!
KRAK
YOUR ANGEL OF DEATH AWAITS.
BATGIRL...
OW! MY ANKLE!
SHRRIP

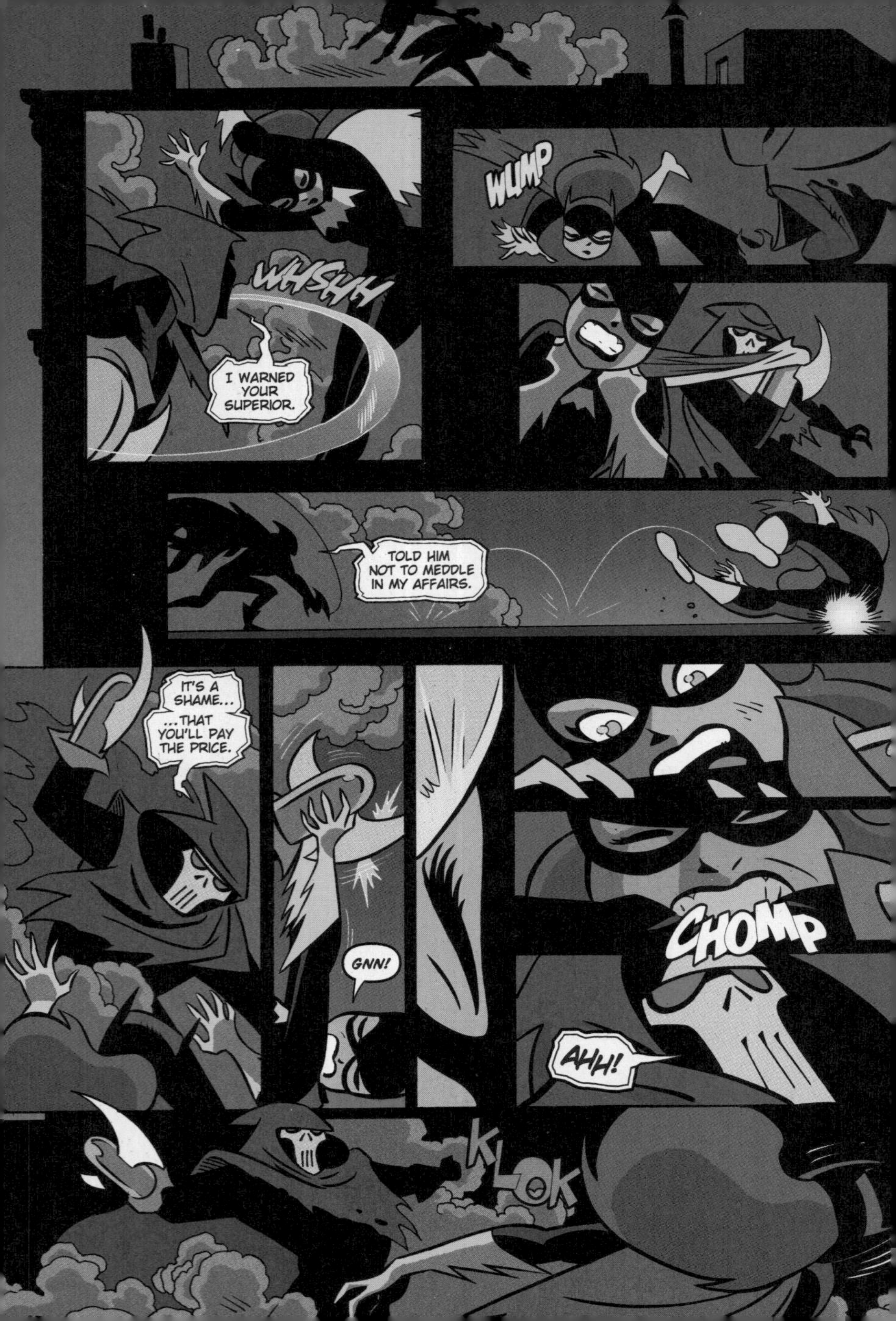
WUMP
WHSHH
I WARNED YOUR SUPERIOR.
TOLD HIM NOT TO MEDDLE IN MY AFFAIRS.
IT'S A SHAME...
...THAT YOU'LL PAY THE PRICE.
GNN!
CHOMP
AHH!
KLOK

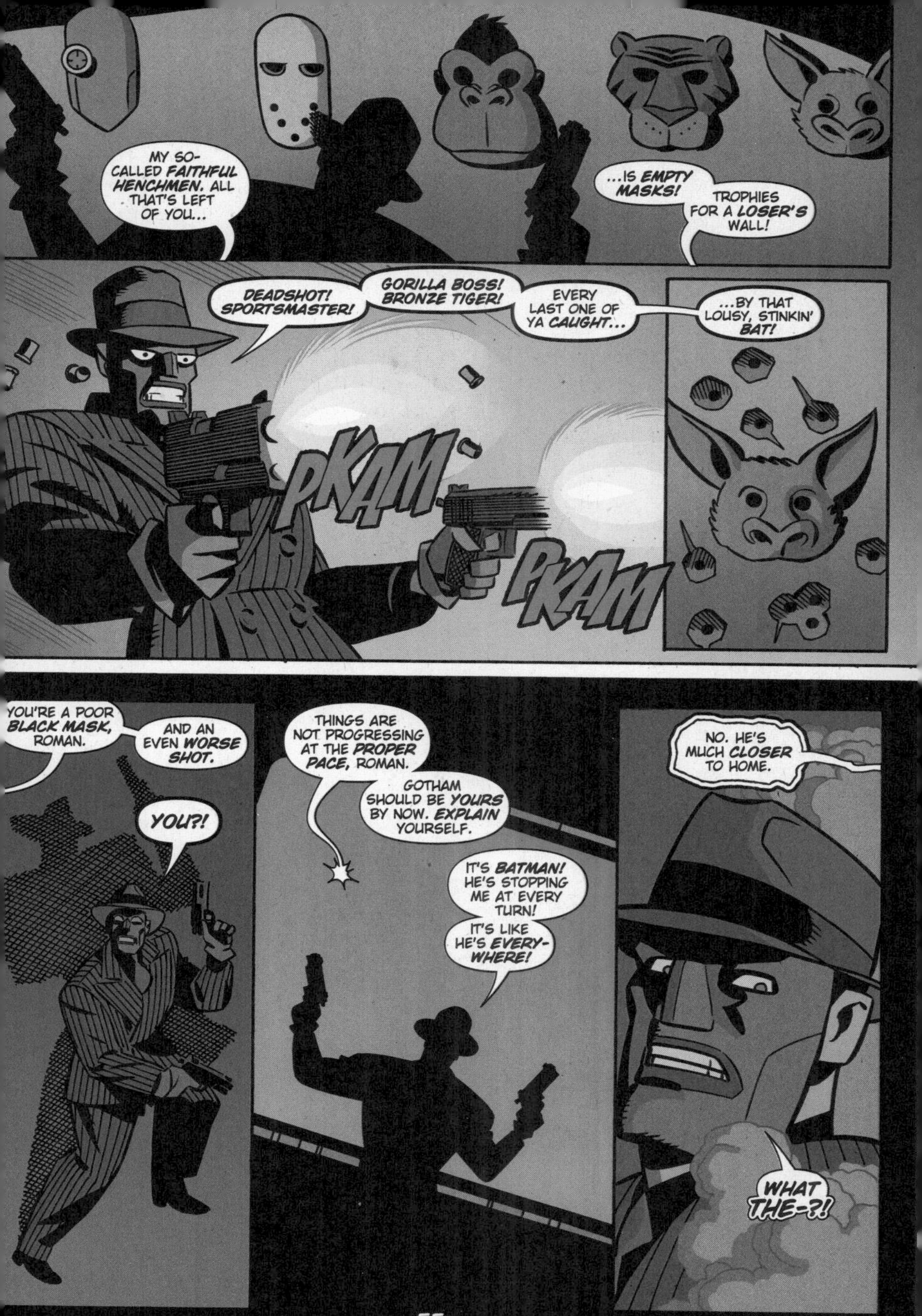

MY SO-CALLED FAITHFUL HENCHMEN. ALL THAT'S LEFT OF YOU...
...IS EMPTY MASKS!
TROPHIES FOR A LOSER'S WALL!
DEADSHOT! SPORTSMASTER!
GORILLA BOSS! BRONZE TIGER!
EVERY LAST ONE OF YA CAUGHT...
...BY THAT LOUSY, STINKIN' BAT!
PKAM
PKAM
YOU'RE A POOR BLACK MASK, ROMAN.
AND AN EVEN WORSE SHOT.
YOU?!
THINGS ARE NOT PROGRESSING AT THE PROPER PACE, ROMAN.
GOTHAM SHOULD BE YOURS BY NOW. EXPLAIN YOURSELF.
IT'S BATMAN! HE'S STOPPING ME AT EVERY TURN!
IT'S LIKE HE'S EVERY-WHERE!
NO. HE'S MUCH CLOSER TO HOME.
WHAT THE-?!

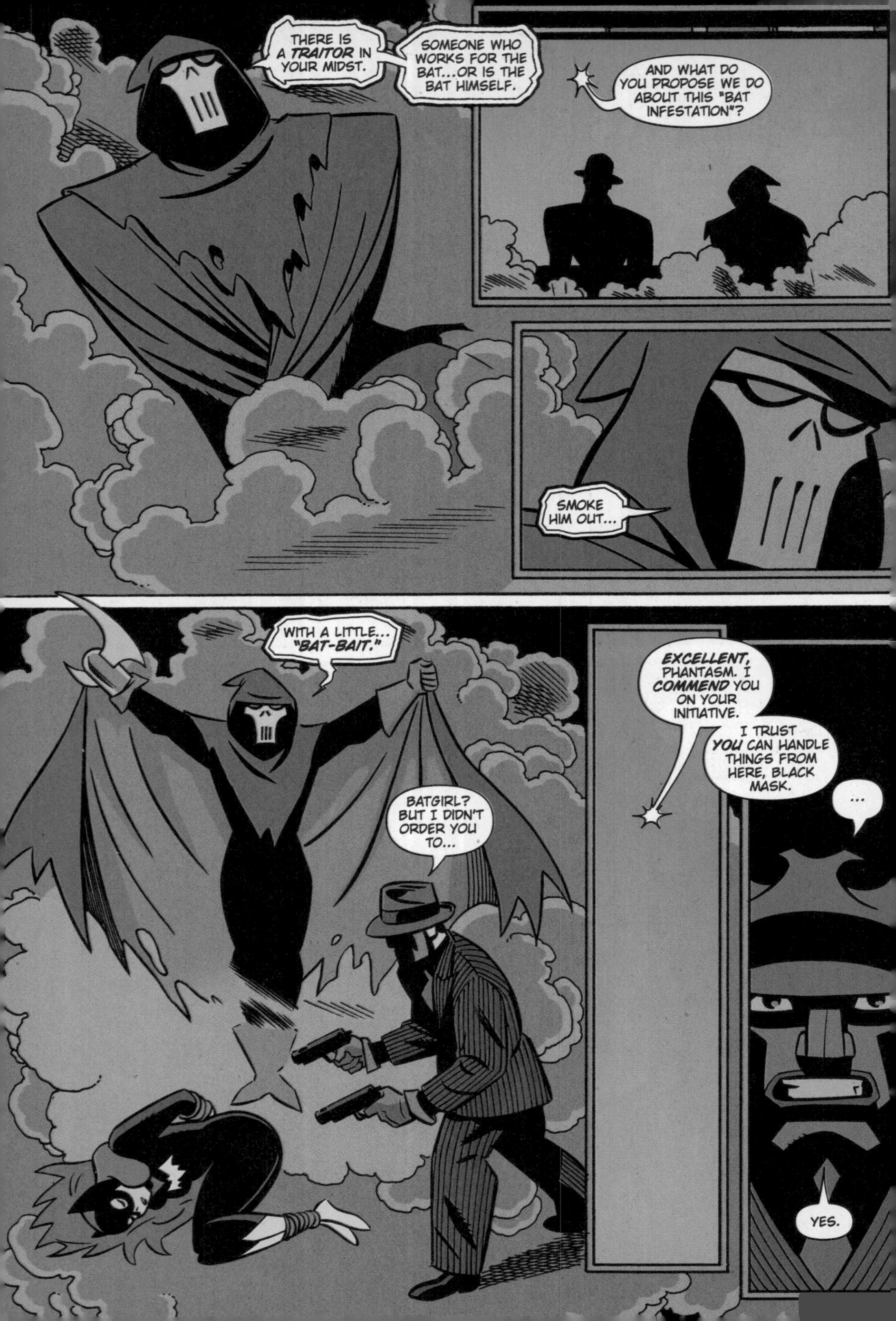
THERE IS A TRAITOR IN YOUR MIDST.
SOMEONE WHO WORKS FOR THE BAT...OR IS THE BAT HIMSELF.
AND WHAT DO YOU PROPOSE WE DO ABOUT THIS "BAT INFESTATION"?
SMOKE HIM OUT...
WITH A LITTLE... "BAT-BAIT."
BATGIRL? BUT I DIDN'T ORDER YOU TO...
EXCELLENT, PHANTASM. I COMMEND YOU ON YOUR INITIATIVE.
I TRUST YOU CAN HANDLE THINGS FROM HERE, BLACK MASK.
...
YES.

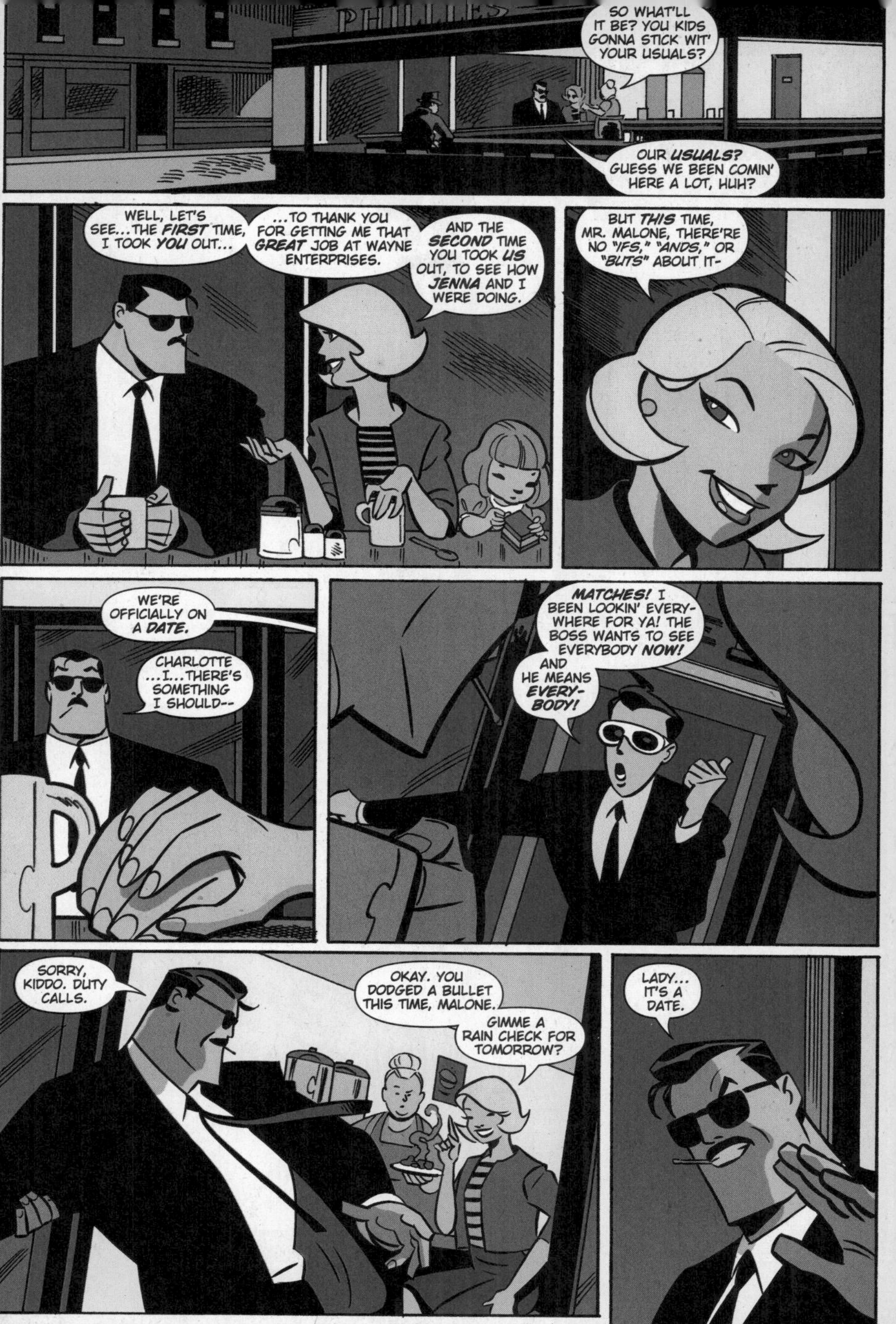
PHILLIES
SO WHAT'LL IT BE? YOU KIDS GONNA STICK WIT' YOUR USUALS?
OUR *USUALS?* GUESS WE BEEN COMIN' HERE A LOT, HUH?
WELL, LET'S SEE...THE *FIRST* TIME, I TOOK *YOU* OUT...
...TO THANK YOU FOR GETTING ME THAT *GREAT* JOB AT WAYNE ENTERPRISES.
AND THE *SECOND* TIME YOU TOOK *US* OUT, TO SEE HOW *JENNA* AND I WERE DOING.
BUT *THIS* TIME, MR. MALONE, THERE'RE NO *"IFS," "ANDS,"* OR *"BUTS"* ABOUT IT-
WE'RE OFFICIALLY ON A *DATE.*
CHARLOTTE ...I...THERE'S SOMETHING I SHOULD--
MATCHES! I BEEN LOOKIN' EVERYWHERE FOR YA! THE BOSS WANTS TO SEE EVERYBODY *NOW!*
AND HE MEANS *EVERYBODY!*
SORRY, KIDDO. DUTY CALLS.
OKAY. YOU DODGED A BULLET THIS TIME, MALONE.
GIMME A RAIN CHECK FOR TOMORROW?
LADY... IT'S A DATE.

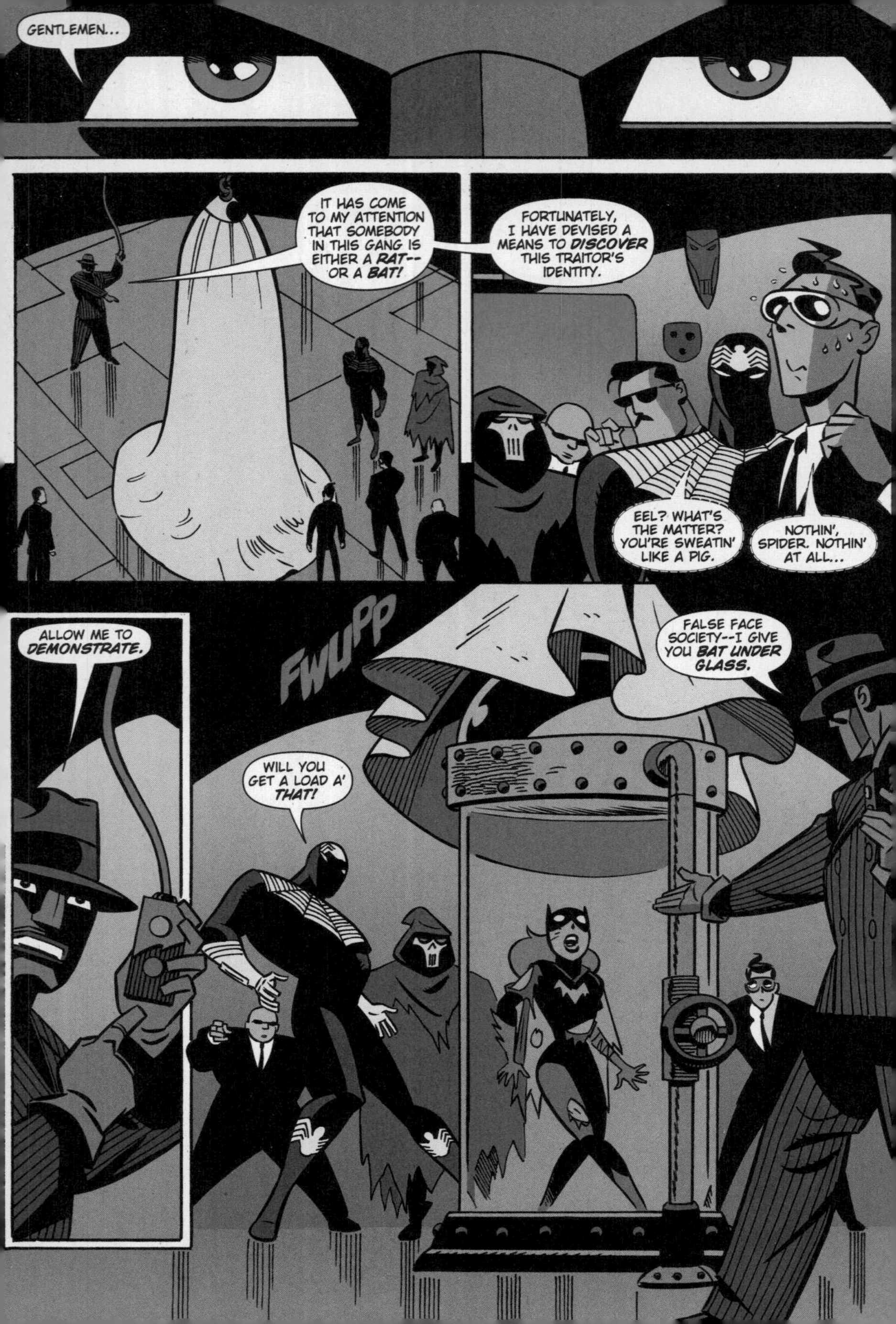

GENTLEMEN...
IT HAS COME TO MY ATTENTION THAT SOMEBODY IN THIS GANG IS EITHER A RAT-- OR A BAT!
FORTUNATELY, I HAVE DEVISED A MEANS TO DISCOVER THIS TRAITOR'S IDENTITY.
EEL? WHAT'S THE MATTER? YOU'RE SWEATIN' LIKE A PIG.
NOTHIN', SPIDER. NOTHIN' AT ALL...
ALLOW ME TO DEMONSTRATE.
FWUPP
FALSE FACE SOCIETY--I GIVE YOU BAT UNDER GLASS.
WILL YOU GET A LOAD A' THAT!

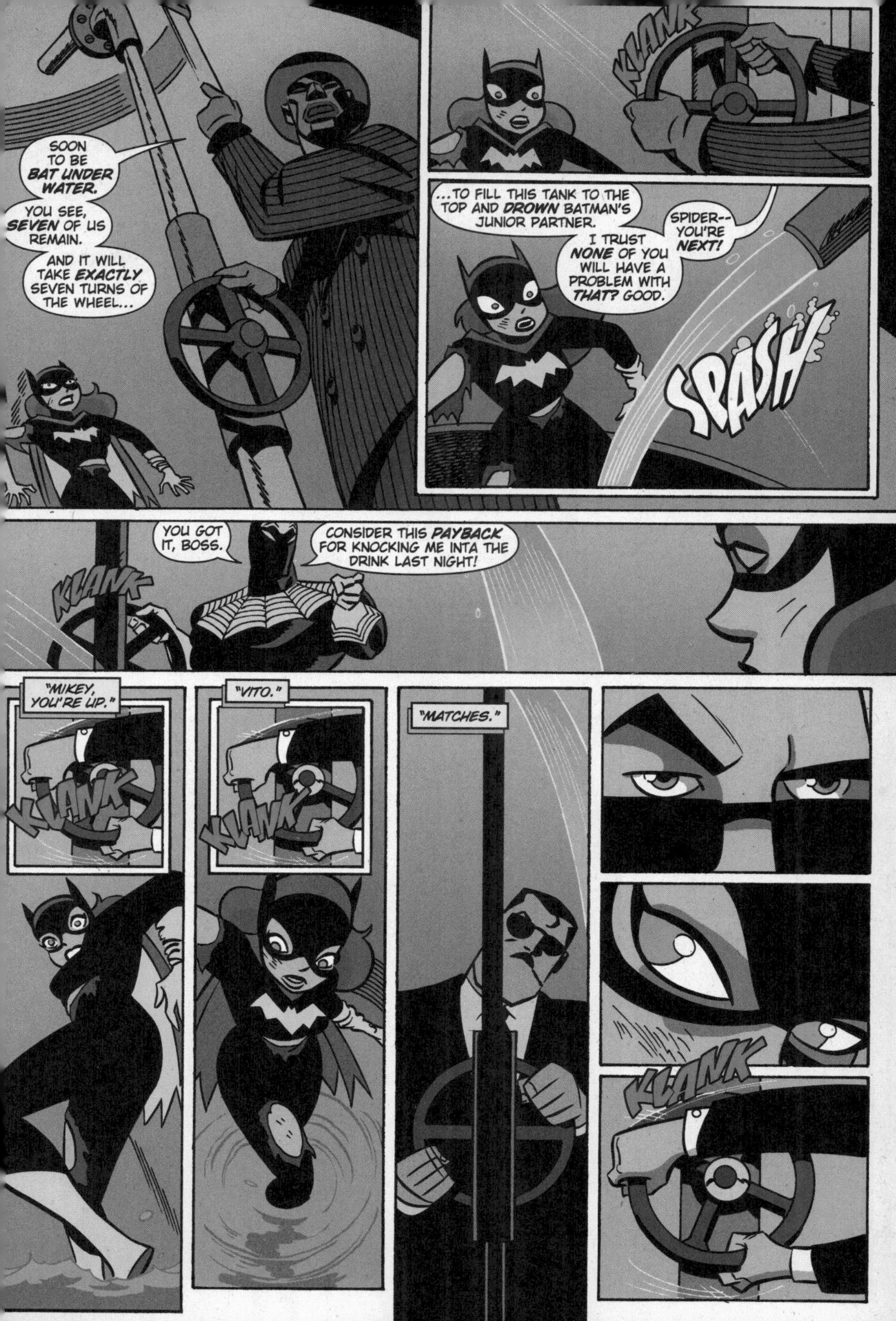
SOON TO BE BAT UNDER WATER.
YOU SEE, SEVEN OF US REMAIN.
AND IT WILL TAKE EXACTLY SEVEN TURNS OF THE WHEEL...
KLANK
...TO FILL THIS TANK TO THE TOP AND DROWN BATMAN'S JUNIOR PARTNER.
I TRUST NONE OF YOU WILL HAVE A PROBLEM WITH THAT? GOOD.
SPIDER-- YOU'RE NEXT!
SPASH
YOU GOT IT, BOSS.
CONSIDER THIS PAYBACK FOR KNOCKING ME INTA THE DRINK LAST NIGHT!
KLANK
"MIKEY, YOU'RE UP."
KLANK
"VITO."
KLANK
"MATCHES."
KLANK

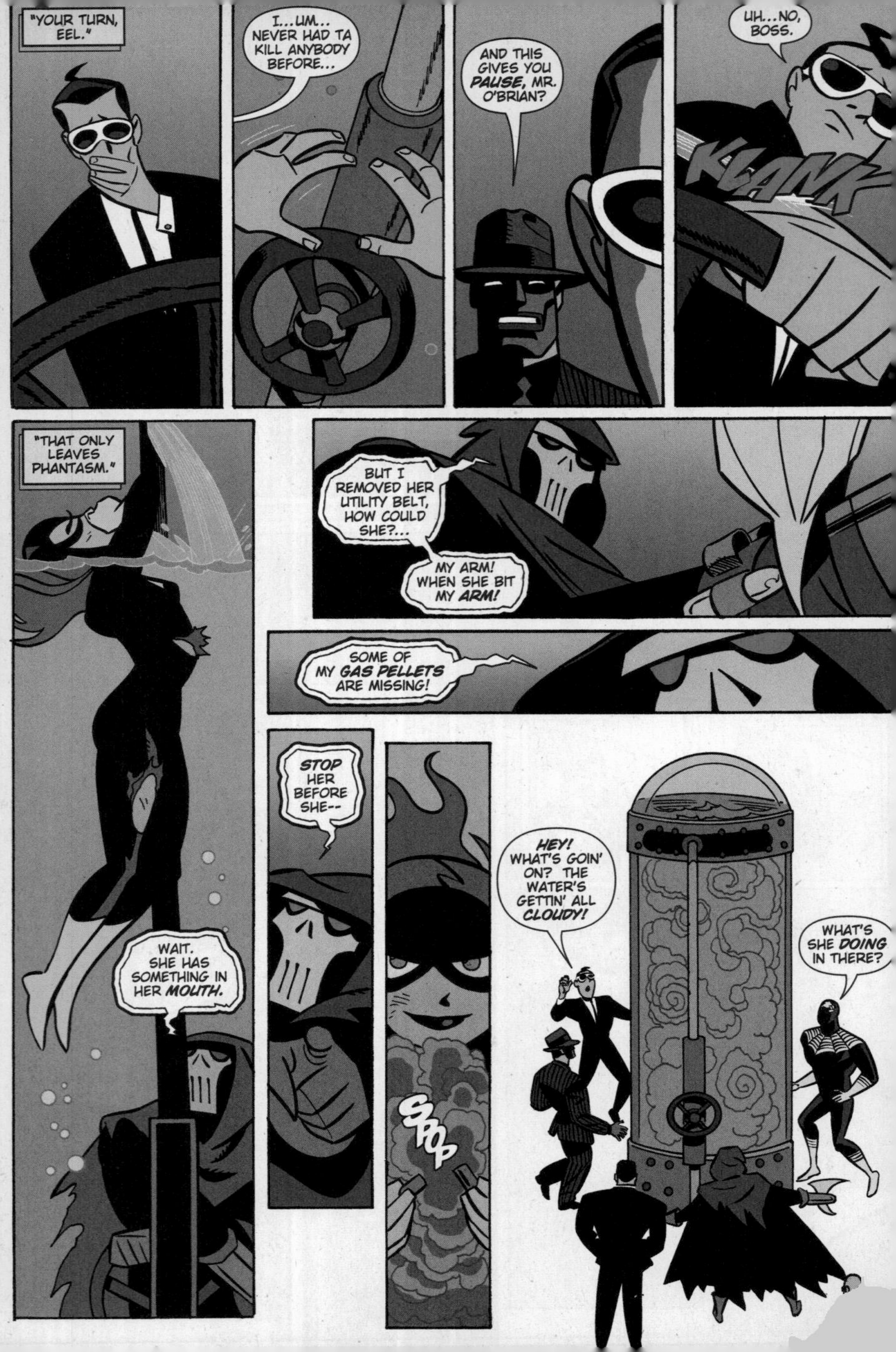

"YOUR TURN, EEL."
I...UM... NEVER HAD TA KILL ANYBODY BEFORE...
AND THIS GIVES YOU *PAUSE*, MR. O'BRIAN?
UH...NO, BOSS.
KLANK
"THAT ONLY LEAVES PHANTASM."
BUT I REMOVED HER UTILITY BELT, HOW COULD SHE?...
MY ARM! WHEN SHE BIT MY *ARM!*
SOME OF MY *GAS PELLETS* ARE MISSING!
WAIT. SHE HAS SOMETHING IN HER *MOUTH.*
STOP HER BEFORE SHE--
SPOP
HEY! WHAT'S GOIN' ON? THE WATER'S GETTIN' ALL *CLOUDY!*
WHAT'S SHE *DOING* IN THERE?

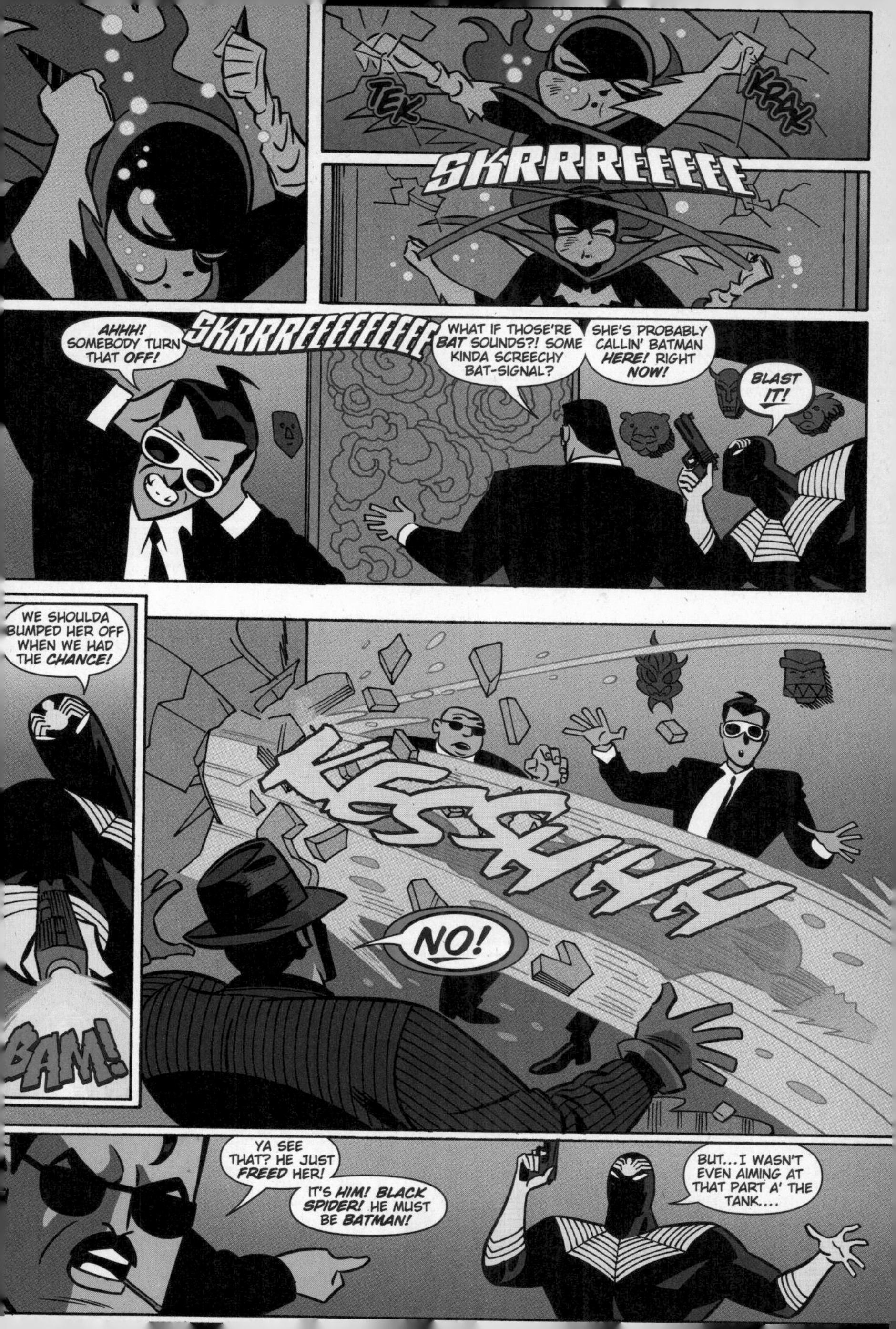
TEK
KRAK
SKRRRREEEEEE
AHHH! SOMEBODY TURN THAT OFF!
SKRRRREEEEEEEEEE
WHAT IF THOSE'RE BAT SOUNDS?! SOME KINDA SCREECHY BAT-SIGNAL?
SHE'S PROBABLY CALLIN' BATMAN HERE! RIGHT NOW!
BLAST IT!
WE SHOULDA BUMPED HER OFF WHEN WE HAD THE CHANCE!
BAM!
KSSHHH
NO!
YA SEE THAT? HE JUST FREED HER!
IT'S HIM! BLACK SPIDER! HE MUST BE BATMAN!
BUT...I WASN'T EVEN AIMING AT THAT PART A' THE TANK....

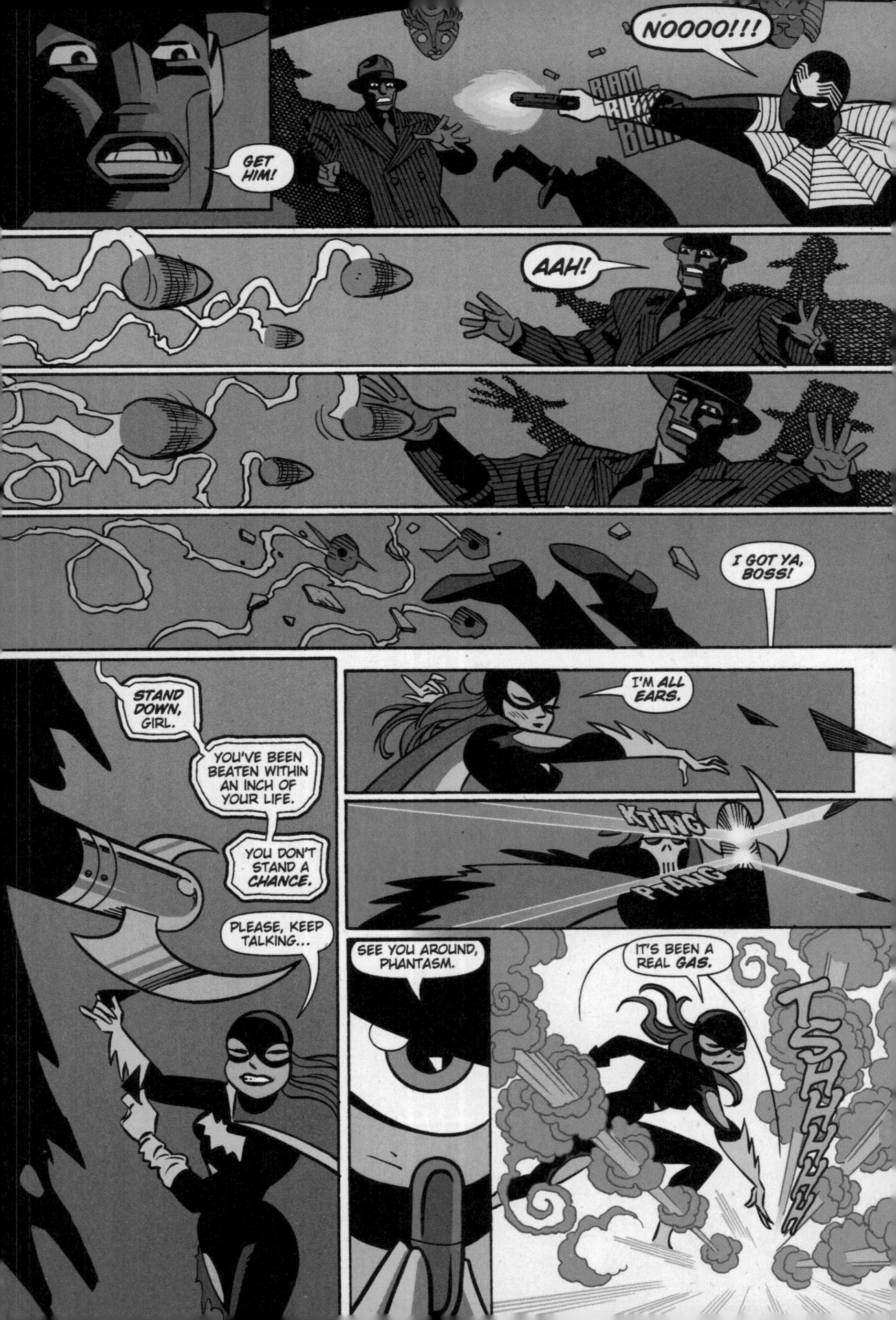
GET HIM!
NOOOO!!!
BLAM BLAM BLAM
AAH!
I GOT YA, BOSS!
STAND DOWN, GIRL.
YOU'VE BEEN BEATEN WITHIN AN INCH OF YOUR LIFE.
YOU DON'T STAND A CHANCE.
PLEASE, KEEP TALKING...
I'M ALL EARS.
KTING
PTANG
SEE YOU AROUND, PHANTASM.
IT'S BEEN A REAL GAS.

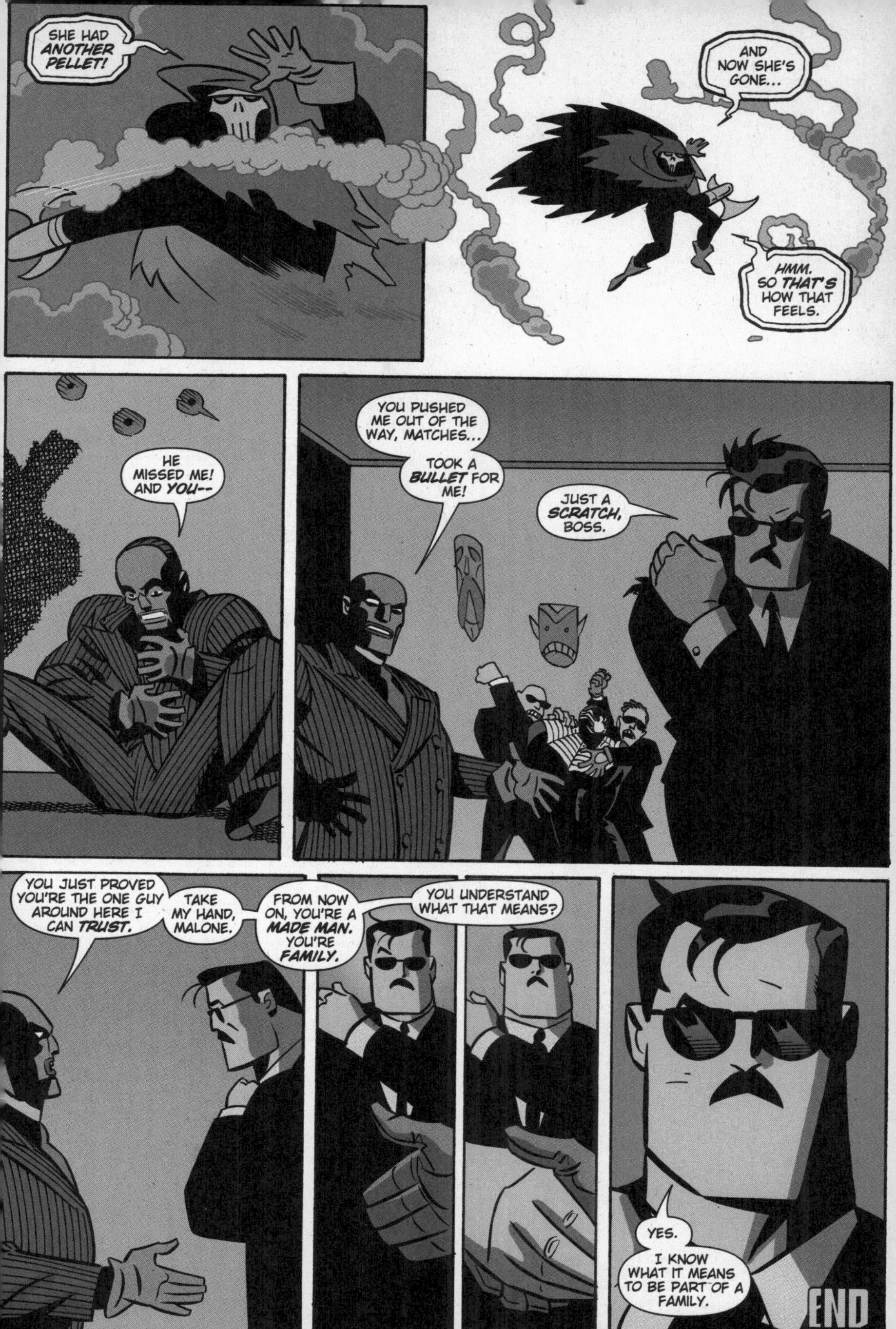
SHE HAD ANOTHER PELLET!
AND NOW SHE'S GONE...
HMM. SO THAT'S HOW THAT FEELS.
HE MISSED ME! AND YOU--
YOU PUSHED ME OUT OF THE WAY, MATCHES...
TOOK A BULLET FOR ME!
JUST A SCRATCH, BOSS.
YOU JUST PROVED YOU'RE THE ONE GUY AROUND HERE I CAN TRUST.
TAKE MY HAND, MALONE.
FROM NOW ON, YOU'RE A MADE MAN. YOU'RE FAMILY.
YOU UNDERSTAND WHAT THAT MEANS?
YES.
I KNOW WHAT IT MEANS TO BE PART OF A FAMILY.
END

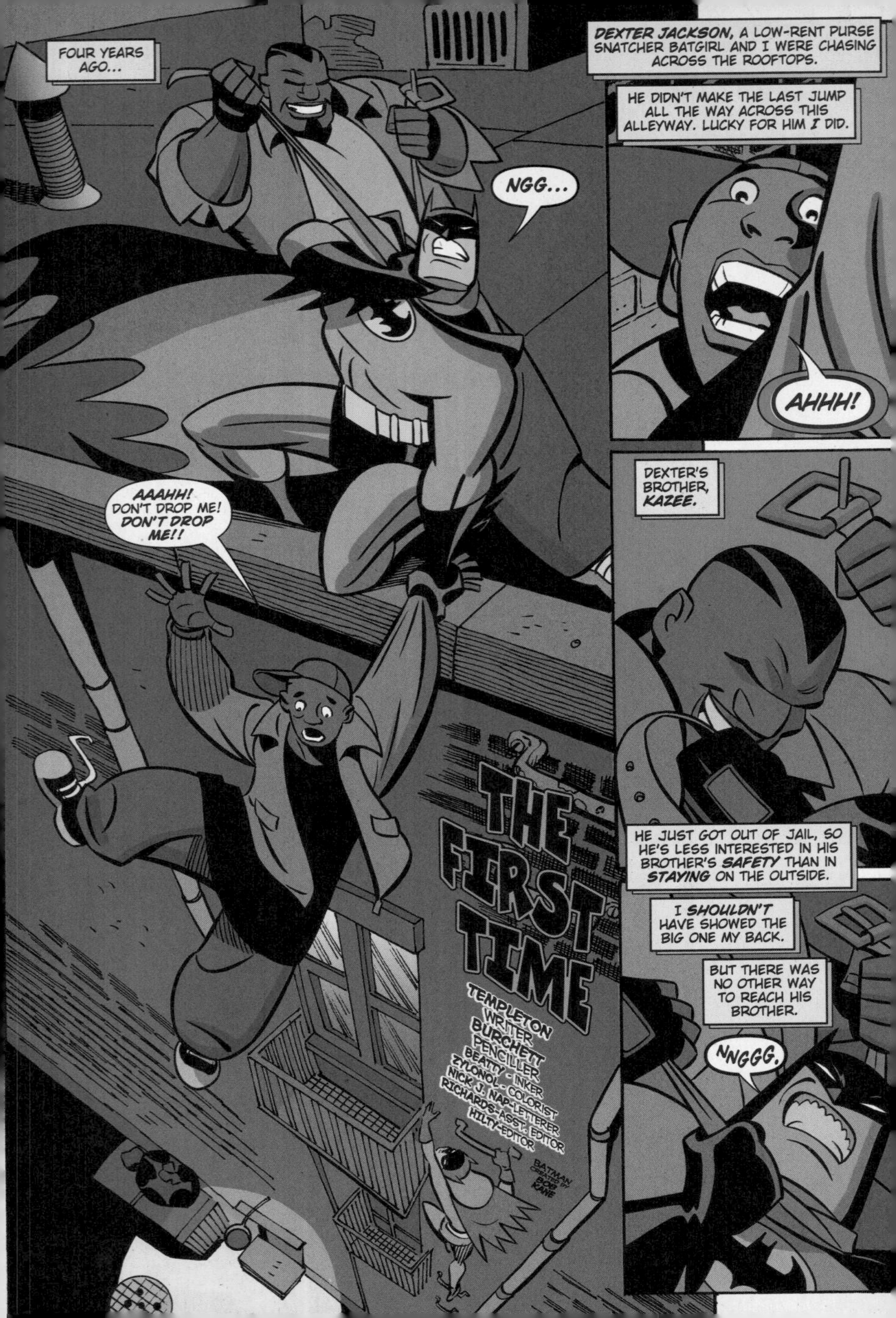

FOUR YEARS AGO...
DEXTER JACKSON, A LOW-RENT PURSE SNATCHER BATGIRL AND I WERE CHASING ACROSS THE ROOFTOPS.
HE DIDN'T MAKE THE LAST JUMP ALL THE WAY ACROSS THIS ALLEYWAY. LUCKY FOR HIM I DID.
AHHH!
NGG...
AAAHH! DON'T DROP ME! DON'T DROP ME!!
DEXTER'S BROTHER, KAZEE.
HE JUST GOT OUT OF JAIL, SO HE'S LESS INTERESTED IN HIS BROTHER'S SAFETY THAN IN STAYING ON THE OUTSIDE.
I SHOULDN'T HAVE SHOWED THE BIG ONE MY BACK.
BUT THERE WAS NO OTHER WAY TO REACH HIS BROTHER.
NNGGG.
THE FIRST TIME
TEMPLETON WRITER
BURCHETT PENCILLER
BEATTY - INKER
ZYLONOL - COLORIST
NICK J. NAP - LETTERER
RICHARDS - ASST. EDITOR
HILTY - EDITOR
BATMAN CREATED BY BOB KANE

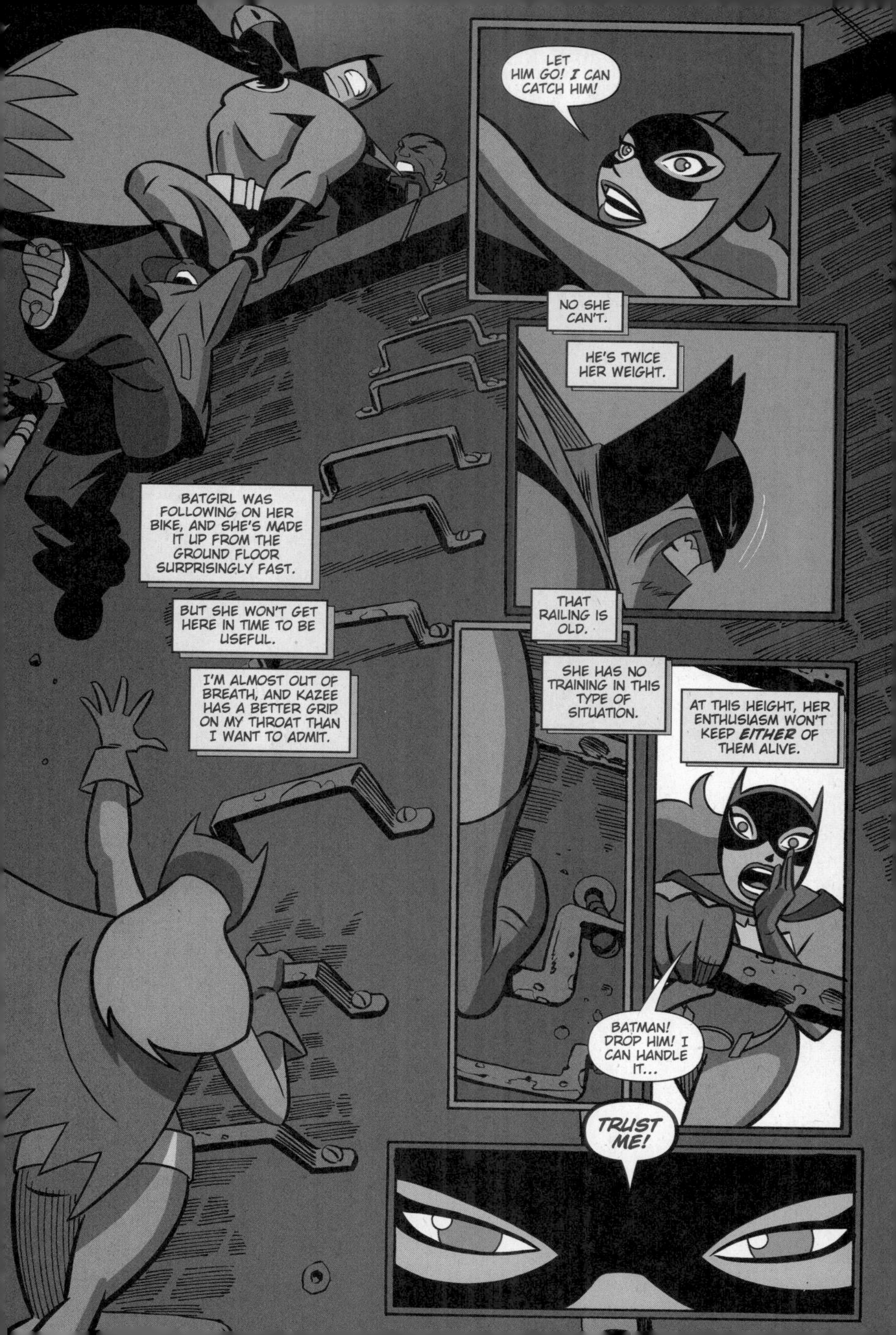

LET HIM GO! I CAN CATCH HIM!
NO SHE CAN'T.
HE'S TWICE HER WEIGHT.
BATGIRL WAS FOLLOWING ON HER BIKE, AND SHE'S MADE IT UP FROM THE GROUND FLOOR SURPRISINGLY FAST.
BUT SHE WON'T GET HERE IN TIME TO BE USEFUL.
I'M ALMOST OUT OF BREATH, AND KAZEE HAS A BETTER GRIP ON MY THROAT THAN I WANT TO ADMIT.
THAT RAILING IS OLD.
SHE HAS NO TRAINING IN THIS TYPE OF SITUATION.
AT THIS HEIGHT, HER ENTHUSIASM WON'T KEEP *EITHER* OF THEM ALIVE.
BATMAN! DROP HIM! I CAN HANDLE IT...
TRUST ME!

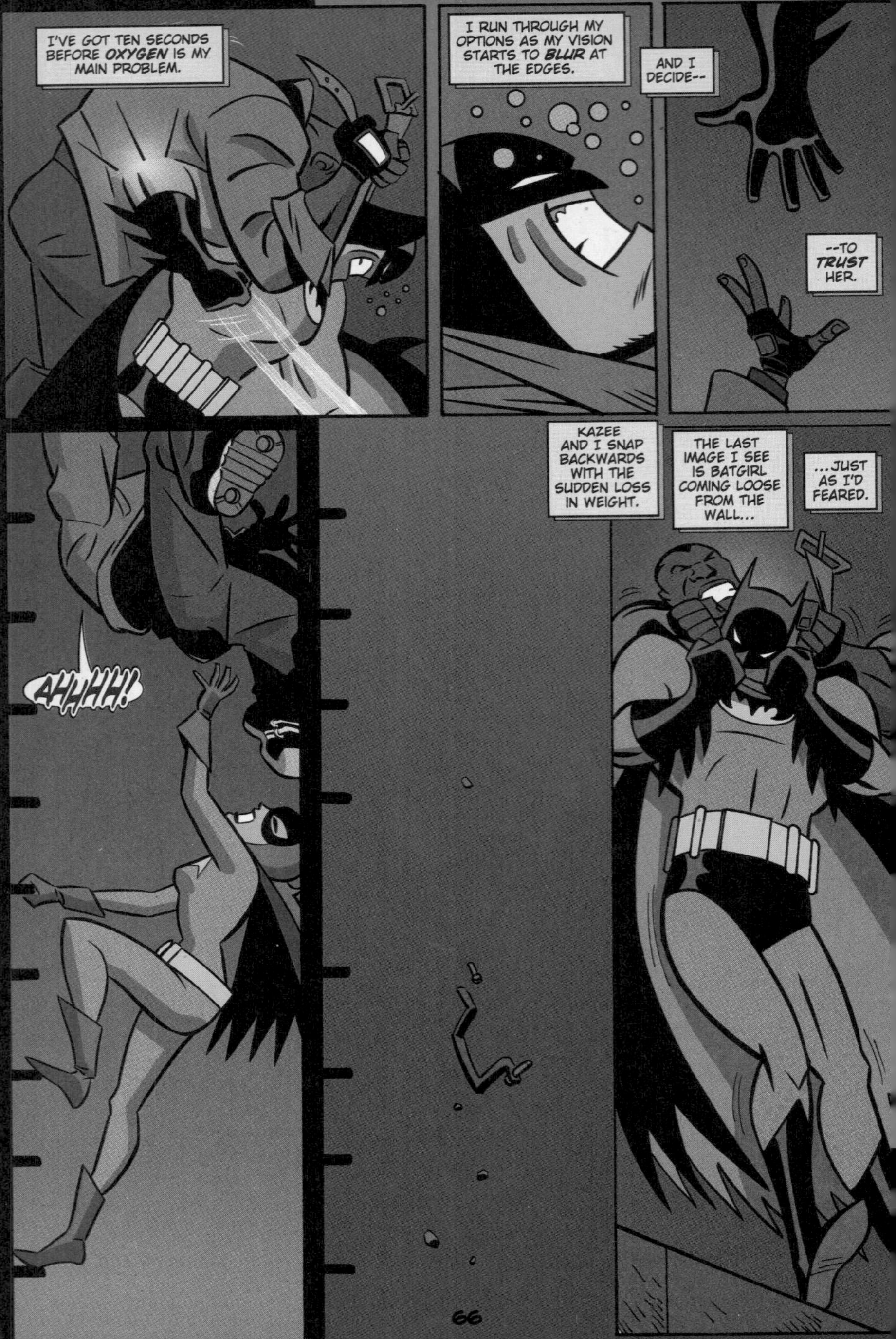

I'VE GOT TEN SECONDS BEFORE OXYGEN IS MY MAIN PROBLEM.
I RUN THROUGH MY OPTIONS AS MY VISION STARTS TO BLUR AT THE EDGES.
AND I DECIDE--
--TO TRUST HER.
AHHHH!
KAZEE AND I SNAP BACKWARDS WITH THE SUDDEN LOSS IN WEIGHT.
THE LAST IMAGE I SEE IS BATGIRL COMING LOOSE FROM THE WALL...
...JUST AS I'D FEARED.

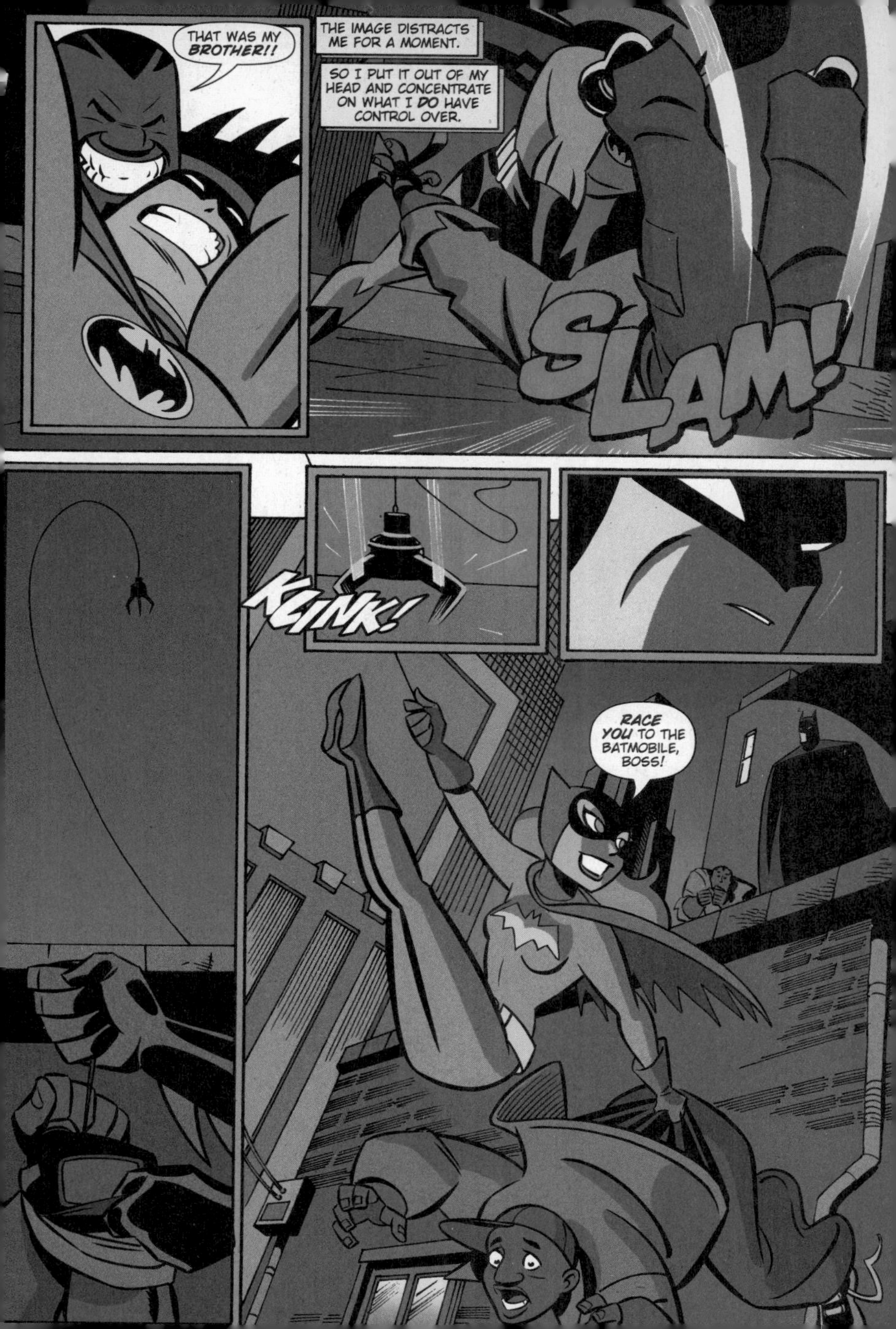
THAT WAS MY BROTHER!!
THE IMAGE DISTRACTS ME FOR A MOMENT.
SO I PUT IT OUT OF MY HEAD AND CONCENTRATE ON WHAT I DO HAVE CONTROL OVER.
SLAM!
KLINK!
RACE YOU TO THE BATMOBILE, BOSS!

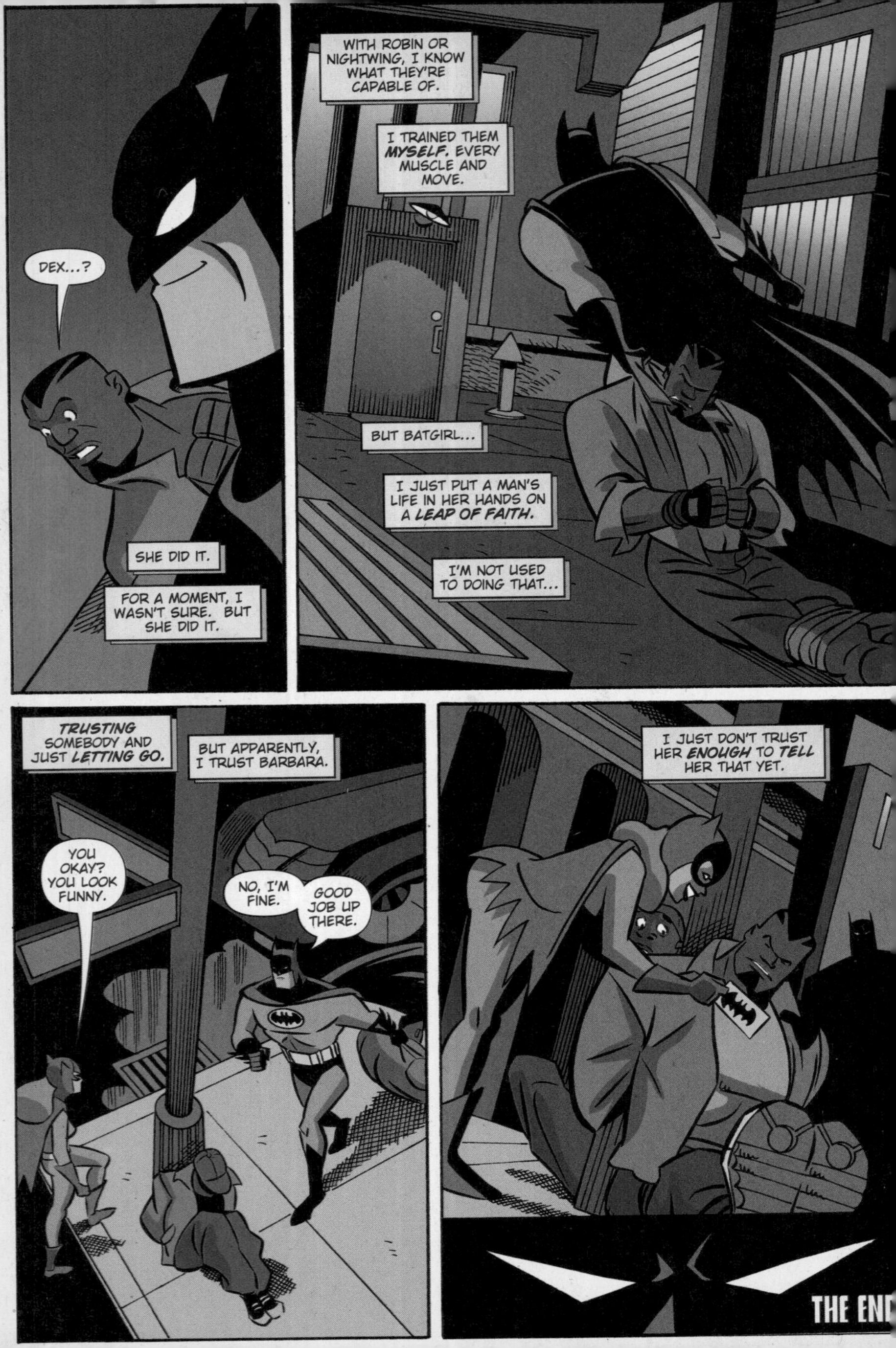
DEX...?
SHE DID IT.
FOR A MOMENT, I WASN'T SURE. BUT SHE DID IT.
WITH ROBIN OR NIGHTWING, I KNOW WHAT THEY'RE CAPABLE OF.
I TRAINED THEM MYSELF. EVERY MUSCLE AND MOVE.
BUT BATGIRL...
I JUST PUT A MAN'S LIFE IN HER HANDS ON A LEAP OF FAITH.
I'M NOT USED TO DOING THAT...
TRUSTING SOMEBODY AND JUST LETTING GO.
BUT APPARENTLY, I TRUST BARBARA.
YOU OKAY? YOU LOOK FUNNY.
NO, I'M FINE.
GOOD JOB UP THERE.
I JUST DON'T TRUST HER ENOUGH TO TELL HER THAT YET.
THE END

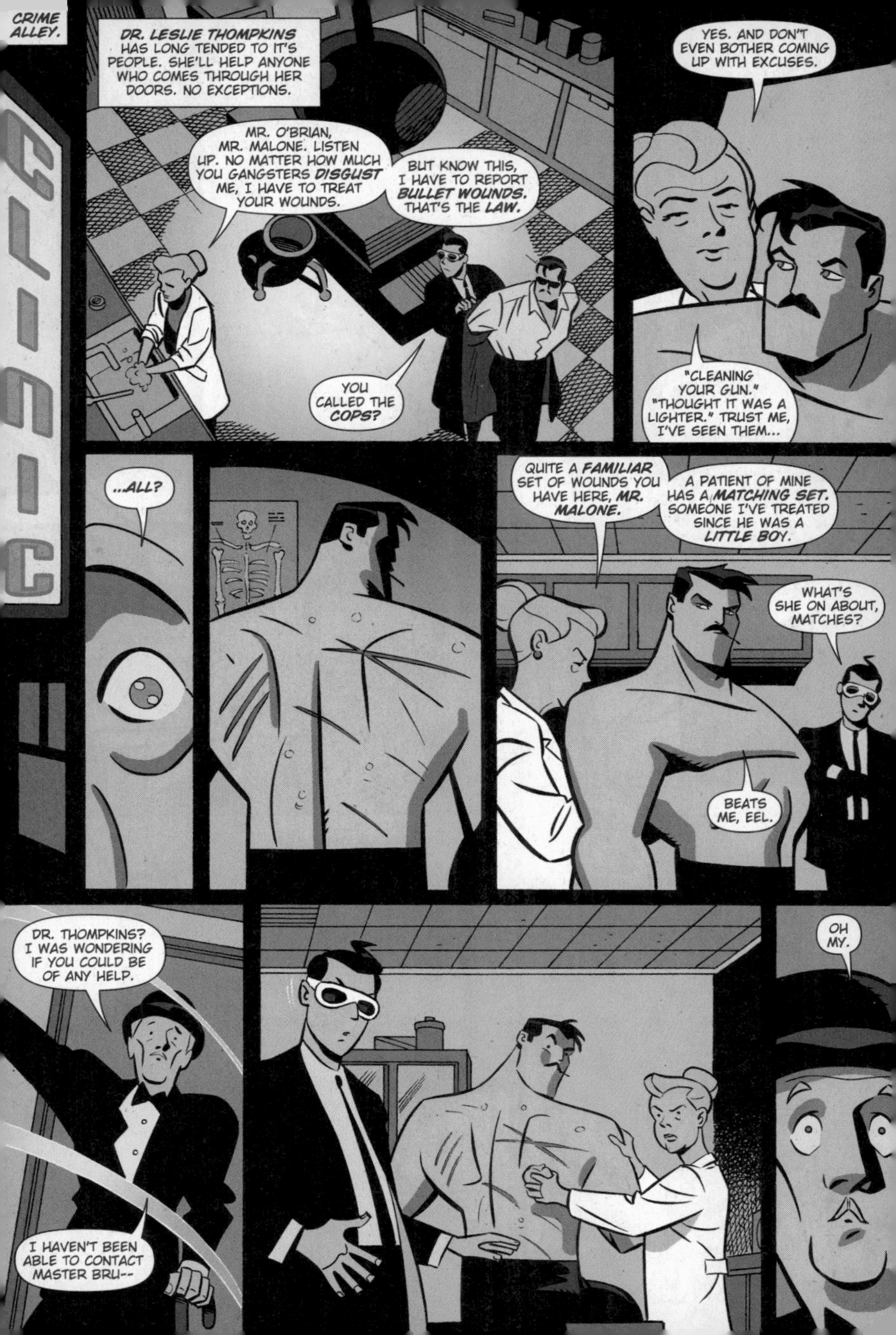
CRIME ALLEY.
CLINIC
DR. LESLIE THOMPKINS HAS LONG TENDED TO IT'S PEOPLE. SHE'LL HELP ANYONE WHO COMES THROUGH HER DOORS. NO EXCEPTIONS.
MR. O'BRIAN, MR. MALONE. LISTEN UP. NO MATTER HOW MUCH YOU GANGSTERS DISGUST ME, I HAVE TO TREAT YOUR WOUNDS.
BUT KNOW THIS, I HAVE TO REPORT BULLET WOUNDS. THAT'S THE LAW.
YOU CALLED THE COPS?
YES. AND DON'T EVEN BOTHER COMING UP WITH EXCUSES.
"CLEANING YOUR GUN." "THOUGHT IT WAS A LIGHTER." TRUST ME, I'VE SEEN THEM...
...ALL?
QUITE A FAMILIAR SET OF WOUNDS YOU HAVE HERE, MR. MALONE.
A PATIENT OF MINE HAS A MATCHING SET. SOMEONE I'VE TREATED SINCE HE WAS A LITTLE BOY.
WHAT'S SHE ON ABOUT, MATCHES?
BEATS ME, EEL.
DR. THOMPKINS? I WAS WONDERING IF YOU COULD BE OF ANY HELP.
I HAVEN'T BEEN ABLE TO CONTACT MASTER BRU--
OH MY.

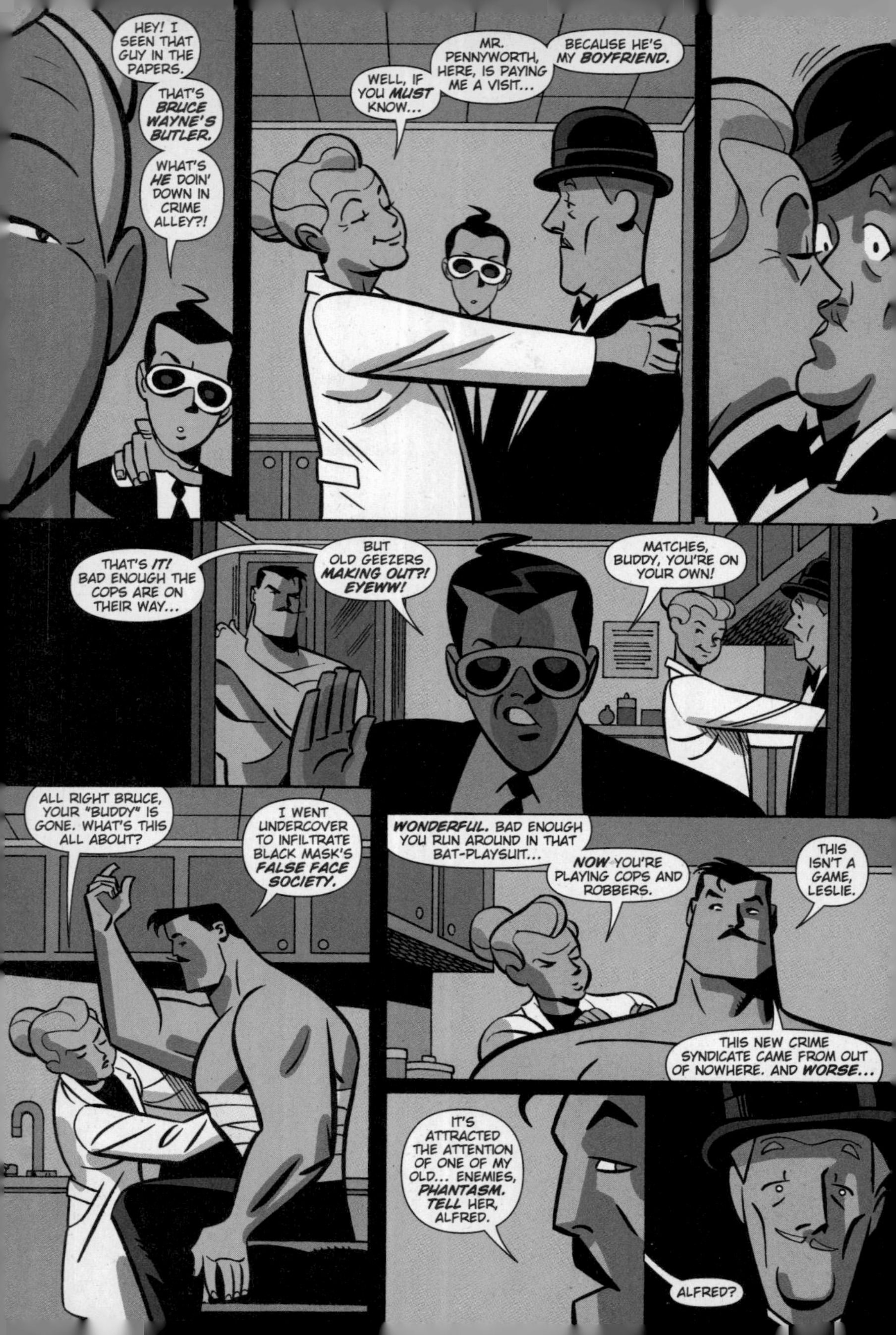
HEY! I SEEN THAT GUY IN THE PAPERS.
THAT'S BRUCE WAYNE'S BUTLER.
WHAT'S HE DOIN' DOWN IN CRIME ALLEY?!
WELL, IF YOU MUST KNOW...
MR. PENNYWORTH, HERE, IS PAYING ME A VISIT...
BECAUSE HE'S MY BOYFRIEND.
THAT'S IT! BAD ENOUGH THE COPS ARE ON THEIR WAY...
BUT OLD GEEZERS MAKING OUT?! EYEWW!
MATCHES, BUDDY, YOU'RE ON YOUR OWN!
ALL RIGHT BRUCE, YOUR "BUDDY" IS GONE. WHAT'S THIS ALL ABOUT?
I WENT UNDERCOVER TO INFILTRATE BLACK MASK'S FALSE FACE SOCIETY.
WONDERFUL. BAD ENOUGH YOU RUN AROUND IN THAT BAT-PLAYSUIT...
NOW YOU'RE PLAYING COPS AND ROBBERS.
THIS ISN'T A GAME, LESLIE.
THIS NEW CRIME SYNDICATE CAME FROM OUT OF NOWHERE. AND WORSE...
IT'S ATTRACTED THE ATTENTION OF ONE OF MY OLD... ENEMIES, PHANTASM. TELL HER, ALFRED.
ALFRED?

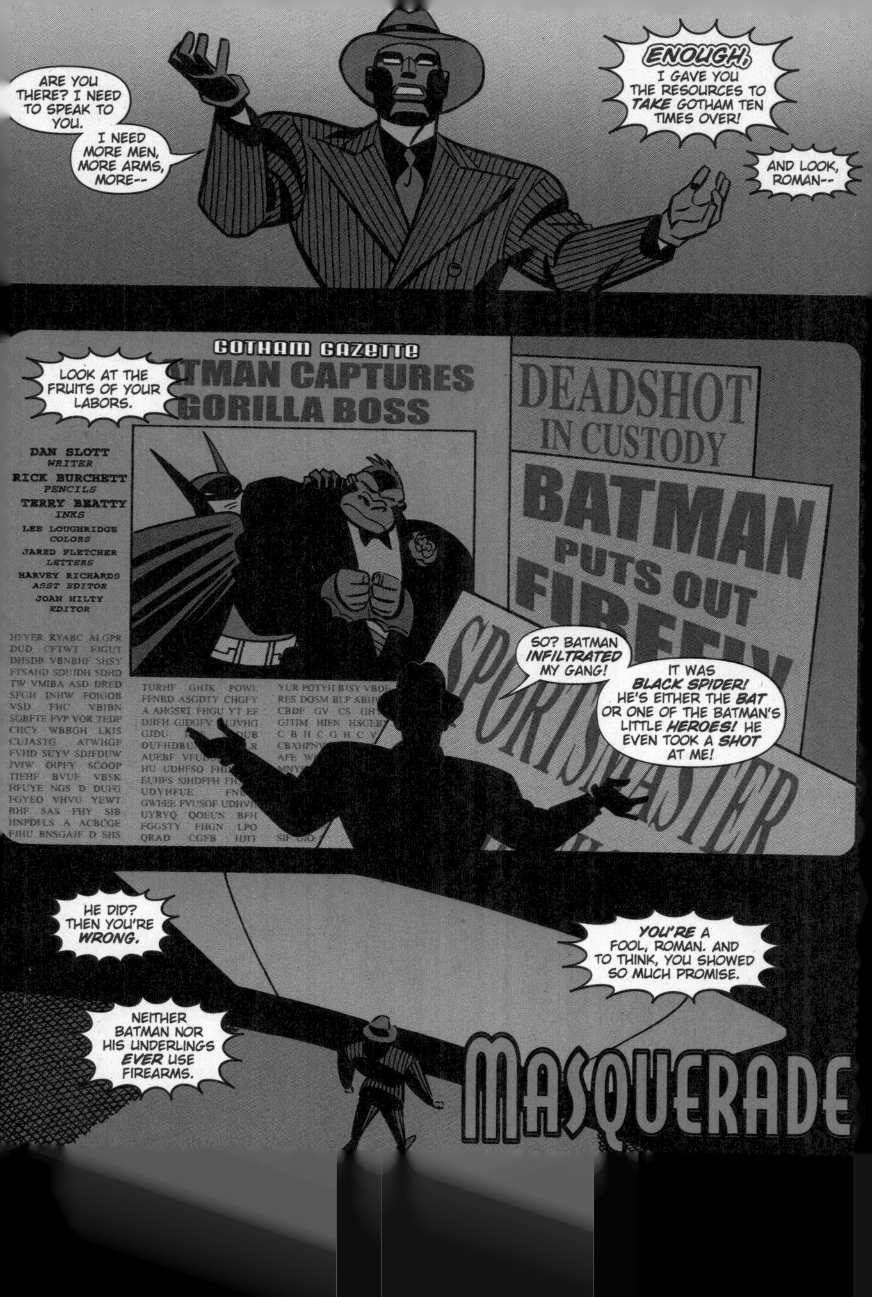

ARE YOU THERE? I NEED TO SPEAK TO YOU.
I NEED MORE MEN, MORE ARMS, MORE--
ENOUGH, I GAVE YOU THE RESOURCES TO TAKE GOTHAM TEN TIMES OVER!
AND LOOK, ROMAN--
GOTHAM GAZETTE
LOOK AT THE FRUITS OF YOUR LABORS.
ATMAN CAPTURES GORILLA BOSS
DEADSHOT IN CUSTODY
BATMAN PUTS OUT FIREFLY
DAN SLOTT WRITER
RICK BURCHETT PENCILS
TERRY BEATTY INKS
LEE LOUGHRIDGE COLORS
JARED FLETCHER LETTERS
HARVEY RICHARDS ASST EDITOR
JOAN HILTY EDITOR
SO? BATMAN INFILTRATED MY GANG!
IT WAS BLACK SPIDER! HE'S EITHER THE BAT OR ONE OF THE BATMAN'S LITTLE HEROES! HE EVEN TOOK A SHOT AT ME!
HE DID? THEN YOU'RE WRONG.
YOU'RE A FOOL, ROMAN. AND TO THINK, YOU SHOWED SO MUCH PROMISE.
NEITHER BATMAN NOR HIS UNDERLINGS EVER USE FIREARMS.
MASQUERADE

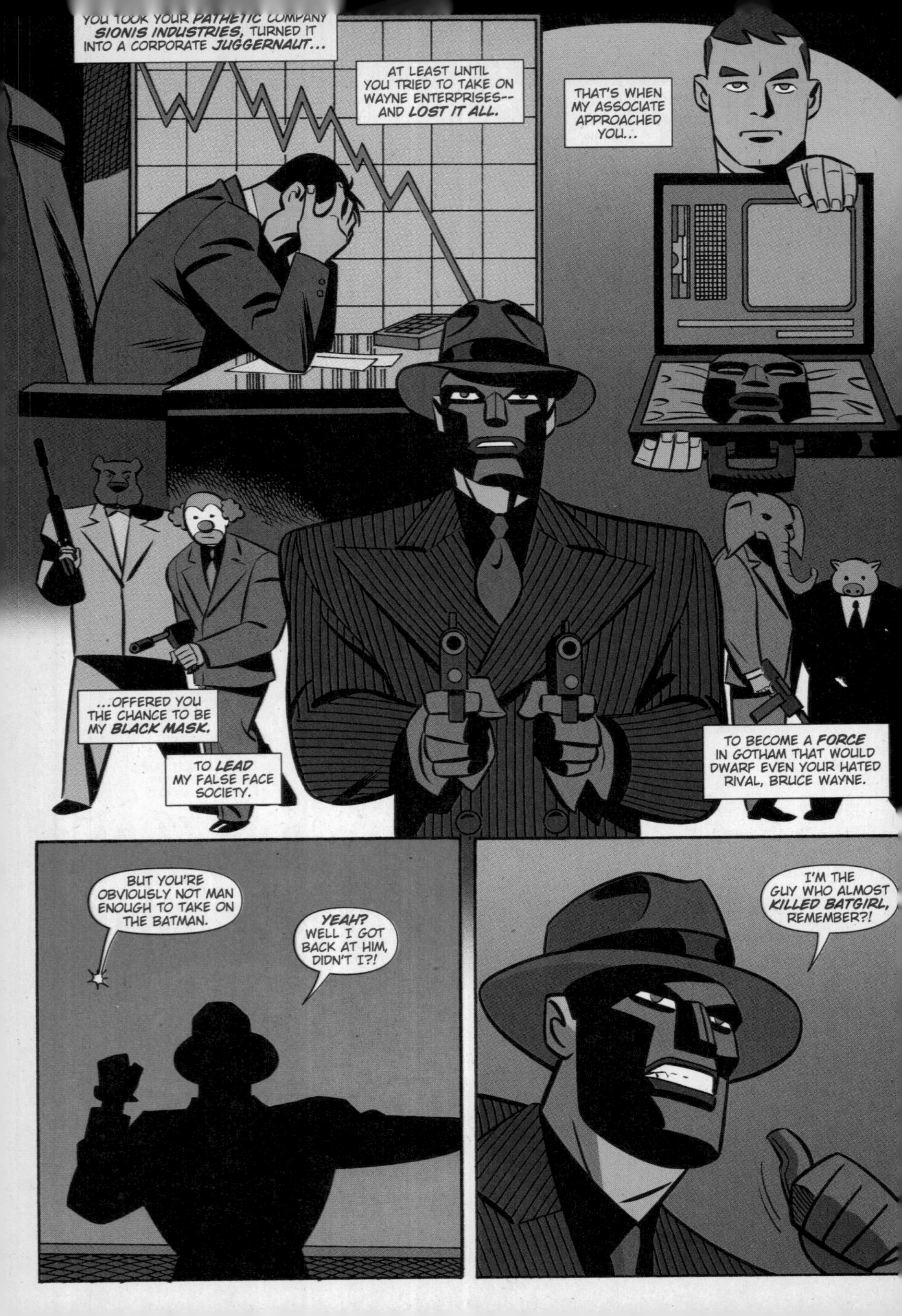

YOU TOOK YOUR PATHETIC COMPANY SIONIS INDUSTRIES, TURNED IT INTO A CORPORATE JUGGERNAUT...
AT LEAST UNTIL YOU TRIED TO TAKE ON WAYNE ENTERPRISES-- AND LOST IT ALL.
THAT'S WHEN MY ASSOCIATE APPROACHED YOU...
...OFFERED YOU THE CHANCE TO BE MY BLACK MASK.
TO LEAD MY FALSE FACE SOCIETY.
TO BECOME A FORCE IN GOTHAM THAT WOULD DWARF EVEN YOUR HATED RIVAL, BRUCE WAYNE.
BUT YOU'RE OBVIOUSLY NOT MAN ENOUGH TO TAKE ON THE BATMAN.
YEAH? WELL I GOT BACK AT HIM, DIDN'T I?!
I'M THE GUY WHO ALMOST KILLED BATGIRL, REMEMBER?!

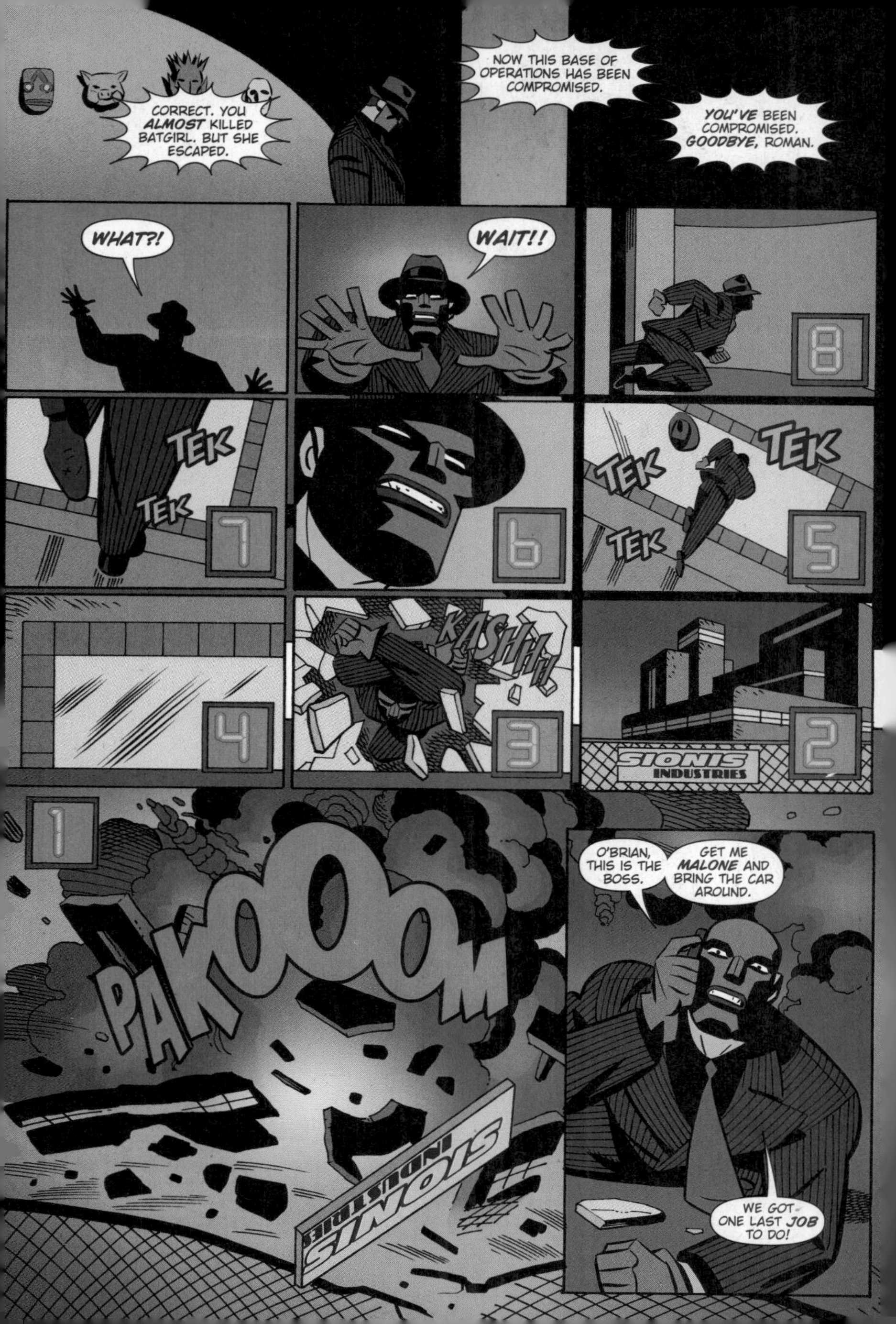
CORRECT. YOU *ALMOST* KILLED BATGIRL. BUT SHE ESCAPED.
NOW THIS BASE OF OPERATIONS HAS BEEN COMPROMISED.
YOU'VE BEEN COMPROMISED. *GOODBYE,* ROMAN.
WHAT?!
WAIT!!
8
TEK
TEK
7
6
TEK
TEK
TEK
5
4
KASHHH
3
SIONIS INDUSTRIES
2
1
PAKOOOM
SIONIS INDUSTRIES
O'BRIAN, THIS IS THE BOSS.
GET ME *MALONE* AND BRING THE CAR AROUND.
WE GOT ONE LAST *JOB* TO DO!

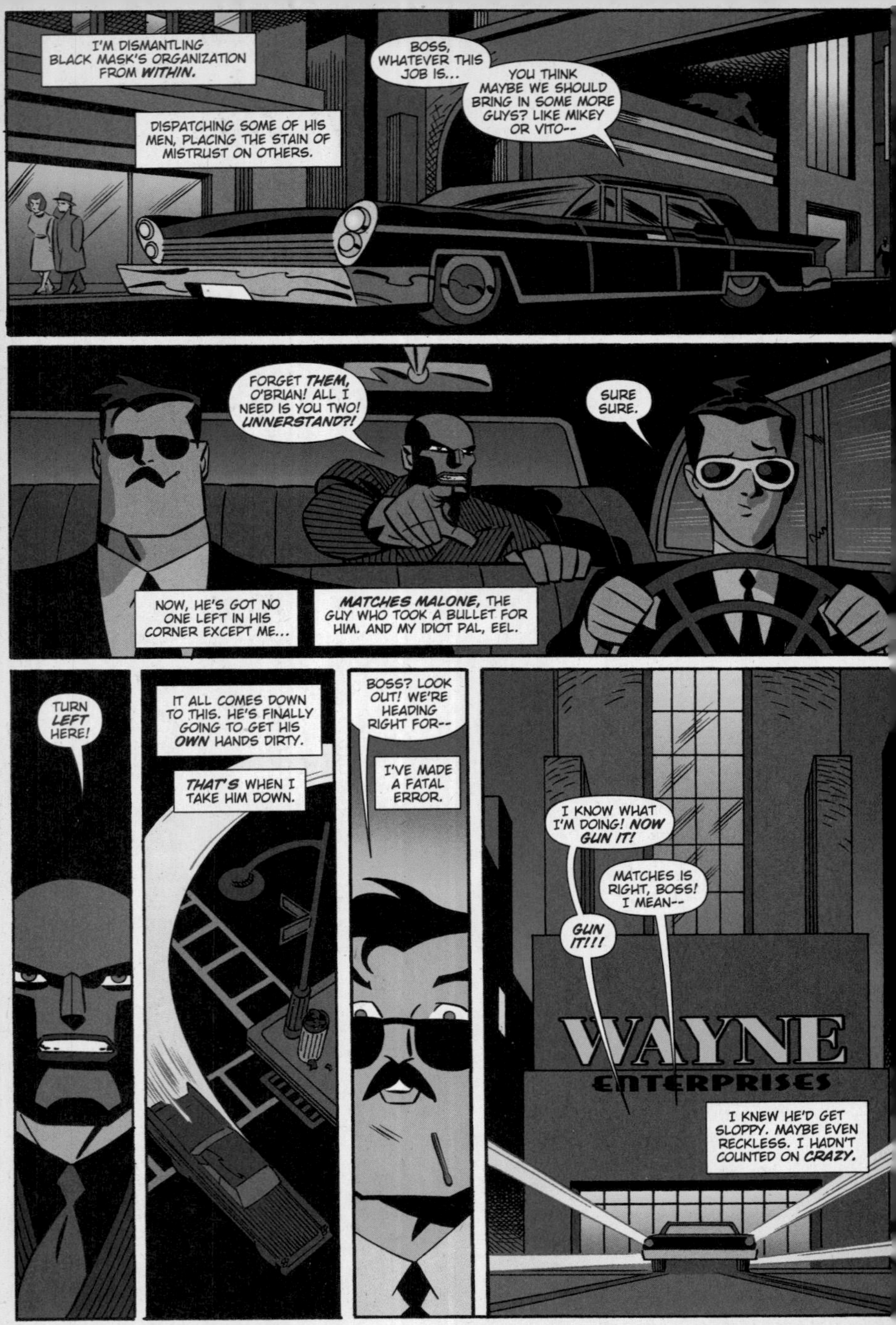
I'M DISMANTLING BLACK MASK'S ORGANIZATION FROM *WITHIN.*
DISPATCHING SOME OF HIS MEN, PLACING THE STAIN OF MISTRUST ON OTHERS.
BOSS, WHATEVER THIS JOB IS...
YOU THINK MAYBE WE SHOULD BRING IN SOME MORE GUYS? LIKE MIKEY OR VITO--
FORGET *THEM,* O'BRIAN! ALL I NEED IS YOU TWO! *UNNERSTAND?!*
SURE SURE.
NOW, HE'S GOT NO ONE LEFT IN HIS CORNER EXCEPT ME...
MATCHES MALONE, THE GUY WHO TOOK A BULLET FOR HIM. AND MY IDIOT PAL, EEL.
TURN *LEFT* HERE!
IT ALL COMES DOWN TO THIS. HE'S FINALLY GOING TO GET HIS *OWN* HANDS DIRTY.
THAT'S WHEN I TAKE HIM DOWN.
BOSS? LOOK OUT! WE'RE HEADING RIGHT FOR--
I'VE MADE A FATAL ERROR.
I KNOW WHAT I'M DOING! *NOW GUN IT!*
MATCHES IS RIGHT, BOSS! I MEAN--
GUN IT!!!
WAYNE ENTERPRISES
I KNEW HE'D GET SLOPPY. MAYBE EVEN RECKLESS. I HADN'T COUNTED ON *CRAZY.*

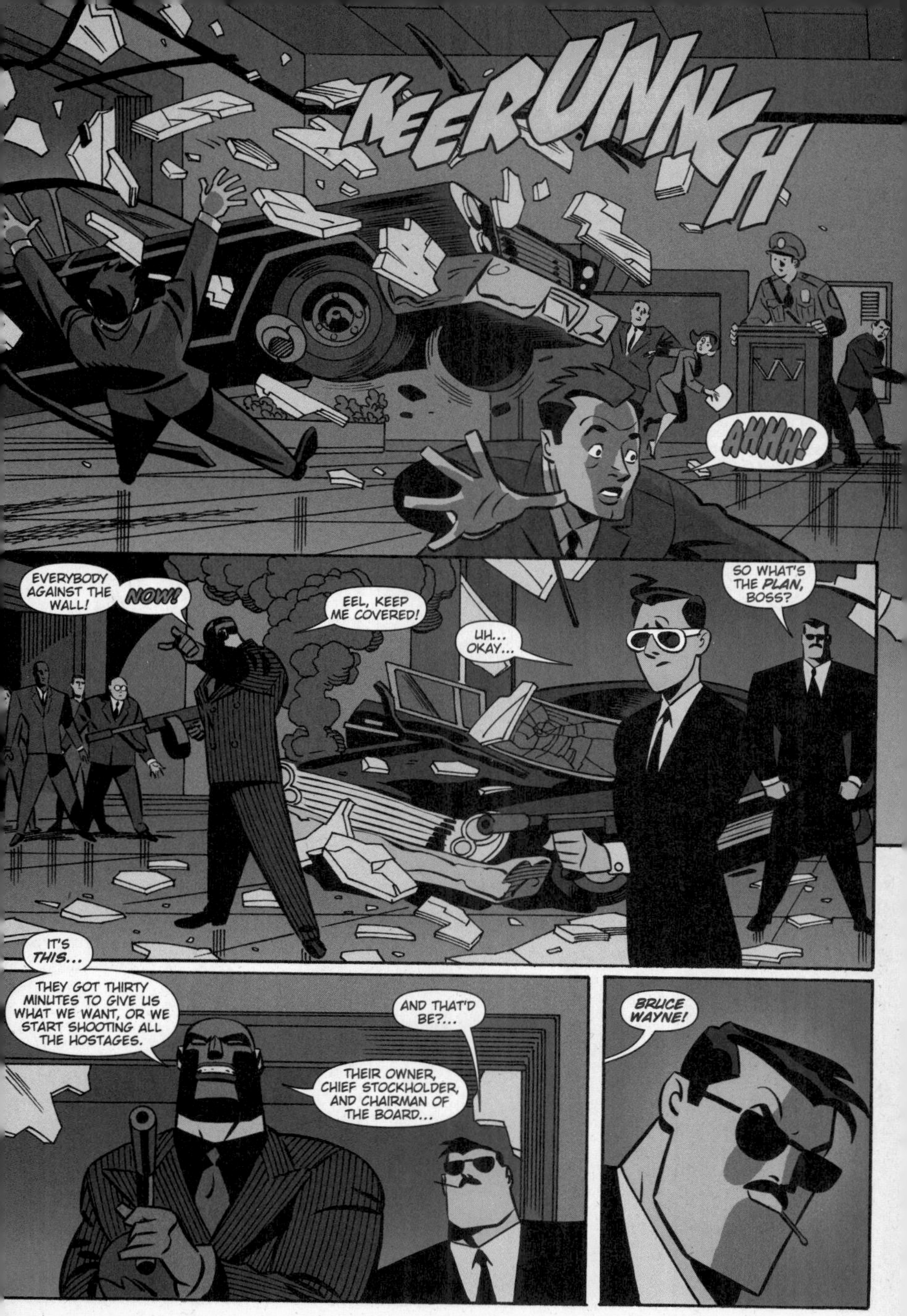
KEERUNNKH
AHHH!
EVERYBODY AGAINST THE WALL!
NOW!
EEL, KEEP ME COVERED!
UH... OKAY...
SO WHAT'S THE PLAN, BOSS?
IT'S THIS...
THEY GOT THIRTY MINUTES TO GIVE US WHAT WE WANT, OR WE START SHOOTING ALL THE HOSTAGES.
AND THAT'D BE?...
THEIR OWNER, CHIEF STOCKHOLDER, AND CHAIRMAN OF THE BOARD...
BRUCE WAYNE!

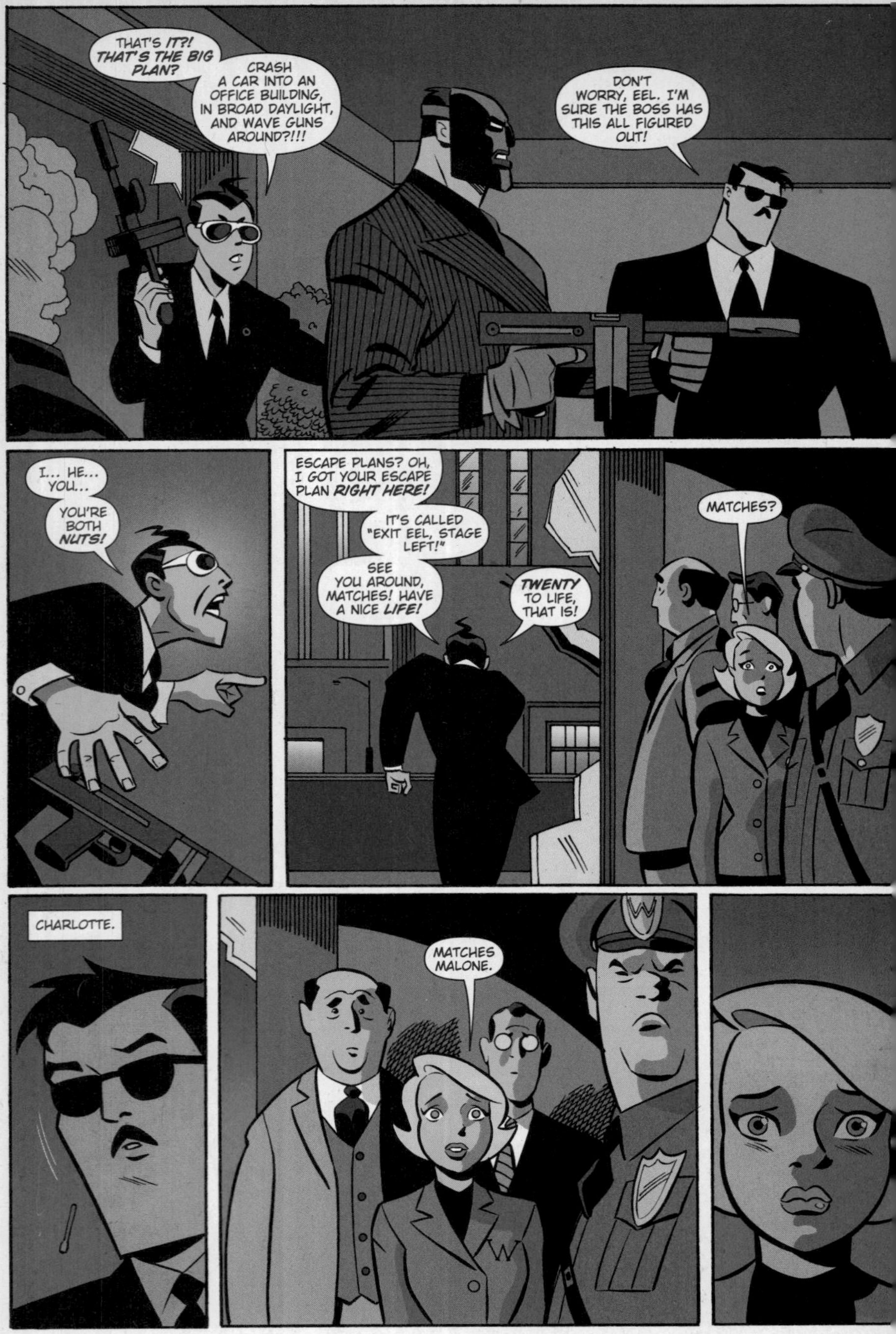
THAT'S IT?! THAT'S THE BIG PLAN?
CRASH A CAR INTO AN OFFICE BUILDING, IN BROAD DAYLIGHT, AND WAVE GUNS AROUND?!!!
DON'T WORRY, EEL. I'M SURE THE BOSS HAS THIS ALL FIGURED OUT!
I... HE... YOU...
YOU'RE BOTH NUTS!
ESCAPE PLANS? OH, I GOT YOUR ESCAPE PLAN RIGHT HERE!
IT'S CALLED "EXIT EEL, STAGE LEFT!"
SEE YOU AROUND, MATCHES! HAVE A NICE LIFE!
TWENTY TO LIFE, THAT IS!
MATCHES?
CHARLOTTE.
MATCHES MALONE.

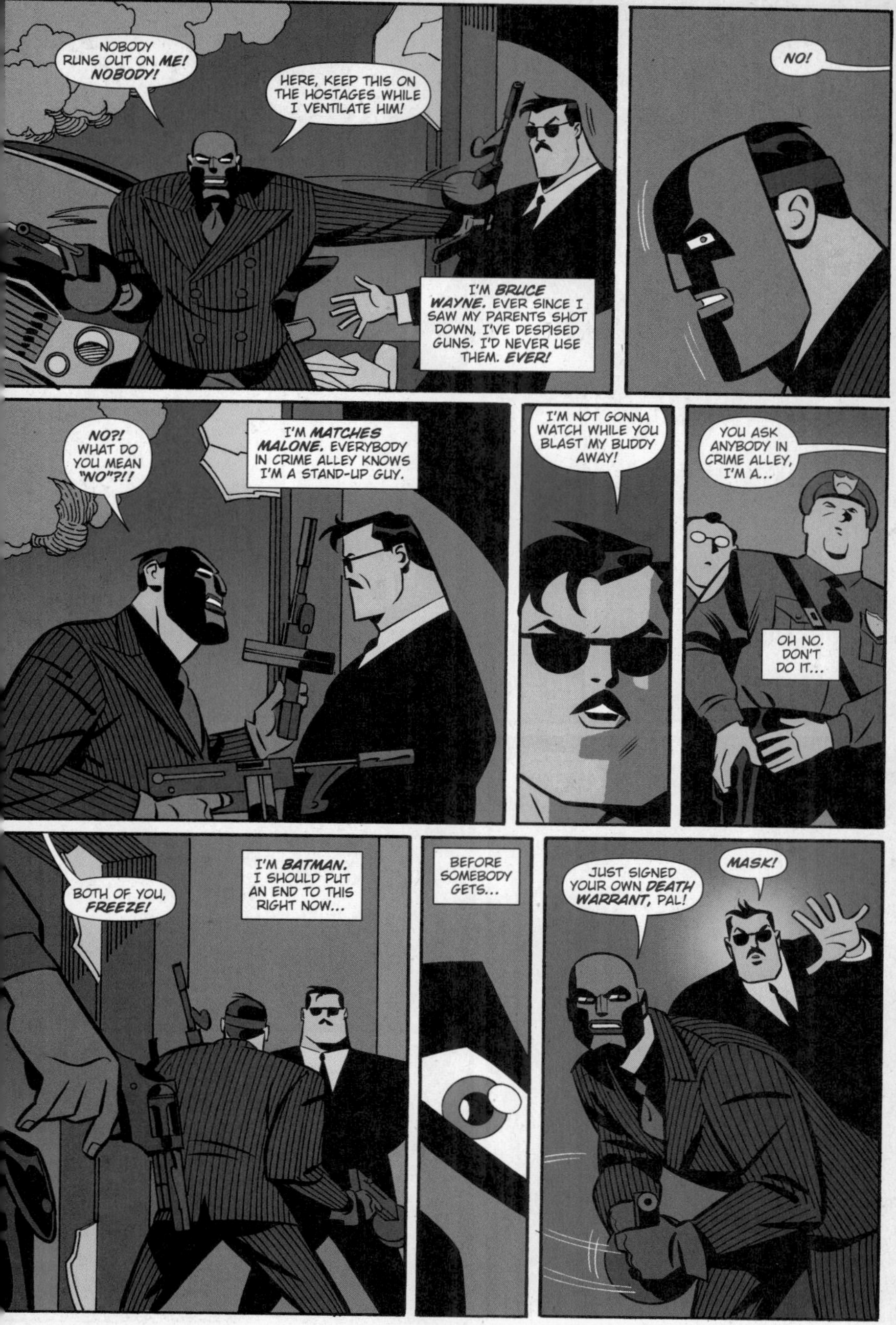
NOBODY RUNS OUT ON ME! NOBODY!
HERE, KEEP THIS ON THE HOSTAGES WHILE I VENTILATE HIM!
I'M BRUCE WAYNE. EVER SINCE I SAW MY PARENTS SHOT DOWN, I'VE DESPISED GUNS. I'D NEVER USE THEM. EVER!
NO!
NO?! WHAT DO YOU MEAN "NO"?!!
I'M MATCHES MALONE. EVERYBODY IN CRIME ALLEY KNOWS I'M A STAND-UP GUY.
I'M NOT GONNA WATCH WHILE YOU BLAST MY BUDDY AWAY!
YOU ASK ANYBODY IN CRIME ALLEY, I'M A...
OH NO. DON'T DO IT...
BOTH OF YOU, FREEZE!
I'M BATMAN. I SHOULD PUT AN END TO THIS RIGHT NOW...
BEFORE SOMEBODY GETS...
JUST SIGNED YOUR OWN DEATH WARRANT, PAL!
MASK!

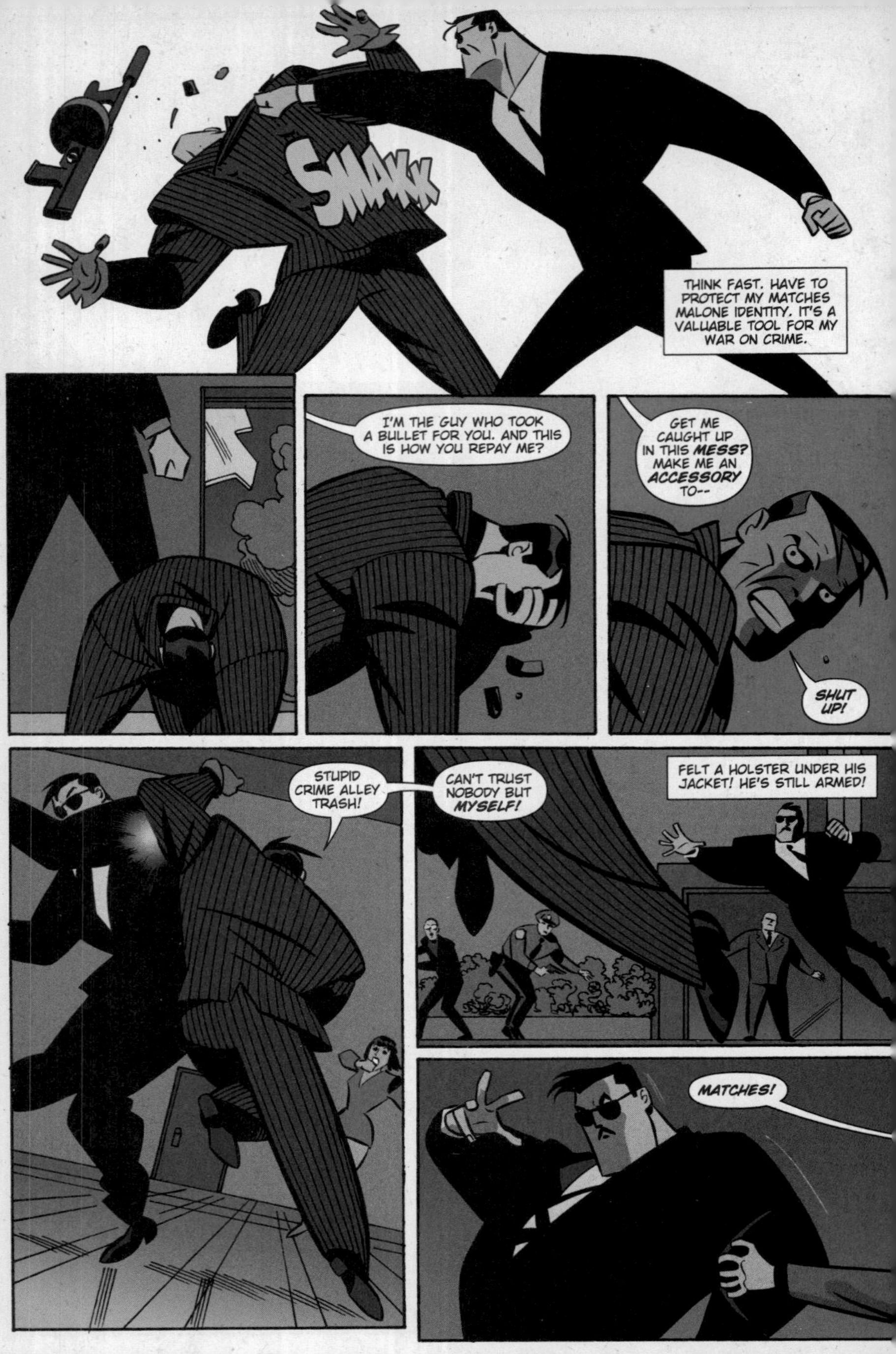

SMAKK
THINK FAST. HAVE TO PROTECT MY MATCHES MALONE IDENTITY. IT'S A VALUABLE TOOL FOR MY WAR ON CRIME.
I'M THE GUY WHO TOOK A BULLET FOR YOU. AND THIS IS HOW YOU REPAY ME?
GET ME CAUGHT UP IN THIS MESS? MAKE ME AN ACCESSORY TO--
SHUT UP!
STUPID CRIME ALLEY TRASH!
CAN'T TRUST NOBODY BUT MYSELF!
FELT A HOLSTER UNDER HIS JACKET! HE'S STILL ARMED!
MATCHES!

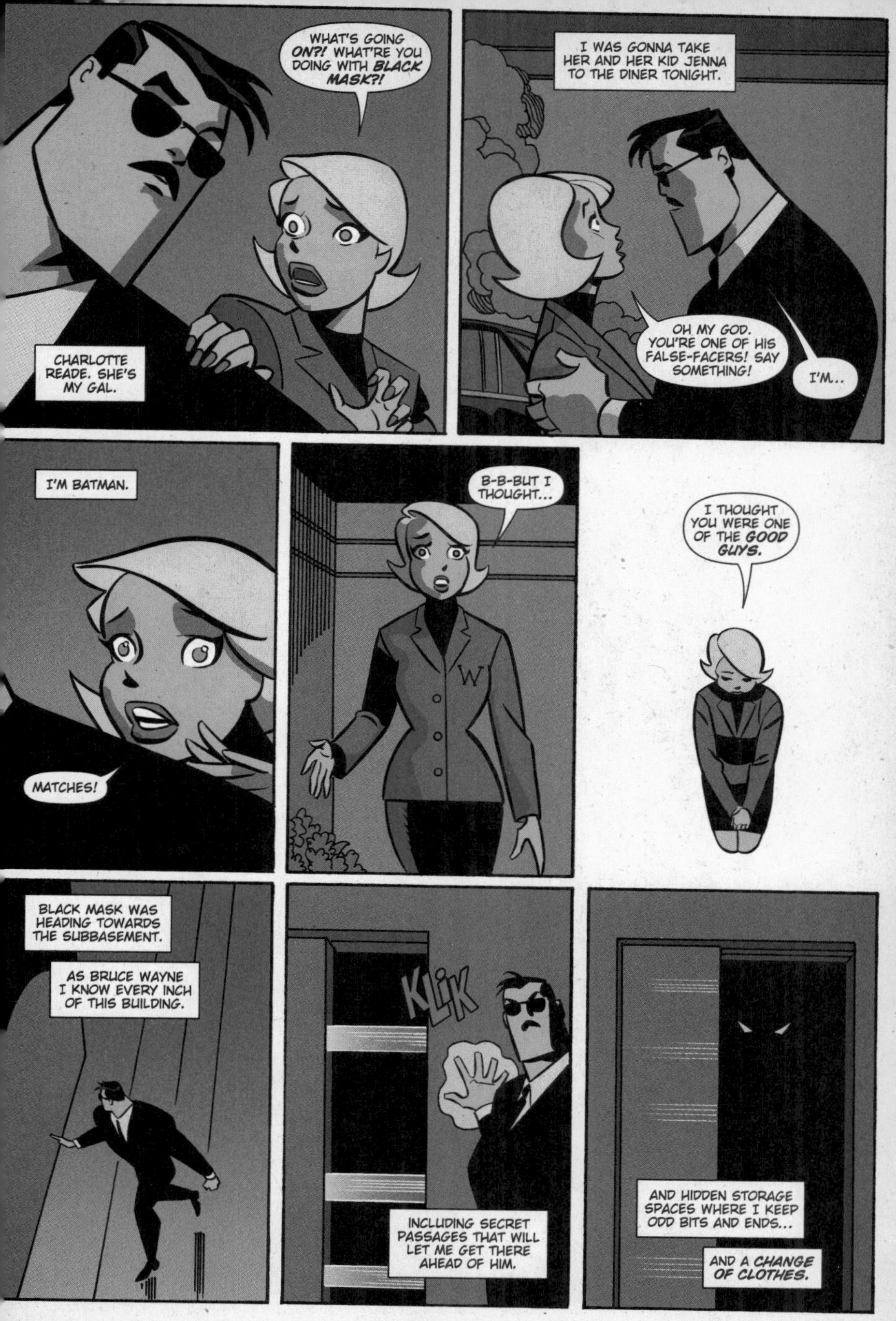

WHAT'S GOING ON?! WHAT'RE YOU DOING WITH BLACK MASK?!
CHARLOTTE READE. SHE'S MY GAL.
I WAS GONNA TAKE HER AND HER KID JENNA TO THE DINER TONIGHT.
OH MY GOD. YOU'RE ONE OF HIS FALSE-FACERS! SAY SOMETHING!
I'M...
I'M BATMAN.
MATCHES!
B-B-BUT I THOUGHT...
I THOUGHT YOU WERE ONE OF THE GOOD GUYS.
BLACK MASK WAS HEADING TOWARDS THE SUBBASEMENT.
AS BRUCE WAYNE I KNOW EVERY INCH OF THIS BUILDING.
KLIK
INCLUDING SECRET PASSAGES THAT WILL LET ME GET THERE AHEAD OF HIM.
AND HIDDEN STORAGE SPACES WHERE I KEEP ODD BITS AND ENDS...
AND A CHANGE OF CLOTHES.

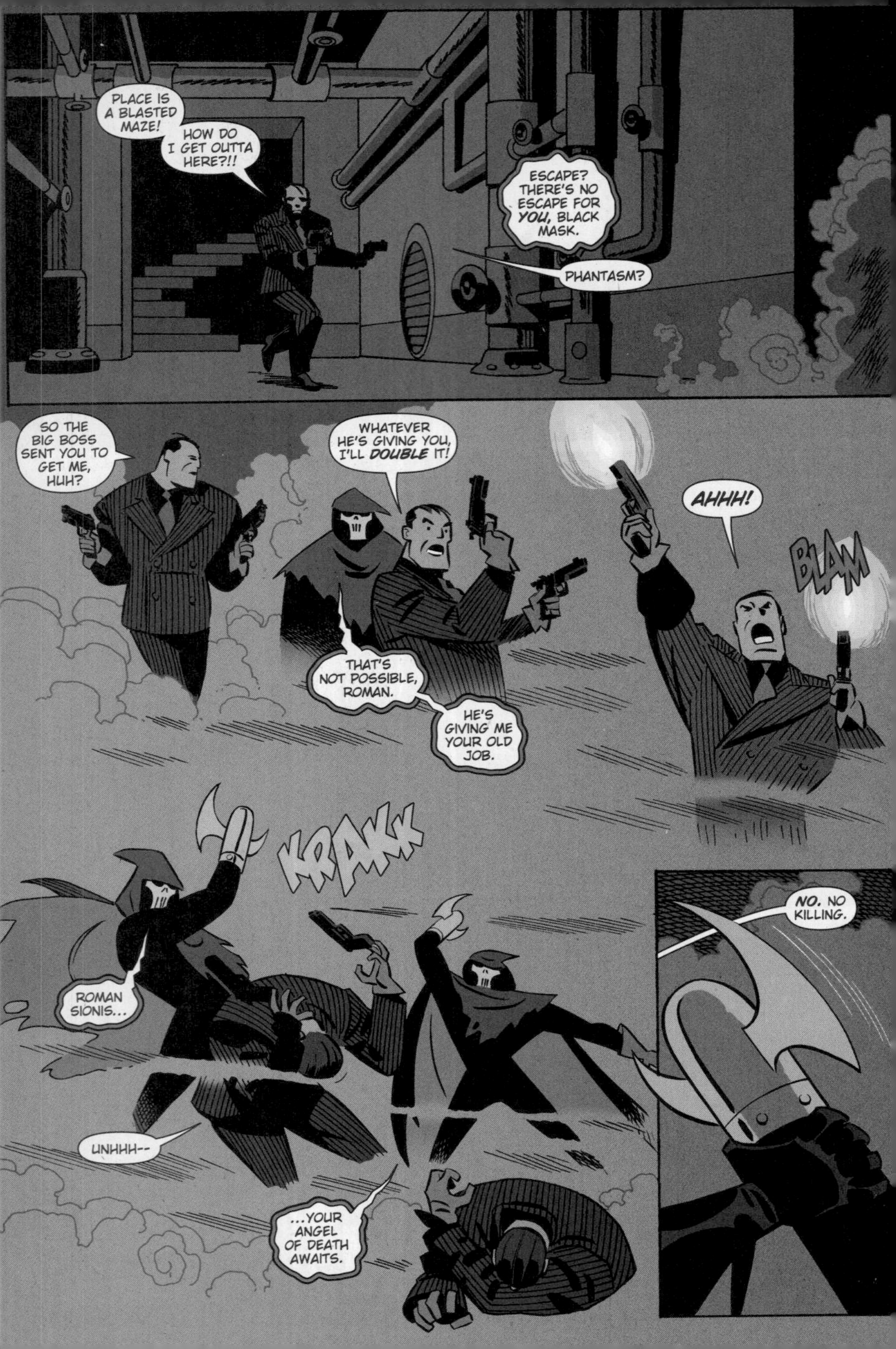
PLACE IS A BLASTED MAZE!
HOW DO I GET OUTTA HERE?!!
ESCAPE? THERE'S NO ESCAPE FOR YOU, BLACK MASK.
PHANTASM?
SO THE BIG BOSS SENT YOU TO GET ME, HUH?
WHATEVER HE'S GIVING YOU, I'LL DOUBLE IT!
THAT'S NOT POSSIBLE, ROMAN.
HE'S GIVING ME YOUR OLD JOB.
AHHH!
BLAM
KRAKK
ROMAN SIONIS...
UNHHH--
...YOUR ANGEL OF DEATH AWAITS.
NO. NO KILLING.

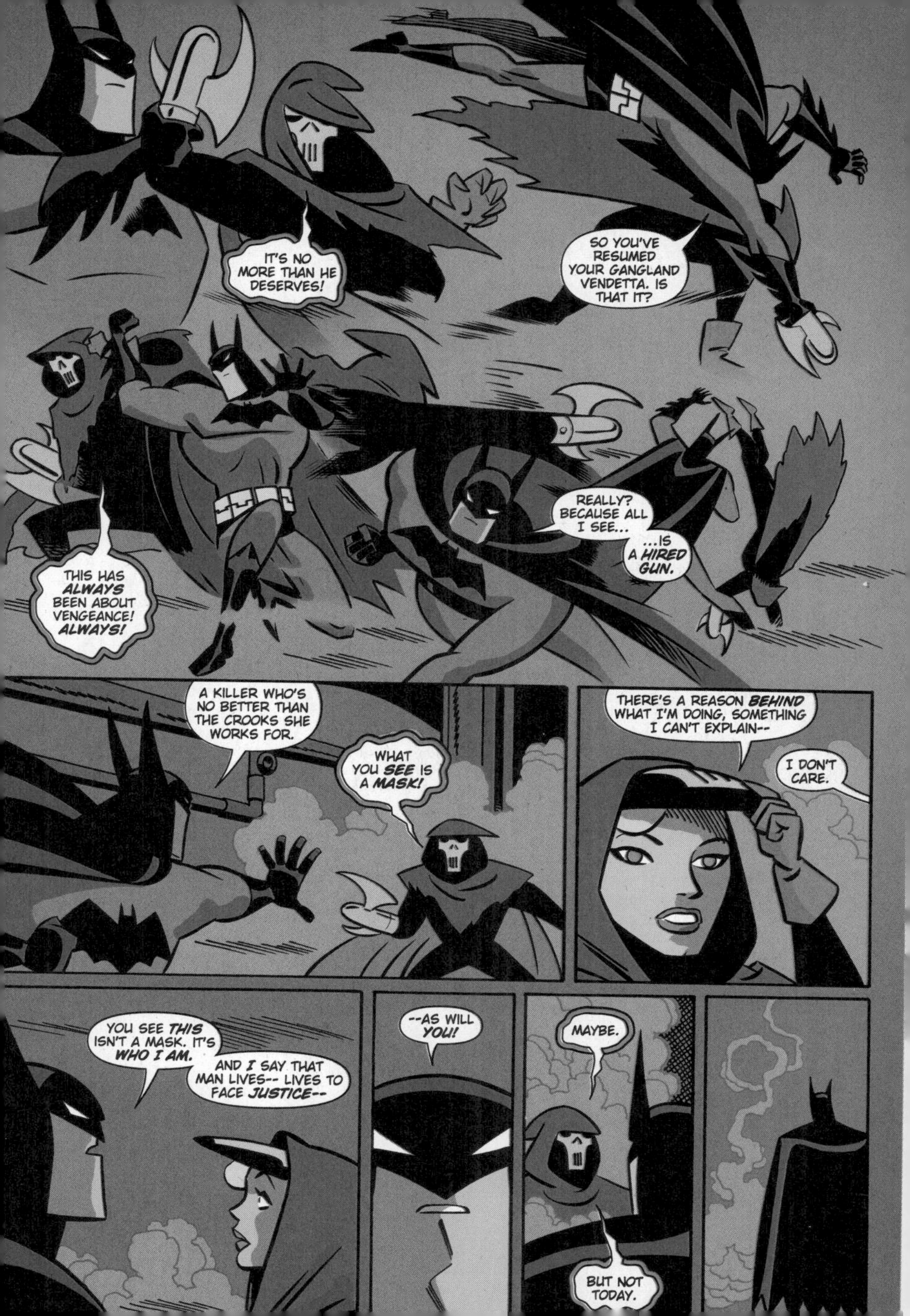
IT'S NO MORE THAN HE DESERVES!
SO YOU'VE RESUMED YOUR GANGLAND VENDETTA. IS THAT IT?
THIS HAS ALWAYS BEEN ABOUT VENGEANCE! ALWAYS!
REALLY? BECAUSE ALL I SEE...
...IS A HIRED GUN.
A KILLER WHO'S NO BETTER THAN THE CROOKS SHE WORKS FOR.
WHAT YOU SEE IS A MASK!
THERE'S A REASON BEHIND WHAT I'M DOING, SOMETHING I CAN'T EXPLAIN--
I DON'T CARE.
YOU SEE THIS ISN'T A MASK. IT'S WHO I AM.
AND I SAY THAT MAN LIVES-- LIVES TO FACE JUSTICE--
--AS WILL YOU!
MAYBE.
BUT NOT TODAY.

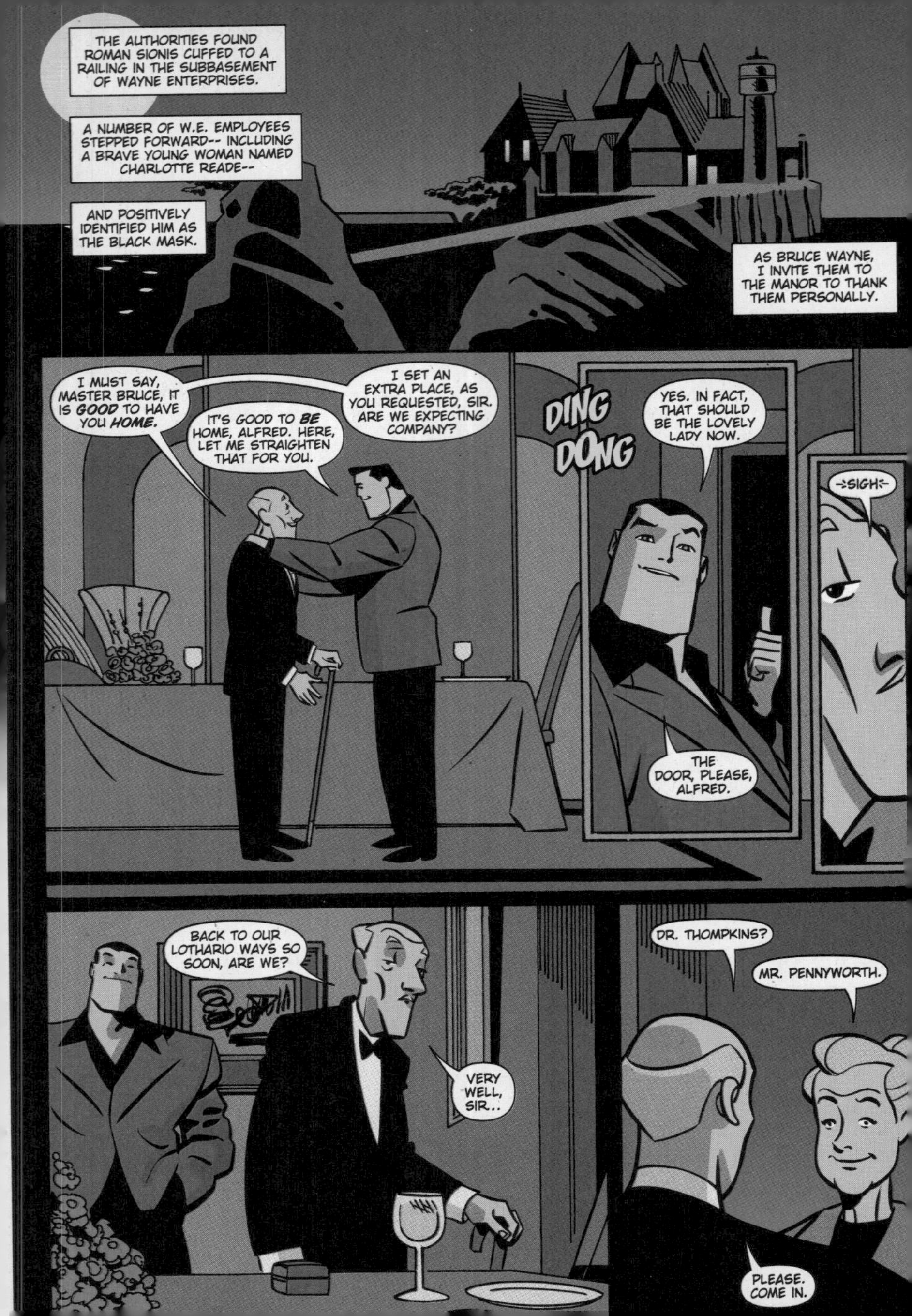

THE AUTHORITIES FOUND ROMAN SIONIS CUFFED TO A RAILING IN THE SUBBASEMENT OF WAYNE ENTERPRISES.
A NUMBER OF W.E. EMPLOYEES STEPPED FORWARD-- INCLUDING A BRAVE YOUNG WOMAN NAMED CHARLOTTE READE--
AND POSITIVELY IDENTIFIED HIM AS THE BLACK MASK.
AS BRUCE WAYNE, I INVITE THEM TO THE MANOR TO THANK THEM PERSONALLY.
I MUST SAY, MASTER BRUCE, IT IS **GOOD** TO HAVE YOU **HOME.**
IT'S GOOD TO ***BE*** HOME, ALFRED. HERE, LET ME STRAIGHTEN THAT FOR YOU.
I SET AN EXTRA PLACE, AS YOU REQUESTED, SIR. ARE WE EXPECTING COMPANY?
DING DONG
YES. IN FACT, THAT SHOULD BE THE LOVELY LADY NOW.
THE DOOR, PLEASE, ALFRED.
-SIGH-
BACK TO OUR LOTHARIO WAYS SO SOON, ARE WE?
VERY WELL, SIR..
DR. THOMPKINS?
MR. PENNYWORTH.
PLEASE. COME IN.

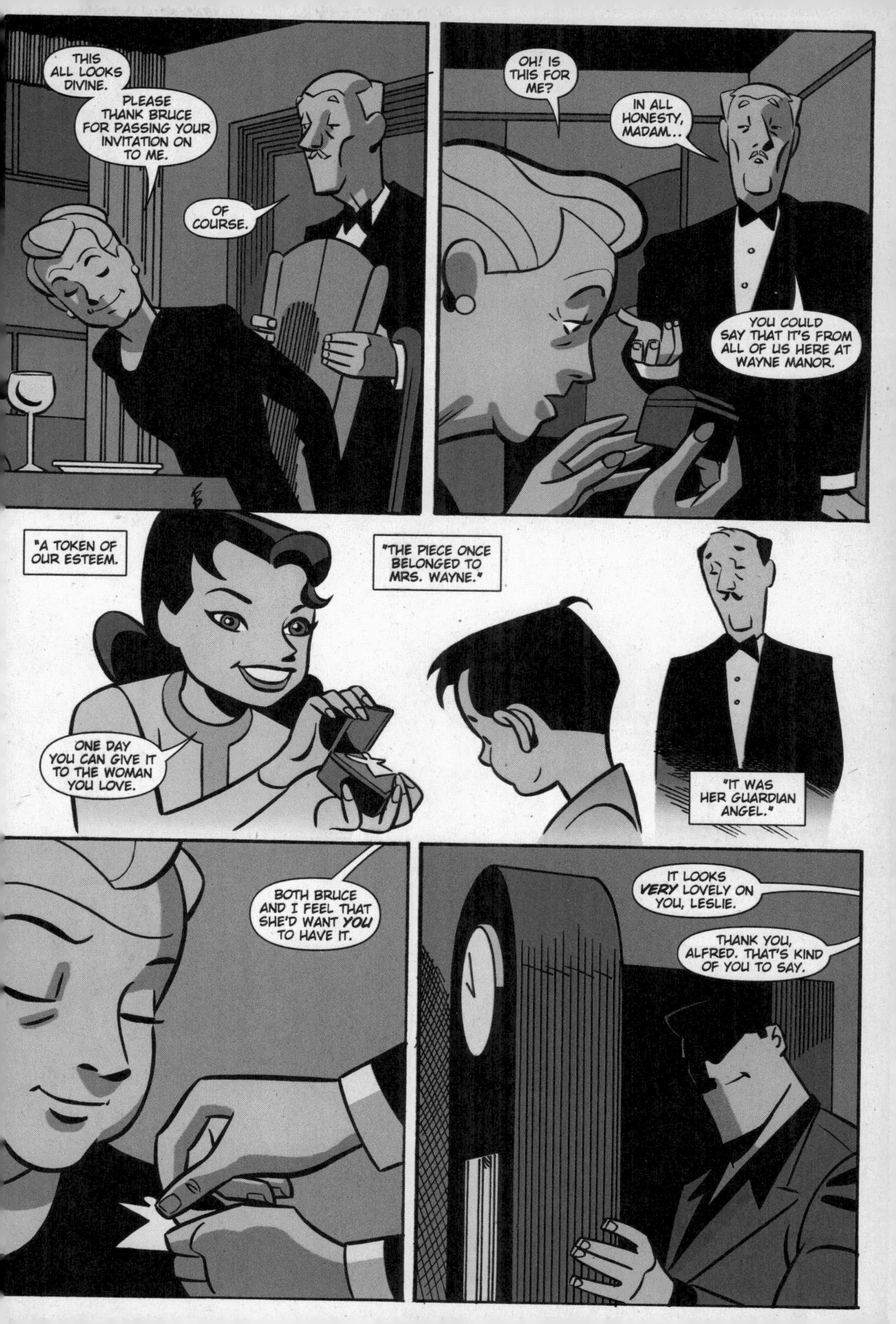
THIS ALL LOOKS DIVINE.
PLEASE THANK BRUCE FOR PASSING YOUR INVITATION ON TO ME.
OF COURSE.
OH! IS THIS FOR ME?
IN ALL HONESTY, MADAM...
YOU COULD SAY THAT IT'S FROM ALL OF US HERE AT WAYNE MANOR.
"A TOKEN OF OUR ESTEEM.
"THE PIECE ONCE BELONGED TO MRS. WAYNE."
ONE DAY YOU CAN GIVE IT TO THE WOMAN YOU LOVE.
"IT WAS HER GUARDIAN ANGEL."
BOTH BRUCE AND I FEEL THAT SHE'D WANT ***YOU*** TO HAVE IT.
IT LOOKS ***VERY*** LOVELY ON YOU, LESLIE.
THANK YOU, ALFRED. THAT'S KIND OF YOU TO SAY.

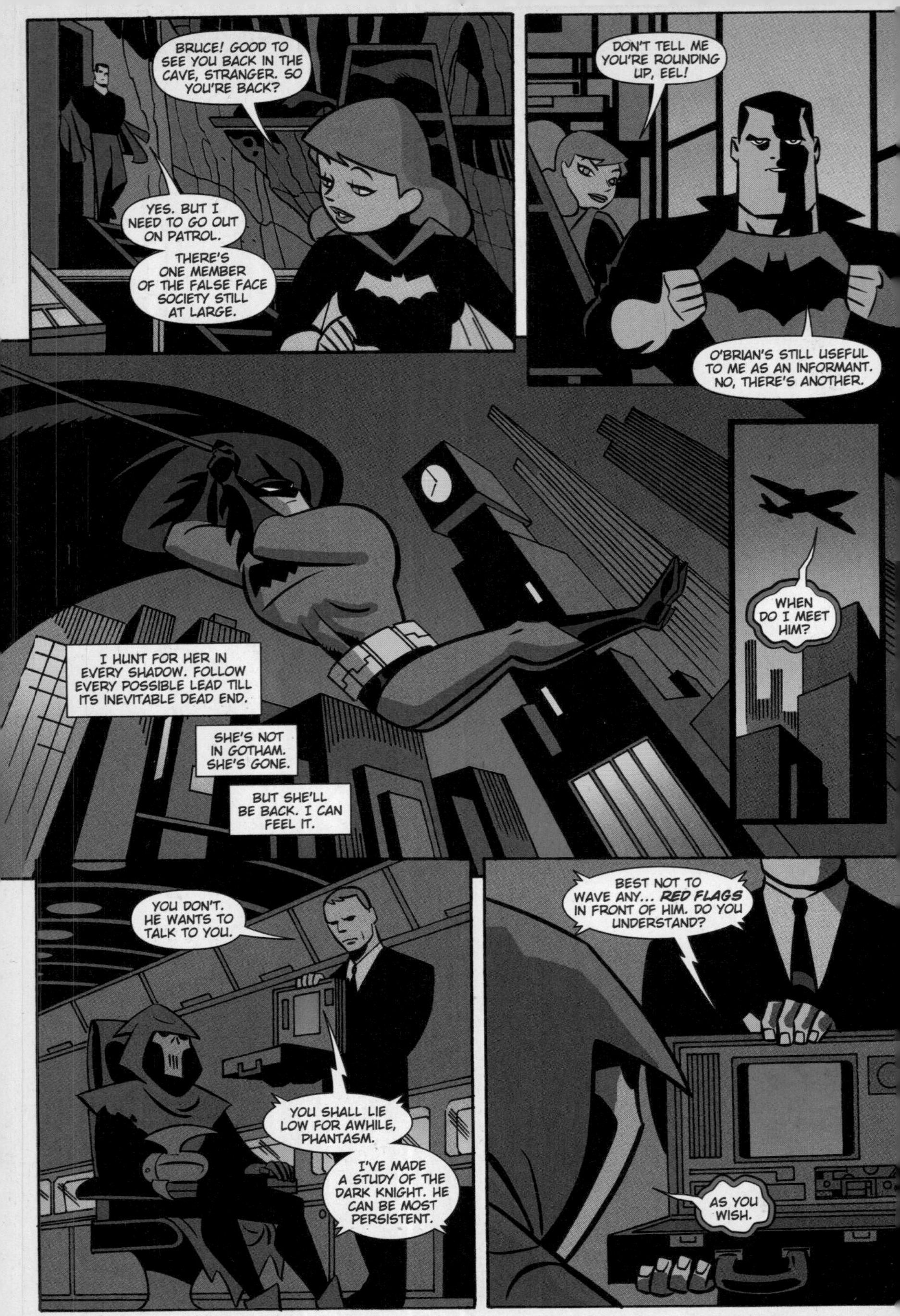
BRUCE! GOOD TO SEE YOU BACK IN THE CAVE, STRANGER. SO YOU'RE BACK?
YES. BUT I NEED TO GO OUT ON PATROL.
THERE'S ONE MEMBER OF THE FALSE FACE SOCIETY STILL AT LARGE.
DON'T TELL ME YOU'RE ROUNDING UP, EEL!
O'BRIAN'S STILL USEFUL TO ME AS AN INFORMANT. NO, THERE'S ANOTHER.
I HUNT FOR HER IN EVERY SHADOW. FOLLOW EVERY POSSIBLE LEAD TILL ITS INEVITABLE DEAD END.
SHE'S NOT IN GOTHAM. SHE'S GONE.
BUT SHE'LL BE BACK. I CAN FEEL IT.
WHEN DO I MEET HIM?
YOU DON'T. HE WANTS TO TALK TO YOU.
YOU SHALL LIE LOW FOR AWHILE, PHANTASM.
I'VE MADE A STUDY OF THE DARK KNIGHT. HE CAN BE MOST PERSISTENT.
BEST NOT TO WAVE ANY... RED FLAGS IN FRONT OF HIM. DO YOU UNDERSTAND?
AS YOU WISH.

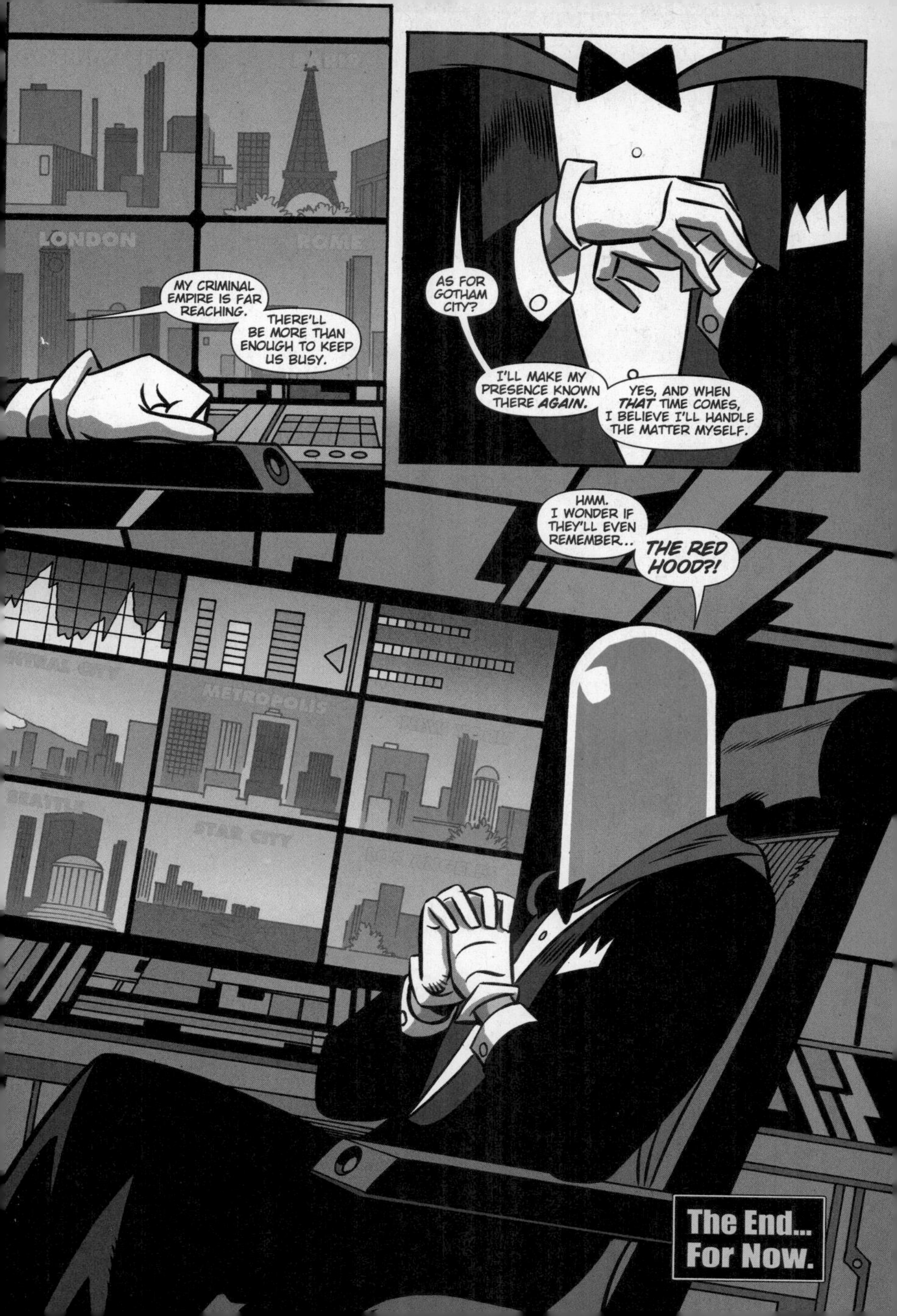
LONDON
ROME
MY CRIMINAL EMPIRE IS FAR REACHING.
THERE'LL BE MORE THAN ENOUGH TO KEEP US BUSY.
AS FOR GOTHAM CITY?
I'LL MAKE MY PRESENCE KNOWN THERE *AGAIN*.
YES, AND WHEN *THAT* TIME COMES, I BELIEVE I'LL HANDLE THE MATTER MYSELF.
HMM. I WONDER IF THEY'LL EVEN REMEMBER...
THE RED HOOD?!
METROPOLIS
STAR CITY
The End... For Now.

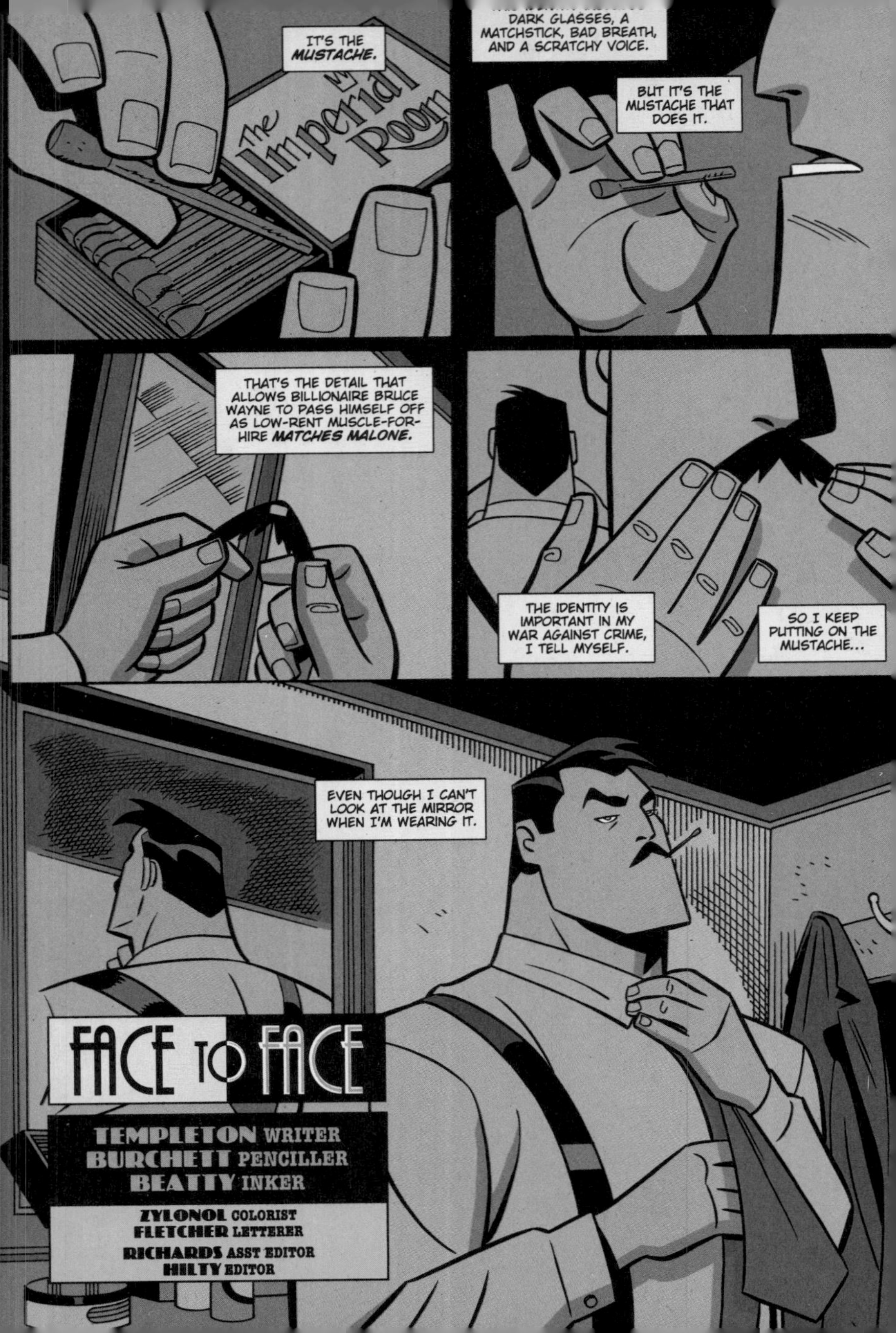
IT'S THE MUSTACHE.
DARK GLASSES, A MATCHSTICK, BAD BREATH, AND A SCRATCHY VOICE.
BUT IT'S THE MUSTACHE THAT DOES IT.
THAT'S THE DETAIL THAT ALLOWS BILLIONAIRE BRUCE WAYNE TO PASS HIMSELF OFF AS LOW-RENT MUSCLE-FOR-HIRE MATCHES MALONE.
THE IDENTITY IS IMPORTANT IN MY WAR AGAINST CRIME, I TELL MYSELF.
SO I KEEP PUTTING ON THE MUSTACHE...
EVEN THOUGH I CAN'T LOOK AT THE MIRROR WHEN I'M WEARING IT.
FACE TO FACE
TEMPLETON WRITER
BURCHETT PENCILLER
BEATTY INKER
ZYLONOL COLORIST
FLETCHER LETTERER
RICHARDS ASST EDITOR
HILTY EDITOR

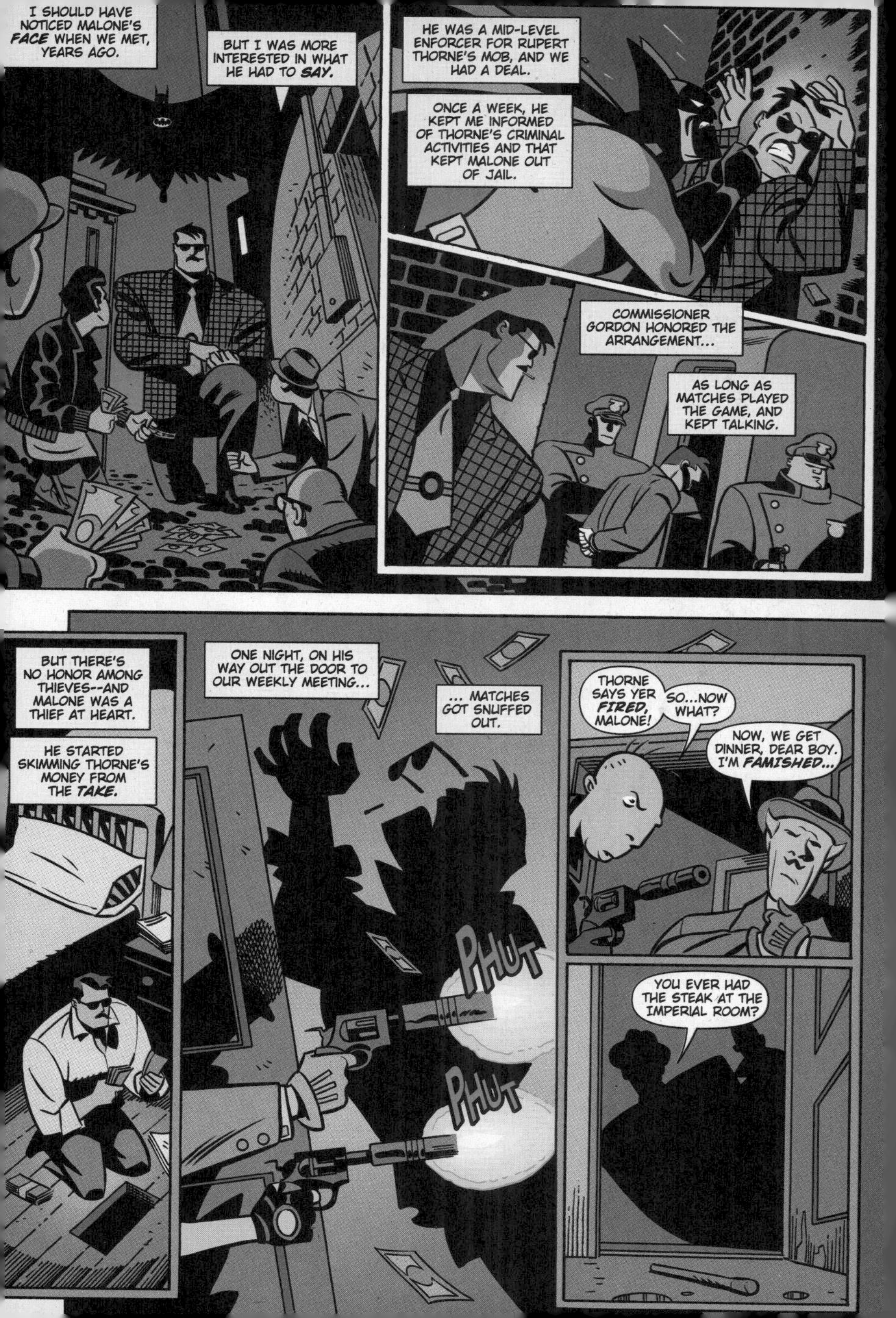
I SHOULD HAVE NOTICED MALONE'S *FACE* WHEN WE MET, YEARS AGO.
BUT I WAS MORE INTERESTED IN WHAT HE HAD TO *SAY.*
HE WAS A MID-LEVEL ENFORCER FOR RUPERT THORNE'S MOB, AND WE HAD A DEAL.
ONCE A WEEK, HE KEPT ME INFORMED OF THORNE'S CRIMINAL ACTIVITIES AND THAT KEPT MALONE OUT OF JAIL.
COMMISSIONER GORDON HONORED THE ARRANGEMENT...
AS LONG AS MATCHES PLAYED THE GAME, AND KEPT TALKING.
BUT THERE'S NO HONOR AMONG THIEVES--AND MALONE WAS A THIEF AT HEART.
HE STARTED SKIMMING THORNE'S MONEY FROM THE *TAKE.*
ONE NIGHT, ON HIS WAY OUT THE DOOR TO OUR WEEKLY MEETING...
... MATCHES GOT SNUFFED OUT.
PHUT
PHUT
THORNE SAYS YER *FIRED,* MALONE!
SO...NOW WHAT?
NOW, WE GET DINNER, DEAR BOY. I'M *FAMISHED...*
YOU EVER HAD THE STEAK AT THE IMPERIAL ROOM?

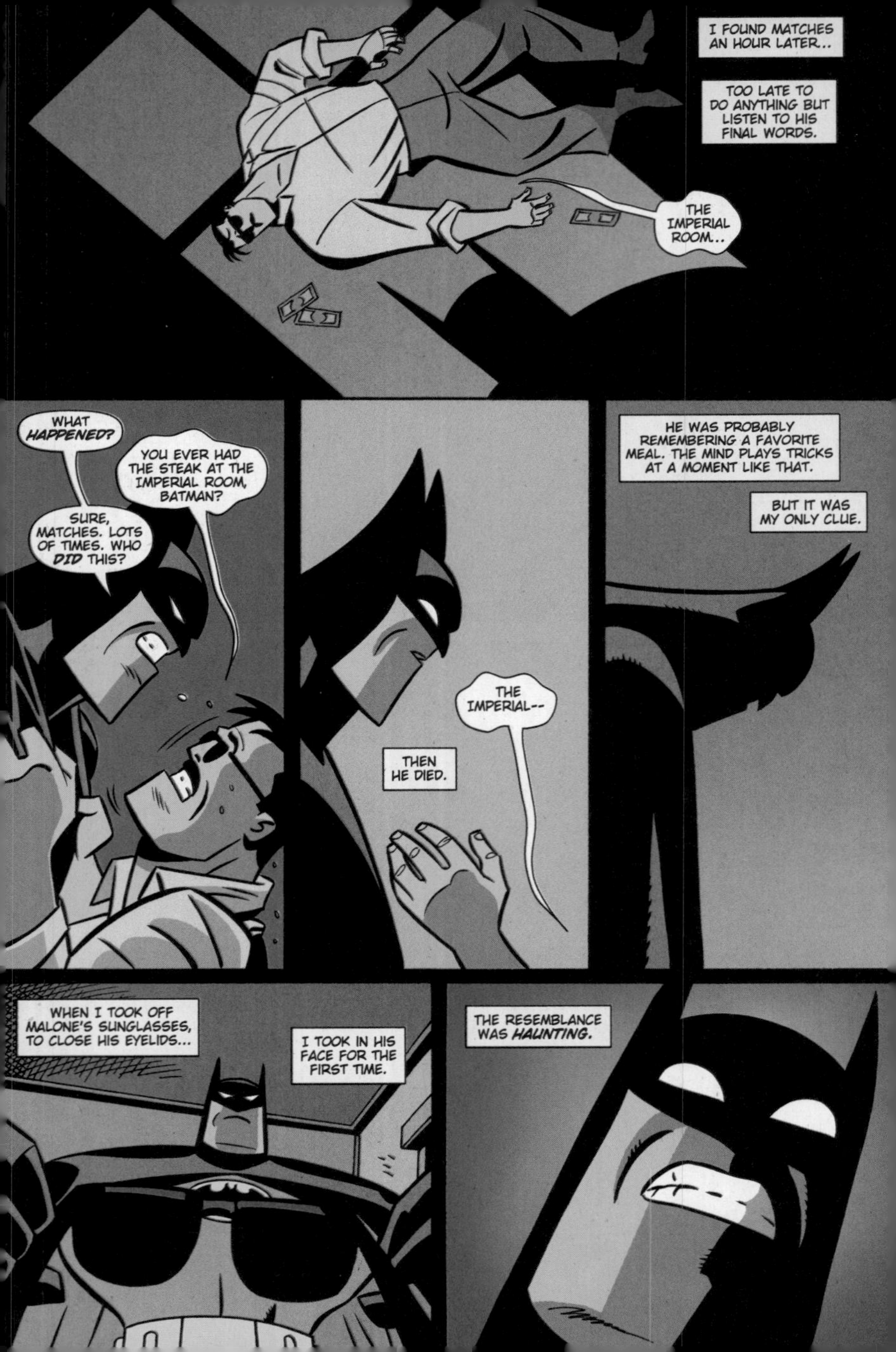
I FOUND MATCHES AN HOUR LATER...
TOO LATE TO DO ANYTHING BUT LISTEN TO HIS FINAL WORDS.
THE IMPERIAL ROOM...
WHAT *HAPPENED?*
YOU EVER HAD THE STEAK AT THE IMPERIAL ROOM, BATMAN?
SURE, MATCHES. LOTS OF TIMES. WHO *DID* THIS?
THE IMPERIAL--
THEN HE DIED.
HE WAS PROBABLY REMEMBERING A FAVORITE MEAL. THE MIND PLAYS TRICKS AT A MOMENT LIKE THAT.
BUT IT WAS MY ONLY CLUE.
WHEN I TOOK OFF MALONE'S SUNGLASSES, TO CLOSE HIS EYELIDS...
I TOOK IN HIS FACE FOR THE FIRST TIME.
THE RESEMBLANCE WAS *HAUNTING.*

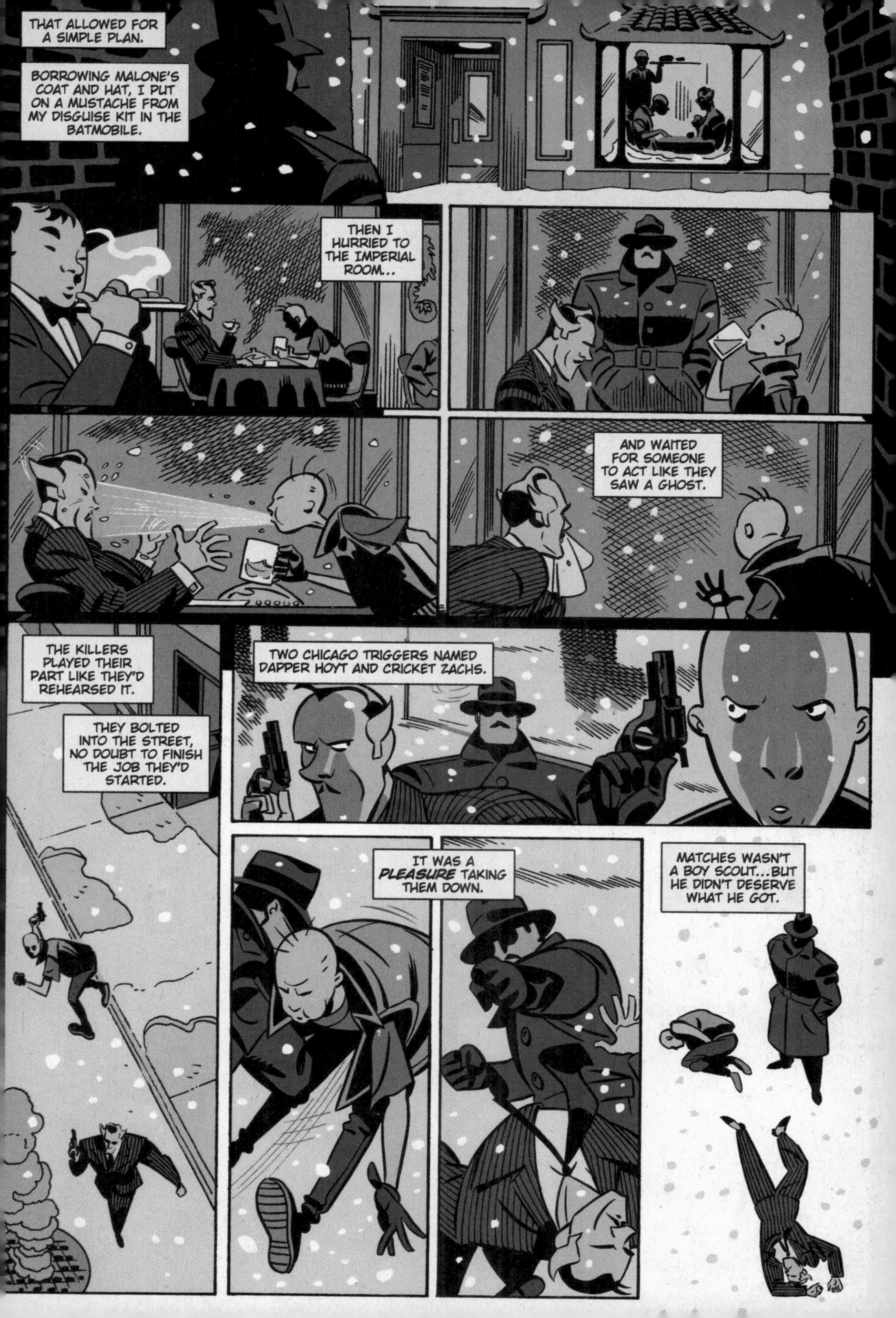
THAT ALLOWED FOR A SIMPLE PLAN.
BORROWING MALONE'S COAT AND HAT, I PUT ON A MUSTACHE FROM MY DISGUISE KIT IN THE BATMOBILE.
THEN I HURRIED TO THE IMPERIAL ROOM...
AND WAITED FOR SOMEONE TO ACT LIKE THEY SAW A GHOST.
THE KILLERS PLAYED THEIR PART LIKE THEY'D REHEARSED IT.
THEY BOLTED INTO THE STREET, NO DOUBT TO FINISH THE JOB THEY'D STARTED.
TWO CHICAGO TRIGGERS NAMED DAPPER HOYT AND CRICKET ZACHS.
IT WAS A *PLEASURE* TAKING THEM DOWN.
MATCHES WASN'T A BOY SCOUT...BUT HE DIDN'T DESERVE WHAT HE GOT.

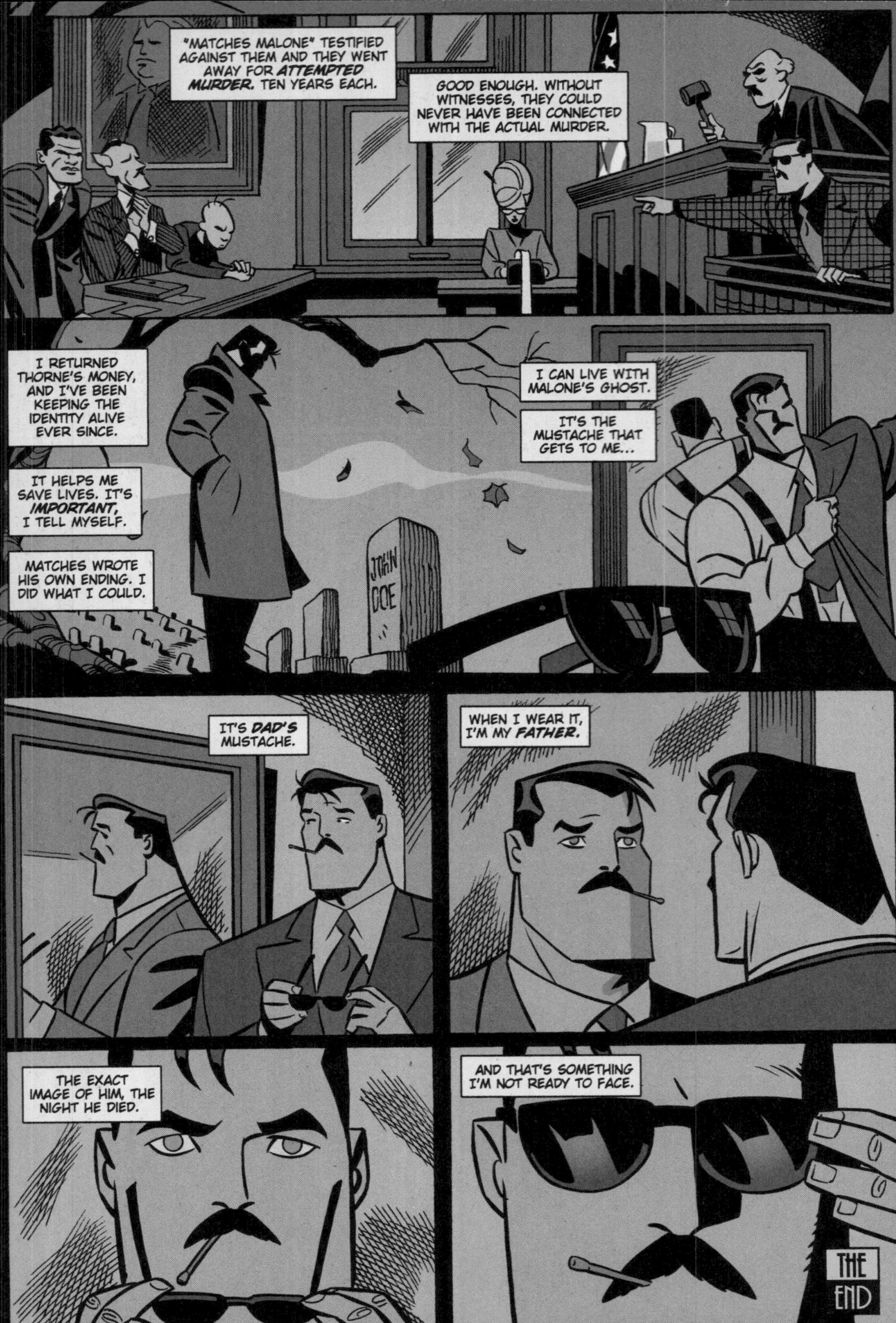
"MATCHES MALONE" TESTIFIED AGAINST THEM AND THEY WENT AWAY FOR ATTEMPTED MURDER. TEN YEARS EACH.
GOOD ENOUGH. WITHOUT WITNESSES, THEY COULD NEVER HAVE BEEN CONNECTED WITH THE ACTUAL MURDER.
I RETURNED THORNE'S MONEY, AND I'VE BEEN KEEPING THE IDENTITY ALIVE EVER SINCE.
IT HELPS ME SAVE LIVES. IT'S IMPORTANT, I TELL MYSELF.
MATCHES WROTE HIS OWN ENDING. I DID WHAT I COULD.
JOHN DOE
I CAN LIVE WITH MALONE'S GHOST.
IT'S THE MUSTACHE THAT GETS TO ME...
IT'S DAD'S MUSTACHE.
WHEN I WEAR IT, I'M MY FATHER.
THE EXACT IMAGE OF HIM, THE NIGHT HE DIED.
AND THAT'S SOMETHING I'M NOT READY TO FACE.
THE END

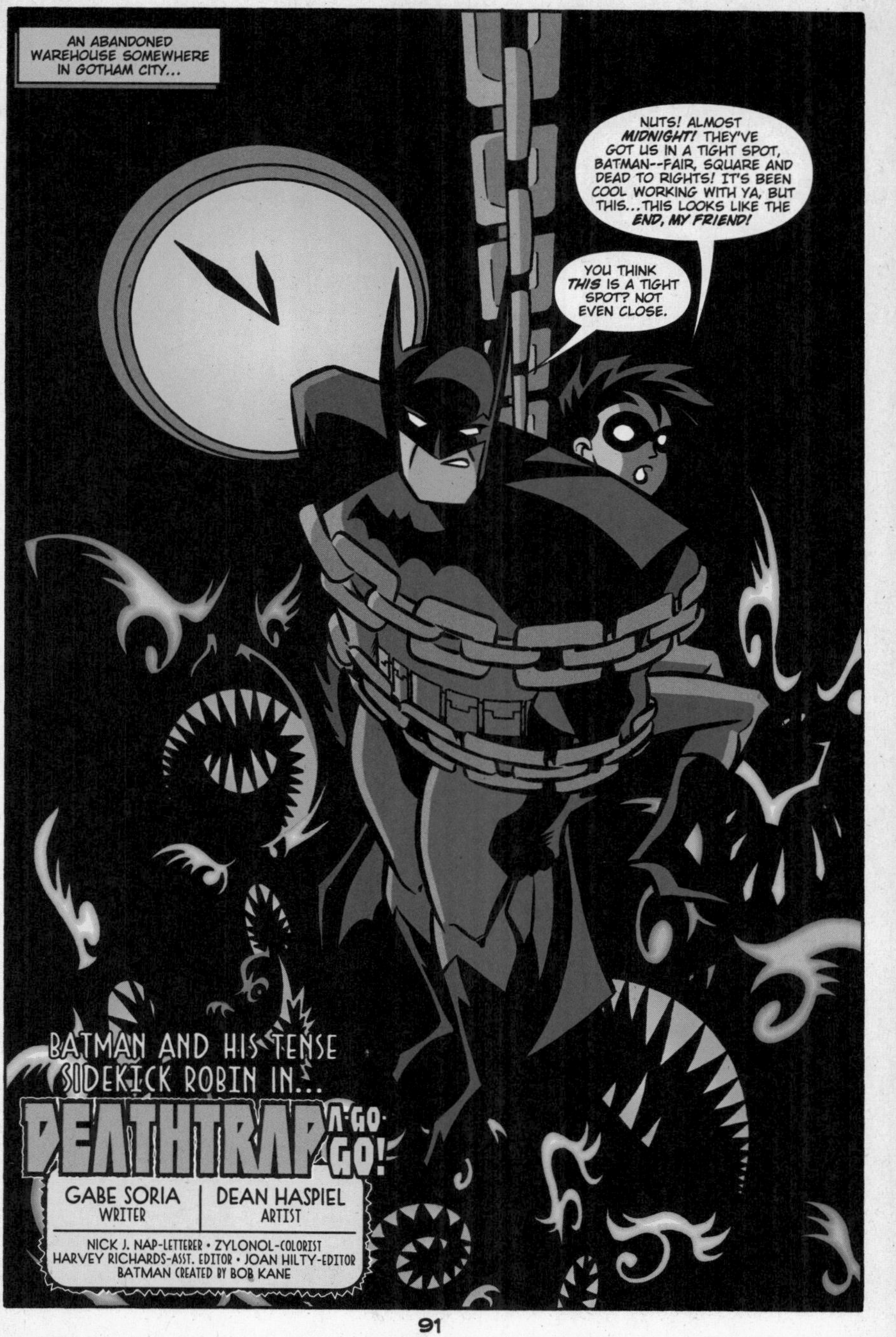
AN ABANDONED WAREHOUSE SOMEWHERE IN GOTHAM CITY...
NUTS! ALMOST MIDNIGHT! THEY'VE GOT US IN A TIGHT SPOT, BATMAN--FAIR, SQUARE AND DEAD TO RIGHTS! IT'S BEEN COOL WORKING WITH YA, BUT THIS...THIS LOOKS LIKE THE END, MY FRIEND!
YOU THINK THIS IS A TIGHT SPOT? NOT EVEN CLOSE.
BATMAN AND HIS TENSE SIDEKICK ROBIN IN...
DEATHTRAP A-GO-GO!
GABE SORIA WRITER
DEAN HASPIEL ARTIST
NICK J. NAP-LETTERER • ZYLONOL-COLORIST
HARVEY RICHARDS-ASST. EDITOR • JOAN HILTY-EDITOR
BATMAN CREATED BY BOB KANE

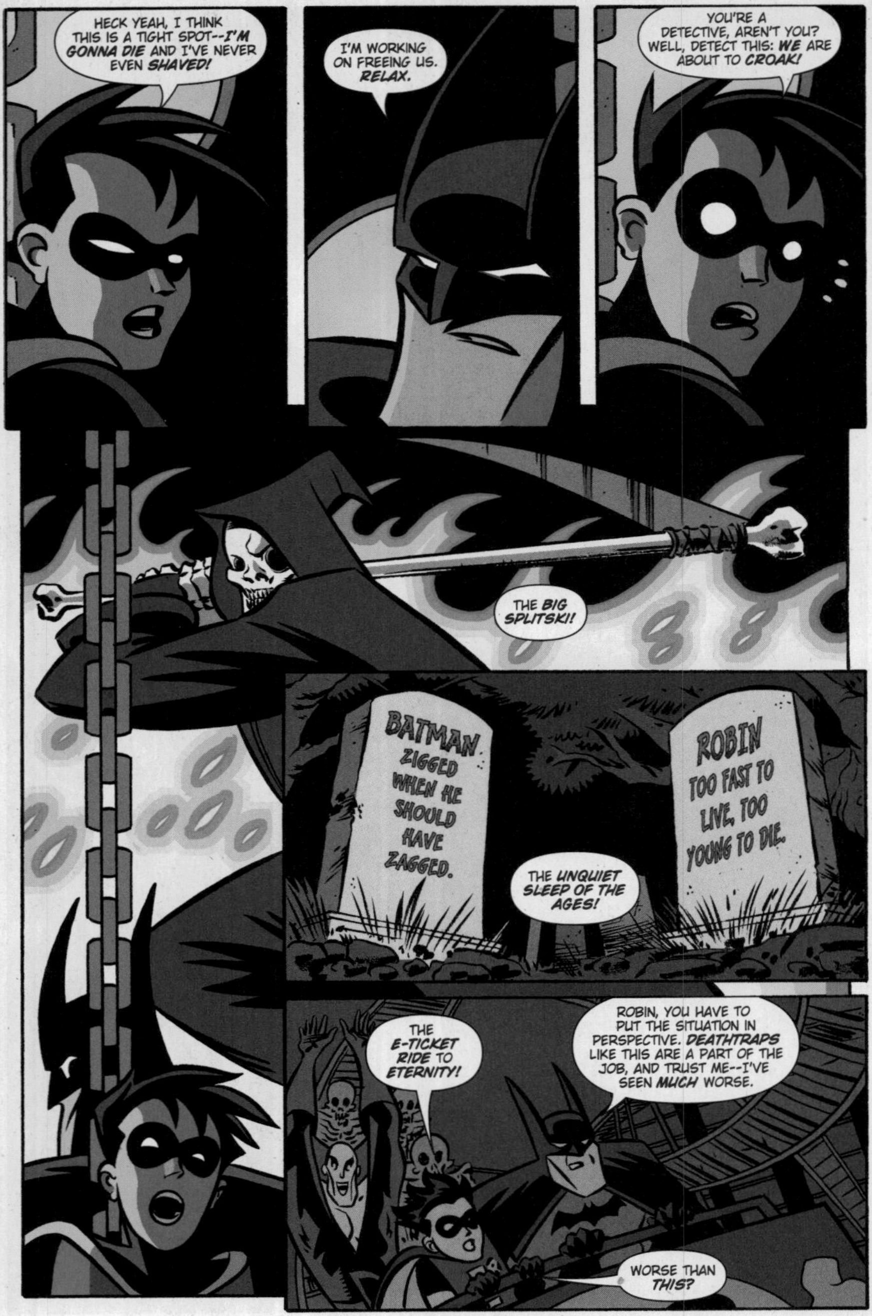
HECK YEAH, I THINK THIS IS A TIGHT SPOT--I'M GONNA DIE AND I'VE NEVER EVEN SHAVED!
I'M WORKING ON FREEING US. RELAX.
YOU'RE A DETECTIVE, AREN'T YOU? WELL, DETECT THIS: WE ARE ABOUT TO CROAK!
THE BIG SPLITSKI!
BATMAN ZIGGED WHEN HE SHOULD HAVE ZAGGED.
ROBIN TOO FAST TO LIVE, TOO YOUNG TO DIE.
THE UNQUIET SLEEP OF THE AGES!
THE E-TICKET RIDE TO ETERNITY!
ROBIN, YOU HAVE TO PUT THE SITUATION IN PERSPECTIVE. DEATHTRAPS LIKE THIS ARE A PART OF THE JOB, AND TRUST ME--I'VE SEEN MUCH WORSE.
WORSE THAN THIS?

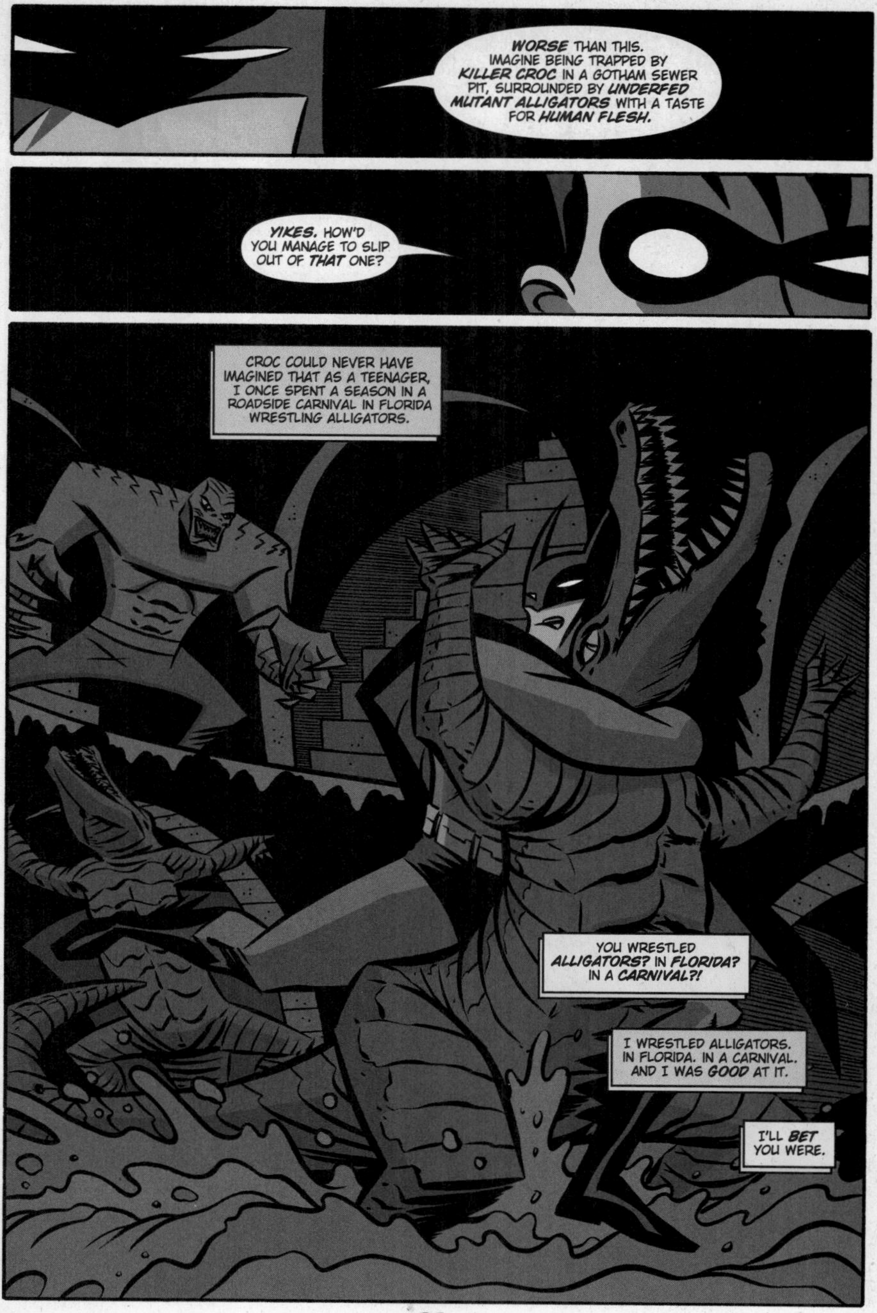
WORSE THAN THIS. IMAGINE BEING TRAPPED BY KILLER CROC IN A GOTHAM SEWER PIT, SURROUNDED BY UNDERFED MUTANT ALLIGATORS WITH A TASTE FOR HUMAN FLESH.
YIKES. HOW'D YOU MANAGE TO SLIP OUT OF THAT ONE?
CROC COULD NEVER HAVE IMAGINED THAT AS A TEENAGER, I ONCE SPENT A SEASON IN A ROADSIDE CARNIVAL IN FLORIDA WRESTLING ALLIGATORS.
YOU WRESTLED ALLIGATORS? IN FLORIDA? IN A CARNIVAL?!
I WRESTLED ALLIGATORS. IN FLORIDA. IN A CARNIVAL. AND I WAS GOOD AT IT.
I'LL BET YOU WERE.

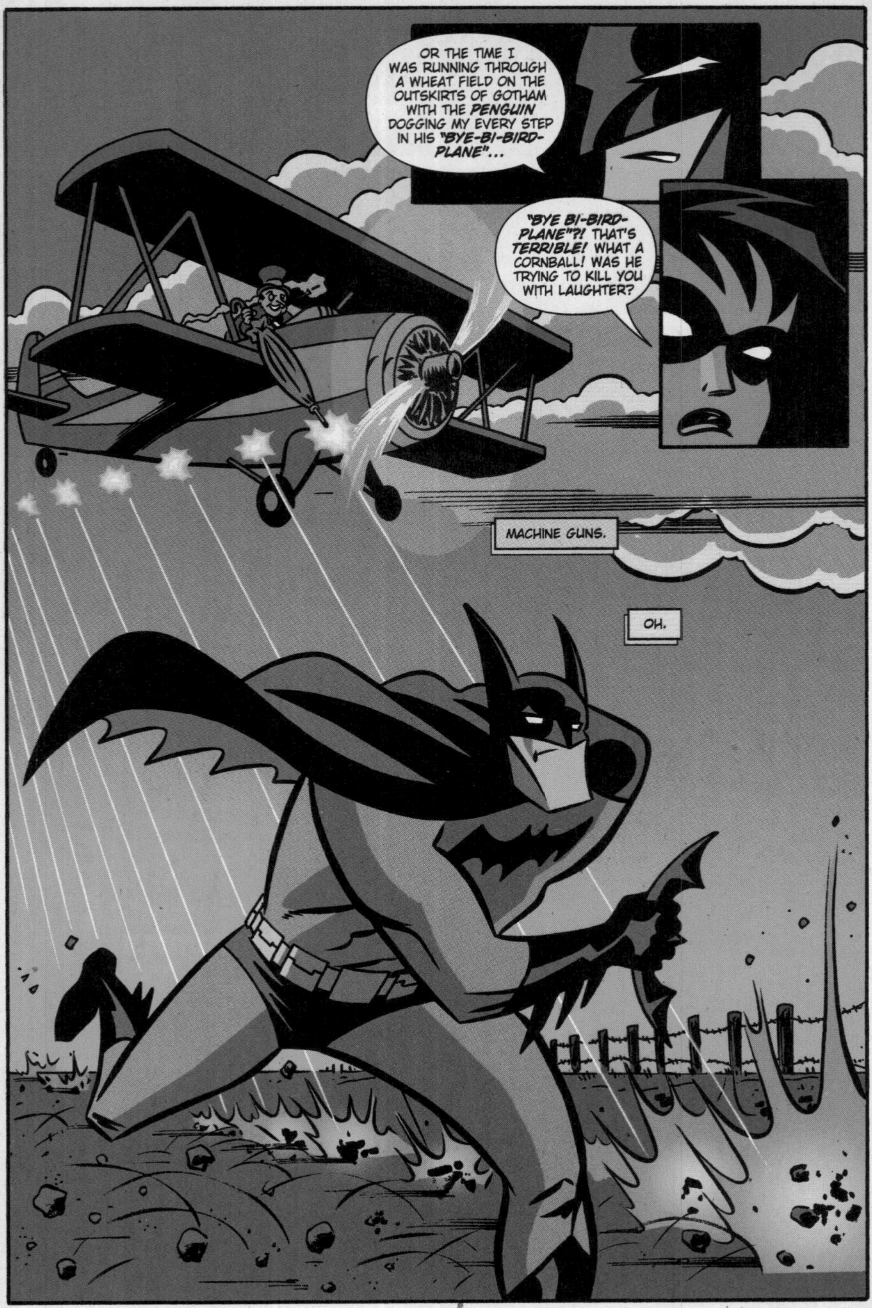
OR THE TIME I WAS RUNNING THROUGH A WHEAT FIELD ON THE OUTSKIRTS OF GOTHAM WITH THE *PENGUIN* DOGGING MY EVERY STEP IN HIS *"BYE-BI-BIRD-PLANE"*...
"BYE BI-BIRD-PLANE"?! THAT'S *TERRIBLE!* WHAT A CORNBALL! WAS HE TRYING TO KILL YOU WITH LAUGHTER?
MACHINE GUNS.
OH.

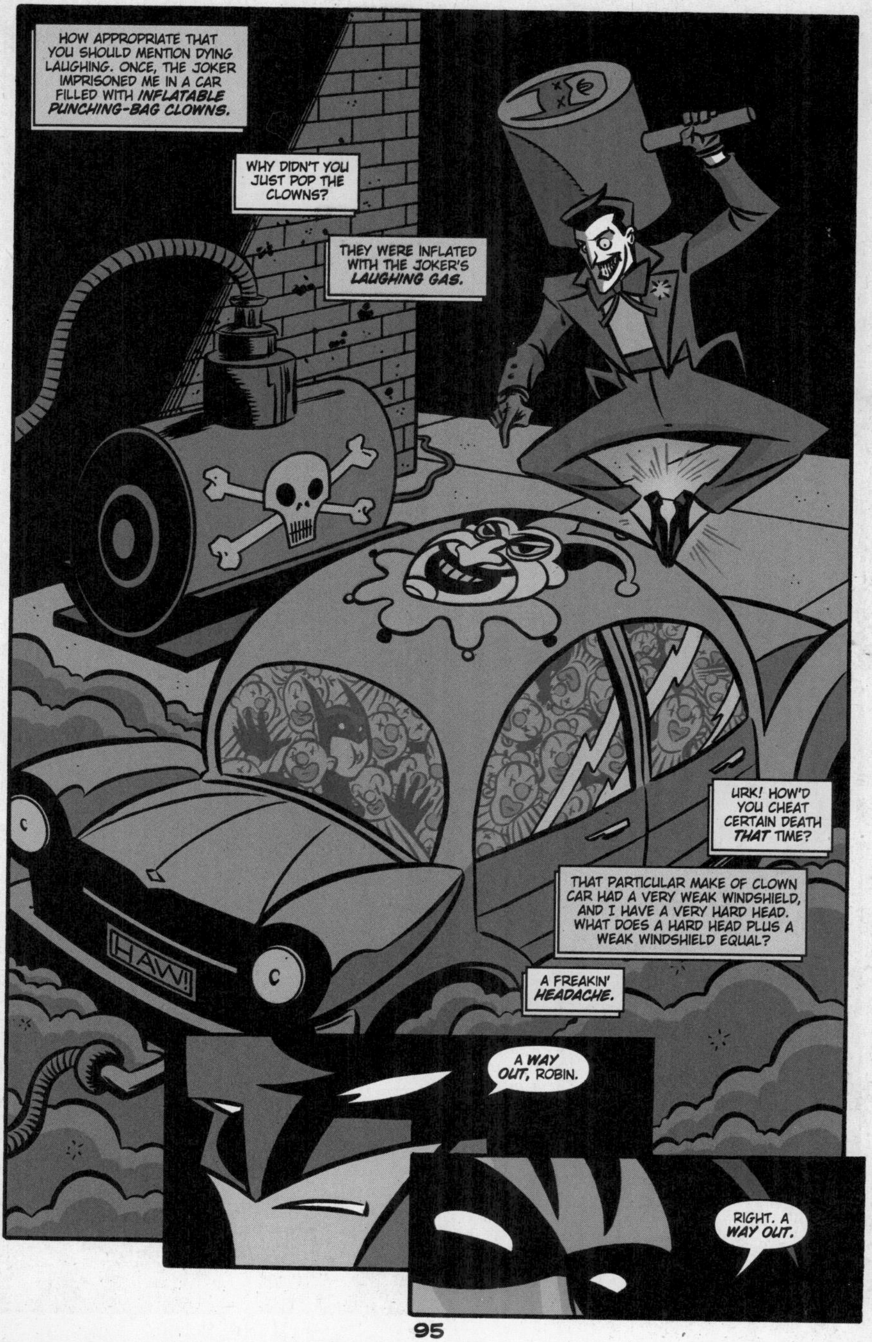
HOW APPROPRIATE THAT YOU SHOULD MENTION DYING LAUGHING. ONCE, THE JOKER IMPRISONED ME IN A CAR FILLED WITH INFLATABLE PUNCHING-BAG CLOWNS.
WHY DIDN'T YOU JUST POP THE CLOWNS?
THEY WERE INFLATED WITH THE JOKER'S LAUGHING GAS.
HAW!
URK! HOW'D YOU CHEAT CERTAIN DEATH THAT TIME?
THAT PARTICULAR MAKE OF CLOWN CAR HAD A VERY WEAK WINDSHIELD, AND I HAVE A VERY HARD HEAD. WHAT DOES A HARD HEAD PLUS A WEAK WINDSHIELD EQUAL?
A FREAKIN' HEADACHE.
A WAY OUT, ROBIN.
RIGHT. A WAY OUT.

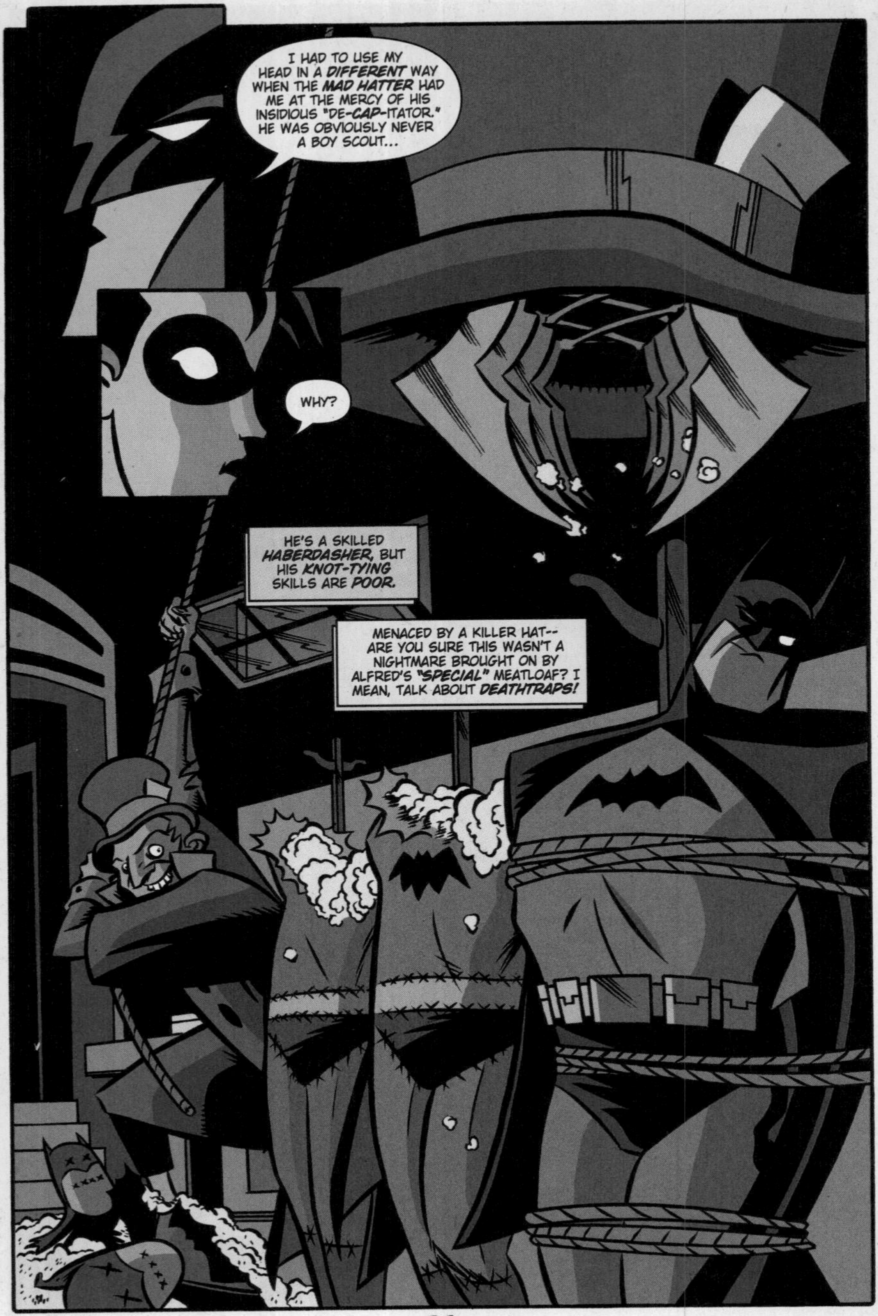
I HAD TO USE MY HEAD IN A DIFFERENT WAY WHEN THE MAD HATTER HAD ME AT THE MERCY OF HIS INSIDIOUS "DE-CAP-ITATOR." HE WAS OBVIOUSLY NEVER A BOY SCOUT...
WHY?
HE'S A SKILLED HABERDASHER, BUT HIS KNOT-TYING SKILLS ARE POOR.
MENACED BY A KILLER HAT--ARE YOU SURE THIS WASN'T A NIGHTMARE BROUGHT ON BY ALFRED'S "SPECIAL" MEATLOAF? I MEAN, TALK ABOUT DEATHTRAPS!

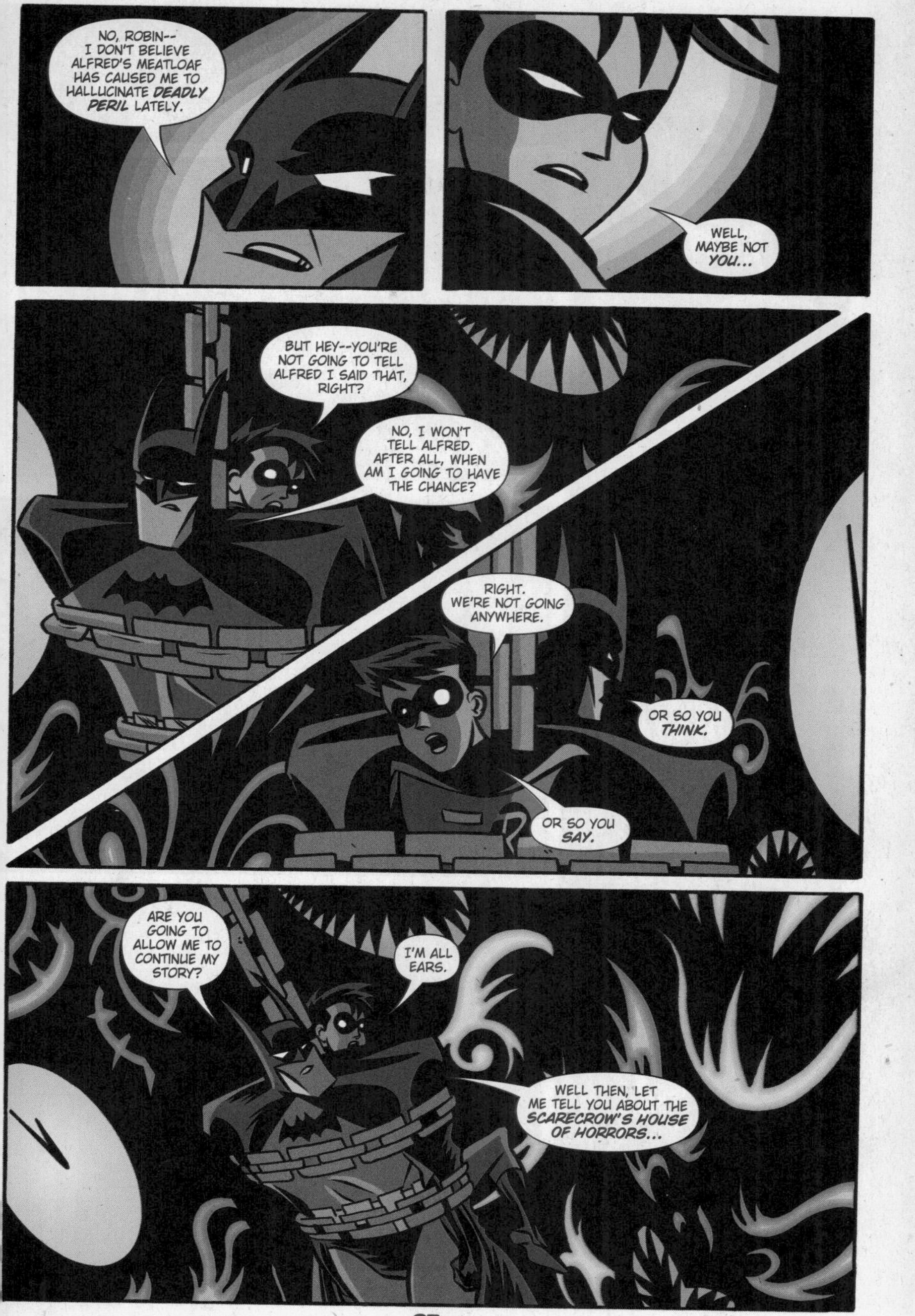

NO, ROBIN-- I DON'T BELIEVE ALFRED'S MEATLOAF HAS CAUSED ME TO HALLUCINATE DEADLY PERIL LATELY.
WELL, MAYBE NOT YOU...
BUT HEY--YOU'RE NOT GOING TO TELL ALFRED I SAID THAT, RIGHT?
NO, I WON'T TELL ALFRED. AFTER ALL, WHEN AM I GOING TO HAVE THE CHANCE?
RIGHT. WE'RE NOT GOING ANYWHERE.
OR SO YOU THINK.
OR SO YOU SAY.
ARE YOU GOING TO ALLOW ME TO CONTINUE MY STORY?
I'M ALL EARS.
WELL THEN, LET ME TELL YOU ABOUT THE SCARECROW'S HOUSE OF HORRORS...

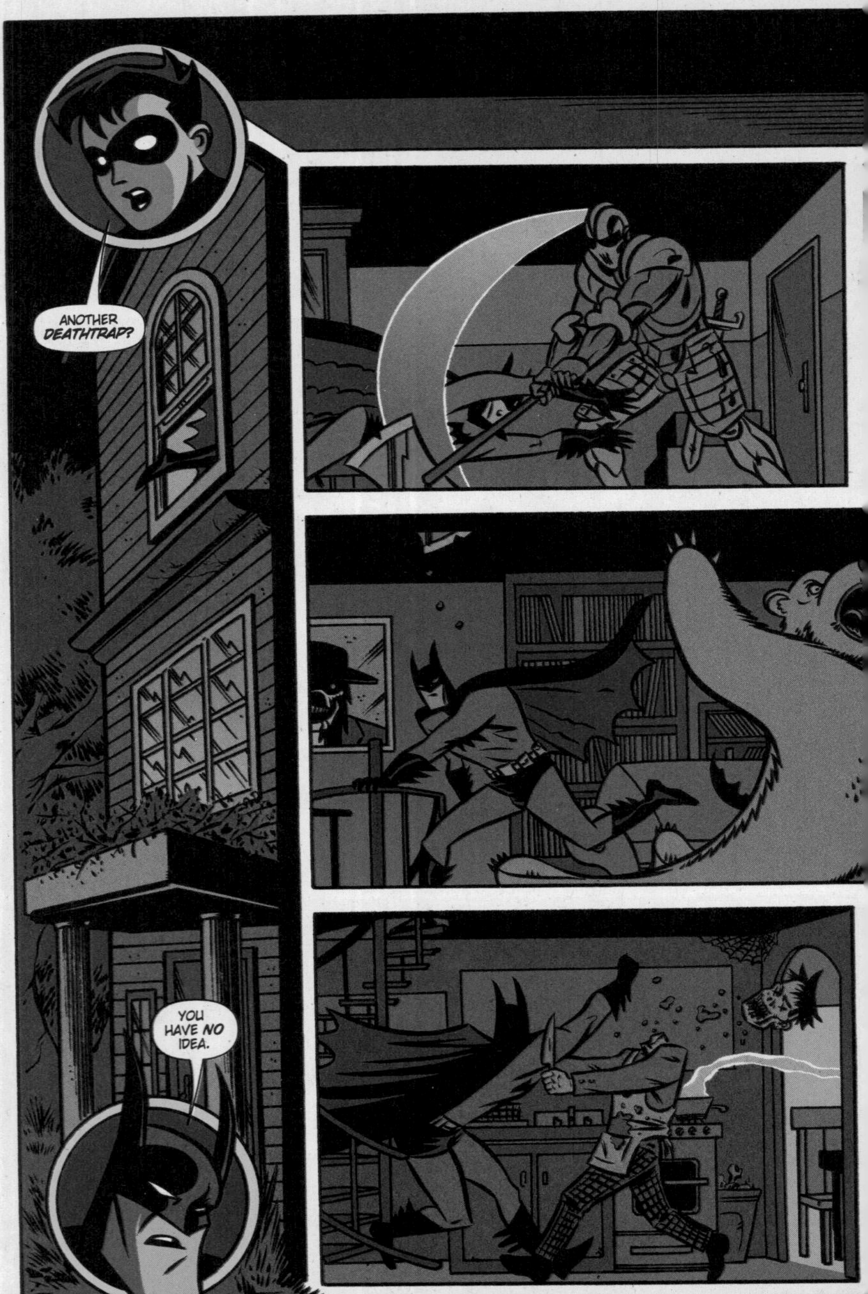
ANOTHER DEATHTRAP?
YOU HAVE NO IDEA.

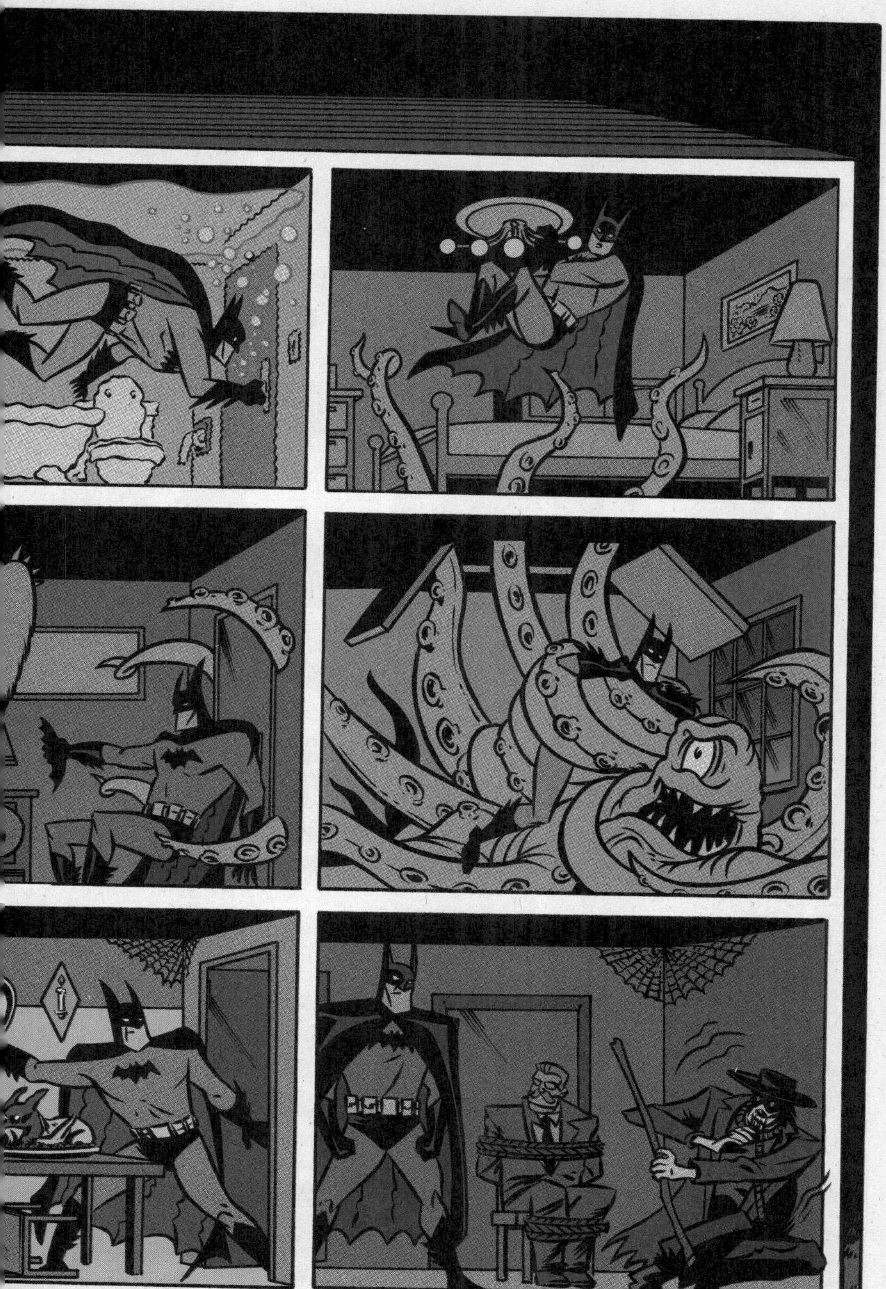

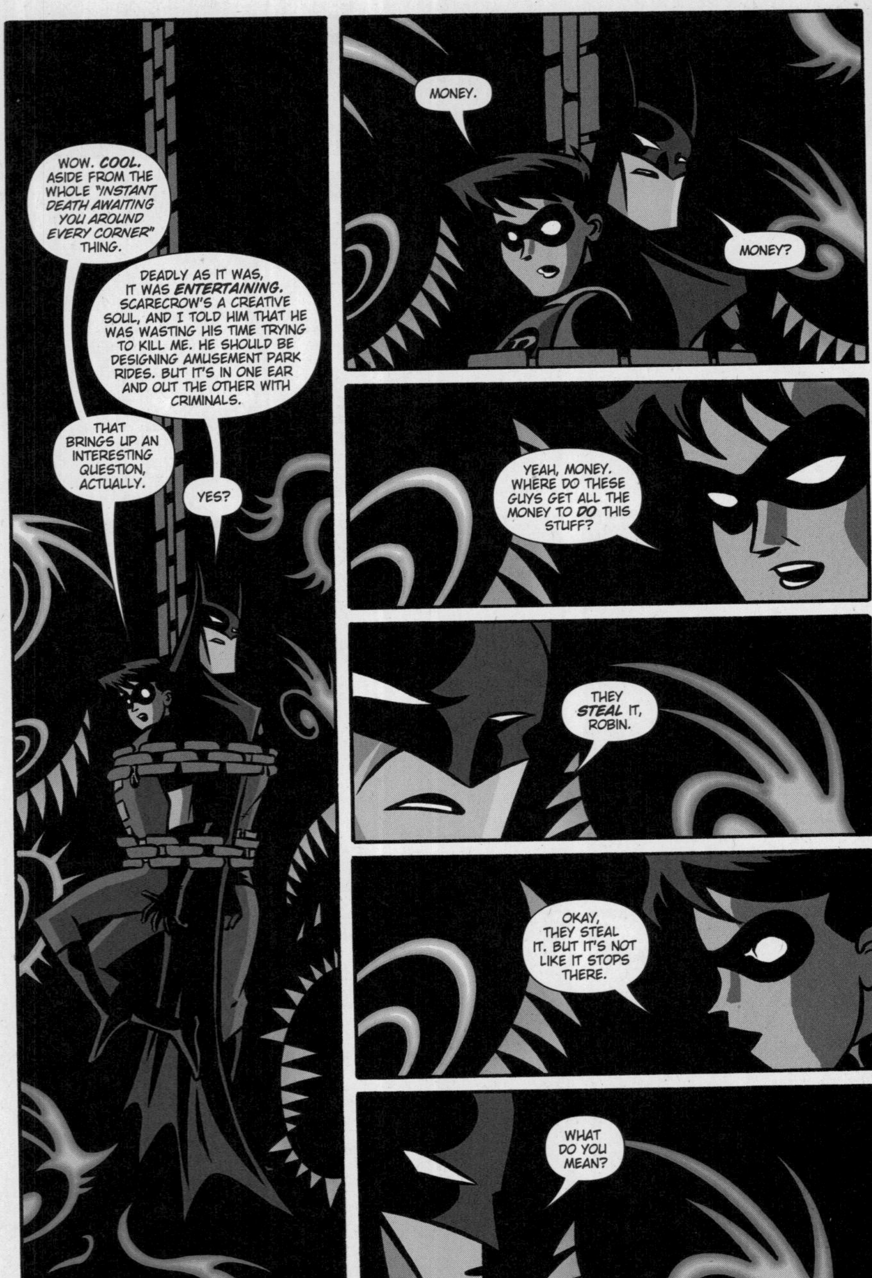
WOW. COOL. ASIDE FROM THE WHOLE "INSTANT DEATH AWAITING YOU AROUND EVERY CORNER" THING.
DEADLY AS IT WAS, IT WAS ENTERTAINING. SCARECROW'S A CREATIVE SOUL, AND I TOLD HIM THAT HE WAS WASTING HIS TIME TRYING TO KILL ME. HE SHOULD BE DESIGNING AMUSEMENT PARK RIDES. BUT IT'S IN ONE EAR AND OUT THE OTHER WITH CRIMINALS.
THAT BRINGS UP AN INTERESTING QUESTION, ACTUALLY.
YES?
MONEY.
MONEY?
YEAH, MONEY. WHERE DO THESE GUYS GET ALL THE MONEY TO DO THIS STUFF?
THEY STEAL IT, ROBIN.
OKAY, THEY STEAL IT. BUT IT'S NOT LIKE IT STOPS THERE.
WHAT DO YOU MEAN?

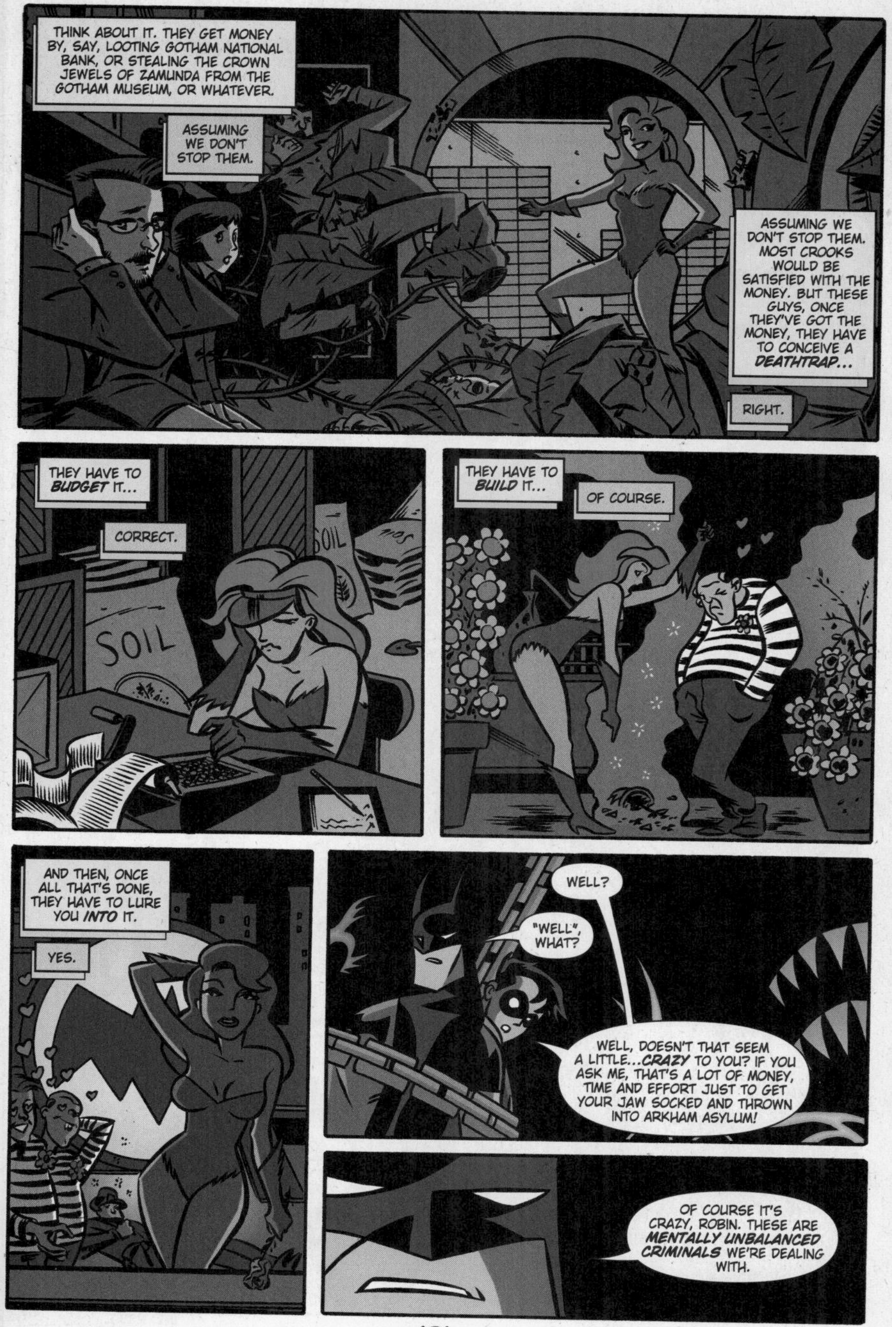
THINK ABOUT IT. THEY GET MONEY BY, SAY, LOOTING GOTHAM NATIONAL BANK, OR STEALING THE CROWN JEWELS OF ZAMUNDA FROM THE GOTHAM MUSEUM, OR WHATEVER.
ASSUMING WE DON'T STOP THEM.
ASSUMING WE DON'T STOP THEM. MOST CROOKS WOULD BE SATISFIED WITH THE MONEY. BUT THESE GUYS, ONCE THEY'VE GOT THE MONEY, THEY HAVE TO CONCEIVE A *DEATHTRAP*...
RIGHT.
THEY HAVE TO *BUDGET* IT...
CORRECT.
SOIL
SOIL
THEY HAVE TO *BUILD* IT...
OF COURSE.
AND THEN, ONCE ALL THAT'S DONE, THEY HAVE TO LURE YOU *INTO* IT.
YES.
WELL?
"WELL", WHAT?
WELL, DOESN'T THAT SEEM A LITTLE...*CRAZY* TO YOU? IF YOU ASK ME, THAT'S A LOT OF MONEY, TIME AND EFFORT JUST TO GET YOUR JAW SOCKED AND THROWN INTO ARKHAM ASYLUM!
OF COURSE IT'S CRAZY, ROBIN. THESE ARE *MENTALLY UNBALANCED CRIMINALS* WE'RE DEALING WITH.

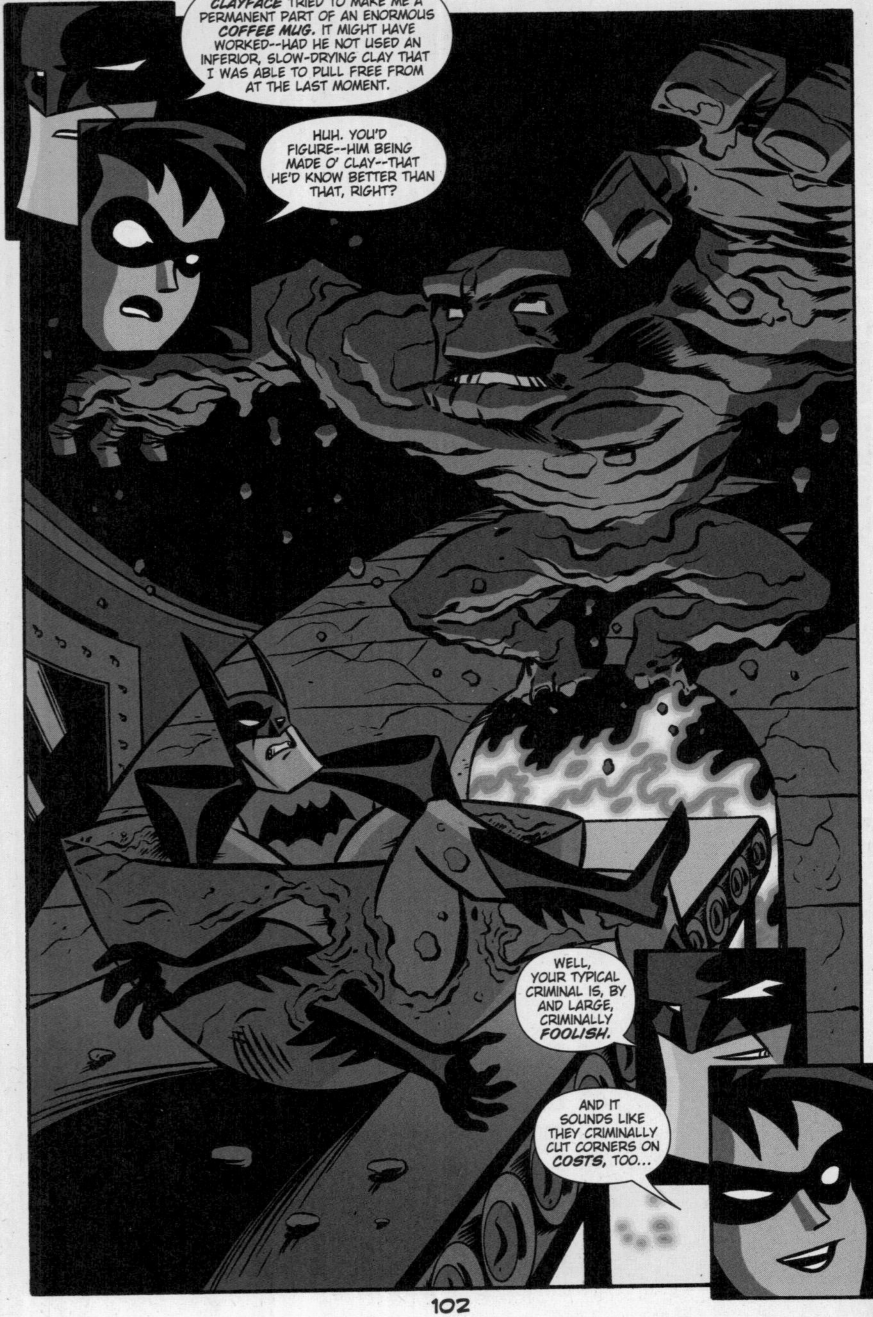
NOT SO LONG AGO, CLAYFACE TRIED TO MAKE ME A PERMANENT PART OF AN ENORMOUS COFFEE MUG. IT MIGHT HAVE WORKED--HAD HE NOT USED AN INFERIOR, SLOW-DRYING CLAY THAT I WAS ABLE TO PULL FREE FROM AT THE LAST MOMENT.
HUH. YOU'D FIGURE--HIM BEING MADE O' CLAY--THAT HE'D KNOW BETTER THAN THAT, RIGHT?
WELL, YOUR TYPICAL CRIMINAL IS, BY AND LARGE, CRIMINALLY FOOLISH.
AND IT SOUNDS LIKE THEY CRIMINALLY CUT CORNERS ON COSTS, TOO...

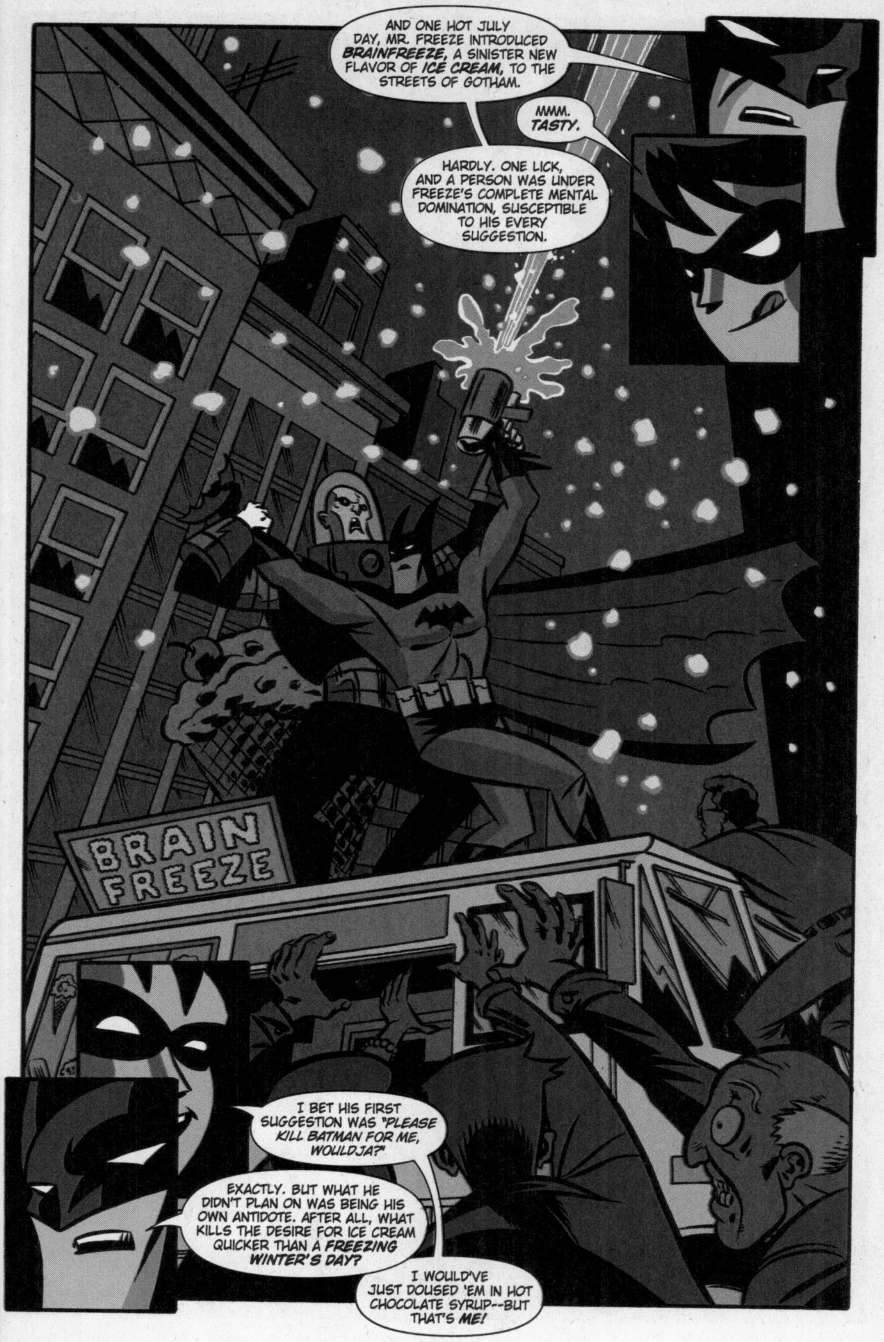
AND ONE HOT JULY DAY, MR. FREEZE INTRODUCED BRAINFREEZE, A SINISTER NEW FLAVOR OF ICE CREAM, TO THE STREETS OF GOTHAM.
MMM. TASTY.
HARDLY. ONE LICK, AND A PERSON WAS UNDER FREEZE'S COMPLETE MENTAL DOMINATION, SUSCEPTIBLE TO HIS EVERY SUGGESTION.
BRAIN FREEZE
I BET HIS FIRST SUGGESTION WAS "PLEASE KILL BATMAN FOR ME, WOULDJA?"
EXACTLY. BUT WHAT HE DIDN'T PLAN ON WAS BEING HIS OWN ANTIDOTE. AFTER ALL, WHAT KILLS THE DESIRE FOR ICE CREAM QUICKER THAN A FREEZING WINTER'S DAY?
I WOULD'VE JUST DOUSED 'EM IN HOT CHOCOLATE SYRUP--BUT THAT'S ME!

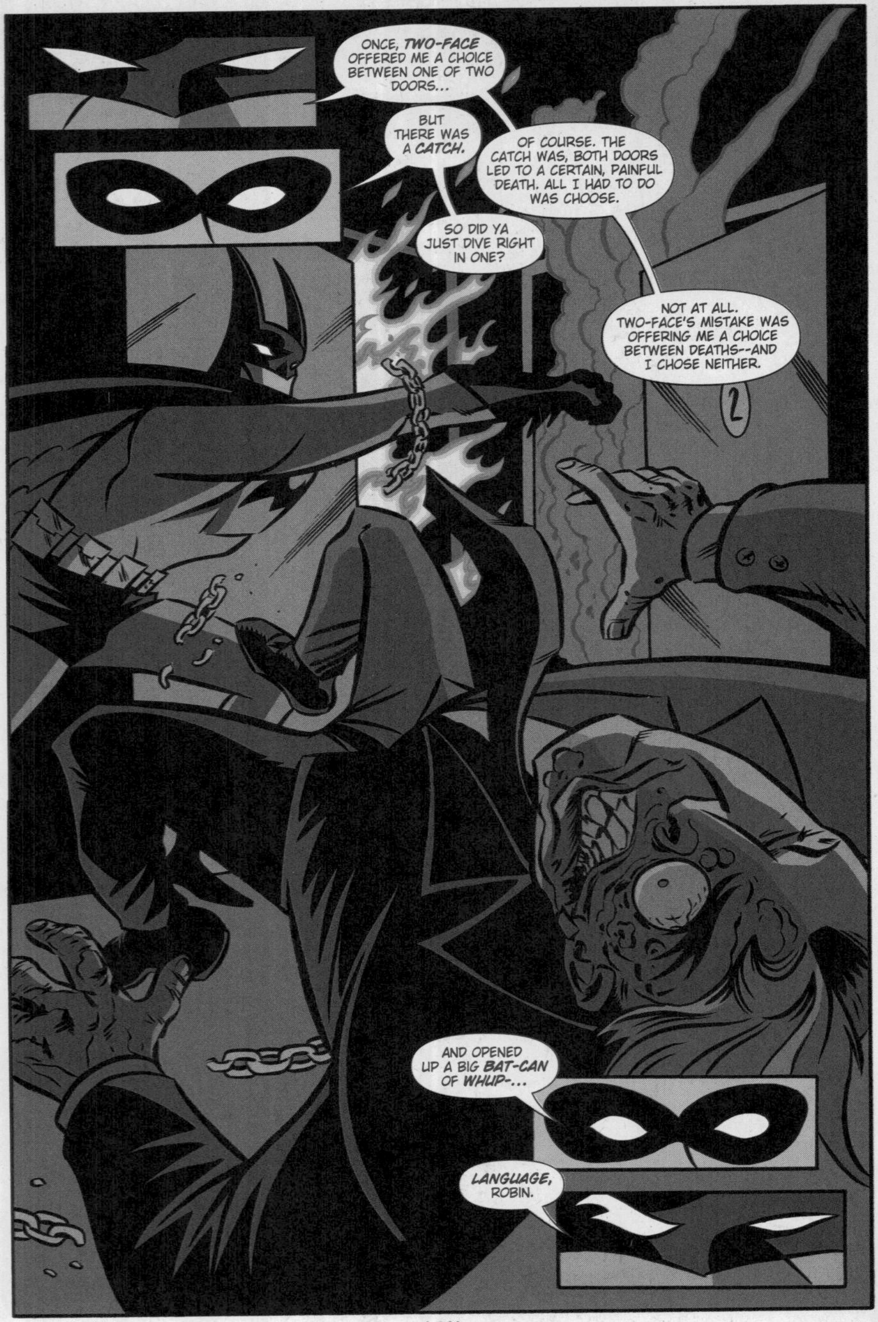
ONCE, TWO-FACE OFFERED ME A CHOICE BETWEEN ONE OF TWO DOORS...
BUT THERE WAS A CATCH.
OF COURSE. THE CATCH WAS, BOTH DOORS LED TO A CERTAIN, PAINFUL DEATH. ALL I HAD TO DO WAS CHOOSE.
SO DID YA JUST DIVE RIGHT IN ONE?
NOT AT ALL. TWO-FACE'S MISTAKE WAS OFFERING ME A CHOICE BETWEEN DEATHS--AND I CHOSE NEITHER.
2
AND OPENED UP A BIG BAT-CAN OF WHUP-...
LANGUAGE, ROBIN.

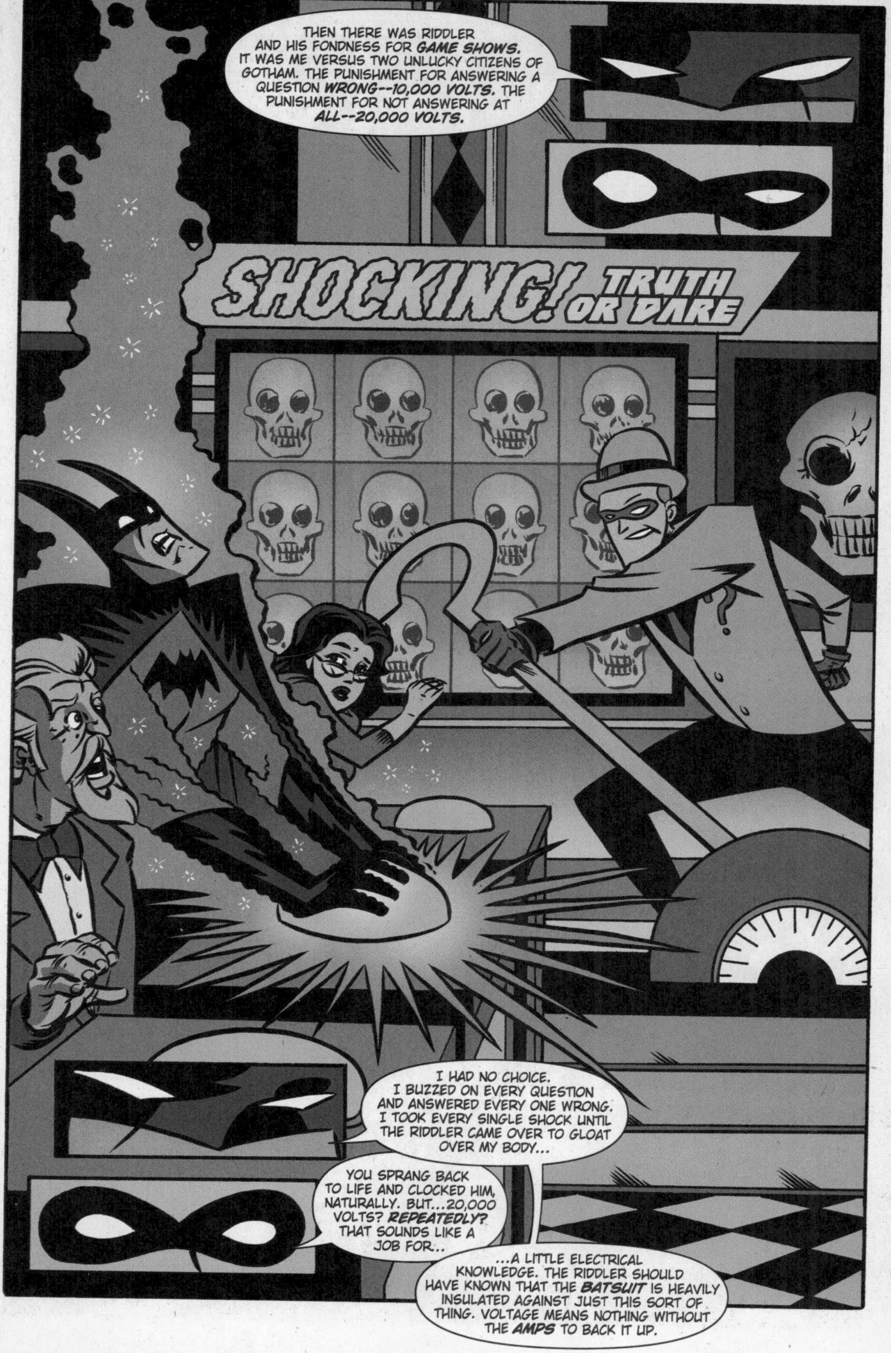
THEN THERE WAS RIDDLER AND HIS FONDNESS FOR GAME SHOWS. IT WAS ME VERSUS TWO UNLUCKY CITIZENS OF GOTHAM. THE PUNISHMENT FOR ANSWERING A QUESTION WRONG--10,000 VOLTS. THE PUNISHMENT FOR NOT ANSWERING AT ALL--20,000 VOLTS.
SHOCKING! TRUTH OR DARE
I HAD NO CHOICE. I BUZZED ON EVERY QUESTION AND ANSWERED EVERY ONE WRONG. I TOOK EVERY SINGLE SHOCK UNTIL THE RIDDLER CAME OVER TO GLOAT OVER MY BODY...
YOU SPRANG BACK TO LIFE AND CLOCKED HIM, NATURALLY. BUT...20,000 VOLTS? REPEATEDLY? THAT SOUNDS LIKE A JOB FOR...
...A LITTLE ELECTRICAL KNOWLEDGE. THE RIDDLER SHOULD HAVE KNOWN THAT THE BATSUIT IS HEAVILY INSULATED AGAINST JUST THIS SORT OF THING. VOLTAGE MEANS NOTHING WITHOUT THE AMPS TO BACK IT UP.

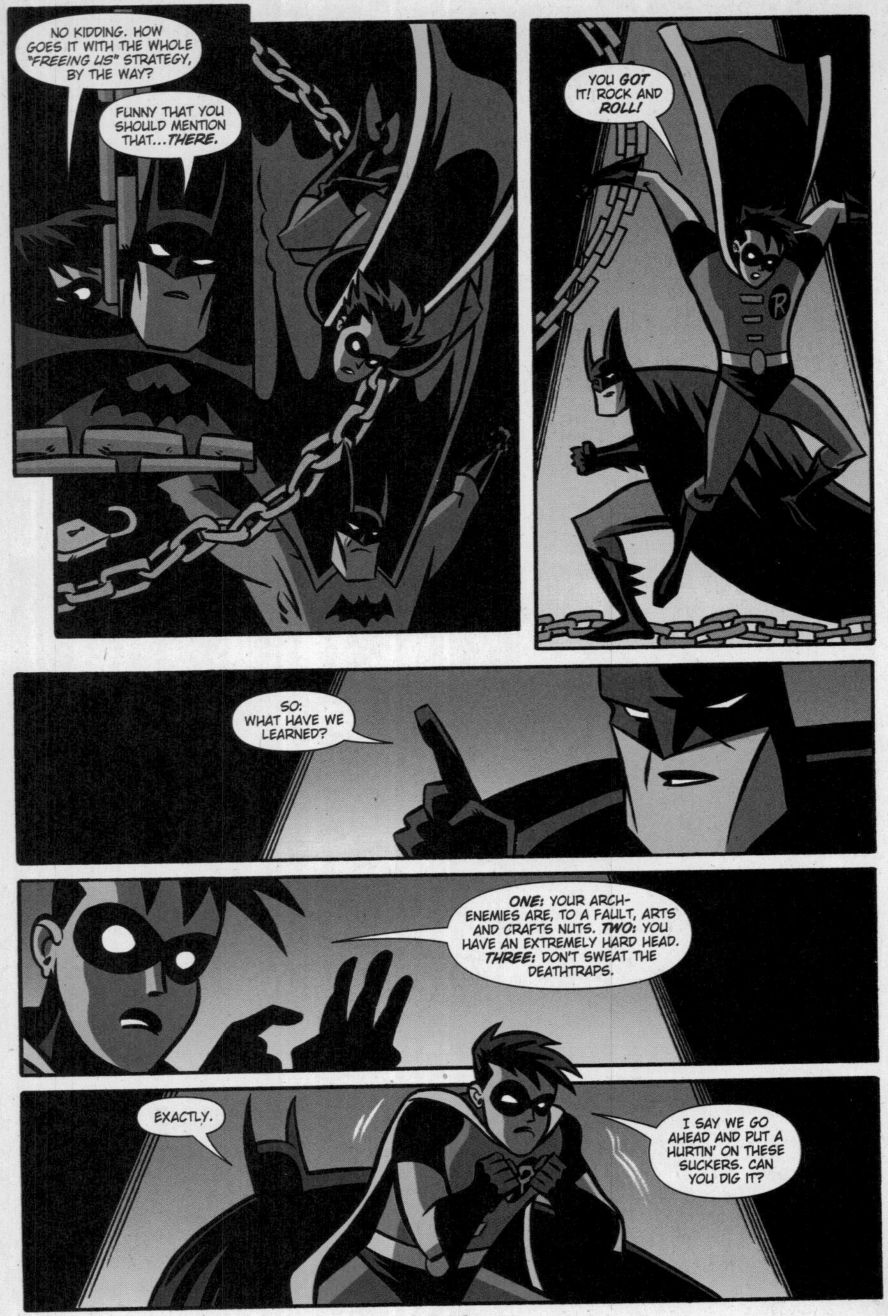
NO KIDDING. HOW GOES IT WITH THE WHOLE "FREEING US" STRATEGY, BY THE WAY?
FUNNY THAT YOU SHOULD MENTION THAT...THERE.
YOU GOT IT! ROCK AND ROLL!
SO: WHAT HAVE WE LEARNED?
ONE: YOUR ARCH-ENEMIES ARE, TO A FAULT, ARTS AND CRAFTS NUTS. TWO: YOU HAVE AN EXTREMELY HARD HEAD. THREE: DON'T SWEAT THE DEATHTRAPS.
EXACTLY.
I SAY WE GO AHEAD AND PUT A HURTIN' ON THESE SUCKERS. CAN YOU DIG IT?

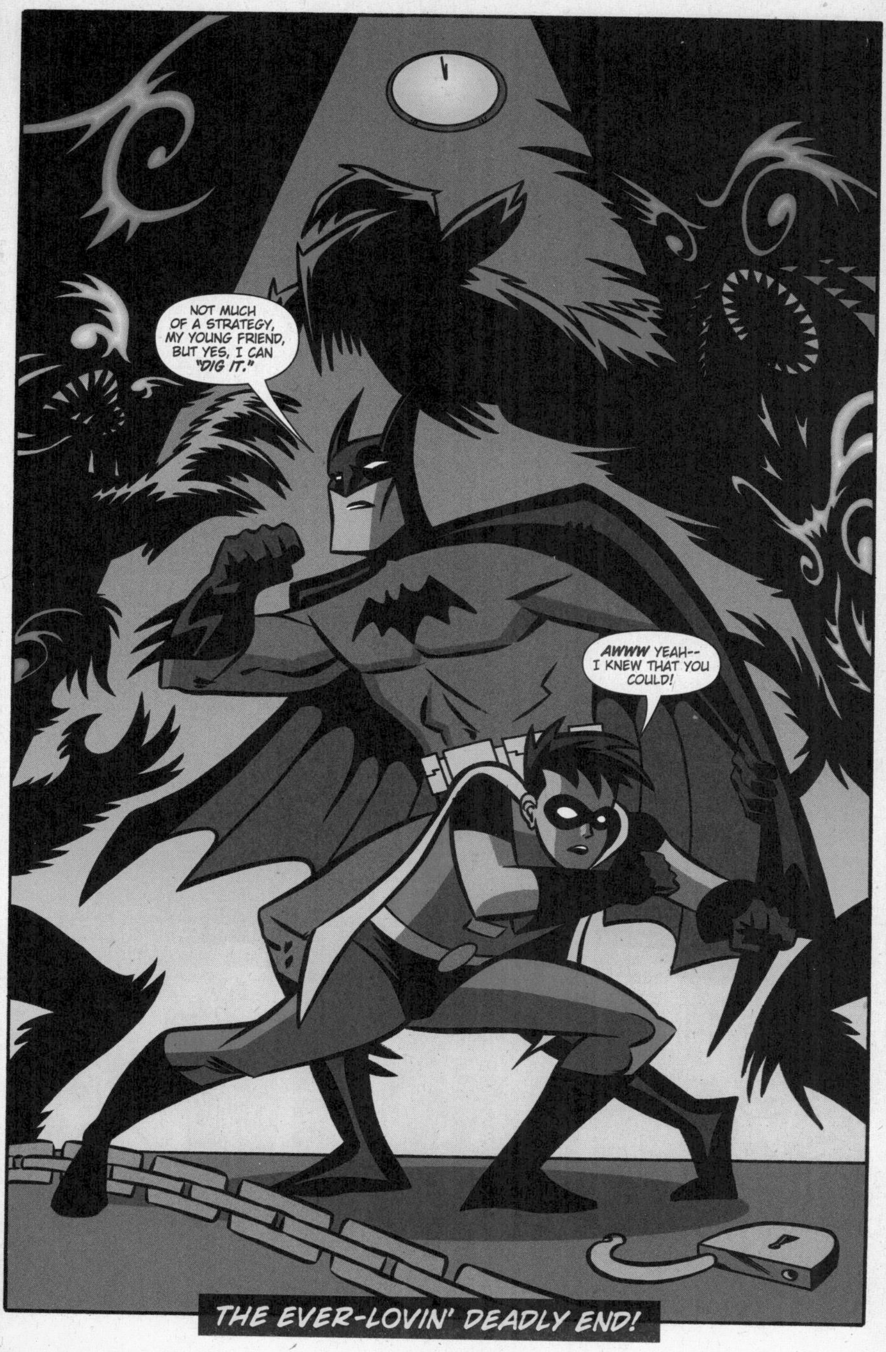
NOT MUCH OF A STRATEGY, MY YOUNG FRIEND, BUT YES, I CAN "DIG IT."
AWWW YEAH-- I KNEW THAT YOU COULD!
THE EVER-LOVIN' DEADLY END!

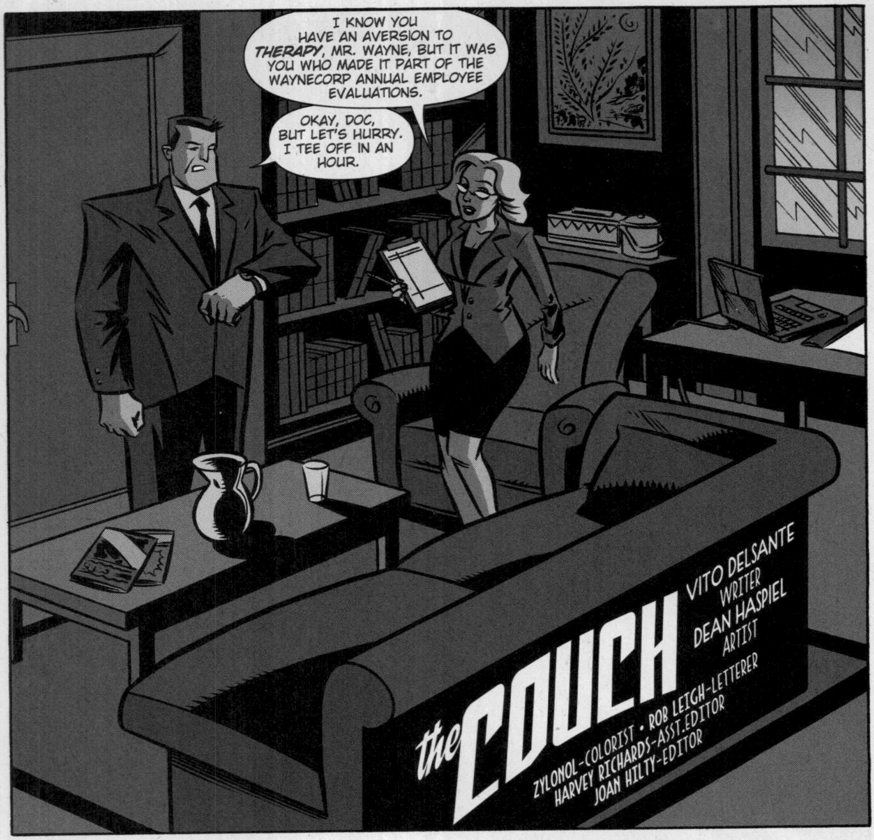
I KNOW YOU HAVE AN AVERSION TO THERAPY, MR. WAYNE, BUT IT WAS YOU WHO MADE IT PART OF THE WAYNECORP ANNUAL EMPLOYEE EVALUATIONS.
OKAY, DOC, BUT LET'S HURRY. I TEE OFF IN AN HOUR.
the COUCH
VITO DELSANTE WRITER
DEAN HASPIEL ARTIST
ZYLONOL-COLORIST • ROB LEIGH-LETTERER
HARVEY RICHARDS-ASST.EDITOR
JOAN HILTY-EDITOR

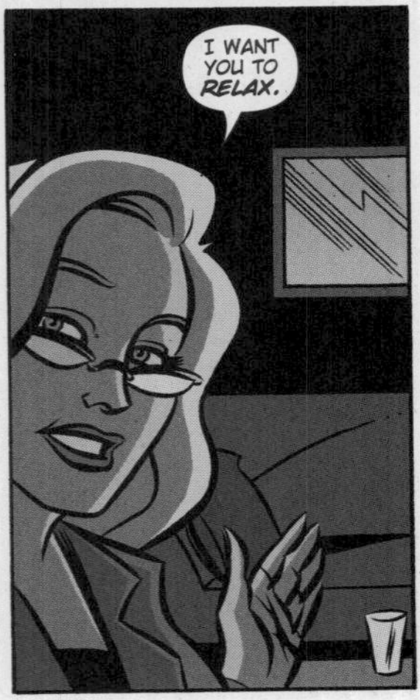
I WANT YOU TO RELAX.

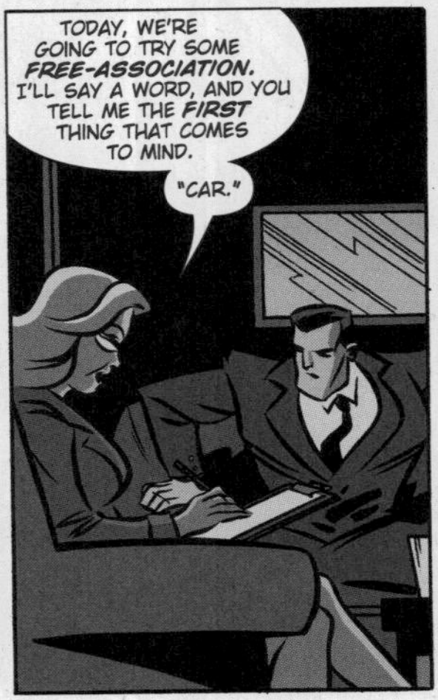
TODAY, WE'RE GOING TO TRY SOME FREE-ASSOCIATION. I'LL SAY A WORD, AND YOU TELL ME THE FIRST THING THAT COMES TO MIND.
"CAR."

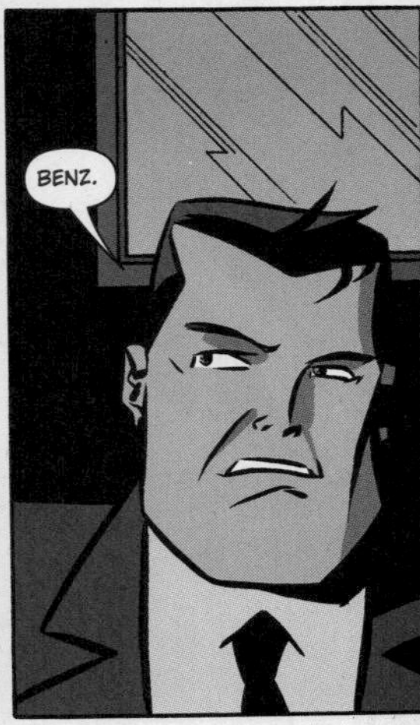
BENZ.

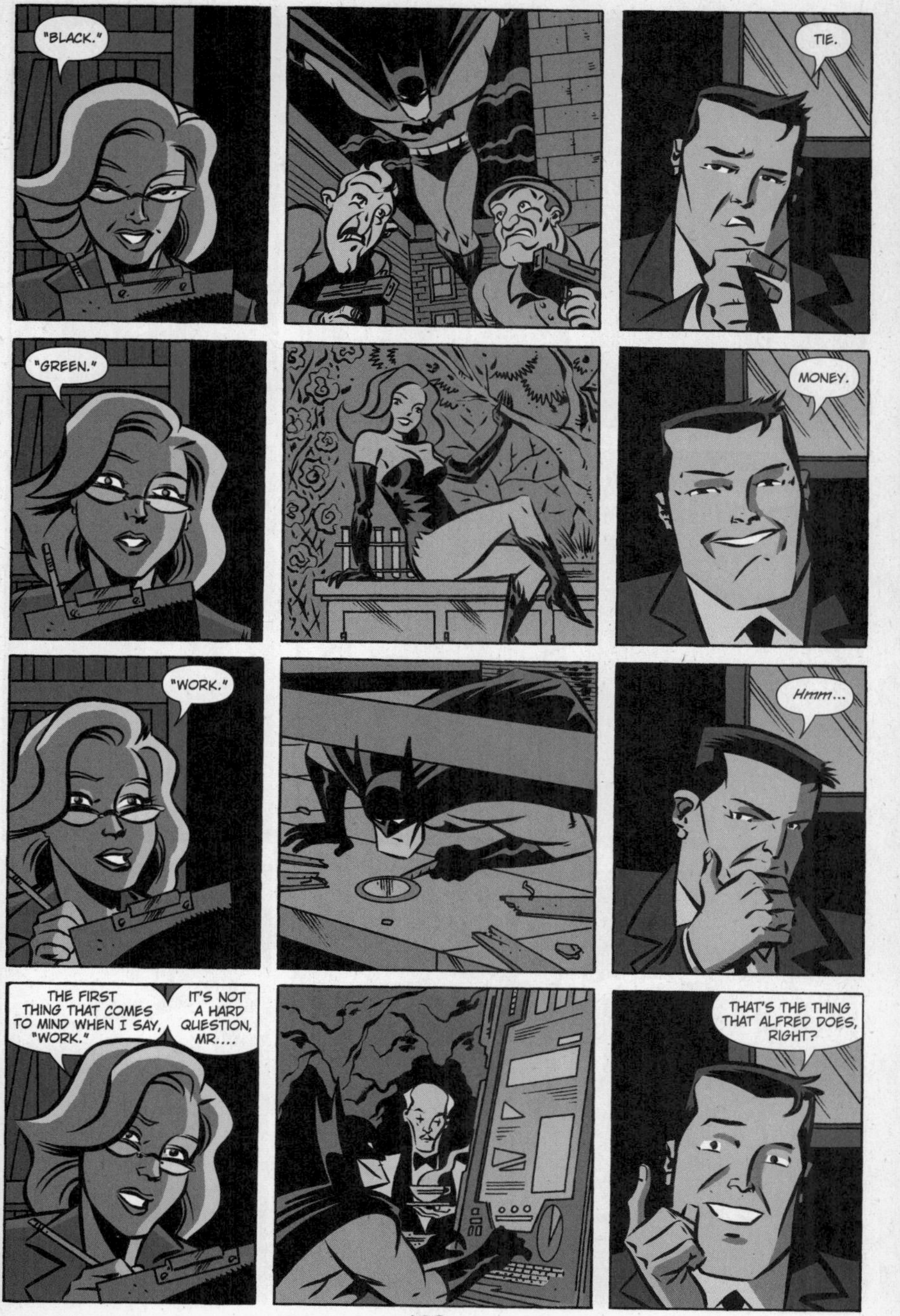
"BLACK."
TIE.
"GREEN."
MONEY.
"WORK."
Hmmm...
THE FIRST THING THAT COMES TO MIND WHEN I SAY, "WORK."
IT'S NOT A HARD QUESTION, MR....
THAT'S THE THING THAT ALFRED DOES, RIGHT?

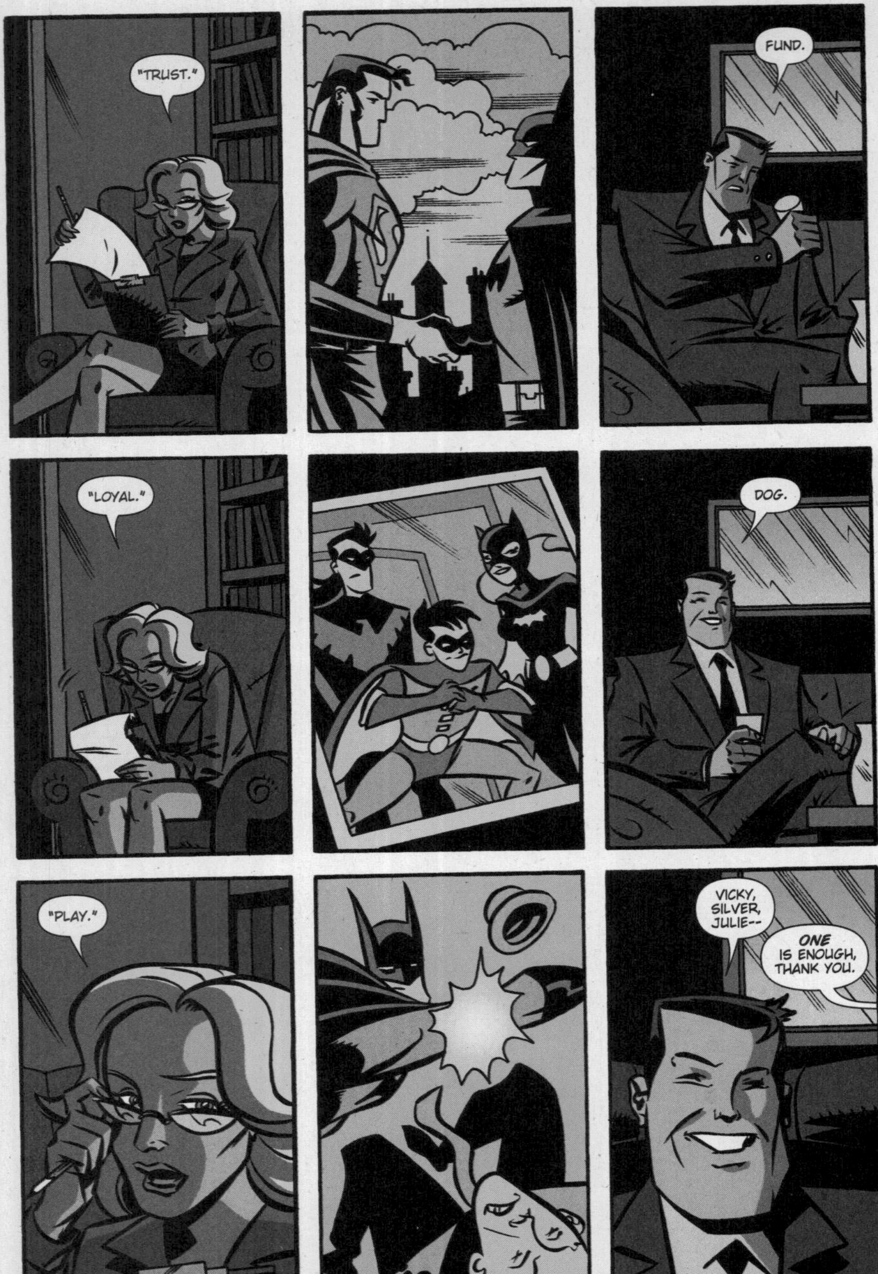

"TRUST."
FUND.
"LOYAL."
DOG.
"PLAY."
VICKY, SILVER, JULIE--
ONE IS ENOUGH, THANK YOU.

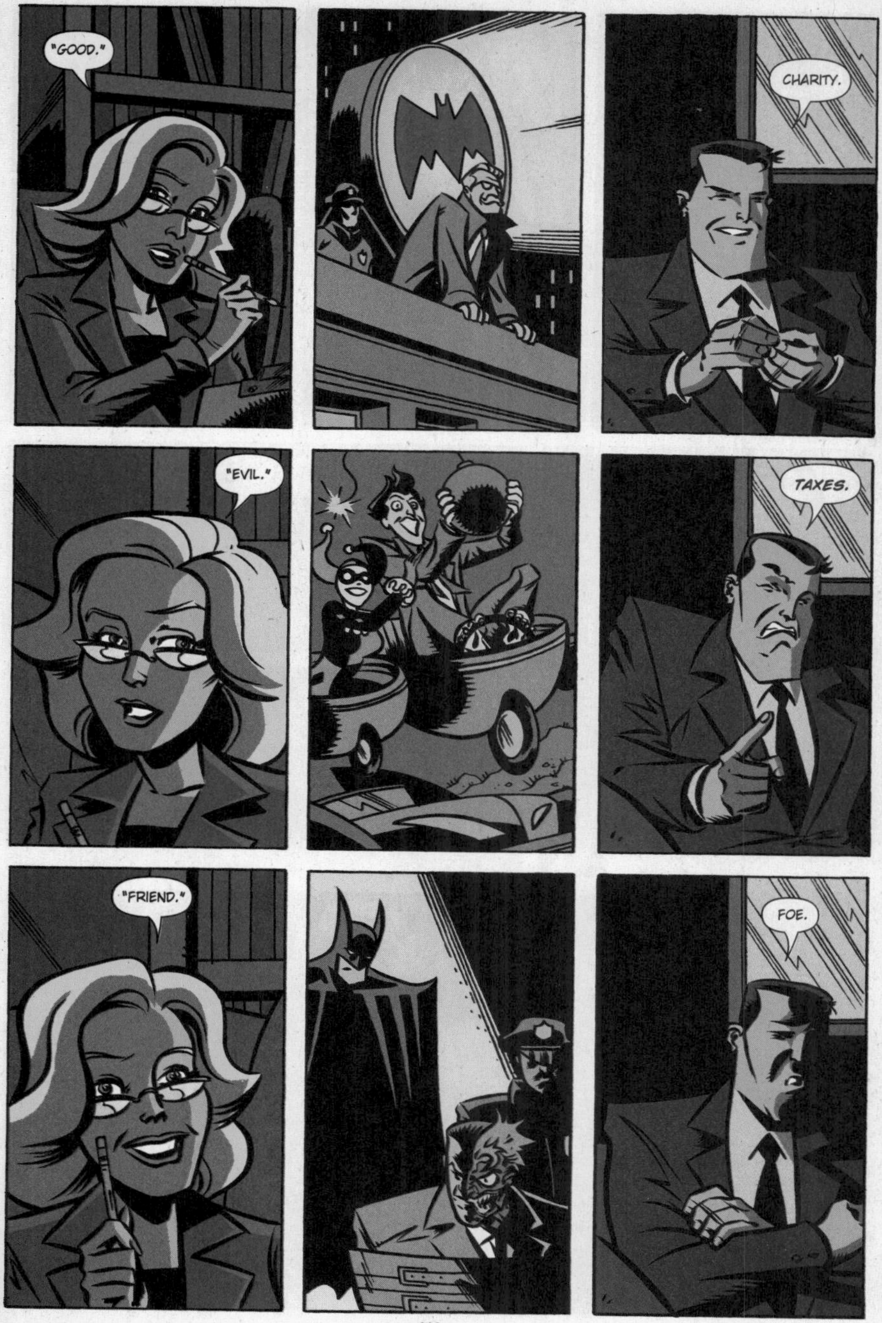
"GOOD."
CHARITY.
"EVIL."
TAXES.
"FRIEND."
FOE.

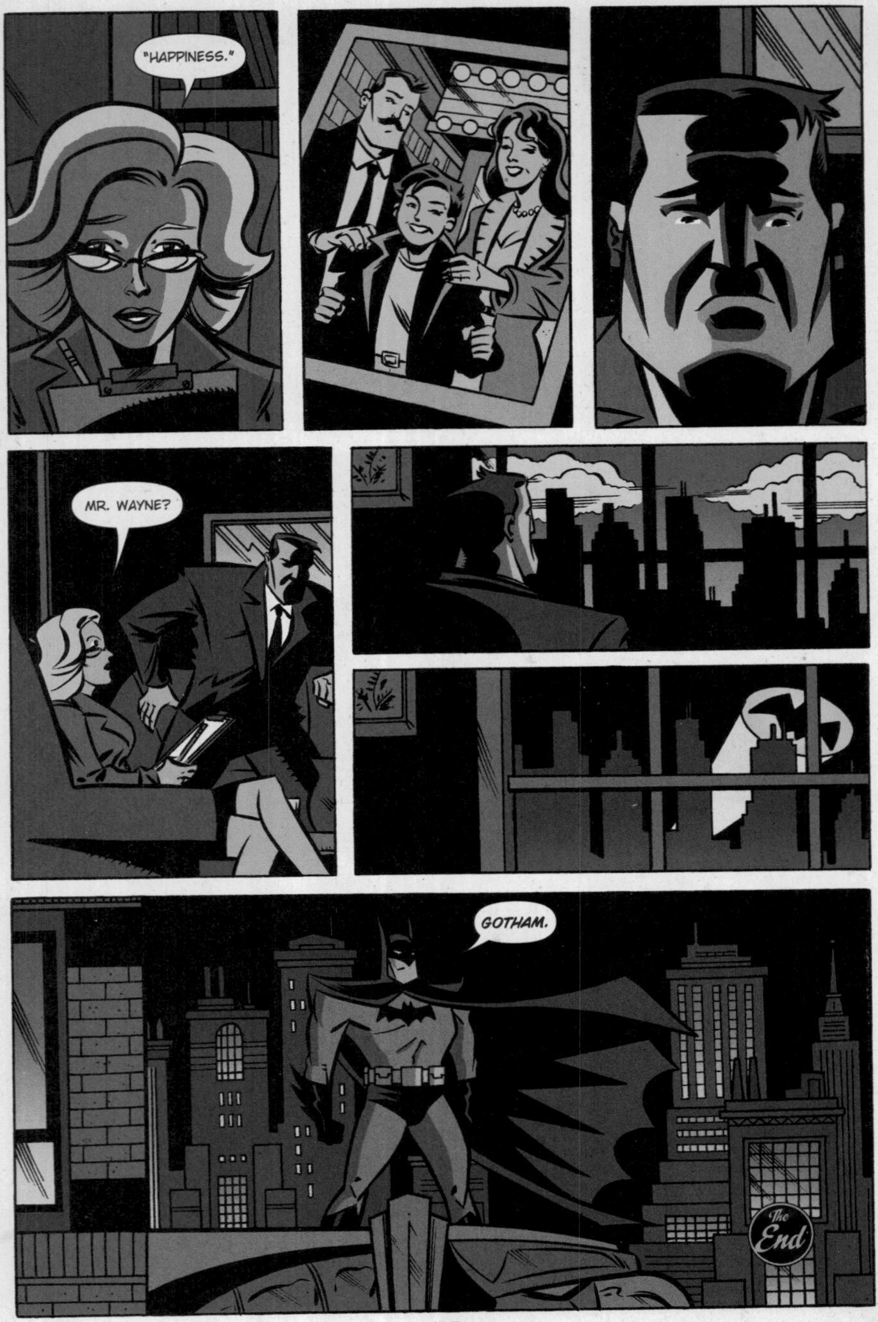
"HAPPINESS."
MR. WAYNE?
GOTHAM.
The End